LADIES OF THE STONE

A Scottish Romance Anthology

ELIZA KNIGHT MADELINE MARTIN
CECELIA MECCA LORI ANN BAILEY

KNIGHT
MEDIA

LADIES OF THE STONE Copyright © 2018 by Eliza Knight, Madeline Martin, Cecelia Mecca, Lori Ann Bailey

ALL RIGHTS RESERVED. No part or the whole of this book may be reproduced, distributed, transmitted or utilized (other than for reading by the intended reader) in ANY form (now known or hereafter invented) without prior written permission by the author. The unauthorized reproduction or distribution of this copyrighted work is illegal, and punishable by law.

LADIES OF THE STONE is a work of fiction. The characters and events portrayed in this book are fictional and or are used fictitiously and solely the product of the author's imagination. Any similarity to real persons, living or dead, places, businesses, events or locales is purely coincidental.

Cover Design by Kim Killion @ The Killion Group, Inc.

THE HIGHLANDER'S QUEST Copyright © 2018 by Eliza Knight

CASSANDRA Copyright © 2018 by Madeline Martin

THE PROTECTOR'S PROMISE Copyright © 2018 by Cecelia Mecca

THE HIGHLAND GUARD AND HIS LADY Copyright © 2018 by Lori Ann Bailey

LEGEND

✺

From within the soul of a special stone, the embodiment of the heart of Scotland, a protector is selected. A woman with a pure heart and the ferocity of a warrior is called to the fairy pools on the Isle of Skye upon the death of the previous protector. However, nature has a way of balancing itself, and so with each call to a Protector comes the call of an evil force, set on using the stone for their own purpose. Â These are the stories of the Protectors of the Heart of Scotland, the stone they seek to keep safe and the love that strengthens and emboldens them.

✺

While beautiful and ethereal in her wildness, Scotland held within her so much power, she could very well tear herself apart. To ensure Scotland's safety, an ancient order of druids decided to safeguard her very heart.

They made a gem of the purest emerald, protected by a necklace wrought of gold, and locked her soul within it, imbuing the stone with magical properties no mortal could ever destroy. For every generation to come, the soul of the stone would select a protector, a woman with a pure heart and the ferocity of a warrior. Upon her death, the immortal stone would then seek the security of its next protector.

But the battle of light and dark is as old as time, and nature has a way of balancing itself—whether for good or evil.

When the reach of the stone stretches toward its next guardian, so too does the call go out to the opposing force—a man whose heart is set on reclaiming Scotland for his own purposes. Both guardian and nemesis receive their mark and are drawn toward the stone that lies in wait within the glittering shallows of the fairy pools, guarded by the Priestess of the Stone.

Scotland's darkest days will emerge if the stone should fall into the wrong hands. The fate of the chosen is a never-ending battle for the stone, Scotland's lifeblood, between the protector and her adversary. For when one dies, a new struggle will begin again until the end of time.

CASSANDRA

MADELINE MARTIN

Together their power is brilliant. But when destiny rivals the safety of family and the whole of Scotland hangs in the balance, can their love survive the required sacrifice?

ACKNOWLEDGMENTS

Thank you to my amazing beta readers who helped make this story so much more with their wonderful suggestions: Kacy Stanfield, Monika Page, Liette Bougie, Tracy Emro and Lorrie Cline. Thank you to Janet Kazmirski for the final read-through you always do for me, and to Tina Conder for her awesome proofreading on this. Thank you to John and my wonderful minions for all the support they give me. And thank you so much to my readers for always being so fantastically supportive and eager for my next book.

PROLOGUE

Durham, England
October 1086

It always rained when a child of the Beaumont bloodline was delivered. And certainly the birth of Cassandra Thomas, daughter of Sir Edmund, was no different. Lightning flashed outside and rain lashed against the shutters. Above the roar of the storm came the lusty, indignant cry of Cassandra, perhaps the most special youngest daughter in a line of gifted youngest daughters.

The Beaumont line contained power, granted only to the last born daughters of each generation. Cassandra's mother swept a hand over the babe's face, immediately soothing the child with her ability to manipulate emotions, and handed her to her own mother who could read one's future.

Cassandra gazed up at her eldmother with large, pale blue eyes, silently curious as if pondering her own fate.

"She will be your final daughter borne," her eldmother said with a tender smile at the newest member of her family, the most special of all her grandchildren. "There is great enchantment within her. She will have a connection to the earth, a skill unlike any we've ever seen, and it will give her incredible strength." She paused.

"What is it?" Cassandra's mother asked.

The eldmother gently lay Cassandra on the bed and removed her swaddling. A whisper of a mark glimmered over the infant's right hip, under the tight curl of her leg against her pink body.

"There is more," the older woman said in a whisper of wonder. "She will be chosen as a Protector which also carries its own gifts." Her eldmother's brow furrowed. "Strength - great strength, especially when her force as a Protector is combined with her blessings as a daughter of the Beaumont bloodline."

"When?" Cassandra's mother sat forward with anticipation, alight with joy to have a child of such importance. "When will this greatness happen?"

The eldmother shook her head with a frown. "It is strange, there is a fog preventing me from reading precisely."

Cassandra's mother settled back into a pile of soft pillows and surveyed the sparse room. "It matters not, surely her abilities will manifest themselves with haste and we shall soon witness their extent for ourselves. After all, how long could they possibly take?"

I

Durham, England
October 1106

Cassandra could not meet the gaze of her family. Her heart flinched at what she would find there — disappointment. It was like this every year on her birthday, the time when most of the Beaumont women came into their powers. The weeks leading up to the annual mark of her birth brought on a frenzy of excitement and anticipation, and the days afterward crashing into the solemn realization that nothing had happened. Again. For over two decades.

She curled tighter into herself where she hugged the tree branch, hoping no one would search the orchard for her. Year after year, she faced this insurmountable expectation. She hated it. She hated it. She *hated* it.

She yanked an apple off a nearby branch and hurtled it out of the tree where it thunked hollowly into something below.

"Och!"

She jerked upright. Dear Lord, she'd hit someone!

Her own feelings of self-pity were shoved aside and she climbed down the tree to discover what hapless soul might have been felled by her inadvertent blow. Her eldest brother, Phillip was on his knees in the grass, cradling the side of his head. Of course it had been him who had come to speak her. He'd always been the only one who had cared about her more than a legacy. To him, she was a younger sister, a person with her own wishes and dreams.

He lifted his hand from his head, revealing a fat red bump. "I should have known it was you based on that hit. No woman can throw like you. Or man for that matter." Quick as lightning, he snatched an apple from the ground and sent it flying in her direction.

She spun out of its way and hefted a fallen apple, this time intentionally tossing it at him and with less force. It landed on his shoulder and sent spatters of juice flying in all directions.

He cried out dramatically and stuck out his tongue. "It was juicy." He grimaced with great exaggeration, looking more like a cat who'd sucked a lemon rather than her regal brother. "Have a care with the soft ones or mother will have my hide."

"She wouldn't dare skin you, Sir Knight." Cassandra curtseyed sweetly to her brother.

He lowered his head and pounced on her, knocking her to the soft grass where several fallen apples jabbed at her back. She shrieked a laugh and shoved at him. He didn't move, the cur. Very well. She'd play by his game. She grasped his right arm and twisted, careful to avoid breaking the bone. He flinched and Cassandra took advantage of the opportunity to duck free of his weight.

"That only took seconds." He grinned up at her. "You're getting faster."

His words reminded her of why he'd spent hours training her, why he felt she needed protection, why she was out in the orchard in the first place.

"What's the point?" She knew she was being sullen, but couldn't stop the words any more than she could quell the resentment.

He hopped up, his expression serious. "Because someday it might happen. And that's a solid reason for me to ensure you can protect yourself."

She opened her mouth to protest, but he cut her off. "Aye, you're strong, but that isn't enough. You need skill, to be able to defend yourself, and even attack, if necessary." His voice lowered. "The path of a Protector cannot be an easy one."

Protector.

He'd said the word. He actually said it.

Cassandra wanted to block her ears from the word, to cut it from her heart or soul or wherever the foulness of it had attached itself to her. But even if she could somehow remove her eldmother's damning prediction, Cassandra would remain trapped by the expectation of a legacy. She was, after all, still the youngest daughter from a string of youngest daughters in the Beaumont bloodline. After years of watching her mother's belly swell to only reveal two more boys and never grow with child again, Cassandra was indeed the last daughter — the youngest — the one whose blood had been imbued with great powers.

Phillip settled on the ground and patted the spot beside him when she didn't join him.

"I don't want this gift," Cassandra said softly.

"I know." He patted the grass once more. "What makes you the most frightened about it?"

She lowered herself to where he'd indicated. He always had a blunt way of saying things that made her look deep into her heart, beyond the gloss of her emotions. She stared at the distant trees, past the orchard and into herself for the answer.

"I'm afraid I'll fail." The confession came out of her mouth so abruptly and accurately, their impact warmed her eyes and nose.

God's bones, was she about to cry? She looked at the scuffed toes of her kidskin shoes rather than at her brother.

"That is daunting." Phillip shifted. He rolled several apples across the green grass, inspecting each carefully. "I hope you don't presume you're not strong enough or skilled enough. I think we've handled that." He glanced back and winked at her.

"What if I'm not the Protector?" She gasped out a breath. There. She'd said it. Her greatest fear. "What if I'm just a normal woman who is destined to live an ordinary life?"

He lifted an apple from the earth and swept the fruit against his shirt until the golden skin gleamed. "That would imply our soothsayer eldmother was wrong, the bloodline of our ancestors doesn't exist and the humming you feel on the ground is..." He lifted his brows in silent question and bit into the apple.

She smiled softly to herself and spread her hands, palm out, toward the tender green shoots of grass. Sunlight from the copse of trees over her head dappled the skin on the back of her hands with spatters of light. Over the years, the steady vibration of the earth's life had become as silent to her as her own heartbeat. She had to concentrate on the sensation now to even acknowledge it.

Phillip waved the half-eaten apple at her. "Go on."

She closed her eyes and inhaled, tasting the sweet apples scenting the air, letting the sun's heat warm her skin and hair, skimming her palms against the cool grass. Her hands hovered and she fixed on the steady drone buried deep in the rich, black soil. It started like a low buzz at first, the way a lazy bee might sound as it languidly flew through a field of summer flowers, then it whirred in a chorus of energy, rising around her, singing to her the beauty of its being. But there was something else. Something deeper.

Perspiration prickled along her brow, but she ignored it and forced her attention on the tenuous connection between her soul and that of the earth. A high-pitched ring echoed in the distance. Not a ring — a cry. Mourning. The hollowness of misery rose over the din of life until it filled Cassandra's ears and mind and heart. Sorrow spread through her like shadows and swept off in rolling waves. So much sadness.

Strong hands caught her shoulders and shook her. The connection severed and she was snapped back, away from her awareness.

"What is it, Cassandra?" Phillip's ashen face was mere inches from her own, his apple lay discarded and forgotten on the ground. "Why are you crying?"

She brought her hands to her face and found them trembling uncontrollably. She brushed her fingertips over her cheeks and they came away damp with her tears.

The deafening cries of the earth had fallen to a whisper with her broken connection. Phillip put his face in front of hers, his blue eyes locked on her. "Look at me, Cass. Look. At. Me." He bit the words out, his tone so stark, it drew her from the horror.

"Breathe," he commanded.

She obeyed. Air rushed into her body and the tension gripping her eased until finally her breath came on its own accord rather than by order.

His brow relaxed, if only slightly. "What is it, Cassandra? What have you seen?"

She suppressed the urge to give in to the threat of her tears once more. "The earth is crying."

"What does that mean?" Fear rendered his pupils to specks of black in his pale blue eyes and sent a jab of ice to her heart.

She shook her head. "I don't know."

"Is it time?" His hands on her shoulders gripped tighter, as if he meant to keep her locked there forever.

"I don't know."

He nodded. "Come, you should be inside."

Cassandra glared at the house. If it was time, she wanted her family to be no part of it. She didn't want their cajoling and honeyed platitudes sending her on her way. "Don't tell them."

He stared down at her for a long pause. His face smoothed for the first time since the awful conversation. "Of course." His expression turned playful and he offered her a deep, groveling bow. "I am eternally at your service, my lady."

She ruffled his dark curls, so like her own, but shorn close to his head to give him an advantage in battle. "I'll hold you to your word to keep mum about telling the rest." Despite her attempt to continue the lighter tone, her voice came out flat and Phillip's mood sobered.

He rose and nodded.

They parted ways at the house as nonchalantly as possible with Phillip striding toward the solar and Cassandra climbing the polished wood staircase to the long hall. A sudden warmth spread over the right side of her hip, like a breath fanning over her skin. A gasp choked from her and she drew back, away from...from nothing. She clasped her hands against the warm spot and looked at the fabric there. Naught showed against the pale pink linen. Its smooth surface lay cool and unassuming against her body, as if the sensation had never happened.

Strange.

She ran to her room on shaking legs and her hands slipped over the latch in her haste. She needed to be alone, to breathe, to relive that moment in the orchard when she experienced the power of the earth weeping even as she wanted desperately to forget it. Her mind swam so fast, it felt as though bits of it were flying loose.

What was happening to her?

Finally she burst through the door and secured it behind her. She grasped the heavy, voluminous skirt of her cote in her fists and yanked it up, over her legs and up past her hip. A mark showed upon her skin where the warmth had flared. It was in the shape of a dagger with the point tilted down to her left foot, mottled brown as though it were simply a birth mark.

But what was the meaning of it?

She stroked a hand over it. The mark was not raised or indented. Nay, it was flush as if it had always been part of her skin.

An image flashed in her mind. Green and blue waters, fed from a nearby waterfall. Grass hugged against every side. The apparition was so close to her, the damp cool air kissed at her skin. A sparkle glinted in the shallows of the colorful water. A green gem? She stepped closer and her feet shuffled under the soft grass underfoot. She dropped the hem of her cote and stretched her hand to the water, reaching, reaching. Her fingers dipped into the icy pool. The vision rippled and disappeared.

Cassandra cried out in disappointment and stared down at her outstretched hands where evidence of having touched water glistened in a slant of sunlight streaming in from the open shutters. Wherever that was, she needed to find its location.

Now.

"Lady Cassandra?" a quiet, feminine voice said. The maid who had been both companion and servant to Cassandra in their twenty years growing up together stood in the doorway.

"I fear I must leave at once, Mary. Please, be so kind as to fetch Phillip." Cassandra looked out to the long road winding from their small manor. The trail pulled at her, beckoning with urgency. "And tell no one else of my departure."

Edinburgh, Scotland

THE SEVENTH KNIGHT STAGGERED BACK AND SCRAMBLED TO KNEEL in resignation before Fergus the Undefeated. The conquered knight leaned heavily against his blade, and gasped to reclaim the breath knocked from him. Rain pattered down on their chain mail, leaving the padded clothing beneath soaked through to the skin. The squires would be required to apply a solid rubbing of oil to the chain that evening.

Six others had come before the newly fallen man, and each had clamored with as much haste to draw the line of surrender in their battle. Fergus had purposefully made sure never to hurt another of his fellow knights at practice, but apparently his efforts had not subdued their fears.

He clasped the man's lifted hand and aided him to his feet. "Ye did well." Fergus clapped him on the back and instantly regretted it when the man winced.

"Sir Fergus." A young man with tousled blonde hair stood bravely in front of him. His chain mail was new enough to reflect the gray sky with a gleam like freshly wrought silver. "I would be honored to fight ye, The Undefeated."

"Ye may want to try when yer armor shows the effects of war a bit." Fergus made to flank the young knight, but the lad cut in front of him once more.

The young man set his chin stubbornly. "I've been watching ye for years and now I can finally have my chance."

"For years?" Fergus chuckled, flattered despite himself. Who was he to stop a lad from his dream? "Ready yerself."

The young man's eyes went wide in his face with eagerness. He shoved his head into the equally new helm and held his sword. Fergus huffed out an exhale and concentrated on his opponent the way he always did during battle, utilizing his gift.

He shoved through the emotions and thoughts and fears emanating from his foes; those were merely distractions. Nay, he wanted the movement of energy around them, the tick that would betray the move they thought before their body had time to execute.

Likewise, Fergus directed a fraction of his attention on himself, to absorb the force his body created with each move, masking them completely from even the most astute of opponents.

The lad's intended movements radiated from his left arm. Fergus blocked the hit before the young knight could attempt the strike.

The wind shifted and carried with it a sweet, familiar fragrance. Apples. Fergus' nostrils flared at the aroma. There were no orchards nearby, at least none he'd noticed, and it was nearly too late for apple season. A hum crackled in the air and brought on a wet, earthy scent, like rain. Fergus' hair stood on end.

Magic.

His heart slammed with a frenzy in his chest. The presence of it hissed everywhere, reminding him of that night.

Nay.

He wanted to clutch his head in his hands and roar until his throat bled, he wanted to claw at his chest until his heart was a pathetic pulsing bloody pulp in his palms. He would endure any injury over the memories of *that* night.

Fergus jerked to the side, as though doing so would wrench the memory free and fling it from his mind. But it was not that night that came to him. The rain parted and peeled away the gray sky for sunlight to pour in. Fergus squinted against the brilliance, but did not pull away his gaze.

A woman's face appeared at its center, one he'd never seen before. She was young, her skin practically white against the dark mass of curls spilling over her shoulders. Her gaze flicked up and met his, a piercing blue. A flush of pink showed on her cheeks and lips, giving her the allure of true innocence. Confusion crossed her comely features. Her hand moved over her right hip, the opposite side as his mark, but in the same place, and he knew.

The stone had passed to its new Protector.

A dulled practice sword thwacked against his chest, but he did not move.

The former Protector was dead. She'd hidden herself away for well over a decade, impossible to find despite Fergus' efforts to find her. He'd searched with desperation, all to no avail. There was a new Protector now, which meant he would have another opportunity to lure her back to King Edgar, and there would be another opportunity to claim the stone as his.

His mind spun with possibilities and what they might bring to him. After years of fruitless searching, and as many years of separation from the son he had never met, he may finally have his opportunity.

The practice sword skimmed off the shoulder of his chain mail. Fergus had completely forgotten their mock battle. He turned his head to regard the youth, and the young man stepped back. Rightly so.

Power thrummed through Fergus' veins with all the force of a decade of rage and loss and longing. A single blow could kill the lad.

"We're done," Fergus said flatly.

The lad nodded. "Mayhap again? At another time?" He watched Fergus with a hopeful expression.

"There is business requiring my attention."

The young man gave a slight bow. "It was an honor to fight with ye."

Fergus inclined his head respectfully and quit the training yard for the palace. Inside, King Edgar sat on his throne as he did most days, his elbows rested against the carved sides of the regal seat, his fingers steepled between them. He flicked a hand outward in dismissal of others.

"Leave us," King Edgar's voice echoed in the large stone room.

Advisors and petitioners alike silently obeyed the order, streaming past Fergus' large frame in a clatter of footsteps on the stone floor. The last man out pulled the massive doors shut behind him, letting them close with a deafening slam. Silence followed while the king stared down at Fergus.

There was an arrogant victory about the king, not outwardly, but a glow deep inside his chest where the rest of him was rotten and dark. He already knew.

"The Protector is dead." Fergus spoke as if he was unaware of the king's knowledge. Likewise, he concentrated on keeping his own emotions and thoughts contained within himself.

He was not certain how the king came upon his uncanny revelations, whether he himself had power, or someone else in his employ did, but Fergus knew better than to let his own thoughts be read and heard.

King Edgar's eyes widened. "I am aware. Which means a new Protector will have been found. I'm assuming ye can find this one."

Fergus gave a sharp nod.

The king's fingers separated from where they steepled together and clawed over the arms of his throne like long limbed insects. "I was too lenient last time. I see as much now."

Fergus said nothing, focusing instead on muffling the rapid beat of his heart and silencing his racing thoughts.

"Find the stone this time and bring the lass here." The king paused to lift a gilded chalice from a tray beside his throne. He drank long and deep so the lump in the middle of his long, skinny neck bobbed several times before he set the cup aside. Moisture clung to his upper lip, but he did not blot it away. "Ye have two moon cycles to bring them both to me."

"If I do not?" Fergus pressed.

"There will be consequences." King Edgar's mouth curled up in a wolfish grin. "Consequences ye willna like."

Fergus did not respond. Why bother when he had no choice?

The king swept the back of his hand toward Fergus, dismissing him as one might wave away an annoying fly.

Fergus put his back to the king and walked the long stretch of flagstone leading to the door. His feet echoed off the cold stone walls. He used the sound to keep himself in the moment, to lock his concentration to hold his thoughts to himself.

"Do not let me down, Fergus the Undefeated." The title was said with a drawn out taunt.

The Undefeated. How Fergus hated the name, the intentional mockery King Edgar had bestowed while knighting him after that damned night. For truly there was no man as defeated in all the land as he.

2

The call of the stone was stronger on Skye, pulling Cassandra beyond the desire for sleep or food. Her bones ached from the constant sway of the saddle and hunger gnawed at her belly. It had been well over a fortnight since she'd left her home in Durham, perhaps longer. Some of her travel had been ridden on the back of her horse, some thicker areas walked through by foot, and still others requiring a vessel to carry her over water.

The skies rained down upon her for the better part of a week. She was drenched and her hands were locked in clawed fists from her grip on the reins. Though it was not yet winter, the cold froze her breath and her constant shivering left her back and ribs aching.

She had not known what to expect in being the Protector, but it was certainly not this.

Her upper body lay against the horse's neck, seeking whatever heat she might gain from it. The beast trudged along, heedless of her suffering.

Cassandra blinked her heavy eyes once, twice. The third time they remained closed and a peaceful warmth spread through her, as though she were back home in the sunlit meadow of the orchard. She tried to push that memory from her mind, for it was too painful to recall – a time when she had been warm and well fed, when expectation was the worst of her worries.

Only it was not the orchard which blossomed in her thoughts, but a terrain very much like what she traveled in presently along with a man.

His chain mail initially made her assume the knight might be Phillip. But nay, Phillip had a brown steed and this man rode one as black as night. The man's dark hair was longer than Phillip's, coming down to his shoulders rather than cropped neat and close. Hoofbeats echoed in her head, growing louder, faster. Closer.

His expression was ferocious where it fixed on the path before him, his jaw locked with steely determination. He straightened and turned his head toward her, his gaze so dark his eyes appeared to be black. Their stares locked and she knew he could see her from wherever he was, as clearly as she saw him.

She drew a sharp inhale and sat upright on her steed, no longer weary. The image cleared away as though it'd never been there, much as the waters with the glittering gem had done when she'd first gotten the mark. And like the gem, she knew the man to be real.

An urgency filled her, stronger than before, pulling her, driving her to make haste to the fairy pools. The horse rode onward on powerful legs as though drawn with the same level of intensity as she. The wind roared, and the landscape flashed by with incredible speed.

All at once, her horse stopped and nearly sent her flying over its neck. Mist hung in the air like a gauzy curtain, blocking their path. Cassandra rocked in the saddle and clicked her tongue. The horse did not move. She looked behind her where there had been no haze, and once more to the front where it blanketed the trail.

The horse stamped its hoof to the ground. Restless, the beast shifted, only to stop and rear back.

Clearly it would not go any further. Perhaps it could not. Cassandra patted its neck and leapt to the ground. She drew her pole arm from the saddle. If nothing else, she would not be unarmed. Not with images of the knight still pounding through her mind.

She drew a deep breath and plunged into the fog. The air within was dewy and cool and thick enough, she could scarce see two paces in front of her. She clung to her pole arm and tapped it along the ground in an effort to avoid any large objects which might impede her path.

Water trickled in the distance. Her heart pounded and her blood roared through her veins. She was close. So close.

The wall of vapor cleared away and opened to a sunlit mountainside. Emerald grass shone in the golden light and large pools of blue-green water sparkled under wide-open skies. Her racing heart slammed to a stop.

She knew this place.

The gem had been there. She surveyed frantically over the surface of the clear water to the shallow depths beneath. No stone glinted back at her. She glanced up the sloping face of the mountain and found a number of such pools, all linked together with trickling streams and waterfalls. One of them must contain the stone.

She strode up the steep side to the next bit of water and glanced about the shimmering surface. Something flew past her peripheral on the opposite side of the multi-colored pools, silent and unexpected. A man.

He raced up the side of the mountain as though his life depended upon it. She straightened in shock. His movements had been too fast, too soundless.

Without hesitation, she ran after him, following on her side of the water. Clearly he knew where the stone was, given his haste, and it was not where she had wasted time searching.

His dark gaze met hers and her step faltered. It was him. The man she had seen only moments ago in her mind.

He stopped as well and stared, his powerful chest rising and falling beneath his chain mail with rapid breath. Lines creased the skin between his heavy, dark brows, as though he were concentrating. He was larger in person than in her vision. Much larger. He could crush her if she were a normal woman. Was this man someone she ought to defeat?

They stared at one another for the span of a long heartbeat before the urgency shrieked at her, spurring her onward once more.

He darted forward the exact moment she did, as though their

bodies were connected. That's when it caught her eye. The glimmer of a sparkle in the depths of a pool between them.

The stone.

Cassandra charged into the thigh deep water. Its chill hit her like a punch, but she pressed onward, dragging her heavy skirts behind her. Her legs burned with the effort, yet still she moved too slowly. The man roared with each step, for surely his chain mail dragged him back as much as her skirts did her. Together they raced with torturous slowness.

Her heart threatened to leap out of her chest. This was her destiny. She could not fail.

The rock beneath her foot shifted and slipped out from under her, sending her sprawling face first into the water. As she fell, the man lunged and thrust his hand into the water where the gem sparkled.

She floundered in the pool in an attempt to find purchase on the slick ground beneath her. Finally her feet caught and she launched herself to standing once more. He might have claimed the stone, but she would not fail.

FERGUS GROPED BLINDLY IN THE WATER, SKIMMING OVER THE ROCKY floor in an attempt to claim the gem. Finally he caught at a chain and the stone pulled safely into the cradle of his palm. Energy seared through him. Hot. Bright. Powerful.

Too powerful.

His bones shuddered and his skin burned. Pain seared through his gut and spiraled outward as though the force of it intended to tear him apart. Everything in him screamed for him to let go. But he did not. He had too much to lose to fail now.

Nay, he clasped his other hand over his fist, securing the stone lest it wrench free.

His blood heated in his veins, igniting with raw strength.

She was worried about him.

The thought carried in on the overwhelming surge and settled him back into the quiet path of pools trickling down the mountainside. He opened his eyes to find the woman standing a pace away from him, the determination on her face softened by the glow of concern in her eyes.

What had once been a lightly pulsing sense of awareness had taken on a more poignant quality. He could not only assume her thoughts, he could practically hear them.

She thought the stone was hers, and intended to get it back.

Nay, he could actually hear them.

She meant to get it back by any means necessary.

Fergus removed one hand from the stone and pulled free his sword. It hissed menacingly from the scabbard. It was meant to intimidate, but she did not back down.

His chest tightened. He did not wish to battle this young woman. Her body was slender within her cote, her arms impossibly skinny in the tapered sleeves, like sticks he might snap. And yet defiance shone in her pale blue eyes and her sharp chin set in a stubborn glower.

She would not go down without a fight.

Damn it, he didn't want her to go down at all.

"I dinna want to fight ye, lass." He stepped back and slipped the stone's simple gold chain around his neck. The heat of it warmed through his chain mail, the padded shirt beneath, the linen under that and to the skin of his chest.

Instead of answering, her energy arced out toward him in preparation to attempt a hit. He stepped to the side, and her energy shifted to follow him. The move was immediate and without hesitation. Too fast.

Never had an opponent moved so quickly before. This baffled him and cost him a fraction of a second before he could think to move again.

Her pole arm slammed into his chest hard enough to tear the breath from his lungs. He gasped for a drag of cool air and his chest ached with the effort.

What the hell? How did that scrap of a lass get a hit like that on a man his size?

The lines of her energy drew back again and this time he treated her preparation with more consideration. He lifted his sword to block the blow as the pole arm came down on him.

How did she move so bloody fast?

Her heel slammed into the back of his knees, catching him off guard. The hit rocked his balance and sent him careening backward into the pool. She was on him, her arms coiled around his, her legs entwined with his, a viper of death intent on drowning him. Her fingers patted over his chest, seeking the stone.

The stone. The stone. The stone.

Her destiny.

He grasped the back of her dress and ripped her from his body. She flew off him, arms and legs outstretched in a fruitless attempt to cling onto him. The woman fought like a damn harpy.

He dragged himself to his feet, sending water flooding off him and dripping from the tightly linked chain mail he wore. The armor weighed practically more than he did. It was a wonder she hadn't succeeded in drowning him.

She lay face down in the water, unmoving.

Shite.

He stared at her, but saw no ripples in her energy. She'd die if he left her as she lay. If she did, a new Protector would be chosen, and who knew where he'd find the next one.

He heaved a sigh, waded to her still form, and dragged her from the water. She weighed next to nothing, even with her clothing and hair sodden. A sputtering sound gurgled from her chest. He tilted her above the water, and she gave a savage choking cough that expelled the liquid from her lungs.

Cold. She was cold. Freezing.

Jesu, her discomfort was so intense, an icy chill settled into the depths of Fergus' very bones and cooled him as well. He set her on the sunlit grass and felt the heat of it seep into her back as surely as though it were him lying there.

Her eyes remained closed, her lashes a dark sweep against pale cheeks. He stared down at her for a long moment, transfixed by her beauty. Again.

The last time had almost cost him the stone. But then, she'd been so lovely when she'd stumbled after catching sight of him. As though she had been as taken aback.

Those beautiful blue eyes had focused on him and his world had fallen away. Those luscious black curls now lay in thick, wet waves, but he could all too easily recall how they shone glossy about her fair face. Despite being so very cold and still, her lips were brilliant red and stood out like rose petals against her porcelain skin.

Had he not experienced the hit she'd delivered him, he would have thought her the most delicately beautiful thing in all the world. He stroked a hand down her smooth cheek and her breath drew in, swelling her bosom upward.

She liked his touch. She found it warm. Comforting.

He snatched his hand back. He had no right to touch her. She was his enemy.

It was that final thought which brought him to his senses and reminded him of his obligation. He could not waste any more time, not when he knew the price of his delay.

A feminine whisper sounded on the wind, distant and impossible to decipher. His hair prickled and a chill shivered over his skin.

He narrowed his gaze and surveyed the surrounding area. The sound intensified, a chant of lyrical vowels and hard consonants echoing in his mind. It filled his head until it crushed against his brain and threatened to crack open his skull.

He clutched his head in his hands and grunted through the agony. The pain did not abate. He tossed his head from side to side, but the scent of magic was everywhere. Foul and inescapable.

Leave.

The word resonated through his suffering. He backed away and the hurt ebbed. He staggered back further and the torturous grip eased from his temples.

A figure stood in the distance, her body masked in a green hooded cloak. She lifted a hand, the action so smooth, it didn't generate any pre-movement energy, as though she knew how to absorb her actions before moving the way he did.

Magic crackled in the air and left a heavy scent of moisture, redolent of the moments before a torrential storm. Lightning streaked across the sky, yet the rain did not come. His skin hummed with the power flickering and snapping around him. Such incredible energy. So much. If he could harness it, learn to use it, he would be unstoppable.

"*Neathu,*" she whispered.

A blanket of milky fog rolled in front of him, draping his view of the Protector and the witch.

Fear grappled Fergus momentarily. The Protector was lost to him. He needed her. Damn it. He needed her.

The witch had spent almost all her energy on him. A few more moments would have killed her.

Even her thoughts in his mind were faint with exhaustion. If he had withstood the affliction of her curse a bit longer, he would have won.

As it was, he had not truly lost.

He curled his fingers against the stone. He had it, and the Protector would try to get it back. Rather than stumble blind through the mist, he would bide his time. She would find him, and when she did - he would convince her to join him.

He would have the stone and the Protector, exactly as was deemed necessary by the king. Then, at long last, Fergus would have his son.

3

Cassandra startled awake and grasped at empty air. There was no stone. No pools. No man. Firelight flickered off natural stone walls and the roar of swiftly falling water came from somewhere very nearby. The sweet scent of burning sage hovered above the musty odor of a cave long left damp.

The small pallet she lay upon, however, as well as the simple table and chairs by a lit fire, indicated someone resided in the cave. The man?

"Ye're awake." A woman's voice spoke gently and echoed within the enclosed space. She straightened from where she'd crouched before the fire and drew back her green hood to reveal thick raven locks and a strong chin. Her eyes were pale, though it was difficult to discern their color in the gilded light of the fire.

A sense of peace exuded from the dark haired woman and although Cassandra did not know who the stranger was, she had no fear.

The woman smiled kindly. "Welcome to Skye, Protector."

"A terrible Protector I've turned out to be," Cassandra said miserably.

The woman blinked at Cassandra. "Ye're English?"

"Aye."

"I dinna expect the Protector to be English." The woman's soft laugh was without malice.

"You are sure you have the correct woman?" Cassandra asked, unable to stem the tide of hope rising in her. None of this had been as she expected. After a lifetime of preparing for this moment, surely she could not have already failed.

"Do ye bear the sign of a dagger on yer right hip?"

Cassandra nodded.

"Then aye, ye're the keeper of the Heart of Scotland." The woman's expression sobered. "The former Protector died days ago and the transfer of the mark would have happened then."

Cassandra put her hand to the symbol on her hip, so recently emblazoned on her skin, she could still recall the strange wash of heat. "How do you come by such knowledge?"

"I am a priestess of the stone." She inclined her head. "I am called Morag and have been given information passed down through the centuries to bestow upon ye."

Cassandra's shoulders relaxed somewhat. Having someone to guide her on her quest would make it easier, would it not? Countless questions buzzed through her mind and came to rest on the large man with dark eyes who had been at the pool. The way he'd looked at her, as though he were mesmerized by her. It was too easy to bring to mind again and again. In fact, it did so without her meaning to.

But, nay, she would not ask about him. Not yet. "Has the stone been in the water for centuries?" she asked finally.

"When a Protector dies with the stone in their possession, the stone returns here to the mystical fairy pools and waits to be claimed."

"I didn't claim it." Cassandra shifted her gaze from Morag to the crude table. A massive chunk of cheese rested on the wooden surface along with a loaf of bread. Despite the pang of Cassandra's regret at having failed to get the stone, hunger rasped within her belly.

"It isna always so." Morag approached the table, lifted a slender knife and sliced a thick wedge of cheese. She handed both the cheese and loaf of bread to Cassandra.

The bread was warm against her palm, and crusty, as though it'd been not long out of the oven. Her mouth watered with urgency. Instead she swallowed and shook her head. "I cannot take your food."

Morag was already walking away. "Eat. Recover yer strength. When ye have gotten the rest and sustenance ye've deprived yerself of, and when ye've learned enough of yer task, then ye may go after the stone. Then ye will be ready."

Cassandra daintily broke a corner of the cheese off to nibble at in a ladylike fashion. No sooner had the creamy, sharp cheese touched her tongue, a ravenous hunger nearly took over. She tried to chew with decorum, but her mouth watered too ferociously.

Morag placed a cup of wine in front of her. Cassandra had not been so thirsty until that very moment, when faced with the prospect of drinking again. Her throat burned for liquid. She lifted it with shaking hands to her lips where she drained the sweet wine in two large gulps. Her mouth had been so very dry, her stomach so empty. It was a wonder she had been able to make it as long as she had on so little.

"The stone enhances one's powers." Morag refilled the cup from a ewer of wine and placed a hunk of dried beef in front of Cassandra. "Everyone has special abilities granted from the stone, and they will grow stronger when it is on their person. Each skill is different, as is each person's experience in getting their mark, claiming the stone, taking guardianship of the stone..." She trailed off with a smile. "I believe you understand."

Cassandra nodded and bit an unladylike chunk from the bread. The crust flaked apart against her tongue, and her teeth sank into the tender white center. She almost moaned with delight.

"He mustn't be allowed to keep the stone," Morag warned, her tone ominous.

A trickle of icy fear crept up Cassandra's spine. She set aside the cup and stared at the priestess.

"He sought the stone for selfish purposes." Morag set the ewer upon the small table. "His intent is not to ensure the safety and prosperity of Scotland like you. If he is allowed to keep the stone, Scotland will suffer for his avarice. The earth will lose her balance and great storms will plague Scotland with famine and pestilence and death to follow."

"When will this happen?" Cassandra demanded.

"Some will begin immediately, but the worst will follow in two moon cycles."

"I must go now." Cassandra leapt to her feet, but exhaustion caught at her and she stumbled backward.

Morag smiled sadly. "If yer fate is as yer predecessors, ye have a lifetime of battle ahead of ye. The war between light and dark is one driven by the balance of life and will ensue until the end of time. Rest, my dear. Ye may leave in the morning. Then yer fight will begin in earnest."

The man's image filled Cassandra's mind. The impossibly large man with dark eyes and dark hair, the way he'd stopped in his desperate charge to stare at her, as though he were fascinated. Curious, mayhap. Her pulse flickered at her memory. She had not been unaffected. Would she truly need to battle him?

She supposed she would discover as much once she found him, and she knew she would. The earth hummed beneath her feet with an eagerness to lead her to him. She would have to reclaim the stone, even if it did mean a fight. Though in the depths of her heart, she hoped it did not.

THE WOMAN HAD BEGUN TO FOLLOW FERGUS THE PRIOR DAY. HE'D sensed her presence as soon as she'd left the veiled cover of the mystical pools. She moved swiftly, and with purpose, and yet even though he was just south of the Isle of Skye, she took long enough to strain his fragile patience.

Fergus paced his narrow room in the inn. It had already seemed small when he'd first rented the chamber, but now its walls threatened to crush in against him with more insistence, its ceiling impossibly low. Anticipation was getting the better of him.

He put his hand over the stone where it lay tucked beneath his leine. Power pulsed against his skin. But it was not anything he would possess forever. Even if he had intended to keep it for his own, he would never grow accustomed to its warm, unnatural glow.

It didn't stink of magic. Not like the witch had. But it was reminiscent of it all the same, filled with too many bitter memories. The sensation of it prickled at his skin. He wanted to scrub his hands over his body and remove every bit of it from his person. If the stone did not heighten his ability to read people, if he did not need it on his person to bring to Edgar in bartering for his son, he would throw the blasted thing away.

For now, it was half of what the king required. Once Fergus had the woman in his possession, he would make haste to Edinburgh where King Edgar awaited the woman and the stone. The idea of it was simple, an exchange of sorts - the stone and the Protector for the boy.

The boy.

Fergus snorted derisively into the empty room. He didn't even know the lad's name. In every way, he had failed as a father. First he'd failed to protect the lad's mother, then when he'd been persuaded by the king to join his guard, he'd accepted in the hopes of finding the lad within the keep somewhere. All attempts to locate his son had met with more failure. The king was a crafty devil.

The sweet scent of apples caressed Fergus' senses and took the edge off the restlessness rattling through him. She was near.

He lifted his pack from the floor and strode from the crude rented room. It would be better for her to assume she caught him rather than discover him awaiting her arrival. His horse whinnied upon his arrival, the massive black hooves stamping into the hay-covered earth in the stable.

Fergus swung into the saddle and urged his steed through the streets, away from the dismal village. The sun shone openly upon him, the sky a stretch of clear, cloudless blue. He rode on for the lesser part of an hour when he sensed her. The force of her energy swelled against him, rendering her presence unmistakable. An eagerness sizzled through his veins and surprised him.

He could too easily recall the flush of her cheeks and mouth, the gentleness of her face. She intrigued and enticed him, a delicate wisp of a thing who hit stronger than any knight he'd ever fought.

Then again, mayhap it had been his surprise at finding she could hit at all. Perchance she was not as strong as he remembered. Soon he would find out, and this time he would pay careful attention.

Only her attack did not come when expected. She hung back, hidden from sight. Indeed, if it wasn't for the wavering warmth of her presence lapping at his awareness, he would have assumed she'd left.

Like a true warrior with proper training, she bided her time, her patience immeasurable. She didn't attack when he'd stopped to camp, nor when he'd hunted his supper, or even when he'd stopped to eat the roasted meat. Nay, it was long after he'd lain still in his bedroll, beyond the time it took before the fire smoldered into glowing red embers. That's when the sweet scent of summer apples filled the cave where he'd taken refuge.

Her movement rippled through his consciousness though her feet made not the slightest shuffle. She crept close enough so he could feel her like a wave of heat. His nostrils flared at her delicious scent, as though he might devour the smell as readily as he could the fruit.

She stood over him, but did not move to attack. He curled his hand around the hilt of his dagger and waited.

Nothing happened. Her breathing remained smooth and even, while her movements did not arc out toward him to indicate her intention of an attack. What the devil was she getting at?

He opened his eyes and stared up at her. She did not flinch from his glare.

God's teeth but she was beautiful. A dark cloak had been pulled over her black curls. It shaded her face and left her eyes glowing pale and luminous in the firelight. She crouched near him, yet her hands were free of a weapon.

"Why do ye no' attack?" he demanded.

"I do not wish to fight," she answered simply. Her voice melted over him like honey, light and feminine, quietly breathy.

"Because ye will fail," he surmised.

"I do not fear defeat. Nor do I fear you." She tilted her head. "I think I may be one of the few who does not."

She was correct, but he would not give voice to such affirmations. Not when he was unsure what she was about. He sensed curiosity from her, but naught else. No malice, nor ill intent.

"I believe you do not wish to fight me." She eased from her crouch into a more comfortable sitting position beside him, her legs crossing beneath the heavy length of her skirt. The wool lay against her calves and outlined the fine curves. "You said as much before. Do you still feel that way?"

This lass made him think little of battle and more of loving. A strange consideration, as he had not been tempted in many, many years. Not since Allisandre. Ten long years ago.

He sat up in his bedroll and assumed a similarly relaxed posture with one arm casually slung over his bent right knee. "I dinna want to fight ye. But I fear it may be unavoidable."

Her eyes settled on him, pale in the firelight. But he'd seen them in the daylight and knew them to be the fairest blue, like an iced loch in the middle of winter and rimmed with a ring of sapphire. They were fringed with lashes as dark as her black curls, and just as thick. Eyes that could steal a man's soul.

"Because you have the stone," she whispered.

"Aye," he answered in a gravelly voice. "Because I have it and I know ye want it."

4

Cassandra leaned toward the warrior with the dark mysterious eyes, half crawling to the lure of him. His heartbeat mingled with the earth and thrummed in a sweet, enticing melody. She had sensed it before, she realized, when she'd first seen him.

But, at the time, her heart had been pounding too loud in her ears to discern it in the chaos.

She stared down at his massive chest, where a slight lump rose from beneath his chain mail. The stone. Her body edged forward as though drawn toward him. She lifted her gaze to his penetrating stare.

"Aye," she said in a sultry tone she did not recognize as her own. "I want the stone."

His gaze trailed over her body, bold and unabashed. She ought to have been offended by his impertinence and should have been inclined to deliver a righteous slap upon his cheek. And yet her heart pounded too hard for her to move. Her blood ignited with a delicious heat and her nipples prickled with a sexual consciousness she'd not yet experienced.

"Is that all ye want?" he asked in a thick brogue. His eyes glittered with understanding in the low light.

His brow was creased with a lifetime of worry, but his lips were full and supple beneath his neatly trimmed beard. She found herself watching his mouth, wondering what it might feel like against hers, what he might taste like.

"I think ye'd taste like apples." He leaned on one arm, moving closer. "Crisp and sweet and fresh."

The breath fled her lips and her throat went dry. A virgin's fear within her warred with a woman's curiosity.

"That's what ye smell like." His eyes lowered and she realized he stared at her mouth with the same intensity as she gazed at his.

"Like what?" she breathed.

"Apples." He said it in a growling exhale, the sound intimately primitive.

Except it didn't scare her, it excited her. The blood shot quickly through her veins with heat and an anticipation she did not understand. She wanted to experience it all - the quiet, cool night, the wash of flickering golden light, the heady power of the stone blazing only inches from her hand, and that beautiful mouth set beneath the darkness of his beard.

"I smell like apples." Her lips curled at the thought.

"If ye dinna mean to kill me, why come here?" He shifted nearer still, until he was practically bowing over her.

Cassandra's body thrummed with heat and longing. Should she feel this way about the man with whom she was supposed to be locked in a lifelong battle? It hadn't occurred to her to ask Morag at the time.

But then, she had never expected to feel *this*.

The heat of desire was unmistakable. She stared up at him, not backing down from his question.

"Why are ye here, Protector?" His gaze raked down her body.

She arched her breasts upward, her essence alight with sexuality. With need.

"For the stone," she gasped. "For you."

"For me." He caught her waist in his massive arms and dragged her body against his.

A surprised moan escaped her lips. He could kill her right now, drag a blade across her exposed throat while her core burned with lust. She ought to flee.

The earth pulsed under her, almost undulating, encouraging her toward him. But there was something else. Heat rolled off him, like fire, threatening to consume her with the force of his own desire.

He wanted her.

The knowledge of his thoughts rolled in her mind and prickled through her with sharp, tangible awareness.

He ran a powerful hand down her back and clasped her bottom, nudging her hips against his where the heat of his manhood rose hard between them. "This is what ye want?"

Mortification blazed through her. What had she wanted? Not this. It was too much. Too soon. The force of his mind in hers, their shared need welling like fire between them. She had a purpose.

It was not the stone. She needed the stone.

Her teeth sank into her bottom lip and she slid her glance away, her emotions warring. He struggled too, somehow she sensed it.

"Ach, too much then?" He eased back and his touch smoothed over her waist. "Do ye want a lover's touch? Caresses and teasing?"

She trembled. She, who had waited for the honor of her role as Protector, who had learned how to best a man in combat and had trekked countless miles through the rugged Scottish terrain to find the stone, trembled.

The stone.

She needed the stone.

He wanted her to forget.

His palm cradled her jaw and he stared deep into her eyes. His pupils melted into the vast darkness of his irises. Beautiful.

She lost herself in the intensity of his stare, of his desire. His thumb swept over her lower lip and freed it from her teeth. He shook his head in chastisement and gently lowered his mouth to hers.

His beard tickled over her chin as his lips touched hers, warm and surprisingly soft. He tasted of the roasted rabbit he'd eaten at dinner and the sweetness of ale. His mouth closed over her lower lip in a delicate, savoring kiss - this man whose name she did not know, who had something she so desperately needed. She ought to be fighting him, not kissing him.

And yet she tilted her head to return the intimate gesture when the tip of his tongue swept against her mouth. She moaned softly and he grew more daring with his kiss, deepening it with his tongue and stoking the fires of her lust.

He could not stop himself from kissing her, wanting her at his side, and yet he hated himself for it.

She sensed betrayal lingering in his thoughts, so easily read it was as though he spoke to her.

Yet the lust was as apparent, if not more so. His emotions in her soul, his voice in her mind – all of it served only to heighten her own desire. She put her hands to his chest and found them shifting higher of their own volition, toward that lump beneath his chain mail. To the Heart of Scotland.

He jerked back and eyed her with suspicion. "Leave it."

The connection between them fell away and she no longer could sense what he thought, nor could she feel the presence of his emotions.

"Who do you betray?" she asked.

His fingers ran lightly over the ground and his face reflected a furrow of concentration.

"You hated yourself for kissing me, but you couldn't stop." Cassandra frowned. "You are betraying someone. Are you wed?"

"I was." He put his palm to the ground and studied his hand. "Ye can read thoughts as well?"

As well? He had powers as she did? "Only when you kissed me. I could hear what was in your mind, and sense it." Her cheeks went hot. "You knew my thoughts, didn't you?"

A corner of his mouth lifted in a cocky grin in response. "I knew ye would welcome my kiss."

Cassandra pressed her lips together at the still-warm sensation tingling over her mouth.

"I know ye crave more still." His gaze rose from the ground and met hers. "How did ye make the earth sing? Is that what ye can do?"

FERGUS DIDN'T NEED THE WOMAN'S ANSWER SPOKEN ALOUD WHEN

her thoughts registered the answer for him. They came at him in a vivid rush.

She'd always had a connection to the earth. That, and her entire body burned with mortification that he had read her thoughts in that intimate embrace. She didn't like that she didn't know his name.

"I'm Fergus the Undefeated," he offered. "I would offer to stymie my ability to read yer thoughts if I thought the stone was safe from ye. Cassandra." He found the name in her mind and let it grace his tongue.

The flush to her cheeks reddened further still. *He made her feel exposed.*

"Verra well," he acquiesced. "I willna search yer mind, but know I will sense any attack ye plan, aye?"

Her shoulders relaxed and a cool sense of relief washed toward him.

"I need the stone, but I do not want to fight you," she said. "You have to understand that in keeping it in your care, you will destroy Scotland."

Unease gripped Fergus. Was that why King Edgar wanted the stone? To see Scotland destroyed? But why would any king want his country left in ruin?

"I need it," Fergus said at last.

"Your need is greater than the good of Scotland?" Her brows lifted.

This lass had a feistiness to her for being such a wee bit of a thing.

"I need it to save my son," he replied earnestly.

Her brows drew together. He didn't need to read minds to know she was unsure if she ought to trust him or not. In truth, she should not. But he needed her to accompany him and would tell her anything necessary to ensure her compliance.

"He's unwell. The stone will aid him and then ye may have it when I'm done." The lie sat sourly in Fergus' mouth. He had to have her with him. Damn it, he had to have his son back.

"Why not give it to me now?" She held out her hand, as though she anticipated he might actually drop it into the softness of her slender palm.

"I know how badly ye want the stone and I canna trust that ye willna run off with it."

Her hand folded closed. "Very well, but you must allow me to travel with you."

He nodded slowly, as though he were conceding to her request. As though he didn't have to have her at his side. "Ye may travel with me. I go to Edinburgh where my son is." Guilt squeezed at him even as the darkness within him crowded at the barriers he'd erected long ago. He ought to let it in, to embrace the cold detachment it would provide. Part of him was afraid of how much it would control him, and part of him could not allow all his mother's hard work to be destroyed.

Cassandra nodded firmly, clearly assuming the matter was settled, assuming herself the victor in the discussion. Only she had no idea how terribly she had lost.

She unfurled her own bedroll across from his, on the other side of the fire. Outside the cave, lightning flickered and the roar of a fresh rainstorm sounded.

Despite their exhaustion, the night dragged on in restlessness, more in wakeful wariness than sleep, each not fully trusting the other. For his part, Fergus could rely on his heightened awareness. She would never sneak an attack upon him. However, her presence left him unnerved.

It had been years since he craved a woman at his side, over a decade. Not since Allisandre.

Mayhap it was Cassandra's incredible beauty, or the fascination of her being a Protector. Certainly it had something to do with the sweetness of her scent and how badly she made him long for her. Even as he lay opposite, his arms ached to hold her. His eyes refused to close, instead wandering repeatedly toward her smooth face, relaxed in slumber beneath the flickering light of the fire's embers.

At long last, the effects of weariness won out over his thoughts and he gave in to the quiet lull of sleep.

They came in the night, the cowardly bastards, and pulled Allisandre from his arms. The stink of magic hung thick in the air. It clogged in his throat and rendered him frozen in place. The soldiers were quick, sent with purpose, their deeds executed with precision. They clearly had been imbued with a darkness that left their movements unnatural and sent Fergus' heart pumping like a dog on a hunt. Only when they'd jerked her from him did the magical binding break and Fergus was freed to snatch the dagger from beneath the mattress.

Allisandre screamed, a terrified cry that cut him to his soul. She writhed in their shadowy grips, her body swollen with Fergus' child, her bright red hair streaming about her like fire.

There were too many of them and Fergus' body would not obey as quickly as was necessary. It was as though he moved through a bog. Even the sharpness of his senses were dulled, save for the acute agony of loss.

There hadn't been a damn thing Fergus could do to protect his pregnant wife. Nay, they had dragged her from him as he watched, helplessly. He had lost everything.

The air shifted, and the scent of magic prickled his nostrils like an impending rainstorm. The intent of movement drew his awareness with the beginnings of an attack. Fergus grasped the dagger from under his pillow and threw it with all his might at whoever planned to attack him. His actions were so fast, his target would never have been able to dodge the lethal blow.

He did not open his eyes, not wanting to see Allisandre being dragged away in the moonlight again. Then another scent appeared beneath the foulness of magic and made his eyes fly open. Apples. Sweet and fresh.

Cassandra.

He sat up, fully awake, painfully aware. Her ragged breath pulled his attention to where she sat against the rough cave wall, her eyes open wide in shock with the dagger caught between her hands.

5

Cassandra stared at the tip of the dagger, barely one inch from her face. Had she not had the skill and strength to catch it, the wicked blade would have soared straight through her head.

"Cassandra." Fergus called to her in a hoarse voice.

She ought to have been afraid. Her heart surely should race with her death defying catch and how close she was to her own mortality. Yet her hand was steady as she lowered the blade and regarded Fergus. "You threw a knife at my head."

"No' with intention."

"You have tremendous aim without intention." She rose to her feet and handed the dagger to him.

His fingers closed over the hilt and brushed her own. His thoughts poured into her.

He was afraid. Not only of having almost killed her, for she was too important to lose, but also from the magic in the air.

She drew in a deep inhale and recognized the prickling scent of magic from his mind. "You don't like magic. Why not?"

He grasped the hilt more firmly and snatched it out of her hands. "It's nearly dawn."

It was no answer. Frustration tightened through her shoulders. "Why do you worry at having almost killed me?" she asked. "I was under the impression we were supposed to fight one another to our dying breaths."

The lines on his brow creased with intense concentration while he pointedly ignored her. He crouched beside where he slept and rolled his bedding into a neat bundle.

"Are we supposed to fight?" she pressed.

He glared up at her. "We should go."

The magic still lingered in the air, a cool, wet scent. "Where did the magic come from?"

He shot to his feet and glowered at her. "Why do ye ask so many damn questions?"

She stood her ground. "Because you're not answering a single one."

His eyes narrowed. "I almost killed ye."

"I'm not so easily slain." She folded her arms over her chest. "Why do you hate magic?"

"Nothing good ever comes from it." He scooped a handful of water from the small bowl by the fire and splashed it over his face. It dripped from his dark beard. "Maybe ye should be asking, because I haven't an idea."

"The stone is magic," Cassandra pointed out.

He scrubbed a linen over his face. "It's different."

A gray light cast toward the back wall of the small cave, indicating the sun had begun to rise. There would be no point in attempting to go back to sleep.

"We wouldna be here if it werena for this stone." His lip lifted with disgust and his gaze wandered down to his chest where the lump of the stone lay beneath the chain mail he'd slept in.

If she'd had chain mail, she would have slept in it too. "Let me have it."

He smirked. "Is it no' enough ye draw from its power by being near?"

She tried to tamp down the swell of impatience. It would not get her the stone any faster. And he could sense every emotion threading through her.

"It is dangerous for you to keep." She spoke quietly in an attempt to leverage her patience. "You will destroy all of Scotland if it remains in your care."

His somber expression darkened. "Because magic is a terrible thing. Even earthy magic like this."

"That magic will save your son."

She thought he might not have an argument against that. But he turned his head to the side and said, "Magic stole my wife."

He hefted his packs and strode from the cave. Cassandra hurriedly assembled her own effects. A wild chill rent down her spine. She couldn't lose him. She couldn't lose the stone.

The hard packed dirt floor gave way to mud as Cassandra neared the mouth of the cave. Rain continued to pour down without respite. The horses had been tucked beneath a stone ledge that acted as a crude shelter over their heads. If nothing else, it had kept them relatively dry.

Fergus stood beside his horse, tying the packs into place behind his heavy saddle. Phillip had a similar leather seat, reinforced with a pommel to keep him locked into place despite the weight of his chain mail, and studded with metal to offer protection with the luxury befitting a knight.

The thought of her brother seemed like recalling another life, one a world away without hunger and rain, where she had a warm bed and the worst of her troubles was her family's heavy expectation. Phillip's broad smile radiated in her mind and left her heart aching for him and his constant instructions. She missed the comforts of home, but more than anything, she missed her brother.

The rain came down with such terrible might, any conversation between her and Fergus was impossible. Which was well and good, for it did not appear Fergus wished to speak. Indeed nor did she. Not when her soul was pained with the loss of everything she missed.

Together the miserable pair of them staggered through the storm, enduring the downpour as it pelted them with enough force to sting the exposed skin on their cheeks and hands. Their progress was painstakingly slow and the shoreline of the Isle of Skye took the better part of three hours to appear when it ought to have taken a third of the time.

Lightning streaked across the sky and flickered a brilliant light over them. Cassandra turned her face from the ominous sky and regarded Fergus. "We should wait for the storm to pass."

He shook his head and pushed his horse onward to the gravel shore where a lone birlinn lay on its side. The vessel was crude, fashioned from a wooden hull with oars set beneath the narrow row of seats. Fergus hopped down from his horse and approached the simple boat.

The water ahead, their necessary path for quitting the island and making their way back to land, churned and roiled with wild, erratic waves swelling from all angles without any predictable pattern. Cassandra was no sailor, but even she knew navigating such waters would be impossible. "No one will ferry us across. Not today."

"I dinna expect they will." Fergus spoke loudly to be heard over the storm. He made his way back to his horse and removed his packs.

Cassandra watched him warily. "We will not be able to take the horses." Nor did the birlinn belong to them. She could not help but assume it most likely belonged to a simple fisherman, one whose livelihood no doubt depended on the small boat.

"We'll no' be taking the horses." He motioned for her to remove her items from her horse. "They'll be payment for the birlinn."

Within minutes, he had approached a small home in the distance and negotiated possession of the vessel from an overjoyed man who gladly traded the boat for the quality horseflesh he received in return. Securing the vessel though was only the smaller part of their victory. They still had to survive the crossing.

THE WAVES WASHED OVER THE SIDES OF THE SIMPLE BOAT AND sloshed against them. Fergus and Cassandra were drenched, both from the splash of seawater and the deluge still raining down from above. Fergus rowed with all his might, but the birlinn seemed no further from the shore than it had been half an hour before.

Lightning flashed, followed by a crack of thunder so loud, it made their boat vibrate. Fergus' stomach rolled with the waves, knocking and swirling until sweat formed beneath the layers of rain and seawater.

"Let me take the oars," Cassandra shouted.

It was on the tip of Fergus' tongue to refuse to allow a lady to head the rowing. But his stomach lurched in protest of doing anything more than cradling the offending bit of his body and wishing for relief however that might come. He shoved the oars in her direction.

Their hands briefly touched and strength whispered between them. It bolstered his countenance with a reserve he would not have otherwise had. She gripped the oars and drew her body back in a hearty row. The boat bobbed over the waves and glided further from the shore. Several more rows and they were finally making headway through the terrible might of the storm.

Even still as they rowed onward, the helplessness to the violent swaying gripped Fergus once more. His entire world swayed and his body was suddenly too feeble to keep him upright. A formidable wave slammed into the boat and delivered upon them a savage knock to the right. Fergus' body lulled limp to the edge and teetered over the water for a brief moment.

A strong hand grasped his wrist and jerked him back. Again, the strength soared between them, and drove away the debilitating effects of his weakness. But he was not the only one to feel something from their connection.

Power roared through Cassandra's veins and cast a calm through her soul. The stone called to her. He could hear it over the noise of the storm, and his own illness.

She did not know what to do with it. Frustration balled within her and rippled the calm.

Fergus remembered that very irritation when he'd first come into his ability. Not truly understanding it, yet knowing it was there. "Close yer eyes," he ground out.

She closed her eyes, her hand still locked about his wrist. He grasped her other hand with his free one and locked their connection. Her strength hummed through his veins and the storm's roar intensified with her connection to the earth. The sea beneath them pulsed with a thundering heartbeat as though it were locked in battle, and the wind sang in his ears. How did she manage living in such chaos?

He could sense her searching the link between them, testing it, testing him. A shudder wracked through him and a wall went up in his mind to block her from his thoughts. With their shared power, he would need to always be vigilant to keep her from knowing his mind.

Instead, he sent out memories of his own experiences. The way he had learned to tame it over the years, to groom it into submission so he was no longer at its mercy.

Cassandra released one of his hands and stretched her palm out over the water. The energy between them welled and drained from him toward her. Her fingers trembled.

The waves surrounding their boat calmed to a gentle lapping at the sides of the birlinn. Everywhere else, the water roiled and churned and spit angrily at them, yet their vessel remained in place.

Disbelief threatened to overwhelm Cassandra. This was more than she ever thought possible of herself.

And yet she could do so, so much more. Fergus could sense it simmering under the surface of her doubt, like a pot ready to boil over. Only she would have to find it for herself. He knew as much from experience with himself.

Allisandre had known about his skills and encouraged him with them, driving him to push harder and concentrate more. Those sessions had never been helpful and had ended with Fergus exhausted and frustrated, with ripples of disappointment flowing off Allisandre.

He would not do the same now to Cassandra.

They remained stationary in the calm water. Fergus' body, however, continued to suffer the effects of the brutal waves, even though they no longer pummeled against the birlinn. His stomach clenched mercilessly and made him grateful he had not broken his fast yet that day.

Cassandra realized his plight and could not herself row the boat while concentrating on her abilities. She needed her other hand.

Fergus released her hand. The connection cut immediately between them and the boat pitched violently in the water, nearly tumbling them both overboard. His hands shot out and clasped her waist to steady her, to connect them once more. Energy hummed and crackled again, flowing from the stone and through Fergus to Cassandra.

The sea settled near their vessel even as the storm raged overhead. She carefully put out her left hand on the other side of the boat and swept her fingers gracefully forward. The boat glided toward their destined shore, nudged speedily along by ripples of currents beneath the still water beneath them.

He was impressed. Thoroughly so. She had grappled her talents and put them to immediate use. The warmth of her flattered pleasure washed over him, and he knew she heard his praising thoughts.

His other thoughts, though, he continued to keep walled up. The ones of his fear for his son, the truth of his ultimate impending deception of Cassandra, and even the surge of desire gripping him as he held her narrow waist. The warmth of her skin heated his palms through her wet kirtle and her ribs flexed and swelled with each breath. She was life against his touch, slender and beautiful.

They neared the shore when the boat began to slow and began to rock hard from side to side once more. Cassandra's hands lowered slightly and her weight sagged against his hold. Her energy was faltering. But then, she was not accustomed to so fully applying her ability. She flicked her hands forward and a mighty wave crashed into the back of the birlinn. The boat slid quickly over the water and did not stop until it bounced against the rocky shore.

Despite his own weakness and the churning of his stomach, Fergus drew her in his arms along with their packs and hopped from the boat, lest they be pulled back out into the violent sea.

For surely, they might not survive a second time. He staggered to the shoreline, set Cassandra to her feet, and collapsed to his knees, heedless of the sharp stones biting through his surcoat and woolen hose and the icy water lapping over his feet. Cassandra pulled the packs from his arms and hefted the incredible weight into her thin arms without issue despite her exhaustion.

She set them gingerly on the sandy shore and dug through her pack until she produced a twisted root. Using the edge of her blade, she scraped away the smooth brown bark and presented him with a sliver of yellow white root. "Chew on this. It will settle your stomach."

He accepted it and obediently popped it in his mouth. It was spicy and wet against his tongue and produced a sharp juice when he bit down upon it. True to her word, after several minutes, the discomfort passed and he was able to rise to his feet without the world swaying about him.

Cassandra was weak, evidenced by the waning of her arcing energy. Fergus was as well, sapped by the weakness of his body after the violent crossing. They may be on dry land and he may be standing, but they needed shelter to recover or they'd be vulnerable to any kind of attack.

Fergus set his hand to the stone at his chest. Its warmth radiated against his palm, ensuring him of its presence. He couldn't do anything to risk the loss of this stone, not when his son awaited him. There was too much to lose.

6

Shelter was a necessary need. Fortunately, there were several homes near the shore, one of which even opened their door to Fergus. The eye and nose peering with wary curiosity through a slender crack had instructed them toward an inn a furlong or so away. Indeed, they found the aged building with a slight right lean to it, and were able to secure a room until the following morning.

It had been Fergus' intent to provide an additional room for Cassandra, out of respect. However, he sensed fear spike in her at the thought of being away from him. She still did not trust him.

While he could not blame her cautious regard, he did not like it.

After getting a plate of hearty stew for Cassandra and a bit of bread and ale to further ease his own stomach, Fergus led her from the common room up the dark, narrow stairs to the row of rented rooms above. His legs were heavy as lead and his entire body seemed to sag under the burden of exhaustion. Still, he stayed near Cassandra's side should she need him for support. The feat of getting them over the water had greatly taxed her strength and the energy around her wavered like a candle near the end of its wick.

Inside their room, the innkeeper's wife was tying off a string against one side of the wall, so it draped in front of the fireplace. She tugged it with her reddened fingers and turned her cheerful face in their direction. There was a sweetness emanating from her, genuine and kind, the sort he'd only seen in his mother.

"Ach, ye ate faster than I thought ye would." The innkeeper's wife wiped her hands on the skirt of her kirtle in a manner which seemed more habit than necessity. "Ye looked as though ye might need dry things, so I brought ye some of our clothes to wear while ye set yers by the fire." She looked down at herself then to Cassandra and flushed. "I'm no' the wisp of a lass I once was, mind ye, and my husband is no' so braw as ye." Her gaze crept up to Fergus' chest and shoulders. The flush deepened and Fergus intentionally kept himself from her thoughts. "But they'll do fine." She hummed in confirmation to herself. "Aye, fine enough. If ye need anything further, dinna hesitate to give a call."

"That was kind of you, thank you." Cassandra smiled at the woman who nodded briskly, wiped her hands upon her kirtle once more, and departed the room.

On the bed lay two simple tunics, both made of rough wool, as well as two undergarments of linen. It was indeed a kindness for their hosts to bestow upon them when people of their financial standing most likely owned only a few items of clothing.

"We ought to change lest we fall ill." Cassandra set her packs down and stepped toward him. "Do you need assistance with your chain mail?"

God's teeth, did she mean to help undress him? His groin tightened at the very thought.

"I assisted my brother with his chain mail often." She put a hand to where the armor lay heavy against his shoulder. "I do not mind."

"Yer brother is a knight?" He shifted his arms upward and knelt to allow her the ability to draw the bulk of metal away.

"Aye, same as my father."

The weighty mail was lifted off and the rings clinked loudly against one another as she carefully set it aside. She was a knight's daughter. One whose brother had earned the honor as well. She was no simple peasant, though he'd known that from her noble manner of speech and the pride with which she carried herself.

She turned back toward him and scoffed. "You needn't look at me like that."

He raised his brows, pretending he could not sense her thoughts. Keeping himself from hearing her was significantly more difficult than he had anticipated. After a lifetime of being open to the emotions and thoughts of others, it was almost impossible to close it off, especially when his powers were so heightened by the grace of the stone.

She didn't want him feeling guilty about being in this room alone with her, for having held her waist on the birlinn. For having kissed her. She had liked it far too much to regret it herself.

"I'm the youngest daughter of three," she said. "Even if I had not been born under the burden of Protector, marriage would be difficult to obtain unless it was to a local shopkeeper."

Sensual heat radiated off her. He tried to keep his body from responding, for it was more than the energy they shared between them. There was also the simmering heat of attraction, a drawing of two bodies toward one another with the sizzling promise of consensual passion.

"I shall turn my back while ye undress," he said.

She pressed her red lips together and nodded.

Disappointed.

He spun away and tugged at the wet wool of his surcoat to peel it away from his linens beneath. His phallus beat with the healthy thrum of his heartbeat, wanting. He tossed the surcoat to the floor with a wet slap. A similar sound came from behind him where Cassandra undressed likewise. He imagined her, slender and milky white.

His cock hardened.

She wanted him to come to her. There was a frustrating heat between her legs she knew he could ease. She tried to summon an image of his body without clothing but her innocent mind had no reference. She wanted to see, to know, to touch and feel.

He clenched his hands into fists. He could take her. Right now. The temptation was great and it had been so damn long. But she was a maiden. He squeezed his fists so his closely cropped fingernails bit into his palms and reminded himself how he had failed Allisandre.

He summoned a mental wall to block her lusty thoughts and put it in front of his own to keep his thoughts from being read by her when they touched. The effort caused sweat to prickle his brow despite the wet chill settling over his skin. A worthy effort, for the sound of her thoughts went silent at long last.

"Oh." Cassandra's voice startled him from the depth of his concentration. "You are not...dressed yet...I had assumed..." Her stammered words were breathy and disjointed. Clearly she was distracted.

Fergus snatched up the linen and threw it over his head. The underclothes barely reached his knees. The tunic fell similarly short and both stretched tight over his shoulders.

He turned to Cassandra with an apology on his lips and found her slender body lost in a tent of fabric, her tunic as large as his was small. Her shapely calves were visible below the hem where her clothing fell short as his did.

Her gaze slid over him and he did not need to read her mind to know she was seeing what lay beneath the cloth, her innocent interest lit. His body reacted with an eagerness to sate that curiosity, as well as other necessary needs they both shared.

Her hair was still wet and hung in limp curls down her shoulders, some falling down her back, the rest spilling over her chest where it parted over her breasts. The loose fabric did not offer any support to her breasts and left her pert nipples jutting from under the fabric. He wondered if her skin was still cold, if those pink buds would be cool and hard against his tongue while he heated her flesh with his mouth.

"Tell me about your wife," she said softly.

Her request jarred him from his lusty thoughts and guilt slammed hard into him. He busied himself with picking up his clothing to hang on the string set before the fire.

"I need to know," Cassandra said.

"Why?" he asked through gritted teeth. "Why must ye know?"

She lifted her wet kirtle and placed it over the hanging line by the fire. The move was nonchalant, but the gaze she slid him from the corner of her eyes was not. "I would not want to attempt to lay claim to any woman's husband."

THE ADMISSION OF DESIRE OUGHT TO HAVE EMBARRASSED Cassandra, but it did not. Her longing was too great. Fergus put his back to her while he hung up his surcoat on the line.

She recalled all too well every inch of his naked body. His dark hair hanging down the broad expanse of his back, shadowed with muscle. The strength of his legs and his firm arse. It had made her mouth go dry to see him thus and she could not clear it from her mind. She had no wish to clear it from her mind.

He turned slowly to her. His wife was gone is what he'd said before. Did that mean she had left their home as people sometimes did? That she was dead?

Cassandra had been truthful when she'd said she didn't want to lay claim to any woman's husband. And with every molten drop of blood thundering through her veins, she wanted him.

"She's dead." He lifted his hose from the ground and draped them over the string.

Cassandra followed likewise, helping him put up his clothing beside her own kirtle. "Because of magic."

"Aye. Over ten years ago." His jaw clenched.

An ache settled in Cassandra's chest. If ten years had passed and he still mourned her, the affection between them must have been strong. "You must have loved her," she offered weakly.

Immediately she regretted having said such words. She did not want to hear of his love for his wife, no matter how foolish it made her.

His brows furrowed and the creased lines of perpetual worry there deepened. "She understood me," he answered slowly. "And I failed her."

"What did magic have to do with it?" Cassandra was pressing now, practically begging for information, and yet she could not stop herself. This girlish infatuation with the dark knight, the man tied to the same fate as she, the draw between them, was too great to ignore. It wasn't just that she wanted him. She *needed* him. The way one needed air.

He gazed down at her with his dark eyes and all the emotion roiling within. His hand lifted, palm up in silent invitation. He wanted her to touch him.

She lifted her fingers and their skin touched. Power shot through them both, firing through their veins simultaneously.

The memory swirled through her and consumed her thoughts. *The crackle of magic, the helplessness, Allisandre's scream while she clutched her belly. The hard look of accusation as she was dragged away.* She blamed him.

Cassandra blinked and stared up into Fergus' eyes with understanding of what made him hurt.

"It wasn't your fault." She squeezed his hand. "There was nothing you could have done."

"I failed her." The force of his disappointment blazed through her. It wasn't love that cradled her to his soul, it was guilt.

His brow furrowed with pained concentration. "She's dead because of me."

"That was your son in her womb. And now he's ill."

Fergus pulled his hand from hers. "Aye." He backed away from her, as though he meant to put as much distance between himself and the conversation as possible. "She died where they held her, after having given birth to him."

"I will do anything to help you save him," Cassandra vowed. "Anything."

He looked away and she wished they were touching so she could read his thoughts. How she envied his ability.

"It isna always good to read minds," he replied. "I canna keep from doing it. They fill my thoughts even when I dinna want them to."

"Could you read my thoughts earlier?" she asked.

"Earlier," he said in a gruff tone. "In the birlinn."

"More recent than that." She let her memory glide back to the image of him naked, to the heat of her desire even as her body had been so cold while she'd dressed. How she had wanted nothing more than for him to come to her, to touch her.

Her nipples were pleasantly hard and the rasp of the rough fabric against them caused sensitive little ripples of delight. The intimate place between her legs pulsed with mind-numbing need. She wanted his mouth on hers again. She wanted to see the front of his body, to touch it, to explore what the energy they shared between them might do when they were mated together.

"I can hear yer thoughts now," he said tightly.

Touch me. Kiss me. Satisfy this ache within me. She called out to him with her mind. She willed him to take her and yet he did not move.

The cold shame of realization washed over her. He may not want. Her burgeoning confidence wobbled. How foolish to have not even considered—

"Ye're a maiden, Cassandra." His gaze raked over the massive dress she wore and settled on her breasts. "Ye're a knight's daughter." There was more. Something he wasn't saying.

"I have no hope for an advantageous marriage as my sisters do, nor do I desire one. This is my path. It has always been my path."

"Cassandra." Her name came out in a growl.

"The stone and us, we are tied together as one." She put her hands to his chest.

He knew he would fail her too.

Cassandra shook her head. "You won't fail me."

The thought disappeared and the fire of lust took its place, white hot and ravenous. His heartbeat thundered under her fingertips. She stared up in his eyes, lost in the dark depths there, drawn into his power and the force of their desire.

"If I kiss ye, I willna be able to stop." His lust was only barely restrained. She could sense the difficulty he had in maintaining himself even now, and she pried against it with her own will, her own want.

He cupped the back of her head in his large palm and tilted her face up to his. "Ye undo me, Cassandra." His mouth lowered to hers and he kissed her with all the heat of his desire.

7

Cassandra's world lit in the glow of raw energy mingling with beautiful passion. Her own yearning melded with his and roared between them. He caught her more tightly against him and slanted his mouth over hers.

His tongue swept between the seam of her lips, as it had done before, as she'd fantasized about since. She licked at his mouth, eager to match the pleasure he gave. Not only did he like it, she sensed his anticipation as tangibly as her own.

Her hands still rested against his chest, her palms humming with the strength wavering off the stone and whirling about them like brilliant starlight. His mouth ravaged hers in the most delicious of ways. His lips ground against hers, as though he wanted to consume all of her with their kiss. But she knew there was more to what they did than a kiss. She could feel it in the heaviness of her breasts, the heat pulsing between her legs, the hardness of his groin straining against her stomach.

He broke off their kiss and stared down at her with glittering black eyes. His lip curled in a lopsided smile, arrogant and so handsome it caught her breath. "Ach, aye, lass. There is much, much more."

He ran his thumb over her mouth, still tingling from their shared kisses, and ran the digit down her throat. He lowered his head and pressed his lips to her neck. The skin there was far more sensitive than she'd ever realized. Her whole body prickled to life at the simple, intimate kiss. She cradled him in her arms and curled him closer to her.

His hands skimmed down her shoulder, over her back and to the sides of her breasts. She moaned with an innate need and thrust her chest forward. He groaned and swept a finger over her nipple. Sharp pleasure shot through her and she sucked in a breath.

His beard rasped against her neck while the heat of his mouth trailed from her earlobe to the juncture between her shoulders and neck, and down to her neckline. He massaged her breasts in his palms and the blunt ends of his fingers circled the hard points of her nipples, again and again and again until she thought she might die of want.

He chuckled. "Impatient."

Cassandra closed her eyes and focused on the energy between them. She found the thread of his lust and followed its source to what he longed for. Her fingers raked down his chest past where his tight stomach flexed with each hard breath, and to the rigid staff jutting against her.

He hissed an exhale between his teeth and his hips jerked. Sexual delight sizzled through him and filtered through her by her touch. She molded her fingers around the hard bulk, measuring and teasing all at once. He thrust forward and his eyes closed in obvious enjoyment.

She nuzzled his ear, the way he'd done with her and spoke against his ear lobe so her breath whispered hot against his skin. "Who is impatient now?"

He grasped her bottom with both hands and the hem of her skirt lifted. The chilled air of the room swept over her knees. She grasped his shoulders to keep from falling while her world spun. He settled her pelvis against his and the hard length of his maleness nudged against her center.

She gave a little cry without meaning to. A flicker of arrogant pride flitted through him and she might have cast him a teasing chastisement had he not taken that moment to rub against her intimate place once more.

The friction built a decadent heat to what was already warm and aching. She found herself arching against him in a helpless rhythm that only seemed to leave her more frustrated.

Please.

Though she said it only in her mind, his eyes lit with intent. He fisted the fabric at her bottom and raked his hands upward, drawing the tunic and the linen together in one fluid sweep that left her entirely nude. The sudden loss of their touch, their connection, rendered her bereft and alone.

Cassandra's body heated at the vulnerable exposure and her hands lifted to cover herself. Fergus took her hands and shook his head without ever drawing his gaze from her.

With that simple, innocent touch came a barrage of his thoughts. How perfectly lovely he found her. *A goddess.*

She flushed and had only begun to think how she longed to see him when he jerked the hem of his tunic over his head. The breath fled Cassandra's lungs and every bit of moisture fled her mouth. She shifted her legs together, discovering where the wetness in her body had gone in a pulsing madness of need.

Fergus' back had been glorious and impressive. But the front of him…

Cassandra's mouth parted in awe. The massive span of his shoulders rippled with strength that ran over his powerful chest. His stomach clenched with bands of muscles with each breath. The stone was a deep green gem which hung from a gilded chain against his chest. Her gaze lingered there briefly before curiosity drove her onward. A sprinkling of dark hair covered his torso and ran in a tantalizing line from the indent of his navel.

On his hip, the opposite one of her own, was the mark of a dagger, pointing the other direction. Her match. She gasped and met his eye. He nodded in silent agreement. "We are both bound to the stone. To each other."

She put her hand to her own hip and let her fingertip skim over the mark there. Even as she caressed it, curiosity pulled her stare lower still, down, down, down to—

She jerked her gaze away. The column of desire she'd felt beneath the tunic had seemed large, but not quite so long, nor so…alive. It ticked in time with his heartbeat, the head massively swollen as though it were to the point of bursting.

"It's a flattering assessment," he said playfully. "But I assure ye, I'll keep it from bursting until I've felt ye climax around me."

She lifted her curious stare to him once more. Up his sculpted calves, over the strength of his thighs to where the patch of dark, curling hair embraced the base of his phallus. Fear snagged at the back of her mind and warred with desire.

At least until Fergus touched his fingertips to her chin, just below her lips.

He would be gentle. Loving. The way she deserved. He wanted to please her. With his hands. His mouth. His cock.

She gasped softly at the vulgar word and yet her yearning intensified. He pulled her lower lip down slightly and then kissed her with reserved hunger. She didn't want this gentleness from him. She nipped at his mouth and arced her tongue against his to encourage a battle of lust.

He growled, a sound which vibrated through her and hummed at her core. The energy soared between them, bright with the promise of sated satisfaction, an end to the drive of sexual frustration. He cupped her breast and toyed with the nipple as he had before. Without warning and so quickly she did not anticipate his movement, he lowered his head over her breast and pulled one pink bud into the heat of his mouth, suckling. A needling pleasure prickled through her.

She cried out, her voice husky. He secured her to him with his arm about her lower back and walked the fingers of his free hand down from her breast, past her navel to where she burned for his touch. He licked her nipple, slowly at first with the flat of his tongue before circling it and flicking it repeatedly before finally sucking it between his lips once more.

Finally, when she was nearly mad with his caresses, he clasped her thigh and drew her leg over his hip. His skin was hot against hers, the hair of the back of his legs prickly where it brushed her calf and heel. Something blunt brushed the juncture between her legs, hard and hot.

Fergus' body tensed and she sensed the restraint in him become far more difficult to maintain. She pushed her hips forward so the edge of him pushed against her. Their marks overlapped one another, his pointing to the right, hers pointed to the left. Heat fissured between them and raced through their blood.

His arm at her back tightened. The stone pressed between them and threatened to burn Cassandra's skin where its weight bore into her. A headiness robbed her of breath, though she could not tell if it was the stone, or if it was Fergus.

"No' yet." He paused to breathe, and she knew with her heightened awareness they shared that he needed the moment to reclaim his control.

And yet so much of her wanted to shatter it.

His free hand brushed against her inner thigh, caressing while drifting higher up, closer and closer to the heat throbbing between her legs.

"Yer want is making this so damn impossible," he said in a ragged voice. "Knowing how bad ye want me." He gritted his teeth. "How bloody bad I want ye."

His fingers skimmed between her thighs and pleasure threatened to tear her apart, the combination of hers and the power of his. He bowed his head over her and captured her mouth with his as his fingers stroked and stroked and stroked until she cried out with blind need against his lips.

When she thought she could stand the teasing no more, he swept her standing leg from her and wrapped her legs around his waist, carrying her to the bed and carefully lowering them both to the soft surface. His eyes bore down into her, lit with promise and lust and true temptation. Soon this man would lay claim to her and she to him, and their energy would be completely joined in its full magnificence.

FERGUS COULD SCARCELY THINK OVER THE MINDLESSNESS OF HIS yearning. As if it were not already bad enough for him to control himself, the frantic, desperate thoughts of Cassandra pouring into his mind only served to weaken his wavering resolve.

He wanted to hold down her hands, trapping her willingly beneath him and drive deep and hard into her. But she was a maiden. She needed to be prepared.

Her hips arched in the natural rhythm of sex, enticing him toward her. God's bones, she would be her own undoing with such movements. Her breasts strained upward, the nipples pink and hard from his ministrations. His mouth watered to close over them again and suckle until her breathy moans filled the small room.

He shifted his hand between them once more so his fingers glided over her slick center. Her body was ready for him, eager for him.

More. She wanted more.

And God how he longed to give her so much more. He nudged the end of his middle finger against her entrance and carefully inserted it within her. She gave a soft exclamation of encouragement.

More.

Her sheath gripped him tightly. So damn tightly. Sweat warmed his brow and lower back. His cock strained ferociously between them. He moved his finger within her, gentle in his attempt to stretch her to accommodate him.

Her legs spread and greedy desperation hummed through her, a combination of her thoughts and the charge of the earth beneath them. She pushed against him.

Please.

He groaned his own frustration. Wanting to be inside her. Not wanting to hurt her. But God, wanting to be inside her.

In one fluid movement he did not anticipate, she grabbed his wrist, pulling him from her, and flipped him onto his back. Strength sang through his blood and he knew he could have stopped her if he wanted to. Her lips quirked up in a coquettish, confident manner.

She was taking the control.

Fergus lay back, pinned beneath her as she straddled his hips. His mark lay a mere inch below hers, like a shadow. He wanted them pressed together once more, pleasantly warm while their bodies ignited with shared passion. The wet heat of her entrance pressed to the underside of his shaft. He gripped the blanket in his fists to keep from lifting her up and thrusting into her. Her fingers ran over his body, lingering near the stone. He arched his hips upward, grinding their need against one another.

Her lashes fluttered and her teeth sank into her lower lip. Uncertainty wavered about her despite her show of confidence and the intent to be in charge. She was, after all, still a maiden.

He slid his hands over her thighs and held her sweet hips. "It will be easier with me above ye."

She shook her head. "Show me what to do."

He was torn at the idea of her riding him, lost somewhere between desire and fear.

"You won't hurt me," she whispered.

He hoped he did not. He focused his thoughts on showing her what to do, how to raise her hips, how to guide him in, reassuring her he would help.

She lifted her hips and curled her fingers around his shaft. His cock jerked in anticipation and his ballocks drew tight. She angled him upward so he pointed directly where he had been so hungry to enter. Then, ever so carefully, she lowered onto him.

The heat of her enveloped the sensitive head of his cock. He gave a low grunt and forced himself to lie patient and still. Cassandra sank deeper, taking in the top part of his shaft as well. She gave a sigh and he could sense her body tingle with enjoyment.

She nudged her hips up and then slowly returned to the same place. A tight groan slipped from Fergus' throat. It was all he could do to lay in place and allow her to control the pace, the depth. She continued to rock over him, each time she lowered further, and took him in deeper and deeper. Finally, she slid completely down him and the base of his phallus met the apex of her thighs.

She gripped him tightly in her sheath, almost too tightly. But it was more than his own sensations, he could feel hers as well, the way his cock stretched and filled her, the burning insistence of her body to move.

He let her rock on her own several times, her attempts clumsy with untried experience. There had been little pain for her and the delicate thrusts were becoming more desperate. Indeed, his own desires were screaming in his mind, driving him to plunge into her.

"Yes. Please." Cassandra rubbed herself with frustration over him. "Do it. The way you want. The way we both want."

He released one hand from her hips and settled his thumb against the swollen nub at the top of her sex. She drew a sharp breath. He rolled it in time with her movements, speeding when she sped. The waves of her pleasure were overwhelming, hot and delicious, especially when paired with his own experience of her gripping and gliding over his cock. Sweat beaded on his brow.

She was close. So damn close. He quickened his pace on the little bud and her panting came harder. He released her, grabbed her hips and thrust hard into her, plunging in and out. She cried out and arched her back, her small breasts bouncing each time their hips met.

Their bodies were on fire, alight with incredible passion, joined with sensations of both their experiences - gliding and slick, thick and hard, filling and stretching, squeezing, squeezing, squeezing. Her nails dug into his chest and pleasure exploded from him the same time her grip on him spasmed in her crises.

Euphoria took them to another place where they were not bound to the earth, where every nerve of their bodies flared with a bliss neither had ever known. They were joined, they were perfect. They were power. They were undefeatable.

The intensity of it was so great, it wiped clear Fergus' mind for a brief moment and dragged down the wall he had so carefully erected and maintained. Cassandra jerked to stillness atop him. He opened his eyes, still panting with the effects of their unnatural coupling.

Cassandra stared down at him with hard confusion.

He drew up the wall once more, but his correction had come too late. She had already seen into his mind. He tried to push against her thoughts, to scrape away what she knew. He searched, desperate, and discovered nothing there. Nothing but a formidable wall.

8

Cassandra knew everything, including the icy fear prickling through Fergus' veins. Being in such close proximity to him gave her the strength, the knowledge, to close the curtain of her mind and keep him from seeing her thoughts. She only hoped she possessed the strength once they were not touching, when her mind was weakened without the stone.

The coital bliss between them cooled and she climbed from his body. She left her hand resting on his chest, hesitant to remove it and lose the surge in her power. He watched her intently, his brow furrowed in hard concentration.

He wondered what she had seen in his mind, and longed to extract the knowledge from her mind. His racing heartbeat under her palm calmed to a steady thud and still she did not pull away her hand. She knew everything.

He had never seen his son, he didn't even know his name, yet still his love for the child was fierce. The king was using the boy to encourage Fergus to do his bidding. And Cassandra was part of that bidding. The king needed not only the stone, but also her.

Yet there was more, a part of Fergus going deeper than he even realized. There was good in him. A beautiful beacon of goodness shining in the inky darkness within. He had hope – for a family, for love. And she had become part of that hope, even as he knew he would have to turn her over to the king's care. Even as he knew it would most likely end in her death.

The earth's presence crackled around Cassandra. A reminder of the strength she stood upon every day, the strength she had only just learned to draw from. She closed her eyes and pulled the buzz of energy toward her. It hummed through her veins and lit her body and mind with exactly what she needed.

She opened her eyes and removed her hand from Fergus' chest. His mind tapped against hers, and yet she maintained the control to keep him at bay.

"How do ye know how to do that?" he asked.

"A Protector's secret." She glanced over her shoulder at him. While she no longer had his ability to sense emotions wavering off anyone or read their thoughts, she could see the frustration carved on his face.

He rose from the bed, naked and obviously unashamed of his fully nude state. She was not so blissfully uncaring. Her face burned with heat. She had wanted him with a force wild enough to threaten to rip her apart, and what they had shared had been incredible.

All this time, he meant to betray her. And yet since the moment he met her, he did not want to. Every decision was for his son. Could she fault such a noble cause?

"Cassandra." He reached out to her.

She looked at his hand stretching toward her. "If you mean to read my thoughts by touching me, you will only find I have more strength."

"What did ye see?" he asked.

"Enough." She drew the clothing they'd discarded from the ground, grabbing first Fergus' garments in error. "This is yours." She handed it to him.

He accepted the bundle and clutched it to his chest. Cassandra did not hesitate with her own clothing. She pulled the linen and wool tunic on together, the two garments still connected from where Fergus had pulled them from her body.

"I dinna want it to end like this." He took her hand in his.

"As I stated previously, you cannot read my—"

"I dinna want to read yer thoughts." He shook his head. "I mean, aye, I do, but I wanted...I wanted to touch ye. After what we experienced together."

She relented and his strong hand curled against her own.

"I want ye to stay with me," he said. "I want ye to come with me to Edinburgh."

Truth.

She knew his words to be true. She could sense the honesty in him through the touch of their fingers threaded together.

"To heal your son," she said.

Guilt.

It scored into him, white hot and ugly before he could cover it. "Aye," he answered slowly, as if he suspected she did not believe him. "To heal my son."

"What do you think I know, Fergus?" She met his gaze and he shook his head.

"I dinna know, but I dinna want ye to leave me."

Fear.

Solitude.

So vastly empty and alone.

She recalled the glow of hope within him, dimly lit and tucked in a corner shrouded by helplessness. He was not all darkness within. She swallowed.

But what of her path? Was she supposed to aid him? Was she supposed to fight him and take the stone? She wished her eldmother were still alive and could read her future - beyond the fate of Cassandra being a Protector and to where she was now.

If she failed in the task to obtain the stone, it was more than she who would suffer. It was all of Scotland.

"Stay with me," Fergus said gently. He lifted his free hand to her face and ran his thumb down her cheek to her chin, just below her bottom lip.

Her pulse fluttered and despite the uncertainty in her future and the understanding she had to be wary of trusting him, her body warmed with lust. Outside the rain raged against the shutters and thunder grumbled in the distance.

Even if she were to leave now, in wet clothing and amid the mighty storm, she would not have the stone. She needed a plan.

Fergus brought his face closer to hers. His mouth a breath from hers. She found herself tipping her face toward him.

He slid one large hand up the back of her neck to cradle the back of her head. "Will ye come with me?"

Cassandra stared deep into his eyes, cherishing those heady moments before their lips met "Aye."

And even as they kissed and passion ignited their veins once more, she found herself wondering if it would be she who would betray him, or he who betrayed her.

SEVERAL DAYS ON THE ROAD TOGETHER HAD NOT PROVIDED FERGUS the opportunity to fully understand what Cassandra knew. There had been a shift in her, a wariness, and yet she had so successfully erected a wall to prevent him from her thoughts, it was impenetrable. And damn impressive.

It had taken him months to learn how to properly block his mind, a skill he hadn't realized he needed to develop until his meetings with the king. Somehow the bastard always seemed to know what Fergus had been thinking in their prior meeting.

Snow dusted the ground like baker's flour, leaving dots of white mingled with the bits of wilting grass and dry heather. The air held a wet cold to it that pierced one's bones and made Fergus wish they had shared a horse rather than having their own. Though with the terrain being rough through Inverness and the ground slick in places, the animals needed to be spared. Especially when the beasts were as shoddy as they were, having been procured from a neglected stable near their inn.

Had Fergus not known the land so well from his youth, it might have been impossible to navigate.

He slid a glance to Cassandra and found her watching him, as she often did, her expression ponderous beneath the cloak wrapped about her. She was little more than a face from beneath furred hood, emitting occasional puffs of frozen air from her lips. The weather had been uncommonly cold for mid-November.

He could not read her thoughts, but he knew her emotions to be warring. They blurred about her in a confused mass, indecipherable.

There was lust, he knew. Aye, he knew that very, very well. It was a flame they handled often despite the awareness that one of them might end up burned. For there was a distinct lack of trust within her, that he knew with certainty.

They made their way down the steep side of a hill, their progress slow with the mud-thickened earth. Wind howled at them and nipped at their exposed faces.

"Do you find this weather strange?" she asked. "It has never been so cold this early before."

"You are used to being farther south." Fergus guided his horse away from a puddle, unsure how deep it might be.

"I've heard people in the villages discussing it. They have never seen weather such as this in November either." She glanced in his direction, her stare pointed.

He knew where she was taking this conversation, where she had taken it before. The need for her to possess the stone. Yet he knew if she had it, she would leave - to ensure he never had possession of it again. Sacrificing everything for the safety of Scotland - him, what they had, and even his son.

The sacrifice of few for the survival of many.

"I canna give ye the stone," he said resolutely.

"But you must see—" The ground beneath Cassandra's horse slid away, like its skin pulled free from the slippery mud beneath. Her horse's hooves scrabbled for purchase, its mighty hindquarters thrusting against the moving earth threatening to pull it down.

Fergus nudged his horse forward in an attempt to help, but his steed lurched backward to safer ground, its baser instincts falling to preservation.

Cassandra released the reins with one hand and the force of her power swelled thick in the cold air. But without touching Fergus and pulling from the force of the stone, her strength was not enough.

She needed him. He leapt from the saddle. His feet splashed on the sodden ground and threatened to slide out from beneath him as well. Cassandra wobbled on her horse while the poor beast continued to struggle, legs racing against the earth falling away beneath them both.

"Nay, hold the reins," Fergus bellowed.

Cassandra's hand shook with the force of her concentration. Her horse lurched to the right as the ground washed away. It leapt into the air and sent Cassandra flying from its back while its hooves finally found solid ground.

She gave a brief shriek midair and somehow managed to land on her feet, which promptly gave way beneath her.

"Nay," Fergus cried. He lunged for her and caught the front of her cloak as the river of mud dragged her downward. It sucked at her with such strength, it almost drew them both to their demise. But Fergus had the stone, and he called on every last fissure of energy within it to save Cassandra.

He clutched her to his chest, unwilling to let her go when he had come so close to almost losing her.

"I am not so easily lost," Cassandra said.

He looked down and found her gazing up at him. Mud had spattered against her cheeks and her hood had fallen away, leaving her dark curls in a wild disarray. Yet never had she looked more beautiful. More his.

"And I thank God for it." He pressed a kiss to her warm, soft lips, not caring if he got mud on his own face.

Pain radiated from her and he pulled back. "Ye're hurt." He scanned over her, though it was impossible to see anything beneath the heavily furred cloak she wore.

She twisted her lips with frustration. "My ankle."

He had to see the limb, but not here where the ground might once more slide away. A desperate survey of their surroundings revealed the rounded stone entrance of what might be a cave. He lifted her into his arms and carried her to it. The horses had both given to grazing once the excitement of their near death had passed, and so he left them thus.

"It is not so bad," Cassandra said.

Rather than answer, Fergus extended his awareness into the cave in an effort to identify any creatures within. Finding none, he ducked into the low ceiling and carried her to the edge, where he could still see well enough, and set her to the dry dirt floor. Her right foot settled on the ground and she gave a hiss of pain despite her protests of being fine.

He pulled off her shoe and rolled down her thick woolen stockings to reveal her slender calf and a misshapen ankle already beginning to bloom with shapeless blotches of purple and red. Definitely not a good sign.

Cassandra lifted and lowered her foot then turned it side to side. "It hurts, but I can move it. It's not broken."

"Nay, but it still needs care. Ye need rest. And a healer." He, of course, knew the best healer in all of Scotland, though he'd been hesitant to go and see her after all these years. She hadn't liked Allisandre, yet she'd still traveled for miles to come and see him after his wife's death. He should have visited sooner, he knew, but excuses piled upon one another until he had been gone too long and remorse had prevented him from facing his wrong. Guilt had a way of settling in the soul like a stain and keeping one from doing what was right.

It would appear Cassandra's injury would finally make right that wrong from so long ago.

Fergus would finally go to see his mother.

9

It had been over a decade, yet even through the whirling snow and mounds of slushing mud, Fergus was able to find his way home. The manor sat on the outskirts of a small village, away from the bustle and noise. Exactly as his mother preferred.

A simple thatch roof cottage had once sat in its place. When Fergus was first approached by the king for help, it was within Fergus' grasp to barter for a better life. Fergus had been given wealth and had insisted his mother have a comfortable home with worthy staff. Despite everything Fergus' sacrifice afforded them, he knew his mother wished for life as it was before his mark had appeared.

He hopped down from his horse and aided Cassandra from hers. He helped her limp to the door and rapped upon it. Footsteps immediately sounded on the threshold and the door swung open, bringing with it the familiar scent of his childhood - warm baking bread and drying herbs.

The maid stared down her hawkish nose at him and gave a cold smile which only served to thin her narrow lips. Helga lifted a brow and he could read her disapproval as readily as if she'd spoken it aloud.

Too long gone with too little care for his mother. A pity when she loved her boy so completely.

The thought cut into his heart.

Helga's gaze shifted to where Cassandra leaned against him.

"Helga, get Mother." Fergus spoke briskly. Before the bitter woman could think something awful about Cassandra.

"She's in the kitchen," Helga replied dryly. "Of course." She widened the door to allow them to enter. He strode past her with Cassandra clutching his side for support. He'd wanted to carry her, of course, but she'd insisted on walking herself rather than being carried like an invalid.

A sense of appreciation washed from behind Fergus as Helga's gaze burned over him followed by thoughts he never wanted to hear from the old maid.

Cassandra choked on a cough and he knew she'd heard as well. Damn her. He slid her a dark gaze, but her mirthful grin didn't dissipate.

"She'll no' believe ye're hurt with the way ye're smiling," he scoffed.

"I canna imagine a lass who wouldna smile in the presence of my son." The soft voice was exactly as he remembered, kind and gentle and loving.

His heart warmed immediately, and he looked to the doorway where the voice had come from. His mother stood at the center with a wide smile on her face, her eyes crinkled with her joy.

"Ma." His heart caught.

She looked older, significantly so. Her rich golden hair had gone almost completely white with a thin, cotton-like consistency that threatened to fly free of her bun. She opened her arms and came to him, intent on the hugs she insisted she give and he insisted he was too old for.

Still supporting Cassandra on his left arm, he hugged his mother tight to him. Her head barely came up to his ribs, at least that was the same. Her embrace was tight and full of enough love to light up the whole of Scotland. Indeed, it made his heart glow.

She held no anger at his delay in coming to see her, no sorrow at his absence, nor even frustration that he'd brought someone with him. Not his mother. She was simply glad to have her son home, because with him there, her heart was truly complete.

The idea left a knot in his throat. He had never been able to fully read his mother's thoughts, not like now with the benefit of the stone. He knew she loved him, but never had he truly understood exactly how central to her world he was.

"Are ye going to introduce me?" She glanced to Cassandra. "Surely yer mother raised ye better than that."

"This is Lady Cassandra. She is traveling with me to Edinburgh and has injured her ankle." He turned to Cassandra. "This is my mother who will provide ye with the best care of any healer or physician in all of Scotland."

"Ach, listen to him." His mother chuckled. "Ye'd think I'm a healer myself with all his praise. I'm merely a mother who sought the best care for my son when he was ill as a lad."

Despite her humble words, he could sense how his praise made her swell with pride.

She waved him toward her and turned to the kitchen. "Get her to the chair by the fire. It's warmer back here than in the drafty great hall."

Fergus followed his mother to the back of the manor where the massive kitchen was located. As they walked, he took advantage of Cassandra's slow pace to examine the state of the manor. Lucky for Helga, he found it all in good repair, polished and dusted without a cobweb to be seen.

Though he wondered how much his mother allowed Helga to do, though, if anything at all. She had never had much use for the servants and Fergus knew she kept them more to appease him than for her own desire.

A pleasant heat filled the kitchen, even in the frigid temperatures. The entire manor belonged to his mother, yet he knew this room was the only one which seemed to truly belong to her. Herbs swayed from the rafters above, their leaves in various stages of drying, just like when they'd had a small cottage. Several jars of butters and oils were neatly lined on one side of the wall, and his father's necklace - an iron cross from when he'd traveled with the Knights Templar - hung near the shutters, just like when they'd had a small cottage. A sense of peace washed over his mother when she entered the kitchen.

Fergus set Cassandra in the wooden seat before the fire and his mother came forward to sit on a nearby stool. If anyone would make Cassandra's foot right again, it would be his mother.

"Lady Cassandra, may I remove yer shoe?" His mother regarded Cassandra with an imploring look.

Cassandra flushed. "Aye, of course, but please call me Cassandra."

His mother smiled and gently removed the shoe. Cassandra's foot had swollen even larger with a deep purple band at the base of her foot. Fergus' mother carefully examined it, her fingers gingerly moving over the swollen skin. The lines around his mother's eyes remained creased though she was no longer smiling.

Again, he was struck by how much she'd aged in ten years. He had been gone too long. She had done everything for him in his life, and he had remained gone.

He knew she would not judge him, and yet he could not bring himself to tell her about his son. And how badly he had failed.

"It's no' broken, merely a sprain," his mother offered in her assessment of Cassandra's ankle, ignorant to the waves of guilt washing over him. "But ye'll no' be moving on it for a while. I have some poultices and balms I can use to take down the engorgement and to ease yer pain a wee bit." She stood and settled a hand on his forearm where it was crossed over his chest. "Ye're of course welcome to stay here."

Her hope flared so bright, it was practically blinding. And even beneath it all, she only wanted it if Fergus could spare the time.

In truth, he could not, but Cassandra would travel more quickly when healed than she could injured. And further damage to her ankle, which was likely if they continued to press on, would only slow them even more.

They had no choice but to stay. He found himself torn between frustration at the lost time when they were already behind, and gratitude for the opportunity to spend the time with his mother. Once his son was recovered, he would ensure they moved back to Inverness along with Cassandra, near his mother's manor.

He stilled. It was the first time he had considered his future with Cassandra. The image had come so readily, with such assuredness, it was as though there were no doubt in his mind it would be.

A cold shudder rent through his heart. And yet it could not be. For he was almost certain when he delivered Cassandra to the king, she would die.

The following week flew by quickly for Cassandra in the comfortable manor with Fergus' mother, whom she'd been instructed to refer to as Blair. Cassandra had been treated well, with all the love from Blair she had never received from her own mother, and it filled a void in her heart she hadn't known she possessed.

Blair settled comfortably on a stool with a tray at her side filled with various pots and herbs and poultices for healing. She unwrapped the linen from Cassandra's ankle and craned her neck over the injured appendage in careful assessment.

"It's almost completely healed." Blair put a hand to her chest. "I've no' ever seen a sprain as bad as yers mend with such haste."

Cassandra peered at her ankle. It was indeed as it had been before the injury, with no swelling or discoloration remaining. Fergus had constantly hovered near her in the past several days, touching his hand to hers when no one was near in the hopes the energy of the stone would encourage her body to repair itself. It was the only time he would touch her.

Even without the stone, Cassandra would no doubt have still healed well for Blair had provided constant care.

"Your diligence to my health has contributed greatly to the success, I am sure," Cassandra said.

As she always did, Blair waved a dismissive hand in the air as if to clear away the compliment. "Ye've been a fine patient to care for. Ye're a verra kind lass." Blair lifted a sly gaze to Cassandra. "And I canna say I havena noticed how my son interacts with ye."

Cassandra's face grew warm. "Whatever do you mean?"

Blair grinned and her eyes squinted at the corner where a lifetime of smiling had left the skin creased. "I see the gentle touches between ye and my son, the way his gaze seems to fix on ye when ye're near. I've no' ever seen him like this with a lass."

The warmth went hotter still. Lately it had seemed he wanted little to do with Cassandra, aside from her being ready as quickly as possible to travel. She'd tried to read his hesitation toward her but could not. At first she had assumed it had to do with his mother, and the fear she would know he had taken Cassandra's maidenhead. But several times of being alone together had cured such thoughts. Even with no one nearby, Fergus was distant. As though he had wanted to stay far from her.

"What of his wife?" Cassandra asked. Her stomach twisted at the very thought. Allisandre had possessed a part of Fergus Cassandra envied, a part of him she would never have.

Blair pursed her mouth. She lifted the lid from a small clay pot and swept her fingers through the yellow salve within. "He fancied her," she said slowly. "But there was something about her I dinna trust."

Her greased fingers moved over Cassandra's ankle, her touch tender as she massaged the salve over the remnants of the injury.

"Was his wife unkind?" Cassandra had seen, unwillingly, some of the memories in Fergus' head when they touched. While beautiful, Allisandre had seemed short of patience and possessed a cool air about her.

"She came about in Fergus' life after the king bestowed a goodly amount of wealth upon him, and was always after him to get knighted." Blair wiped the remaining balm from her fingertips. "I got the impression she liked Fergus no' for who he was, but for what he might provide her with and who he might become."

Cassandra nodded in understanding.

"Fergus needs good in his life." Blair pushed the wrapped poultice of herbs into a small bowl of water. Threads of yellow green seeped from the linen, coloring the water and filling the air with the sweet spice of herbs. "Like ye."

"Me?"

"There is a darkness in my boy." A somber note dulled the light in her eyes. "I thought it gone from him for good, but I see it now has returned. He had the very devil in him as a lad."

Fergus entered the room and both Cassandra and Blair immediately quieted. He looked between the two ladies. "Ye dinna need to stop speaking on my behalf."

"Your mother was telling me what a difficult child you were as a boy," Cassandra teased.

Fergus smirked.

"Did you have to beat it out of him?" she inquired playfully.

"Ach no." Blair rose from her seat on the low stool, moving with a fair amount of ease for one of her age. "I loved it out of him." She approached her son and drew him into a solid embrace that left his arms trapped against his body. "I cradled him in my arms and I sang him songs from my heart. I kissed away his screams and together we baked away his tantrums. He makes a fine bannock if he's ever inclined to do so for ye."

"Ma." His tone possessed a warning note the sparkle in his eye did not reflect. He liberated one of his arms only to drape it over his mother's shoulders and return the hug. An affectionate smile touched his lips, the same one he wore every time he regarded his mother.

Despite what Blair had said about Fergus having his darkness returned, Cassandra had seen a light reflecting from him when they touched. A light not present before their arrival to the manor. It was a direct mirror of the brilliance surrounding Blair, pure and beautiful. As though being in his mother's presence eased some of what weighed heavily upon him. As though her love were enough to battle every shadow of darkness away.

He gazed down at Cassandra's foot. "Ye look to be completely healed."

"Verra nearly." Blair squeezed him hard once more before releasing him. "She's mended so well." She made her way to the stool once more and pulled the poultice from where it had been steeping in the water. Pale green water dribbled from the herb-filled linen. "She'll be well enough to travel in several more days."

"Tomorrow," he said sternly.

Cassandra snapped her attention to him. "So soon?"

"We've spent too much time here." He regarded Blair and his tone softened. "Forgive me. I will return once I've gone to Edinburgh. There is something verra important I must attend to."

Blair smiled up at her son. "Of course, my son."

Without another word, Fergus quit the room, leaving a stark silence in his wake.

"I apologize for our abrupt departure," Cassandra offered meekly.

"He doesna like to leave me." Blair gazed thoughtfully to the doorway her son had strode through. "He doesna deal well with unpleasantries like farewells. But I know in my heart he loves me, and I know he will be back again someday." She set the poultice against Cassandra's ankle.

The wet heat of the herbs settled against her skin and sank deep to the injury below with a soothing heat. Blair patiently bound a linen around the ankle. "I'll include several of these poultices for ye to bring with ye as well as a pot of the ointment I've been using."

"How did you get so good at healing?" Cassandra asked.

Blair was quiet so long, Cassandra feared she had asked a question she ought not to have.

"I had a daughter once," Blair said softly. "A wee lass with blonde curls like her da and his large dark eyes. She was born a year before Fergus, but she was a sickly wee thing. She struggled for breath often and raged with fever more times than not. I'd never known much about herbs or healing. Indeed, I could scarce grow a weed." She chuckled softly at her own folly. "But I taught myself to ensure she had the best care I could provide. I learned much over the years from tending to her." Blair lifted the tray and got to her feet. "I suppose a parent will do anything for their child."

Outside a fresh storm howled and rattled at the shutters. "Ye'll need to travel with care," Blair said. "There's been a wild snowstorm raging for the better part of the week. The ground is frozen solid as a stone."

Cassandra nodded. "Thank you for everything, Blair. You've been most gracious and hospitable."

"It's been my pleasure." With that, Blair left the room with her tray of healing tools.

Cassandra stared at the flames dancing within the large hearth before her, savoring the warmth while she still had it. Tomorrow would bring the soul chilling cold once more and the journey that would end in ultimate betrayal.

Only now she had a plan. And it all started with being honest with Fergus about what she knew.

A parent might do anything to save their child, aye, but what might they be able to do with the help of another?

10

There was a dulling of the light surrounding Fergus' mother the morning of their departure. He tried to harden his heart against it, but found the task entirely impossible. Never once did she blame him for leaving, nor did she begrudge the shortness of his stay. Worse still, he sensed a fear in her that it might be the last time she would see him. It was that final thought which caused her brilliance to wane.

He pulled her into his arms and willed the understanding of all the love in his heart for her to melt into her awareness the way hers had to him. However, he was only able to receive emotion and thoughts, not send them. When he finally released her, the glow about her had not renewed any of its vigor.

"Thank you for bringing Cassandra with ye," his mother said. "I enjoyed her company greatly. I see her as being verra good for ye."

He groaned slightly and cast a glance to where Cassandra knelt near a barn cat, stroking its smooth black and orange fur.

"It's been a decade since Allisandre," his mother said gently. "I think this lass is the one to balm the soul, my son. She's a good woman."

Guilt sliced white hot through him. He hated leaving his mother, and how much it pained her for him to do so. He hated that Cassandra was exactly as his mother had said - a good woman, and he hated even more that he would betray her.

He simply nodded. "I shall take yer advice under consideration."

"Ach, consideration. Ye always were a stubborn lad," she said affectionately. "I'll miss ye."

He pulled his mother in for a final embrace and helped Cassandra to her horse after she'd said her goodbyes. His mother had insisted he take her finer horses and leave the nags behind, as she claimed she had little use for good steeds.

Wind and ice pelted at them, making any attempt at conversation arduous. He was grateful for the opportunity to remain silent. The last week had been difficult with her. He had tried to put some distance between them, a necessary amount of space for what he would have to do. He'd touched her only to help her heal and had felt her pain at his detachment.

His gaze wandered to her, simply a face inside a thick band of fur from her cloak. A beautiful face with red lips and cheeks and the tip of her nose he wanted to kiss. Damn it, he wanted to kiss all of her, to pull her into his arms.

And he would betray her. Sacrifice her.

A knot formed in his throat, a stubborn obstruction he'd found recurring in the last week. He knew the king well enough to know his intentions for Cassandra were not ones of hospitality. No doubt he would kill her.

An icy gust shoved at him and left his eyes watering with the cold. The weather was as miserable as it'd been when they started.

Fergus would do anything to protect Cassandra, sacrifice almost anything to keep her safe – except his son. He had to keep his son forefront in his mind. The lad he'd never met, the one who had waited on him all this time.

Together, he and Cassandra trudged on, their pace slowed over the frozen terrain and mounds of snow, until the sky began to darken. They stopped at a small inn within a village they were lucky enough to stumble upon. Indeed, a frozen night such as this would have been miserable in a cave. Fergus' stomach twisted at the idea of spending the night together in the same room, at the opportunity of being close without the excuse of his mother nearby and Cassandra's reputation to offer distance.

But when the innkeeper led them to their small single room with a warming fire lit in the hearth, and the sweet apple scent of her filled the room, a hunger consumed him. Unfair and insistent. It made him want to draw her slender body against him, both in lust and protection.

For there had to be something he could do. He could not give up so easily on Cassandra. Mayhap once he had his son, he could go back…

"You look so serious as you stare at me," Cassandra said.

Indeed, she looked serious too. The light was gone from her clear blue eyes. The energy arcing from her body was cast in a strange flickering, suggesting she was nervous. He made her nervous.

"Ye needn't be nervous with me," he said. "I'll no' hurt ye."

He regretted the words as soon as they fled his lips. For he would hurt her. He would betray her, perhaps too late to stop her from being killed.

His hands balled into fists. Nay, he would not let that happen.

The nervousness about her shone with more intensity.

"Then you already know," she said softly and looked away. "I thought I'd been so good at hiding it."

He frowned. "I already know what?"

"That I know."

His heartbeat faltered in his chest for a quick second before scrambling to catch the missed beat. "That ye know what?" he asked slowly.

"I know about why you need the stone and I know about your son." Her eyes were large and sad with a heavy, empathetic sorrow. "You've never met him and worry he doesn't even know you exist. You've tried to find him, but to no avail. The only way to reclaim him from where he is being held captive is to give King Edgar the stone. It's why you will not let me have it, even as the world is falling into chaos."

Fergus tried to swallow the sour bile rising in his throat. To hear all his deceit laid bare in such a manner left him feeling vulnerable in a way he never had before, completely exposed. And yet, what she had said was not the whole of it.

He should tell her the rest, to be honest. However, doing so might cause her to leave, and if she left, he would lose his son forever.

"And you have not told your mother," she continued. "About your son."

His cheeks burned with shame. "I couldna bring myself to tell her, for fear it might break her heart."

"And yours," Cassandra said softly. "To say it aloud."

Fergus gritted his teeth against the pain welling in his chest and nodded.

"Please," Cassandra implored. "Let me help you."

There was such earnestness in her gaze, such beautiful hope emanating from her, that he could not bring himself to lie to her. Not again. Not anymore.

She had to know the truth.

CASSANDRA'S SOUL FELT LIGHTER FOR HAVING CONFESSED HER knowledge of Fergus' son to him. However, the gray pallor to his face at her admission made her grateful she had not mentioned she knew of the betrayal.

"Ye're right," he said gravely. "But that is no' the worst of it."

She stood several feet away from him, her arms crossed over her chest to keep from reaching out to him. It was not where she wanted to be. Nay - she wanted to be in his arms, kissing him, letting him strip off her layers of clothing to press the heat of his naked body against hers. But the distance was where she needed to be.

"I know," Cassandra said through the ache in her heart.

He turned away, as though he needed the separation too. As though he could not stand to look at her, and when he spoke, she understood why. "The king doesna want only the stone. He wants ye too."

Cassandra winced at the pain in his words. "I know," she said again.

He turned to her, his brows furrowed low over his eyes as though he were in agony. "Ye knew? Ye knew and ye still traveled by my side the following day? Ye came to my mother's home and ye stayed there, ye ventured on this new part of the journey with me and are sharing a room with me, and ye knew?"

She nodded.

He gave a hoarse cry and ran his hands partway through his hair before stopping and cradling his head in his palms. "Why?" he asked in a rasping voice. "Why would ye do that?" He slid his fingers from his hair and stared desperately at her. "Why would ye stay when ye knew I most likely lead ye to yer death?"

Cassandra blinked back unexpected tears. "I...I need the stone." It was a flimsy excuse and he saw directly through it.

He shook his head.

"I couldn't leave you without your son." Cassandra looked down at the floor, unable to meet the intensity of his bright gaze. "I intended to try to find a way to get the stone back from you while still aiding you in getting your son returned."

"And if ye failed in getting the stone?" he asked.

She lifted her head. "I won't." And it was true, she had it worked out perfectly to ensure if nothing else, the stone would remain hers.

He shook his head, as though none of it made sense to him.

But she knew exactly why she'd done it. She strode forward, reached up and cupped her hands to his face. The growth of whiskers on his jaw rasped against her palms, pleasant and intimate. The connection between them was immediate as always.

Cassandra let her wall crumple and allowed the exposure of her heart to him. She showed him what she'd learned from him, the shock of it all. She allowed him to see her desire to help him recover his son.

But there was more, so much more that she was too afraid to say. She was a coward to do it this way and yet she could not bring herself to speak such words aloud. She showed him her family and how difficult life had been growing up, and how he had made her feel accepted and cherished in a world where she was simply a pawn in the path to greatness. He celebrated her successes while others had constantly complained of her failures.

But most importantly, most pathetically, she let him understand the depth of her feelings for him. This man, who had shown her a world she had always wanted and never thought to possess, she would die for in the pursuit of getting him everything he was missing in life. Because she loved him.

Wholly, completely and most likely, foolishly.

There was only one thing she kept guarded, one small bit she couldn't share.

"Cassandra." He drew in a harsh breath. "Do not love me."

"I cannot make myself stop. Even as I knew you would betray me, I understood your cause and I love you." Saying the words aloud loosened the tight hold fear had on her. It was like throwing wide one's hands in the air and flying free. "I love you, Fergus."

"Dinna say it." He pulled his hands away, but not fast enough, not before she sensed what charged through him. Doubt. Not in her, but in himself.

He would have to believe in his worth before he accepted her love, and before he could allow himself to feel the same way.

"Let me help you," she insisted. "We can work together to save your son."

He strode to the shuttered windows and braced his hands on either side of the frame. His head hung in defeat between his shoulders. "I dinna like this."

She approached him and reached out, hungry to know what it was he thought when he was so guarded with his mind.

"I have to choose between ye or my son."

"I am not making you choose." Her arms longed to hold him. Not only for his thoughts, but for the comfort of his warmth and strength.

"Do ye no' see how much worse it is?" He straightened. "Ye are willingly walking into a trap, mayhap sacrificing yourself, for my happiness."

"You would do the same for me," she said.

He opened his arms and she stepped into his embrace. His arms were warm and strong, the embrace so comforting and rife with power, she melted against him. He nuzzled her, his lips brushing her ear.

Her body immediately lit with desire, raw and desperate. In the previous week they had touched so little, and had no time alone; she needed him like she needed air. His mouth slanted over hers and seared her with the force of his own lust.

She sensed the emotions warring within him, the worthlessness overwhelmed by want. It would all work out. She conveyed the thought to him in her mind in an attempt to share her confidence before giving herself completely to the heat of his touch and the delicious fire it ignited within her.

I have a plan.

11

Cassandra's plan required a week long delay in Stirling upon their arrival. After having taken almost a month to get there, the wait was a generous sacrifice. One they were not pleased with having to make. The length of time for their travel had been unheard of, even in winter as they now were.

The winds blew without cessation and the constant blend of rain and snow left all of Scotland frozen over. It was nearly two moons since Fergus had put the stone around his neck. The earth's pulse was beginning to grow weak beneath Cassandra's feet, pressing her own purpose despite her knowledge of how important Fergus' son truly was.

She hadn't realized how painful it would be to be near the stone, to tangibly understand the debilitating effects on the earth, and do nothing. There was a maternal ache in her chest, and her charge was dying. Scotland needed her.

The understanding tore into her heart and ravaged her conscience. There were times she wished she had not seen Fergus' thoughts, that she didn't know of his son and could take the stone without guilt.

But she did know, and she put her plan into place regardless. At the end of the week, they found themselves anxiously receiving the jeweler

85

they had commissioned to replicate the stone. The slim-figured man with dainty fingers had carefully sketched the stone from Fergus' neck, never once asking why he would not remove it. Now, he pulled out a narrow black velvet cushion and pulled aside a layer of cloth to reveal the replica.

She and Fergus leaned close to the cushion, their breath held to determine if the expense of the remainder of Fergus' gold had been worthwhile. The green stone glittered in the candlelight, the simple gold chain delicate as a cobweb. Perfectly identical.

"It's glass, of course." The goldsmith shifted the cushion beneath the stone. The light caught at it and flashed in the heart of the fake gem as though it were made of fire within. He caught the delicate strand in the frame of his long fingers and held it aloft.

"It doesn't look like glass." Cassandra ducked her head and allowed the man to place it about her neck. The stone settled cool against her chest. But the true Heart of Scotland was warm, imbued with a life of its own.

"It looks bonny on ye, lass." Fergus lightly touched her face.

The glass will warm when ye wear it.

His words whispered in her mind, conveyed through the true stone. She nodded in agreement and tried to quell her doubt that the plan would work. It had seemed feasible before. But now with them being so very close to Edinburgh, so close to whatever awaited them there, she worried it wouldn't be enough.

If they failed, Fergus' son may die.

If she failed, Scotland could die.

Failure could not happen, and yet she had to face the truth of its possibility.

Fergus closed the door behind the departing goldsmith and turned to Cassandra. "Are ye ready?"

Her heart went wild in her chest. She had been born ready, for exactly this purpose. They had waited for this moment, being close enough to Edinburgh to get the stone. And now it was time. Doing it too soon would have the land repairing itself quickly, noticeably. She only hoped it was late enough that real damage had set in.

Fergus pulled the stone from his neck as Cassandra did likewise with the replica. His breath grunted out in a harsh exhale when the stone left its place against his chest. He gritted his teeth and held it to her with a trembling hand.

The blood raced through her veins and the whole of her world focused in on the dangling green gem, like a starving man before a feast, practically mad with ravenous need. She took the gold chain in her hand and vaguely had the sense he removed the duplicate from her. Her breath echoed loud in her own ears and her heartbeat thundered loudly.

Nay, it was not her heartbeat - it was that of Scotland beneath her.

She slipped the stone over her head and a surge flared through her. It expanded inside of her chest where it lay, burrowing deep and exploding outward in rays of energy so bright she thought surely it would extinguish her mortal life. She curled into it, embracing rather than fighting, and let the immensity of it absorb into her.

Strength fired through her, confidence, pure power. She surveyed the world and found it crackling with possibility.

"Incredible, aye?" Fergus asked with a smirk.

His hesitation removing it was understandable now that she had the force of the stone in her possession. It must have taken an amazing amount of will for him to pull it from his body.

"It did," he answered her thoughts grimly. "Though I can scarcely hear yer mind without the clarity the stone afforded me."

She reached forward and took his hand in hers. She wanted him to experience the enormity of her gratitude for what he did with his sacrifice. The earth sang in joy, the beauty of its happiness rose into the air.

Pain edged into Cassandra's awareness and she realized it was not hers, but Fergus'. His hand. She squeezed it too tightly.

She gasped and released him, but he merely chuckled.

"Ye'll get used to yer talent soon." He massaged his hand. "'Tis fine."

He unclasped the shutters and let in the light of a new day. "The snow has ceased. It will take two days at most to get to Edinburgh from here with the ground still mired from the harsh weather." He leaned out and craned his head upward, squinting against the sun. "I only hope the weather isna so bonny it causes suspicion."

Cassandra joined him and gazed out at the bustling square below. Snow glittered against the brightness overhead and jagged blocks of ice had already begun to melt. It was certainly *not* the weather they had experienced without reprieve since Fergus first put on the stone. And yet Cassandra did not think she could bring herself to pull the stone from her chest as he had. Indeed, it would never leave her chest. Not when Scotland sang with such beautiful relief in her soul.

He turned to her. "We must go."

She nodded and gathered her things silently. Despite the completeness of her renewed strength and vigor from wearing the stone, she still harbored some hesitation that her plan would work. Her failure would bring about dire results, all of which would be revealed in two days' time.

Fergus tread heavily upon the ground with an exhaustible weight. It had been that way since he'd drawn the stone from his neck two days ago and given it to Cassandra.

Ever since, he had not seen with the same precision people's emotions. Their thoughts were muted, as though traveling beneath water rather than clear in his mind. He touched Cassandra whenever possible, drinking in the energy coursing through her veins in greedy sips every time their skin connected.

Edinburgh rose before them with its slanted streets and the massive castle atop the hill overlooking all the subjects below. It had been his home for the prior decade and yet it had never felt so foreign.

He wanted nothing more than to go within its bowels, claim the son he had never known and spirit him away from this place with its awful memories and painful past. Throughout the time of their journey, Fergus had sensed Cassandra's doubt at the plan, at her own survival.

Fergus had to concentrate especially hard, not just through his own softened abilities, but also through the column of energy surrounding her. Yet still, he could hear her thoughts: *she was afraid*. Not for herself, or her life, but of failure, and the lives that would be lost.

He clasped her slender hand in his to lead her through the crowded streets of Edinburgh. The power of the stone immediately shot to his palm and radiated out to the rest of his body.

Above, the skies were gray and snow had fallen intermittently through the day. He was glad for the sun having slipped behind the heavy clouds, for it gave the world a less sunlit appearance, one not indicative of the stone being in the Protector's care.

The king clearly had knowledge of the stone and the legend. Surely he would know the adverse effects of Fergus' wearing it. Edinburgh Castle rose before them from its perch at the crest of the tall hill. They were almost there.

Excitement and uncertainty raced through his veins. Cassandra squeezed his hand and her thoughts merged with his own, warm with the recollection of the night before. They had stayed up far later than they ought to before battle. The night had been sweetly spent while they took their time cherishing one another, savoring what might never be again.

Even now, he wanted to draw her in his arms and press his lips to hers one final time. For neither knew the outcome ahead of them.

A flash of red hair showed in the crowd in front of them. Not an ordinary red, but brilliant, that shone even in the muted light of the overcast day. It caught his attention and Cassandra's hand tightened on his.

He'd only ever known one woman to possess such hair. Strange.

The crowd grew thicker when they pressed to the front of the gate. Peasants sought alms and people cried out their need to see the king to settle petty squabbles. The woman with red hair moved through the guards with ease and disappeared into a crowd of nobles within. A chill trickled down Fergus' spine. The likeness was eerie. Aye, that was it, what he was feeling. An eeriness.

He pushed his way to the guards with Cassandra behind him, his bulk clearing the crowd aside for her. The two guards closed the path before him despite his size, and met his gaze with steely resolution.

"I am Fergus the Undefeated," he said with all the authority imbued in such a name.

The guards' eyes widened and they immediately stood aside to let him pass. One of them turned and ran toward the castle, no doubt to inform the king. Cassandra's pulse raced against the heel of Fergus' hand and yet the churning anxiety she'd cast earlier settled to a surprising calm.

She was ready.

She nodded at him, as if to confirm he had heard her thoughts correctly. He nodded in return. For they would do this together, and they would be victorious. They had to be.

Fergus kept his hand clasped around hers though the thinned crowds within the castle did not warrant it. Together they were strong.

They were nearly to the throne room when the woman with red hair turned the corner in front of them, her back facing them. It had been ten years, a lifetime ago, but seeing her from that angle, Fergus knew without question who it was, however impossible it may be.

Or perhaps not. He could have easily been fed lies.

Regardless, he let go of Cassandra's hand in his determination to know, and closed the distance between himself and the red haired woman. She spun to face him, her green eyes wide with surprise, and confirmed his suspicions.

"Fergus," she whispered in awe.

He stared down at her as though he'd seen a ghost, for surely he had. "Allisandre."

12

Cassandra stood rooted in awkward shock. This woman with her flame red hair and luscious curves was Fergus' wife? His *dead* wife?

Quite alive, Allisandre put her hands to Fergus' face and pressed her full lips to his. Cassandra's stomach twisted. It was the very way she had bestowed her own affection to Fergus before. Had she been doing it the same as his wife all these weeks?

Fergus, for his part, stood rigidly in front of Allisandre. "They said ye died in childbirth."

"Clearly I have not." She gave a lovely little laugh and smoothed her hands down the front of her dress as though she were nervous. "They have kept me locked up, summoning me only now. They told me..." She touched her fingers to his lips with wonder. "They told me ye were dead."

Cassandra stared hard at Fergus and willed herself to hear his thoughts. Yet without touching him, she could not hear what he was thinking, not even with the stone. Nay, she was merely left miserable, standing by and wondering. The battle she had prepared to face was a welcome alternative to this.

"They have our son, Fergus." Allisandre drew in a shuddering breath. "They have Geordie."

Fergus flinched at that. The name. The one he had wondered for ten long years. Who was Cassandra to begrudge him this happiness, or worse, keep him from it?

"Do ye have it?" Allisandre put a hand to Fergus' chest, directly over the swell of his firm muscles.

Cassandra had loved to touch him there. She ought to look away, to break the pain of seeing their interaction, and yet found she could not.

"I have the stone," Fergus confirmed.

"Did you bring the Protector?" Allisandre turned and scanned the hallway. Her bright green eyes skimmed past Cassandra and searched the space behind her.

"Aye." Fergus indicated Cassandra who did her best to appear impassive despite the obvious snub.

"Her?" Allisandre's brows lifted with blatant disbelief. "She's a scrap of a thing, isn't she?"

Fergus' jaw clenched. For her part, Cassandra didn't know what to make of his reaction, and wished she didn't care.

Rather than dwell on it, she fixed her focus to the task at hand. After all, she was counting on being underestimated. Instead, she set her mind to the plan. She was there to save Fergus' son, and she was here to see her role as Protector met.

The stone lay against her skin, over her heart, rightfully strung about her neck and carefully hidden beneath the neckline of her wool dress.

The world was setting itself back into position with it in her care. It would not be undone, not even to prevent her own death.

Allisandre turned her back to Cassandra as though she were of little consequence. She reached for Fergus' hand, but he had stepped away from her, putting too much distance between them for her to touch him.

He did not move closer. Instead, he pushed open the massive double doors leading to the throne room.

Cassandra strode behind Fergus and Allisandre, and caught the distinctly sharp scent of magic in the air. Were it not for what she'd seen through Fergus' mind, she would never have been so poignantly aware of its redolence. But with the memory of his association, the knowledge of its presence sent an edge of warning rasping down her spine.

Why would Allisandre smell like magic?

She was so focused on the other woman, she did not realize Fergus had stopped in front of her, and clumsily bumped into the back of him. The image of Allisandre flickered in front of her, shifting from a beautiful young woman with sumptuous locks of red hair to an old woman, plump and gray with age.

Cassandra had stepped away from Fergus once she hit him, the mumble of apology immediate on her lips. But after the flash of an image, she moved forward once more, to touch him again and confirm what she had seen. A guard rushed forward and pulled her back from Fergus before she could touch him. The slam of the doors closing echoed in the greatness of the large, open room. They were trapped within.

She allowed the guard in black chain mail to drag her back, as though she did not possess the strength to fend him off. Let this man think he could easily subdue her. Let them all see and believe as much as well. It would be to her benefit.

It was not time for them to see their folly. At least, not yet.

"Enough," the man said gruffly. He shoved her to the side, putting her at Fergus' left, barely more than an arm's reach from him. Too far.

She stared hard at Fergus in an attempt to reclaim his attention. His gaze remained fixed ahead.

"This is the Protector?" A nasally voice echoed through the room and commanded Cassandra look forward.

On the throne was a slender man with dull yellow hair and shoulders bent forward as though the weight of the world rested upon his rounded back. He openly assessed her with glittering, greedy eyes.

"Remove her cloak and take her bags." He settled back against his throne as though bored. Guards in blackened chain mail came forward and plucked her bag from her grasp. The wet scent of magic clung to each of them.

Something important to keep forefront in her mind.

She unclasped her cloak and gave it to them before they could pull it from her body. It didn't matter. None of it did, for she had no use for anything but the stone, which lay tucked beneath the safety of her kirtle.

The king's gaze slid down Cassandra's body, rude with appreciation. Fergus tensed at her side.

Whether King Edgar noticed or not, he gave a wolfish grin and curled his fingers in a beckoning gesture aimed at Fergus while his eyes continued to feast on Cassandra. "Give me the stone."

Her heartbeat came faster. This was what she had spent the last several months building toward. The journey had stretched out to over two months with injury and weather, love and pain, and it had culminated to this moment.

Fergus obediently pulled off the necklace. The bit of green glass spun on the delicate gold chain and winked in the light from the rows of candles lining the cold chamber. The king nodded to Allisandre who took the replica and carried it to him before resuming her place at Fergus' right.

The king accepted the imposter stone and regarded where it lay cradled in his palm. The length of delicate gold chain draped from between his open fingers. Fergus' body jerked beside her a fraction of a second before the king tossed the fake to the ground and slammed his foot upon it. When he lifted his shoe, a million pieces of dust and shards glittered on the ground.

The weight of every eye in the room fell upon Cassandra and the warmth of the stone against her skin intensified, though mayhap it was merely her imagination, or possibly her nerves. She drew in a long, slow breath to steady herself.

This was what she had truly intended, the part of her plan she had blocked from Fergus. For he would never have agreed to it.

The day she had discovered his true plan to betray her, she knew she needed a way to get the stone from his possession. This had been the only way. In a perfect scenario, the king would have accepted the glass as the Heart of Scotland and she would have walked free with Fergus and his son. In a failed scenario, as Cassandra had feared would come to pass, and appeared to be doing so now, the king would not accept the counterfeit offering.

Most importantly, the stone was in her possession. Scotland was safe. And it would remain so.

Already the scent of magic pressed in on her, and she caught sight of the guards creeping closer through her periphery. Not that she would surrender.

Nay, she would fight.

If she were strong enough, she could somehow save Fergus' son, but the goal of saving Scotland was greater. The stone would not leave her throat, not until she had succeeded and walked from the chamber, or until she died. Either way, her role as Protector, her greater purpose in her short life, would be fulfilled.

But it was not her the guards seized. It was Allisandre. They held her between them and set a blade to her throat.

The king sat forward on his throne and the toe of his shoe ground into the brittle glass beneath. "Give me the stone or she will die."

Fergus turned to Cassandra, his gaze pleading.

Cassandra lifted her head. "Nay."

The king's face colored. "Convince her."

"Please," Fergus hissed. "She has been a victim of this too. It isna right-"

"Nay," Cassandra repeated again, louder this time and with more defiance.

"Convince her or I will kill yer son," the king bellowed.

Fergus' pleading gaze melted to desperation, the pain in his eyes visceral enough to plunge into the most tender place in her heart. "Cassandra," he said in a strained voice.

She turned her face away from him, unable to witness his agony as she gave her final answer. "Nay."

❦

FERGUS STARED AT CASSANDRA IN DISBELIEF. SHE HAD CONDEMNED his son to death. Geordie. The lad he had never met, never held in his arms. The boy whose name he had only just learned minutes before.

Cassandra's face remained fixed toward the king, as if she could not bear to look at him. Indeed, how could she with what she had just done?

"Dinna do this." Fergus stepped toward her and grabbed her arm. The energy of the stone crackled through her and raced into his body. The thoughts and emotions of others whirled around him with Cassandra's thoughts rising above them all.

Look at her.

He knew who Cassandra meant. He put his attention to his wife, the woman he had once loved for her beauty and the fresh smell of rain about her. The woman he realized he no longer felt anything for.

Not that it meant she ought to die.

Allisandre struggled against her captors. Even in her terror, her face remained youthful and supple, her skin without the slightest wrinkle. She looked exactly as she had the day he'd met her twelve years ago. Beautiful. Perfect.

Truly look at her.

Fergus fixed his gaze harder. Her image flickered, briefly like the wavering heat of a flame. The memory of her smell locked in his brain, the delicate scent flooded with the horrors of his nightmare. It wasn't an essence of something fresh upon her all those years - it was magic.

Beyond her block.

Aye, Allisandre's secrets. The ones she insisted all women had, her smile cold with warning when she'd said it. It had worked when he was young and infatuated, his experience untried and without the aid of the stone. He drew deep from the stone and glared at the woman struggling against her captors.

Except she was no longer there. Gone was the woman of unnatural timeless beauty and in her place was an old woman with frizzing gray hair and breasts that sagged against her soft belly.

He staggered back, as did the others, all horrified by her dropped mask.

"Do not touch her," Allisandre shrieked. Her hand shot up and Fergus flew into the air, torn from Cassandra's grasp.

"Ye love me, remember?" She grinned at him with yellowed teeth.

Fergus hung aloft only a second more before Allisandre whipped her hand to the right and sent him soaring across the room. His body crashed hard into the stone wall. His chain mail absorbed none of the impact and instead shoved it painfully against his body. The force holding him slipped away and he dropped several feet to the floor below. Agony exploded at his left side and he curled around it, hissing out his discomfort.

"Allisandre," he ground out.

Cassandra raced toward Allisandre at an unnaturally fast pace, but Allisandre cupped her palms toward Cassandra and she stopped in place, struggling against an unseen force. Magic was thick in the air, cloying where it lodged in the back of Fergus' throat.

A hearty laugh came from the front of the room. The king clapped his hand upon his thigh, the way he might do for a troubadour's performance. "Ye were right, Lachina. He dinna ever suspect ye."

The old woman smirked at the king. "He canna track people who dinna exist."

Fergus' mind reeled. The thoughts and emotions of the room were murky to him, a blur throbbing in time with the ache in his skull. What in God's teeth were they talking about?

The king grinned, his eyes lit with victory. "Guards, collect the girl and bring her to me. She has something I want."

Fergus' awareness latched to the king's and saw exactly what the king wished to do with Cassandra. His muscles flared with white hot heat and he roared in protest. He moved forward three steps. Four. Five, pushing through the magic binding him.

Allisandre put up another hand and stayed him. Fergus growled and fought, even while his brain reeled. Not Allisandre. Lachina?

"Who are ye?" he demanded. "What happened to Allisandre?"

A handful of men in black chain mail surrounded Cassandra and locked their hands over her slender arms. One soldier stood behind her, his elbow crooked under her chin at her throat.

The witch rolled her eyes at Fergus. "There never was an Allisandre, ye fool. It was how we were able to trick ye into believing she was dead. If she were a real person, dinna ye think ye'd have felt her?"

He shook his head, refusing to believe what Lachina said. After all, he had held Allisandre in his arms, he had kissed her, and he had stared into those brilliant green eyes. A shiver rattled through him. The memory surfaced, real and true - the unnaturally green eyes and the intensity of her stare, as though she meant to devour him. Or control him.

Nausea rolled through his stomach. All of it had been a lie. His life had been a lie.

The men pushed Cassandra to the dais where the king drummed his fingers over the arm of the throne with dramatic impatience. Fergus fought harder against the unseen wall holding him back, but it did not yield.

He had been lied to, deceived. A horrifying thought shot through him, as sharp and painful as a marksman's arrow. Lachina was too old to bear a child.

His heart slammed against his ribs. "What of my son?" he asked in a voice he could not keep from trembling. "What of Geordie?"

The king glanced to the witch with the mirth of those sharing a cruel joke. Together they gave a malicious bark of laughter.

His stomach slid lower.

Nay.

"Dinna be so foolish." Lachina shook her head, her eyes sparkling. She slid another look to the king, but he was occupied with Cassandra who stood a foot away.

"Did ye no' hear what I told ye before?" Lachina's bushy gray brows crinkled her forehead upward. "Ye canna track people who dinna exist."

Fergus gritted his teeth and a knot of tension tightened at the back of his throat. "What do ye mean?"

"Ye know what I mean," she snarled.

The king reached for Cassandra, his slender white hand stretching toward her neck.

"Say it," Fergus demanded. The vehemence of his voice echoed off the cold stone and shot back at him.

"Did ye ever once feel the lad in yer mind?" the witch countered.

"Say it," Fergus roared. His vision dotted with white and his palms tingled.

"Ye daft lout." The witch spat upon the ground. "Yer son dinna ever exist anymore than yer wife did."

Fergus ceased fighting the magic and staggered back against the wall. That was it. The entire life Fergus had sacrificed for, what he had led Cassandra to her death for and abandoned his mother to a lonely estate for, all of it had been for naught.

He balled his hands into fists at his side and howled with the force of a demon. He had lost everything.

13

Cassandra had bided her time, and guarded her talents until now. The king had his suspicions about her, she'd seen as much in his thoughts when Fergus had touched her arm.

King Edgar thought her too slight, too insignificant to be a threat - even with the stone's power behind her. He had underestimated her. They all had.

Exactly as she had planned.

Fergus' agonized cry reverberated through her and left her heart trembling with sorrow for his loss. There was no son to rescue. There was nothing more to save, except Scotland.

Cassandra gripped the guard's arm locked over her throat to hold the man against her back, and bent over while drawing him forward. The man fought against the momentum with a speed only an enchantment could afford him. But her action had been too sudden, too unexpected. He flew over her head and collided with the king.

The men surrounding her glided forward, so quickly she almost didn't have time to stop them. She drew all the force of her strength, unrestrained for the first time in her life, and enhanced with the force of the stone. Her fist connected with the first one and arced onward, to the second, the third, the fourth, and fifth. The men were launched into the air and landed nearly ten feet away from her. Three rose, two did not.

In fact, two were no longer there.

Cassandra crouched to the ground and splayed her open hands over the stonework there. She pushed her energy out and let it connect with the earth. The building groaned and dust sifted from the rafters. The flagstones underfoot trembled, a low vibration first before growing to a rattle. An unseen force wrapped around her. Squeezing, squeezing, squeezing, like a giant fist. The air crackled.

Magic.

She gritted her teeth and shot upward, breaking through the invisible hold. She put her hand to the floor and it rumbled violently. Deep fissures cut into the ground and jagged outward like the rays of a sun.

Something dark flew at her, but she deflected the advance of a soldier with the shift of her forearm. Another came at her so quickly, she was forced to lift her other arm. When the third came at her, she had no more arms. The man struck her in the face full force. She rocked backward and the grip of magic closed around her once more.

"Kill her," the king snarled in the distance. "But get that damn necklace first."

Cassandra flexed her body with the exertion of energy and ripped through the shell of magic. This time she focused her attention on the witch. Cassandra wrenched a clawed hand upward. Green vines snaked from the cracked floor and slithered toward Lachina. The woman backed up, but there were more coming from behind.

Lachina swept her palm outward, fighting the stone's strength with magic. Some vines shrank back, but still others crept forward. Fergus staggered as the force keeping him held fell away, and ran toward Cassandra.

She vaguely heard his hoarse cry call her name, but she could not let her attention fix on him. Not when she had a very potent witch to contend with. A witch who was losing the battle.

A soldier cracked his fist against Cassandra's head. She rocked, briefly acknowledging the pain of the strike. Sweat beaded on her brow as she fought the resistance from the witch and kept the vines racing onward. They had spiraled up the woman's red skirt and twisted about her waist.

Another guard darted at Cassandra and swept his leg against the back of her knees while yet another still threw a solid kick directly into the center of her chest. Pain exploded at her breastbone and stole the breath from her lungs.

Her connection to the earth faltered for a brief moment and the vines shrank back.

Yet another man moved behind her in a blur of motion. He clutched her shoulders and jerked her backward. Cassandra lost her footing and connected with the hard ground.

In that brief moment, before she could suck in a deep inhalation to clear her mind, the soldiers were on her. Their black chain mail moved about with a speed that made them no more possible to capture than wisps of smoke. Brutal hands turned her over and jerked her arms back. She snatched her limbs back and leapt deftly to her feet.

She would not go down so easily.

The breath wheezed from her chest, each one as painful as though she drew in fire instead of air. Blood dotted the floor at her feet and a swirling in her head told her the strike to her temple had done some damage.

The stone may have imbued her with strength, but it did not increase the durability of her mortal body. Even with the soldiers charging at her, the witch was the greatest threat.

Cassandra swept her hand and drew all the breathable air toward her in a rush. The men coughed and choked, their magic as unprepared for the inability to breathe as her ability had been against protecting her from strikes.

Cassandra shoved her hands toward Lachina who wrestled with the vines still locked over her shins. The stone burned against Cassandra's chest, but she ignored it and let all of herself be consumed with its strength. It blazed through her like the light of the stars and the moon and the sun all at once. White flooded her vision and streaked from her fingertips.

Her throat rasped with a scream and the vines redoubled their effort until they had wrapped the witch completely. They coiled over her shoulders, her throat, her face, the top of her head, and then she was nothing more than a writhing mass of rapacious vines pulsing and flexing around her.

The surge calmed and pulled with it the unnatural strength. Cassandra staggered back and gasped in a burning breath. The air whooshed back into the room.

"Dinna stop, ye fools." The king's impatience pitched into something of a shriek. "I want that bloody stone now."

A soldier flew at her, but not in attack. He skidded over the floor before coming to a stop inches from her feet and fading. Another figure rushed in front of her, the movements slower, more natural. Fergus. He was at her side. His dark eyes met hers and he held out his left hand, his less dominant one when fighting.

They always were stronger together.

Cassandra placed her palm in his and the energy between them surged anew.

※

Fergus hadn't realized how badly Cassandra had been wounded. Not until he touched her and was slammed by the wave of pain rolling toward him. Still, he kept his alarm guarded from her awareness. Though her body was badly battered, and her energy flagging, he sensed in her a determination that would not be stopped. Fear would only minimize her skills.

Damn Lachina for having kept him captive by her magic, away from the fighting. It had been torture watching her take hits he could have prevented. The fight had been unfair – until now.

He shared his ability with Cassandra, allowing her to see the intended movements of their foes at a speed she could match. The breath rasped from her mouth, but her strikes were sure and lethal. With hands clasped tight, the two of them fought side-by-side, talents and efforts combined.

The soldiers had lost the advantage of magic. One by one they fell beneath the power and the skill afforded to Cassandra and Fergus by the stone. Every now and then, a soldier might get in a punch or a kick, for it was impossible to block so many coming at once.

Cassandra tensed at his side.

The witch is connected to them.

Fergus flicked a glance at Cassandra. He'd thought Lachina dead beneath the vines.

Cassandra punched a man in the throat. Through her, Fergus felt the crunch of the soldier's windpipe against her knuckles as he lurched back and disappeared.

If she is dead, they will be gone.

Fergus nodded at Cassandra's thoughts, unspoken and yet fully understood between them. She would concentrate on her skills while he defended them both. Cassandra closed her eyes, fully trusting in his capability. He sensed the hum of energy rising in her and filling her palm, which she closed into a fist. The vines acted on her will and squeezed.

The guard in front of Fergus flickered in and out, like a sputtering candle. Lachina's control was fading with her life.

"Harder," Fergus demanded. He gripped Cassandra's free hand and fought with his right hand, his blade cutting down man after man, bastards in blackened chain, a bloody endless supply of them.

The crowd of soldiers pressed forward with a renewed effort, a desperate effort, jabbing with fists and blades. With the benefit of the stone, every one of their intended actions were visible to Fergus, and easily blocked. It was a defense he didn't have the ability to wield ten years earlier when he was not strong enough.

Blood welled between Cassandra's fingers and dripped from her fist. She did not register the pain he felt from her, but instead tightened her fist even more. The soldiers began to fade, their movements growing slower, more clumsy.

And then one ran forward from the crowd, crisply outlined where the others blurred, his movements faster than even the stone could register. A knife glinted. Too fast. Too fast.

It punched forward, not at Fergus, but at Cassandra, and lodged in her side.

Her head fell back and a soft cry escaped her lips. All at once the soldiers faded from view and Cassandra drooped. Fergus caught her with his free arm and carefully lowered her to the ground. The breath hissed in her chest and blood bubbled at the corner of her mouth. He'd seen this type of injury before. One he knew to be fatal. Pain filled his chest, not only from the burning of the difficult breathing she suffered from, but also from the ache in his own heart.

He couldn't lose her. Not when he'd lost so much that day. She released his hand, severing their connection, and gripped the hilt jutting from her side, her skin white against the polished onyx. "The king," she hissed.

"Nay," he cried. But even as he spoke, he knew he could not stop her from pulling the blade from her body. The dagger loosened with a wet sucking sound followed by a choked exhale. Blood dotted her lips.

She shoved the dagger to him, still glistening red. "The...king..." she wheezed between the words with pained breath.

As she spoke, a shuffle met Fergus' awareness. The distinct sound of someone trying carefully and discreetly to flee. Fergus honed his attention on the slender man, and narrowed his eyes like a predator ready to catch its prey.

The king's movements fanned out long before he took them, easily apparent after the magically imbued guards, giving Fergus enough time to properly aim his blade. He touched Cassandra's hand, now freed of the dagger and drew from the waning power of the stone to send the dagger launching toward the king with all the force their combined strength could possess.

The weapon punched into the king's chest with such force, it sent him careening backward into the far wall where he slunk like a discarded poppet. He did not rise. Hell, he didn't even struggle, the bastard. So damn easy to kill without his army of magic at his back.

Cassandra choked and the hand under Fergus' flinched. He snapped his attention to her as her body relaxed, relinquishing her mortal struggle. His heart sucked up into his throat.

"Cassandra," he said tightly. He shook his head, unable to say more against the tension in his throat.

Her bloody fist loosened, her fingers unfurling to reveal where her fingernails had scored deep enough into her palms that the white tendons beneath showed. Immediately the vines gripping Lachina uncoiled and fell limp. The witch was nowhere in sight, the same as the men she controlled.

Fergus wrapped his hand against Cassandra's, but felt nothing. No force of the stone, no wild connection of energy. No pulse.

Heat prickled at his eyelids. He had failed her. It was as it had been ten years before, but this time with someone real. Someone he…

Someone he loved.

She wavered, the same as the soldiers had when Lachina was dying. The stone disappeared for a moment before reappearing faintly, more like a skein of sunlight than a physical form. Cassandra was dying.

14

Fergus could not lose Cassandra. He squeezed her hand in search for the stone's connection to flare between them, a sensation he had too often taken for granted.

Nothing happened.

He pulled deep from the anguish inside him and a cry escaped him, raw and savage. His voice echoed around him again and again and again through the vast stone chamber. A mockery of his pain, of his loss. Because he could not lose her. He would rather die than have her taken from the earth.

He didn't know why he did it, but he took her clasped hand and set it over his heart. "Take my life," he said, muttering as though in prayer. "And give it to her who is worthy."

Her fingers fell limp over his own and her form flickered.

"Take it," he cried.

A bone-searing pain bolted through him, as though his soul were being sucked from his body. He jolted forward with the force of it. It pulled at him, suckling the life from his body and funneling it into Cassandra through their joined hands.

"Stop." Her voice was weak, but it was the most beautiful sound in all the world.

"Live, Cassandra," he said through gritted teeth. "Live."

"Not without you." She jerked her hand from his.

Energy sparked between them with streaks of magic stretching between their fingers like ribbons of lightning. She gasped for breath and then gave a soft laugh. "You saved me, Fergus."

He shook his head. "Nay, lass. It's ye who saved me."

She ran a weak hand through his hair. "You were killing yourself."

"I was giving ye life." He stared down at her, unable to take his gaze from the soft curls of dark hair falling about her fair face. Her lips were as lush and red as they'd ever been, her pale blue eyes bright with unshed tears. "I love ye, Cassandra."

She blinked, but a tear escaped the corner of her eye. "And I you, Fergus. I think I have since the day I met you."

"And I ye." He smiled to himself at the memory. "Since the first time I saw ye in the apple orchard in a vision." He eyed the blood at the side of her gown where it stood bright against the pale lavender. "We must leave from here. Can ye walk?"

She nodded, but still winced as she rose. Her gaze immediately fell on the king and she lifted her beautiful gaze to Fergus in question. "We are free?"

He smiled, the first carefree smile he could remember in far too long. "Aye," he answered. "We are free."

"But at what cost?" she fingered his hair.

He frowned with confusion.

"You have a strip of white that was not there before. I worry..." She pursed her lips. "I worry what you have sacrificed in saving me."

"I would have sacrificed it all," he vowed.

She smiled sadly. "I know."

She closed her eyes briefly and waved a hand. The vines sucked deep into the cracks within the floor and the fissures sealed upon themselves. Save the dead king crumpled in the corner, it was as though none of it had ever happened.

Cassandra's brow furrowed and a wild wind billowed outside, rattling doors and windows. Thunder shuddered overhead and the roar of a sleeting rainstorm immediately followed.

She opened her eyes and smiled. "A little chaos to aid in our escape while you clear the memories of those who saw us."

He shook his head, but she nodded. "You can. I saw it." She linked her fingers with his. "Or rather we can together."

They clasped hands and breathed as one. They expanded their minds in unison, threading it through the whole of Edinburgh, locating and plucking their images from the minds of all who saw them until they never existed in the memory of the people.

"What of him?" Cassandra asked when they were done, indicating the king with her mind.

"There is much family strife." Fergus stared at the limp form of the king who had threatened him for the whole of a decade. "Let them think it was his uncle who killed him."

She nodded and allowed Fergus to offer her the support of his body as he led her to a back room where he knew there to be an unseen exit. Her movements were slow, her breathing labored. While her presence no longer flickered with the threat of death, she was still not recovered.

"I'm well enough," she argued and then stumbled.

He caught her before she fell. His hand had splayed over her slender stomach by accident. A heartbeat thundered against his palm. He jerked his hand back in wonder.

Cassandra's eyes went wide, having experienced the same realization as he. Her skin held a sickly pallor and her brow glistened with an unhealthy sheen. "Fergus..." She put her hand to her flat stomach that would not remain so for long.

He nodded, hearing her thoughts before she could get them through the emotion clogging her words.

"I do have a son." He stroked her face. "And a wife." He grinned. "If ye'll have me."

Tears shone bright in Cassandra's eyes. "Nothing would bring me greater joy."

"Nor I," he said. "Save seeing ye safe." He hefted her feet from beneath her and cradled her to his chest as though she weighed nothing, for surely to Fergus the Undefeated she did not.

She relaxed into the embrace of his arms, the glow of contentment spreading between them both from their own joy and through the elation of the other. "I happen to be acquainted with one of the best healers in all of Scotland," she said with a smile.

Fergus grinned. "Then mayhap we should go see her."

Cassandra nodded. "Indeed we should."

They slipped discreetly and unseen from Edinburgh, and ventured to Inverness on sunlit paths until they were once more met with happiness and love and the quiet joy of Blair.

EPILOGUE

June 1109

Giggles erupted from the other side of the garden wall. Cassandra turned to Blair and the two of them shared a smile.

"I believe I hear the sound of a wee lad on his way to see his Ma." Blair lifted the basket of freshly snipped herbs to her side.

"And his Grandmama," Cassandra said with a wink.

"Ach, aye, from time to time he's glad to see me as well." Blair's eyes sparkled as she said it.

Though it was hardly from 'time to time' for little Niven when it came to his eldmother. Fergus rounded the corner to the garden with the toddler on his back. The boy squealed with delight and put his dimpled hands over Fergus' eyes in his excitement.

"I canna see," Fergus cried with great theatrics, which only served to send Niven into greater fits of giggles.

Fergus plucked the boy from his shoulders with both hands and gently set him upon the ground. Niven toddled over the uneven ground to Cassandra and Blair with his clumsy gait, and caught his fists into the skirts of both. "Are you tired, my little love?" Cassandra asked, hefting his scant weight into her arms.

He rubbed at his eyes and shook his head. His lower lip thrust outward in a miserable pout and he met her gaze with the dark, soulful stare he'd inherited from his father. He shifted in Cassandra's arms and the weight of his head settled against the crook of her neck. The gentle blend of rosemary and lavender and little boy sweat rose from his silky dark hair.

Cassandra drew a deep breath of her son and her heart swelled with all the joy he brought to her life. She brushed her lips over his silky hair in a cherished kiss. He pushed her away moodily.

"Are ye sure ye're no' tired?" Blair walked her fingers up Niven's soft arm to the crook of his delicate neck.

He scrunched his shoulder to his ear and shoved at her.

"Not in need of a nap, indeed," Cassandra said slyly.

Blair laughed in her good-natured way. "I had a lad once who was far more a beast than my wee little Niven. Have ye heard that story?"

Niven shifted his head under Cassandra's chin to regard his eldmother. Fergus met Cassandra's eye and together they grinned, already knowing where this was going.

Niven shook his head against Cassandra's neck.

"Ach, it's a fine story." Blair held out her hands and the little boy pulled away from his mother with arms outstretched toward his eldmother.

"I loved the demons out of him." She pulled him into her arms and winked at Cassandra, knowing there was a need for privacy between her and Fergus. Especially this day of all days.

"I hugged it out of him." Blair strode away with the boy in her arms and squeezed him a playfully large, rocking embrace. "I kissed it out of him." The pucker of a dozen kisses led them from the garden to where they could no longer be heard.

Fergus regarded Cassandra from the corner of his eye. "Ye have something to tell me." He concentrated a moment longer. "And ye're blocking it from me." He untucked Niven's small wooden sword from his arm and propped it against the backside of the bench. The pretend weapon had been a gift from Phillip on his last visit to see them. He'd brought gifts for them all, including apples from the orchard, and news of home.

In truth the only thing that had interested Cassandra were the bits involving Phillip and the details of brave things he'd done - as was told in a boisterous tone with many different character's voices and much drama.

"Maybe you should learn not to read a woman's thoughts." Cassandra gave Fergus a coy smile and settled onto the stone bench beneath the shade of an apple tree.

Fergus had planted it when they'd arrived back in Inverness with Blair. And when Cassandra was fully healed, she had pressed upon the earth to help make it grow. In the summer, its shade was the coolest and in the summer and early fall, its apples were the sweetest.

Fergus took her face in his hands. His touch blazed through her veins like fire. Still. After over two years and a child born, each touch was as intense as their first.

"You cannot get through my defenses so easily, Fergus the Undefeated," she chided.

He nuzzled his lips to hers and teased her mouth apart for his tongue to sweep against hers.

"I think you cheat," she murmured.

He leaned back and grinned. "So I do. And so I will until ye tell me."

She took his hand and put it to her lower stomach where she sensed he could discern the healthy, steady thrum of another small heartbeat. Another child.

"A girl," he breathed. "Ye're no' happy."

Cassandra shook her head in protest and put her hand over his. "I do not want our youngest daughter to go through life as I did, beneath the burden of obligation."

Fergus nodded. "I know what ye intend to do. But are ye no' sure it will be a curse upon our bloodline?"

Cassandra smiled at her husband and all the warmth of her love for him glowed through her. "I assure you, it will not."

She closed her eyes and, with the power drawn through both of them and the stone, she drew from the earth a promise that no one would remember the skills of a youngest daughter when she died, so the future generations would not be birthed into a life of expectation.

Her stomach grew warm and Fergus settled his hand over her more securely, as though he meant to protect her.

"She will have a good life," Cassandra reassured her husband.

"The way we do." He put his palm to her cheek once more and she flushed beneath the tenderness of his affection.

"Aye," she whispered. "She will be happy and she will be loved."

"And truly, there's no' anything else to need in life." With that, he kissed her sweetly and soundly, with the promise of so much more to come.

Madeline
Martin

ABOUT THE AUTHOR

Madeline Martin is a USA TODAY Bestselling author of Scottish set historical romance novels. She lives a glitter-filled life in Jacksonville, Florida with her two daughters (known collectively as the minions) and a man so wonderful he's been dubbed Mr. Awesome. All shenanigans are detailed regularly on Twitter and on Facebook. Madeline loves animals in sweaters, cat videos, and working out (to support her love of wine and Nutella). As she is unable to have pets herself due to allergies, she has acquired a plastic Halloween skeleton named Nick and a small robot named Meccano - both of whom are dressed up regularly by the minions.

Newsletter: http://eepurl.com/bijiij
Website: http://madelinemartin.com

ALSO BY MADELINE

WICKED EARLS CLUB

Earl of Benton

HEART OF THE HIGHLANDS

Deception of a Highlander
Possession of a Highlander
Enchantment of a Highlander

MERCENARY MAIDENS

Highland Spy
Highland Ruse

NOVELLAS

The Highlander's Challenge

HIGHLAND PASSIONS

A Ghostly Tale of Forbidden Love
The Madam's Highlander
The Highlander's Untamed Lady

- facebook.com/MadelineMartinAuthor
- twitter.com/MadelineMMartin
- instagram.com/madelinemmartin
- bookbub.com/authors/madeline-martin
- goodreads.com/MadelineMartin

THE PROTECTOR'S PROMISE

A Border Series Novella

CECELIA MECCA

Two bitter enemies. One sacred vow. Will the passion that flares between them consume everything they love?

ACKNOWLEDGMENTS

As always, I would like to first and foremost thank my editor, Angela Polidoro. Her brilliant insight continues to amaze me each and every time. I would also like to thank Carolina Valdez Schneider who goes above and beyond as well as Kim Killion who designed the beautiful 'Ladies of the Stone' cover. Last but not least, to my real-life knight in shining armour. . . Though he wields a spreadsheet rather than a broadsword, my husband Mike is the hero of my life story.

I

Isle of Skye, Scotland, 1273

"Give me a reason not to kill you."

With the tip of his broadsword to his attacker's throat, the Lord of Camburg stood immobile, waiting for the Scotsman's answer. The guard stared back at William.

No response.

He tried again. "What are you guarding?"

Nothing.

He'd not traveled all this way, from the borderlands of North West England, to be stopped so close to his goal.

Suddenly, the big, bearded man who'd tried to lop off William's head from behind shifted before his eyes. A scared young boy, too young to grow a beard, lay in his place. The vision disappeared, and William found himself staring once again at the man who had followed him from the moment he'd begun his ascent up the mountain. The winding path had hidden his pursuer from sight, but the silence had done nothing to mask the big man's telltale footfalls.

The visions came more often now. He had gone years without them, but since arriving in Scotland, they occurred nearly every day. Most often, they were altered versions of that which was in front of him and other times of what was to come. Perhaps whatever was at the top of this mountain might provide some much-needed answers. He hoped so since they were becoming harder and harder to disguise.

Though he would likely regret it, William pulled back his sword. The fleeting visions that had plagued him his entire life had come more readily each day of this voyage. They showed him glimpses of the past or the future, and after seeing the lad the guard had been, he could not harm him. Sheathing his weapon, he moved away from the guard, who scrambled to his feet.

"I am guarding no one," the man insisted.

He lied.

"We shall see." William pointed to the path ahead of them. "Lead the way."

They had nearly arrived. He knew neither what nor whom he sought, something he would never willingly admit to his friends or foes. They'd think he'd descended into madness if he told them, and William may be inclined to agree. But the call that had taken him away from Camburg Castle across the borderlands and to this mountain had been too strong to ignore. Now, after days of aimless wandering with only the strange pull to guide him, William was close.

This man's presence told him as much.

"If you attempt to harm her, I will kill you," the Scotsman said as he picked his way along the rocky path.

"*Her?*"

The guard spun around, his brows furrowed. "Who are you?"

Finally, perhaps, he could get some answers. "An answer for an answer."

The guard responded with a curt nod.

"Who do you protect?"

"Scotland." He answered so quickly, William would have been inclined to believe him if not for the outrageousness of his response. Then again, he'd come here alone, for no better reason than he'd felt drawn to. There was no denying his situation was outrageous.

"Who do you protect"—he pointed—"up there?"

"Scot—"

"You are telling me Scotland resides at the top of this mountain on the Isle of Skye?" He was losing patience. After days of questions with no answers, he was ready for real information. "Try again."

"The Priestess of the Stone. But you knew that already."

Priestess? Stone? What had he stumbled his way into?

All the same, he was a man of his word—he'd promised to answer the man's question in exchange for information. "I am William Thornhurst, son of Lord Ranville and seneschal of Camburg Castle."

"Why are you here?" The man's hands twitched at his sides, reaching for a sword that was no longer there.

"I don't know," he answered honestly. Though he had dozens of questions to ask—Who was this priestess? What was the significance of the stone? Why had he been drawn to this secluded place?—the guard's expression threw him off. The man looked at him as if he'd just seen him for the first time before averting his eyes and looking around frantically, as if searching for an escape.

"An answer for an answer," he reminded the guard. "Why do you look at me that way?"

The man's chin lifted. "You will find out soon enough."

With that, he turned away once again and ran ahead. If he hoped William would follow, running headlong into some trap, he would be disappointed. Instead, he continued to make his way up the mountain, listening and waiting. This was not his land, and the guard's knowledge of the terrain would be a profound advantage for him should he decide to make another attack.

William should not have let him live.

The irrepressible urge to come to this place had begun the morning he'd awoken with that odd mark on his hip. Appearing while he'd slept and seemingly in the shape of a small dagger, the mark ushered a new reality into his life, one filled with the visions of his youth. Nothing had made sense since. Though his men were not surprised he'd wanted to travel alone up north, they'd insisted on joining him. And so William had snuck off under the cloak of darkness, driven by fleeting visions of his destination—the renowned pools of Skye. The visions had served him well in the past, and so he trusted them now once again.

William stopped, the sound of a waterfall ahead drowning out everything else. He could be more easily ambushed now, so he forced himself to slow his steps. Turning another corner, his eyes bulged at the sight before him.

Was it from this world?

Though the oak trees that dotted the landscape had become smaller as he ascended the mountain, one in front of him stood tall and proud next to a waterfall, defying logic. The coloring of the pools at the foot of the small falls baffled him—he'd never seen such shades of green and blue in nature—and the moss-covered rocks that cradled the pools appeared almost unnatural in their smoothness.

A woman stood at the center of them.

Her hooded, dark green cape revealed nothing more than the lower portion of her face and narrowed eyes. The guard that had fled earlier stood by her side, eyeing him warily.

William approached them with equal wariness, watching the lady's back straighten as the guard spoke to her. The waterfall drowned out their words, but he didn't need to hear them talk to notice the change in her expression. It had turned almost . . . murderous.

"Stop there," she called, the lilt of her voice what he imagined a siren's call would sound like. Oddly, he heeded her bidding.

"Go," she said over the sound of the water descending into the pools below. "Go back to England. Forget this place."

Did she really believe he'd traveled this far only to turn back? He needed answers!

"Why did you call me here?"

The words made no sense, even to his own ears. As he said them, memories flashed before him as clearly as if they'd just happened to him. His father introducing him to Sir Richard. The look on Richard's face when he told William his father had died, leaving him an orphan. The first time he met Lady Sara, the girl who'd been his childhood companion, the girl who was too fine of a lady for a lowly baron's son to wed. Richard granting him Camburg. His visits to court. His dream of attaining his own title, one not handed to him by an indulgent overlord . . .

The priestess watched as the memories pounded through him, each leaving behind enough emotion to bring him to his knees.

"Tell me what it means," he demanded, knowing somehow that she would not.

"Go," she shouted, the word etching itself into his very soul.

Instead, he took a step toward her . . . and then saw it.

Disguised as a regular rock, the gray stone in the center of the shallow pool at her feet gleamed a brighter green than anything found in the natural world. She had not called to him. That stone had summoned him, as mad as that sounded. She did not want him to know it was there, and while it had already turned back to gray, William had seen it for what it was: a relic. One that would help him on a mission that he should be back at Camburg preparing for even now. The king's regent would not be happy if he learned of William's journey. But somehow, when he saw the stone, he knew it would help him capture Moordon Castle.

He jumped into the pools, stumbling toward the stone before the priestess or her guard could even realize his intent. Grabbing the stone, William ran faster than he'd ever run in his life. As he navigated roots and pebbles, nearly falling down the steep incline, William did not pause to look for his pursuer, though it did surprise him that the man hadn't yet caught up. Instead, he made his way as quickly as possible down the mountain, anxious to get away from it all.

The guard . . . the priestess . . . this island. Away from Scotland and the strange forces that had drawn him there.

#

"My lady," one of Marion's guards called from behind, "there is nothing here but more trees and rocks. We should turn back."

She'd heard that same refrain for the last hour, and Marion was no more inclined to do so now than she had been earlier though she felt the stone's pull less now than she had earlier in the day.

Since embarking on this journey, the men who had been told to follow her orders had done everything but. She'd invoked her father's name, her mother's admonitions, and every other argument she could think to make.

Yet, as men were wont to do, they simply refused to listen. So she had stopped trying to convince them. Forging ahead of each of the men sent to protect her, Marion wound her way around the muddy path leading toward her destiny.

And then it was there before her.

"Priestess of the Stone . . . ," Kenneth muttered as he nearly knocked her over from behind. She supposed it was her fault for stopping so abruptly. But at least Marion could cease trying to convince the men, most especially her father's captain, of the existence of the Priestess of the Stone. For standing in front of them, just under a massive oak tree that should not have stood so tall this far up, was the very woman they'd journeyed here to find.

Some said her hair was the same color as Marion's, a flaming red not often found even in these parts. Others believed the priestess was an old woman, her wisdom a testament to her advanced age. Neither tale had any truth to it, for the priestess had flung back the hood of her cape, revealing black, flowing hair. At least one aspect of the stories was true—the woman who guarded the heart of Scotland, the stone that would be entrusted to Marion, was beautiful.

Marion felt surprisingly calm as she made her way toward the priestess. Her mother had assured her that she had nothing to fear, but she'd always wondered how she could know such a thing. The legend was, after all, just that. No one had met the priestess before, and her location had always been a well-guarded secret. Until now.

"Come," the priestess said, the soft lilting voice comforting her.

Marion obeyed, walking around the glittering blue and green pools to reach the priestess, who held out her hands. She chanced a glance over her shoulder. Her guards were gaping at them, their mouths hanging open.

Instead, Marion placed her hands on top of the priestess's outstretched ones. They were so soft and smooth, just like the even tone of her voice.

"I've been waiting for you."

"My mother bade me come," she said, her tongue heavy and awkward. "The mark appeared on my hip, and I was drawn here." Just as the legends foretold, it was the shape of a small dagger. It had appeared after a strange rumbling shook the earth. After four and twenty years of hearing the tales, Marion had understood at once.

The previous protector had died. She was being called to take the woman's place.

Back home, at Ormonde Castle, Marion had sometimes been accused of being haughty rather than poised, but standing next to this priestess, she felt like a young child, her words forming slowly and awkwardly.

"A wise woman," the priestess said. "We've much to discuss, and quickly." She glanced down at the pools. "The stone has been taken."

Had the priestess not held her hands firmly, she may have fallen at that declaration. "Taken?"

Marion followed the woman's gaze and saw nothing but calm, green-hued water and rocks in the pool at her feet. She glanced then at the guard who stood not far from them.

The priestess tugged on her hands. "Aye. And there's much for you to learn. But as I said, there is no time. You must act quickly to recover the stone."

Marion allowed her hands to drop when the priestess let them go.

"You have been chosen as Scotland's protector. Now that you've been summoned to protect it, the dark forces that oppose us, that oppose *you*, have stirred to life once more. I know not why it happened, only that it has."

Marion didn't understand. She'd never heard there was another side to the ancient tale. Her mother had said nothing of dark forces. Of anyone else trying to take possession of the stone.

"An Englishman by the name of William Thornhurst. He took the stone and disappeared earlier today," she explained. "You can detect ill intent, can you not?"

"Aye, or at least, I believe so. I have always been able to sense when someone wishes harm to myself or someone I love. 'Tis why my mother was not surprised to see the mark. She always believed I would be the next Protector of the Stone, knowing each garners a special ability from it."

"I do not understand this man's ability, but he was able to recognize the stone from where it was hidden, disguised as an ordinary rock. Though without my enchantment, it will now appear as it is, a precious emerald hanging from a chain of gold."

Now Marion knew why the priestess continued to glance down into the pools.

"He has likely returned to England. To Camburg Castle. You must find him and recover the stone. He will reveal his purpose before two moons pass, so you must act quickly. Trust the stone or—"

"Scotland will suffer." Her duty was clear, and Marion would not disappoint the priestess. Or her parents. Or Scotland. She would recover the stone from this Englishman before the time was up.

"Be careful," the priestess said. "He is smart and strong. And—"

She hesitated.

"And?" Marion prompted her.

"Handsome."

She nearly asked, *Why should that matter?* but held her tongue.

"Do not be deceived by him. The last time the stone fell into the hands of an Englishman, Scotland's king lost Northumbria to King Henry."

"Surely that was not because—"

"The fate of our land rests on the possession of that stone."

The priestess was so confident and serious, Marion did not doubt the truth of her words.

Marion surprised herself by taking her advisor's hands once again and squeezing them.

"I will recover the stone and protect it for the remainder of my days," she said. "I will not disappoint you."

For the first time since they met, the priestess smiled. As did Marion.

She had meant every word.

2

"Lady Marion?"

Though the leader of her guard, Kenneth, had been more receptive to her orders since the pool, he clearly found it difficult to accept the idea that she was in charge. Marion liked to think it was because he'd known her since she was a young girl and not because she happened to be a woman. She'd tried hard to remain patient, but her patience was running out.

"We must not stop," she repeated, looking around in horror as the men set up camp. "My mother—"

"Is not here," he muttered.

Marion often wondered why, if she could sense malintent, the gruff captain did not give her the familiar sensation of cold washing over her body. The strange bouts of cold chills had scared her as a child until she'd discovered the pattern to them. Since then, she'd been revered— by her parents, their people, by everyone who mattered—for her unique ability. The captain, however, did not seem to share their respect. Perhaps the reason she didn't feel any malintent was that he believed he was serving her best interests. Even so . . .

Mustering her best imitation of her father, the powerful Scottish border lord whom none would think to question, Marion approached the overly large captain. "Either we continue riding or we risk losing him. And once he reaches Camburg Castle—"

"We have no way of knowing how far ahead—"

"If we continue through the night, we will catch him by morning," she said forcefully.

Even though he'd been told to follow her orders, and he'd now seen the priestess and the pools with his own eyes, Kenneth frowned. He was going to deny her once again.

"You don't know that."

Marion could argue. She could attempt to convince him. But how could she possibly make the stubborn, overly practical Scotsman understand she could sense the stone? As soon as she left the glen, its pull had tugged her in a new direction—the feeling as undeniable as the fact that this conversation was not getting them any closer to their destination.

Instead, she yawned. A fake yawn that turned very real—they'd set a brutal pace since leaving Skye. And still, the Englishman eluded them.

Well, no longer. "Perhaps you are right," she lied.

And without further discussion, Marion pulled the bedroll from her mount and followed the guard's lead. If Kenneth looked at her strangely, it was because he was unused to her acquiescence. And, may the saints forgive her, she was so driven by desperation, she was about to do the very thing she'd promised her parents never to do.

The guards would be furious when they realized she'd ridden off alone.

As would her parents, but luckily they were back home, safe in their beds, while she battled her fear of the dark. When she finally untied her mount and made her way to the edge of camp, Marion stopped one last time. This close to the border, many dangers lay ahead. But none terrified her as much as human predators, namely reivers. Scottish, English . . . it mattered not. Either might do her harm.

"Truly, lass? You would travel across the border, at night, alone?"

Consarn it. "I'm not sure what you mean?"

The captain was not amused.

"Kenneth, please listen to me. Do you not believe I . . . know things . . . even though I wish it were not so?"

"My lady—"

"I've no wish to navigate this land alone, but you refuse to heed me," she said. She needed to make him understand. The pull toward the stone became stronger with every step, and somehow she just *knew* if they kept going—

"Very well."

Kenneth managed to surprise her.

"You will get yourself killed if you ride off alone," he mumbled. Then he shouted to the others, most of whom were apparently already awake. "We leave—now."

Marion smiled, grateful she would not be forced to extreme measures. And although their path was only lit by moonlight and their pace was slow, their efforts were rewarded.

Just beyond a thicket of trees, barely discernible but growing larger as she approached, stood a lone figure beside a horse. Without a word to Kenneth or the others, Marion spurred her mount forward, for she knew at once this was William Thornhurst, the Englishman who'd stolen the Stone of Scotland. *Her* stone. Or rather, her countrymen's stone and the one that would bring peace and prosperity to them. She felt it pulling her closer.

When she was nearly upon the thief, he pulled out his sword.

Would he kill a woman?

When she halted in front of him and dismounted, Marion thought two things at once.

The cold had not gripped her as she'd expected it would.

And the priestess had been right . . . he was quite handsome.

#

It was only when the riders behind her came into view that William drew his sword. Four men following a woman.

Though not just any woman.

A redheaded, green-eyed beauty who appeared as if she'd like nothing better than to murder him.

"Give me the stone," she demanded in a seething voice. He couldn't reconcile her voice, so commanding and low for a woman, with the smattering of freckles across her nose. Had the priestess sent this group after him?

Her guards were getting too close. Four. I need an advantage.

Without hesitating, he reached out and grabbed the Scotswoman—her accent left no doubt that she was one—and spun her around. Just as her men approached, he lifted his sword until it hovered just beneath her chin.

"That's close enough," he shouted. Not surprisingly, her men stopped far enough away to give him a few moments to consider his next move.

"Let go of me!" The way she twisted in his arms and brushed her bottom against him made William suddenly wish he wore a hauberk. This was not a convenient time for an arousal, though he could certainly understand his body's response.

"Stop moving," he whispered in her ear. "Or I will kill every one of your men."

She complied. Perhaps she assumed he meant those words, though in truth he did not. Though he did need the stone, even if he did not understand why.

Rather than cower, however, as a woman in her position should do, the woman lifted her chin and continued to issue orders.

"Give me the stone," she demanded.

"A bad idea, old man," William shouted to the apparent leader of the guards, who had begun to dismount. He tightened his grip against the redheaded woman.

"You have two choices," he tried to reason with her. "Forget the stone, and ride off with your men when I release my grip. Otherwise, you're coming with me." It was the only way he'd maintain any kind of advantage.

She apparently did not care for either choice.

Turning to her men, she shouted, "He's not going to—"

He moved his hand swiftly from her shoulder to cover her mouth. When she tried to bite him, his gloves prevented any damage.

Moving toward his horse, William thought of how best to get them mounted and away from her guards. He envisioned each possible maneuver—and its follow-through—and decided in a trice. Once again, he did not hesitate. With his sword arm, he grabbed the horse's reins, and he swung himself up with his other hand, never releasing his grip on the woman. Blocking out the sounds of her guards' advance, he sheathed his sword and pulled her up and in front of him.

"Continue to squirm and you'll fall. Sit still . . . you may survive the day."

Thankfully, it was enough to stop her. For now. But the others were nearly upon them. And though William had crossed the border into England earlier that day, this was not a familiar path to him. Looking for an escape, he relied on speed to put distance between himself and his would-be attackers.

There!

The old Roman road split just ahead. As soon as the others rode over the ridge behind them, her men would see which path they took . . . unless they were already long gone. But which path *should* he take? The main road? Aye. They would likely think he'd take the one less traveled.

His eye judged that he'd taken the turn just in time to lose them.

But he kept going at a gallop, working under the assumption the pursuers were just behind him. He only slowed after riding for what seemed like hours, though he knew from the sun's position it had not been so long.

"They'll kill you when they find us."

"They are welcome to try."

For the first time since he whisked her onto his horse, the Scotswoman turned to look at him. A pert nose. Full lips. Her outfit and demeanor told him she was a lady, and a brave one at that.

"Why did you take the stone?"

"Why do you want it back?"

She turned back around, the unladylike huff prompting his next impertinent question.

"You the daughter of . . . whom exactly? A great border lord? Perhaps the king of Scotland himself?"

"My father," she spat out, "is an earl."

"Ahh," he mocked. "An earl. Of course."

"He is no castellan." Her taunt hit too close to the mark. His relatively lowly position had made it impossible for him to marry another earl's daughter . . .

"You never answered my question," she said. "What does the Lord of Camburg want—"

"How do you know who I am?" Her words surprised him for a moment, but hadn't he guessed she had some connection to the priestess? "The priestess sent you." He didn't expect a response, but as the road narrowed and wound its way through a thicket of trees, she answered anyway.

"She did not *send* me. The stone you carry is rightfully mine. It belongs to Scotland. It belongs—"

"You know what it is?"

"You don't?" She turned around again, and by God, if she kept doing that, he'd be near crippled with desire by the time they made it back to Camburg. He'd obviously been too long without a woman. "Then why did you take it?"

When she blinked, her dark lashes kissed the creamy skin beneath. William had never kidnapped a woman before, but he found it was an exceedingly difficult task. The last time he'd been this distracted by a woman . . . in fact, he had never experienced anything like this.

His only answer was not much of one at all. "It . . . called to me."

Her eyes widened. "That's it? You really don't know?" Then something changed in her expression. Whereas it had been angry before, it softened. And then, unfortunately, she turned back around.

"Will you tell me?" he heard himself asking.

"Aye," she said. "I will. But you must promise to give it back—"

"I cannot tell you why, only that I know that I need it."

Her shoulders slumped. "Then I tell you nothing."

He'd expected as much. "Will you at least tell me your name?"

She folded her arms in front of her, forcing him to tighten his grip lest she fall off the horse.

"You know mine. At least—"

"Lady Marion, daughter of Archibald Rosehaugh, 3rd Earl of Ormonde."

Right. An earl's daughter. And an only child like Sara, no doubt.

"Court," he responded.

She turned again. "Pardon?"

"Court. My given name is indeed William, but I've gone by the name of Court since coming to Camburg."

"Court," she repeated. "As in—"

"Aye, the king's court," he said, preparing for her laughter, which surprisingly never came.

"I'd give you leave to call me Marion," she said. "But since I am your captive—"

"Marion." He said it as much to infuriate her as to test the name on his lips. He was not disappointed.

"*Lady* Marion. Or better—"

"Marion," he repeated. "You are not my captive for long. When we return to Camburg and your men arrive, I will happily give you over to them."

"Lady Marion," she corrected. "And how are you so confident my men will not find us before then?"

Court leaned down to whisper in her ear. "Because, *Marion*, I've no wish to be found. And when I want something, I get it."

3

He obviously thought highly of himself. Marion was not accomplishing anything by demanding he relinquish the stone. He'd refused to give it to her more than once, not that she'd really expected he would simply hand it over. But it was clearly time for a new plan.

"Court," she said sweetly, imitating her flirtatious cousin and trying not to laugh at the poor effort, "do you perhaps have anything to eat?"

Though they'd stopped once to see to their needs, she and her captor had spent the remainder of the day on horseback. And though she no longer feared for her life, Marion was hungry, tired, and more than a little annoyed.

"When we camp for the night, I'll catch something for us. And Marion?"

"Yes, Court?" She found she rather liked the sound of his common name on her lips.

"It won't work."

She could have feigned ignorance, but it wasn't worth the effort. Frustrated, she silently railed against her "special ability." For something so unique and special, it was really of no use to her at all. Not

THE PROTECTOR'S PROMISE

when she hadn't felt the slightest chill since meeting her nemesis, who was surely the most dangerous person alive at the moment.

Giving up, she tried for a more practical approach. "What are your intentions?"

"With you," he said, shifting behind her, "or the stone?"

She shifted as well, trying to find a comfortable position.

"Stop," he growled out.

Marion turned, trying to understand what she'd done wrong now. "I didn't do—"

His expression forced her mouth closed. She swallowed, knowing that look. Too many suitors had sought her favor over the years for her not to understand desire when she saw it. Refusing to look away, Marion stared into a set of hazel eyes that looked more blue than green or brown. With a square jaw and short, blondish-brown hair, her Englishman was no less handsome than when they'd met earlier that day. And the way he looked at her . . .

Marion spun back around.

"Your intentions with me," she said finally.

"I already told you, I intend—"

"But we are not near Camburg," she pointed out. "It will take—"

"Just one more full day of riding. We are closer than you think."

Marion knew enough of England to know Camburg was just south of the border, but she'd lost track of where they were exactly. Now that the stone was within her reach, nothing guided her forward except . . . well, him.

"As for the stone, I have no intentions toward it. I know only that it belongs to me. It pulled me toward it, and I had no choice but to listen."

Marion did not bother arguing with him. She knew exactly what he meant by that, even if he did not. They had ridden past the thicket of trees and now made their way through a wide-open field. She watched as the sun began to dip below the horizon.

"Why are there no other travelers? Where are we?"

"We've ventured off the main road." Court pointed to their right. "Your companions are likely west of us, but they'll eventually circle back as they approach Camburg."

"We're off the main road?"

"Aye, we have been for some time now."

She looked down, and while there were few hoof marks beneath them, it appeared very much as if the road was well traveled.

"Have you ever left Ormonde?"

"Of course." In fact, she had not, with the exception of this journey. She'd begged to visit Edinburgh many times, of course, but her parents had claimed it was much too dangerous given the possibility she was "Scotland's chosen one." Heaven and the saints above forbid anything should happen to her.

Then, when the mark appeared, they finally trusted her to know where to go and what to do . . . and here she was, the prisoner of some English knight intent on— "You're planning an attack?"

If he was the opposing force, according to the priestess, he would be the one to throw Scotland into chaos if he kept the stone. Which meant Scotland would suffer so long as it remained in his hands. And according to the priestess, the suffering would begin within two moons of his possession of the stone.

His silence was all the answer she needed.

"Where?" she demanded. "When?"

Court stopped the horse and dismounted, reaching up for her. She pushed away his hand and followed him down without any assistance despite the size of his destrier. She followed Court and his massive black warhorse toward the sound of rushing water.

"Are we stopping for the night?" Since she sensed Court had no wish to harm her, Marion was not in a hurry to reach Camburg. Once there, they would part ways, and the stone would be locked away inside an English holding and lost to her. Until they arrived, she still had a chance.

"Aye," he said, tying his mount to a nearby tree. Though not as thick as the forest they'd passed earlier in the day, this stretch of land would provide cover.

Finished with his task, Court walked toward her. "If you run," he said, watching her intently, "you will only get yourself hurt. On the morrow—"

"I won't run," she said. "That stone you're carrying is mine. And until I have it—"

He laughed, dimples forming on both cheeks. Though he must be at least twenty and eight, Court's smile made him appear younger.

"You are laughing now, but I doubt I will amuse you later."

"You are a tenacious little lass, aren't you?"

"And you are a stubborn, arrogant boar."

He took a step closer. "You know me well, it seems."

"Your kind, aye."

Taunting her captor would not help her accomplish her goal, but it seemed she couldn't help it. Every time Marion opened her mouth, she was surprised at what came out of it. She'd never speak to her father this way, let alone any other man of rank. And yet . . . Court seemed almost pleased by her behavior.

Perhaps she shouldn't be so surprised. Her nemesis was, after all, the worst kind of man.

An Englishman.

"My kind," he said, his voice not as light as it had been earlier. "And what *kind* is that, my lady?"

"The *kind* that would steal from the most holy of persons, put a knife to an innocent maiden's throat and—"

"Innocent? Maiden?" He laughed again, and this time Marion nearly gave in to her urge to kick him.

"You are despicable."

Instead of responding, Court smiled. A lazy, half smile that said he didn't believe her. And with that, he turned and walked away.

After a few moments, she realized he wasn't coming back. Using the time to see to her needs, Marion continued on toward the water, where she washed herself as best she could before returning to their makeshift camp. It consisted of nothing more than a small clearing and, after she pulled it down from his saddlebag, a bedroll.

Court returned shortly after she'd begun to gather sticks into a pile for a fire. He tossed his own logs on top and proceeded to gut the hare he'd caught. Marion made a sound of disgust and turned her back.

"You prefer just to eat it then. No interest in how your meal is prepared?"

She crossed her arms and remained silent. Staring off into the darkness, she listened to his movements behind her. Just as she'd done many times before, usually when someone teased her about her "abilities," Marion contemplated how to get out of the situation with her dignity intact. She'd only turned around because she could not tolerate the sight of blood, whether it be from a hare or a man. But now she refused to look at him because he expected her to. And because she'd not admit that flaw to him.

And she'd called *him* stubborn.

"Do you plan to starve, my lady?" he mocked.

Given a cue, Marion did turn then. And gasped.

Court leaned over a fire roasting their meal. He'd removed his surcoat and chain mail. Clad in only a long linen shirt, the neckline open, and woolen hose, he looked dangerous . . . and delicious. With such a wide chest and thick arms, the Englishman could no doubt crush a man's skull with his hands, and then carry a maiden to his tent.

"See something you like?"

#

Court certainly did.

He'd had no intention of making camp this early, but every time Marion shifted, her backside brushing against him, he became more and more uncomfortable.

"Aye," she said. "Dinner."

He really should leave it at that, but something about Marion made him want to misbehave.

Walking toward the fire, she placed her hands over the flames and rubbed them together. The warm summer days often, like this one, turned into much cooler nights.

"Mmm," he murmured, her murderous glare warning him away. At least, it would have warned off a more cautious man. Court ripped off a piece of meat and handed it to Marion as she lowered herself onto the makeshift seat he'd provided. He watched as she opened her mouth and brought it down on the roasted rabbit.

"Is it safe to have a fire?" she asked.

He concentrated on the flames rather than the redheaded beauty who was likely contemplating how to kill him in his sleep. "As safe as it can be in the borderlands."

Which meant it was not safe at all. But if they were discovered, it would not be the fire that gave them away. The little-used road would not hide their tracks, ensuring he would have a mostly sleepless night.

"So where is it?"

Court wasn't foolish enough to look down at his waist, the pocket he'd sewn into his hose to keep the stone safe. Instead, he continued to gaze into the fire. The sound of crickets was the only accompaniment to the crackling of the wood.

"Why did it call to me if I was not meant to take it?" he asked between bites, aware she would not answer him.

Marion licked her fingers. God . . . why had he looked at just that moment? "Tell me who you plan to attack and when, and I will tell you what I know of the stone."

Court pressed his lips together. He tore off another piece of meat and handed it to her. When their fingers touched, she pulled away as if she'd been burned.

A smart lass.

"I cannot give you details, but if you tell me why I was called to that place, I promise to tell you something."

When she peeked up at him, light from the fire dancing across her face, Court's sight fluttered and he had his first vision of his companion. No longer haughty, the earl's daughter was replaced with a passionate woman, lips parted and eyes hooded.

"What is it?"

He closed his eyes and waited for it to pass.

"Court?"

"A vision," he murmured, opening his eyes.

"You had a vision? Of what?"

If he dared to put to words what he'd just seen, his Scottish maiden would suffer quite a shock. Instead, he offered what he knew. Which was not much.

"I've had them my whole life," he admitted. "Sometimes years pass between them. But since the stone's pull began, I have them much more often."

"What do you envision?"

He shrugged. "I don't know. The person in front of me. But different. They seem to give me some sort of insight."

"What did you see when you looked at me?"

He didn't wish to lie to her, but he was even less eager to answer her question.

"The guard. The one with the priestess," he offered instead. "I saw him as a young boy, scared and alone."

Thankfully, she didn't continue to question him.

Placing a piece of meat daintily inside her mouth, she looked every bit the lady—her log a throne and the trees her lady's maids. He smiled as he watched her finish eating.

"These visions," she began, "are your special ability."

"My—"

"Special ability," she repeated. "Though I'm unsure exactly what it means. Mine is much simpler."

He shook his head, not understanding.

"Did no one ever explain your gift to you?"

"Gift?" He laughed. "Curse, you mean?"

She sighed. "Aye, that too."

"Nay," he said, standing. As he made his way to the saddlebag, he continued, "My mother died in childbirth. My father followed her not many years later. No one knew of my *gift*. Until now. If they had *gifts* of their own, I never knew it."

He pulled the leather waterskin from the bag and walked back to the fire.

"I fostered with Richard Caiser, Earl of—"

"Kenshire."

He wasn't surprised Marion knew of him. Though Richard had died more than two years earlier, passing the earldom to his daughter and her husband, all in the borderlands knew of the man. Some said he'd been more powerful, and certainly more beloved, than the King of England.

"Aye. He knighted me. Entrusted Camburg to me. And said nothing of my gift or ability or however you speak of it. Although I doubt he, or anyone I know, would believe such a thing."

The corners of Marion's mouth lifted in a small smile. Sympathy? Surely not. Well, he'd promised her information, and information he would give. Some.

"On a recent trip to London, Edmund of Almain ordered me to take . . ." He hesitated. "A keep." Moordon Castle had at one time merely been a keep. So this was not truly a lie.

"In Scotland?" she correctly guessed.

He nodded.

"Is this . . . Edmund of Almain one of the king's regents, then? Why would he order such a thing? Why now?"

Court had asked the man that very question. Though it was true these lands had become unstable recently, the border lines had been drawn more than thirty years earlier. The English and Scottish Wardens held monthly Days of Truce to ensure peace continued to reign between the two nations. And yet Edmund had told him it was an edict from the king himself—that Moordon would provide the foothold they needed in the event war broke out.

"He is one of Edward's regents," he answered. "While Edward continues his crusade abroad, he left his duties to two men. Any one regent would have gained too much personal power. But Edmund, along with—"

"Robert Burnell, the king's chancellor. I know some of your English politics."

He was impressed. "Aye. And as to your question of 'why now?' I do not ask, but simply follow my king's orders." For an order from the regent was the same as an order from the king himself.

That Edmund had promised him the very thing he'd always wanted, a title and land of his own, Court kept to himself. Halbury Castle was not nearly as grand as Camburg, but it would be his own.

Marion fell silent. He handed her the waterskin, and she took it. She drank deeply, her elegant neck stretched back, and then returned it to him. A lone drop of water had escaped onto her bare chest.

Don't look.

"Before meeting the priestess," Marion said finally, her tone serious, "I had no way of knowing what was true and what was legend. Growing up, the healer in my mother's village told tales of the Ladies of the Stone, women chosen throughout time to protect the stone, a symbol of Scotland herself. It was said that our lands would remain safe so long as the guardian kept the stone safe. From the priestess, I learned that if the stone fell into the hands of . . ." She looked at him with the same malice that had been directed at him earlier that day. ". . . *you* . . ."

His eyes narrowed.

". . . Scotland would be in danger. For each guardian, there is a nemesis—someone who is called to take the stone. To use it against Scotland. When the protector and her nemesis die, the stone finds its way back to the pools to be guarded by the priestess until it can be claimed once again."

"And you are that guardian?" Her tale was too fantastical to be believed. If it weren't for—

"I am."

She said it so confidently that Court froze. Her eyes held his own, never wavering.

"How could you possibly—"

"When I first told my mother of my ability to sense danger, she did not believe me, of course. It was only after many years of warnings that she and my father finally understood. And then, of course, there was the mark."

His skin tingled. "The mark?"

So it was true. Everything she told him, as much as it sounded like a jester's tale of fancy, was true.

"Do you have it?"

This time he looked down to where the strange mark had appeared just a fortnight ago. His clothes hid it from sight, but he could almost feel it burning his flesh.

"I have one as well," she said, pointing to her right hip.

Court groaned inwardly, imagining—

"Where is yours?"

He almost asked if she'd like to see it. But Court caught himself before he let the impropriety slip. Instead, he pointed to the exact same spot, but on his left hip. His mind reeled with revelations. The first thing he would do once back in Camburg was to seek out the advice of the elders. Surely there must be an English legend similar to her Scottish one. In her version, she was the protector, he the enemy. But perhaps his people had their own version of the tale.

"So you know now why you were called to the stone." She smiled sweetly. "Now you know why it is mine. I'd like it back."

4

Though Court never looked down, his hand moved toward his side protectively. By all the saints, how could she steal it back if he kept it there? Her first failed escape attempt had not gone well, but this time Marion had to get it right. Once at Camburg, the stone would be lost to her forever.

"I cannot give it to you."

She'd expected him to say as much.

"But don't you see—"

"I see only what you tell me, Marion. Your version of the legend."

A shiver ran down her arms. Her name had never sounded so . . .

"It will aid my cause," he blurted out. Court tossed the bones of his meal into the fire. He looked at her, as if awaiting confirmation. The revelation seemed to surprise him even as he said it.

She'd said too much. Belatedly, Marion realized if Court had not known of the stone's importance, he may have been more inclined to give it to her. "Think first, speak later," her tutor had often said.

So much for that lesson.

"If your cause is to start a war along the border," she said, preparing to stand, "then, aye. The stone may prove useful."

"Sit," he asked. Only the softness of his tone stayed her. "We are at an impasse, it seems. But can we not put aside our differences—"

"Differences?" She shook her head, astounded. "We are enemies, Court. You aim to hurt my people—"

"Who refuse the call for peace. The border has become unstable—you know it as well as I do. Those who remember how it was before the Days of Truce say it will only get worse. Blackmail, increasing raids—"

"On both sides," she spat back.

"It would be foolish not to prepare for the worst."

She disagreed. "Surely you don't ask me to condone an attack against my own country?"

"Surely you don't ask me to disobey orders from my king?"

Marion opened her mouth and then closed it again.

What would I do in his position?

They glared at one another, Marion wanting nothing more than to reach over, grab the stone, and get away from here.

Away from him.

Not true.

She pushed away the thought, stood, and marched over to the bedroll. A thin linen blanket and makeshift pillow made from grass and leaves were to be her only protection for the night. Trying to ignore the sound of her companion moving around camp, Marion closed her eyes and breathed deeply, taking in the smell of moss and . . .

Court?

He lay behind her, pushing her over and nearly off the bedroll. Without turning, she asked, "What are you doing?"

He shifted against her, pulling the blanket over his body. It was just large enough to cover them both, but . . . did he really think to sleep this way?

"Attempting to get some rest," his deep voice answered.

"Surely not like this?" She shoved him with her backside, attempting to regain some of the space she'd lost when he lay down.

"Surely not," he answered.

Marion turned from her side to her back in order to see him. With two hands propped behind his head—at least he'd given her the pillow

—he appeared quite comfortable. A man who would steal the stone, attack her country, and cause Marion to fail at her purpose in life . . . and she was drawn to him like a starving man would eye a banquet. A dangerous, virile, and attractive man. "This is not . . . proper."

He turned his head slowly, raising his eyebrows at her. "You are really concerned about propriety? After all that has happened today?"

"And they call *us* barbarians."

"Who does?"

Was he serious?

"You. The English."

Court turned onto his side, propping his head on his hand. "Have you met an Englishman before?"

"Of course." And that was the truth.

"And he dared to call you a barbarian?"

She thought about the question for a moment. "No, but—"

"I do not think that."

She tried to slow her rapidly beating heart by willing it so, but instead it did just the opposite.

"You don't?" she managed.

"No," he said, looking at her lips.

Was he going to kiss her?

"I think you are extraordinary."

It was so unexpected, Marion simply stared at him. What did she say to such a thing? That she felt the same way? That her traitorous body seemed to forget this man had stolen her destiny from her?

Foolish chit, he only thinks you're extraordinary in the way everyone else does. How could she have forgotten?

"Because of my gift," she said softly.

He didn't answer at first.

Finally, he asked, "You sense danger?"

"Of sorts." She pulled the blanket over her chest. It was getting colder with each passing moment. "I sense when someone means harm."

His jaw shifted, the slight tick a sign that he was annoyed, or perhaps anxious?

"What is it?" she asked. Court's eyes darkened. Something had upset him.

"And that is what you sense from me?" he finally asked.

She really should lie. The more information she gave him, the more power Court would have over her. "No."

They were so close that Marion could feel the rise and fall of the blanket as he breathed.

Too close.

Her answer seemed to startle him.

"Why?"

Marion wished she knew. "Mayhap it does not work on you?"

"But I saw a vision of you earlier. I saw—" He cut himself off. This time, there was no mistaking his expression. So he'd not been truthful. But he clearly didn't wish to voice the reason for his lie.

"You said your last vision was of the guard . . . Never mind," she said, then blurted. "'Tis not important. We really should—"

"I saw your eyes hooded and lips parted, as if you'd just been thoroughly kissed."

She accidentally looked at his lips then. They were so . . . full.

"I saw the passion in you, Marion."

Oh God . . . the priestess . . . anyone. Please help me.

"But you don't know why? Or what that means?"

He shrugged, and though it appeared a casual gesture, Marion could tell it bothered him, not to understand.

Court turned from her then, muttering something about sleep.

She did the same, turning so their backsides were touching. But she would not think of that. She'd not think of where and how they touched.

No, she would not think of it at all. Certainly she would not try to imagine what his buttocks would look like—

Stop!

Marion closed her eyes against the vision, but it stubbornly refused to go away.

#

Court could not tell if she slept or not. Even if he hadn't been intent on keeping watch, he never would have been able to sleep with her so close to him.

What had initially seemed a rational decision was proving to be anything but. He'd thought he understood pain. Certainly he'd suffered the day Richard Caiser sent him away from Kenshire. And the day he'd nearly lost his arm in a battle.

But lying beside this beautiful, willful woman with the knowledge that he could never so much as touch his lips to hers . . . he would take a few battle wounds instead.

Glad they'd not encountered anyone yet today, he also knew sleep would have to elude him this night. It was simply too dangerous, with potential adversaries all around, including the one lying so peacefully next to him.

Had he been asleep, he may not have noticed her hand ever so gently lifting his shirt. He'd like to believe he would have woken, though, when those dainty fingers so nimbly pulled on the pouch that contained the treasure she sought.

Did she really think to steal the stone while he slept? And then? Did she intend to take his horse and escape alone?

He really had never met such a bold, determined woman before. It was too bad she was attempting to steal that which he couldn't give her. Part of him wanted to see what she would do next, but he couldn't risk it.

He caught her hand, grabbed it, and brought it around his chest. Rolling toward her, Marion nearly lying atop him now, Court watched her expression turn from surprise to something else.

"Trying to seduce me?" he asked.

Her face was close enough to his that Court simply had to lift his head and their lips would be touching.

"Of course not." Her green eyes flashed, annoyance mixed with the same desire he felt for her.

"Maybe you should be."

Before he thought better of it, Court lifted his head and kissed her.

Or tried to at least. It became immediately apparent she'd not been kissed properly before, so instead of pursuing his suit, Court pulled away. He very much wanted to be the one to instruct her, but with her breasts pushed against his chest and her body so dangerously close to his hardened manhood, he knew it was not a sound idea.

Regretfully, he pulled his hand away and stood.

"Go to sleep," he said, too harshly.

"Court?"

He made his way back to the fire. He tossed a log onto it and sat.

"I will not apologize for trying to take what's mine."

He looked up just as Marion had reached the center of camp. She stood above him looking . . . well . . . damned beautiful. "As I will not apologize for stealing something I wanted."

"The stone—"

"I wasn't talking of the stone."

Why was she so taken aback? Surely she had noticed he desired her.

"I propose a truce."

She sat on her own log, thankfully too far away for him to touch her.

When he looked up, her expression was completely transformed. Another vision. This time, Marion appeared crestfallen. As suddenly as it came, the vision disappeared.

She watched him, waiting. "Another vision?" she guessed.

He swallowed. "Something happened recently," he said, not knowing if it were true, unable to detect if the vision was a part of Marion's past or future. "Something that made you feel extremely sad?" he guessed.

"Likely when I learned you'd stolen the stone from the priestess."

But he was already shaking his head. "Nay, before that."

She looked down. Toward her hip. Toward the mark.

"What is it, Marion? What happened?"

Marion shook her head.

He stood and walked toward her. He bent down, the desire to comfort her overwhelming.

"I didn't want it to be true." She spoke so quietly, it took Court a moment to realize what she said.

"The calling," he guessed. Though her head was still bent, he could see her eyes close briefly. A blessing . . . and a curse. The thing that made her special, or so she believed.

And he had claimed it.

Court lifted her chin, forcing her to look at him.

"The truce? If you'll have it still."

Even frowning, Marion was extraordinarily beautiful. He couldn't believe what he was about to say, and yet the words left his lips nonetheless. "You can have it."

God, he was a fool.

"The stone," he clarified. "It's yours—"

Marion wrapped her arms around him so quickly, the movement nearly toppled them both. As good as she felt so close to him, he pushed her away, not wanting her to misunderstand. "After the attack. I need it to carry out my orders. Then the stone is yours."

She sank back down as he continued.

"You can stay at Camburg until it is over. And then you may take it back to Scotland."

Scowling, as angry now as she had been happy a moment ago, she said, "Very well."

He propped his hands on his knees, still squatting in front of her. "Will you tell me what the vision was about?"

"It was that morning." She looked down at her concealed mark again. "The day it appeared."

"Your parents must have been—"

"Proud." She laughed—a hollow, empty sound that reminded him of the vision. "They were proud, and excited, and a bit nervous too."

"Then why—"

"I did nothing to deserve it."

When she looked into his eyes, Court saw himself. Hadn't he always questioned whether he deserved Richard Caiser's sponsorship? The opportunities that had landed in his lap?

"They were not proud of me. This gift . . . I can't control it. It's just like my ability to sense malintent . . ."

Though she stopped, Court could understand all too well. This was why he felt a burning need to prove himself, to show everyone, once and for all, he deserved the opportunities he'd been given.

He could have told her she was special for much more than her gifts, that he'd never met a woman like her. That he wanted nothing more than to press his lips to hers and lose himself trying to fulfill his earlier vision. Instead, he stood, reached out his hand, which she took, and guided her back to their bed in the forest.

Once they were lying down again, he lifted the blanket over them and said, "This time, do try to keep your hands off me."

He smiled when she chuckled, but his merriment was short-lived. As she moved into a comfortable position, Court prepared for a long, long night ahead.

5

She awoke nestled in Court's arms, a feeling so unusual that her first instinct was to scramble away. Her second was to move closer, which was exactly what she did until his pained moan from behind stopped her. The sound sent a rush of feeling through Marion. Of all the men her father had presented to her as possible husbands, none had ever made her skin tingle and her heart beat as quickly as this Englishman.

This Englishman who was now pulling himself away from her.

"Not yet," she heard herself saying. "I'm cold."

She was no such thing. The heat from his body fended off the crisp morning chill just fine. But when Court wrapped his thick arm around her shoulder once again, she sighed and moved closer to his warmth.

They had lain that way for what seemed like hours, though only a few moments had passed, when a familiar feeling came over her. But this was not the slight chill that had warned her of danger before. It was as if she'd stepped out into the coldest of winter days. So cold it hurt as she sucked in her breath.

"Marion?"

Court must have sensed it too, for one moment she was contemplating the wisdom of her hastily uttered command for him to stay, the next, she was lying on her back, Court peering over her, his eyes wide and brows wrinkled.

"Danger," she managed to say, watching Court jump to his feet, sword immediately in hand. The bitter cold lessened, though it did not go away completely. Marion rubbed her arms to warm herself, coming up behind Court.

"My dagger."

He spared her the briefest of glances before walking toward his horse and pulling the weapon from where it had been hidden among his belongings. Handing it to her silently, he looked in both directions, and when she nodded toward the north, Court motioned for her to move around him.

When she did, he untied his horse, his movements quick and silent, and pointed to the stirrup. Marion let him assist her in mounting, and as she silently grabbed the reins, still holding her dagger, he whispered to her, "Stay here. If you see anyone but me approach, ride away as fast as you can."

After pausing to be sure no sounds reached them, Marion whispered back, "I will not leave you."

"You can, and you will."

With that, he strode toward the ridge that hid them from view but also concealed whatever enemies neared them. Marion looked up to the sky, the sun finally having made an appearance, and waited.

I will not leave you.

It was as if her words had forgotten to reconcile themselves before escaping her mouth. She should have said, *I will not leave the stone.*

Court moved toward her so silently that she didn't notice his approach until he was nearly upon her. He mounted behind her and spurred the horse to a slow canter. She wanted to ask what he'd seen, but they sped up before she could speak. And as she had the day before, Marion silently admired his horsemanship. They navigated the terrain effortlessly, and only when he finally slowed again did she ask what had happened.

"A gang of reivers," he replied.

"How many?"

"At least ten."

She didn't ask if they were English or Scottish because it didn't matter. A reiver's allegiance was to clan and family first. Ten of them riding together could only mean one thing—a raid. Besides, had not she felt their intent?

He navigated off the main road and onto a path marked more by overgrowth than evidence of other travelers. "I'd hoped to be at Camburg by nightfall, but we'll be lucky not to have to make camp again now."

"Will my men be there before us?"

"More than likely, aye."

They rode at a more reasonable pace, Marion's backside beginning to ache from the brutal pace they'd set the day before.

"That could have been . . . interesting," Court said.

Marion had just been wondering what would have happened had her ability not given them advanced warning.

"You said you've had this—gift—for many years?"

"Aye, though never like that before. The cold . . ." She shivered thinking about it.

"Is it the stone, then?" he asked. "Does it make the sensations stronger?"

Marion thought back to what the priestess had told her—precious little, and nothing of her ability. "I'm not sure," she said. "There's much I still do not know. Just that when I'm close to you . . . to it . . . I feel at peace. After the mark appeared, I felt unsettled, as if something were missing."

"I felt the same."

A noise startled her, but when she saw the movement in a bush just ahead, Marion realized it was an animal of some kind.

"Are you scared?" His voice was like the blanket he'd pulled over her last eve. Comforting and warm. The voice of her enemy, but he felt less like one with each passing moment.

"Nay," she said honestly. Oddly, she had never felt truly scared of him, with the exception of the moment he'd held his sword to her throat. But even then . . . Marion should have been terrified—freezing —but she'd had no premonition of coming danger. Was it the stone that prevented her from sensing a threat from Court? Or could it be that he did not pose a threat at all?

Impossible.

So long as he held the stone and intended an attack on Scotland, he posed a very real danger, indeed.

"Where do you intend to attack?"

"You know I cannot tell you that."

"When?" she tried again.

"Marion . . ."

"Then why?"

"That you already know. I've been ordered—"

"To do so. But that does not answer my question."

As they rode through an open field, the marshland giving way to rockier and slightly steeper terrain, Marion decided she would learn everything she could about her English knight in order to convince him to relinquish the stone before his planned attack.

"Do you always follow orders?"

"Of course," he said, without hesitating.

"Even if it hurts others?"

He hesitated. "In war—"

"But we are not in war, Court. We are at peace. Our countries—"

"Peace," he spat. "What do you believe those men back there intended? To break their fast with us?"

"Reiving is a way of life along the border."

"And stealing cattle or sheep is one thing. Murdering innocents, quite another. Surely you know the borderlands become more dangerous with each passing day? Bribery abounds, mistrust threatens to rip apart the tenuous peace."

She turned to peek at him. "An attack will most certainly help matters, then."

Court's eyes narrowed and he slowed until they were at a complete stop.

"What do you want from me, Marion? You want me to call off the attack? Tell the king's regent I refuse to follow his orders on the request of a beautiful Scottish woman I met while on my way back from the pools? The very same place I was called to find after a mark appeared on my hip one morning, one that apparently signifies I am the nemesis of the protector of Scotland?"

She turned her body as much as was possible in the saddle they shared. Though his words mocked, Marion heard something behind them that gave her hope.

He did not want this attack any more than she did.

"Do you believe it is the right thing to do?"

He continued to glare at her.

"Would you do it if—"

"Nay." His hard tone was directed at himself, and not her. She would not let him intimidate her.

"And your overlord? Geoffrey and Sara of Kenshire, do they believe—"

"Nay," he said again. "Is that what you want to hear?"

"I just want the truth. Nothing more."

"The truth?"

Court's eyes darkened and dipped to gaze at her lips. When he looked back up, Marion's heart began to thud so loudly it was a wonder he couldn't hear it.

He dismounted and helped her do the same. Without looking at her, Court moved his horse off the road. He tied their mount and walked back toward her.

"The truth is that I want you, Marion. More than I've ever wanted any woman before. Though you'd sooner slit my throat than come willingly to me, it hardly seems to matter. I'm drawn to you as surely as I am to the stone."

I want him to kiss me.

"That is not true."

"I am not drawn to you?" He took a step closer. So close she could smell the mint he'd chewed earlier that morn.

"Nay, that I would sooner slit your throat than come willingly to you." A dangerous statement, but a true one nonetheless.

"Do not," he said, shaking his head. "Do not give me permission."

This time, it was she who took a step toward him. It made little sense, but Marion would have plenty of time to rue her actions later. For now, she'd speak from the heart.

THE PROTECTOR'S PROMISE

"I want you to kiss me," she said, proud of her bold proclamation.

For a moment, it appeared as if he would do it, but instead, Court looked away. She'd been a fool to say such a thing. Marion turned from her adversary and walked away.

#

Court watched her go from the corner of his eye. It was for the best. Nothing good would come of giving into that which could not be. There were too many reasons not to kiss her.

She was a noblewoman and therefore a virgin. The exact kind of woman he had done well to avoid all these years. Even if it were not for the fact that she claimed they were mortal enemies . . .

Dammit.

Court reached her in a few strides. He grabbed her arm, spun her around, and pulled her toward him in one swift motion. When she parted her lips just before he lowered his own, Court's body immediately responded, and he reminded himself to slow down.

His tongue showed her how to respond, and she did, opening her mouth almost immediately. Court took full advantage, his tongue capturing hers as his mouth slanted to the side for greater access. When her arms wrapped around him, Court pulled her closer.

She learned quickly, and soon the kiss spiraled deeper into a descent that would be hard to pull out of. He could not get enough of her. Court was desperate to tear off the travel-worn gown and touch every inch of skin beneath. In anticipation, his hands moved to her cheeks, wanting to come into contact with her smooth skin. He guided her, kissed her, and nearly lost himself to the sweetness that was Lady Marion of Ormonde.

Pulling away from her took every bit as much strength as lifting a broadsword for the very first time. Only his honor—and the horror of disrespecting her—gave him the ability to do so. Her lips, swollen from his kiss, were slightly parted. Her eyes, wide and bright, just as they'd been in his vision.

"My apologies," he said, taking a step back.

"But I asked you to do it. What are you sorry for?"

Indeed, what?

"That we had to stop."

Her look told him he hadn't needed to stop at all. The reivers had obviously taken the main road or they'd have caught up with them before now. Only his honor had forced them apart at this moment.

"You don't know what you ask for," he said, realizing the truth of his words. Marion's dazed expression told him as much. This was likely the first time she'd been thoroughly kissed. Experience told him where a kiss like that would lead, so it was his duty to stop it.

By God, he'd wanted anything but.

"We need to go," he said before he changed his mind. Her expression closed down at once, and she merely nodded.

It was only hours later, when they stopped for a brief respite, that either of them spoke again.

"You're hungry?" he asked, already knowing the answer. They'd eaten little, but if they continued to push on, he and Marion could still get to Camburg that night. They'd passed the only other keep between the border and Camburg Castle, an abandoned pele tower that was once fortified by Clan MacAdder, a clan no longer. This close to the border, only those with strong alliances and plenty of men behind them could survive.

"Aye," she said, walking back toward him from where she'd seen to her needs behind a thicket of bushes.

"If we stop now, I fear—"

"I can wait."

She raised her chin. But Court finally recognized the gesture for what it was—not haughtiness but pride.

"You are a remarkable woman," he said honestly, wondering if she knew it.

"My ability is—"

"Nay." He walked toward her. "I don't speak of your ability but of you. For someone who has been sheltered much of her life . . ." He shook his head, not trusting himself to finish.

"You are not bad either . . . for an Englishman."

He couldn't help but smile. "High praise from the Protector of the Stone."

Damn. Why had he reminded them both of their situation?

She didn't look angry. Instead, she crossed her arms in front of her. "So are you the Man of the Stone, then?"

He wished he knew.

"I am nothing. Just a simple knight following orders."

When she continued to watch him, Court's heart picked up its pace. It was as if she tried to look beyond his words. As if she could see *him*.

"Tell me something of Richard Caiser," she said as she walked back toward the horse and mounted for the last time. He raised himself up behind her, prepared for another torturous ride with Marion so close he could feel her, smell her . . . Without the mail and surcoat he'd left behind that morning escaping the reivers, precious little separated them, which would make this day an even more difficult one than the last.

"He was the most honorable man I'd ever known."

Court told her of how he came to squire for Richard Caiser. Of his childhood at Kenshire and of his desire to please the man who'd felt like another father.

"You speak little of the daughter."

With good reason.

"Sara and I were . . . are . . . quite close."

"What is she like?"

He conjured her in his mind, the girl who'd become a woman right before his eyes.

"She is like you in many ways," he said, realizing the truth of his words. "Strong-willed and resilient. She'd have been a great warrior if she had been born a man."

"You don't believe a woman could be a great warrior?"

Court imagined Sara in the boys' breeches she'd worn so often when they were growing up. In fact, the last time he'd visited Kenshire, the countess greeted him dressed that way.

"I don't doubt one could," he amended. "But few are trained for it."

Then he remembered the dagger he'd taken from Marion yesterday. The one she wore on her hip even now.

"You know how to use that," he said, patting her hip and wishing he had not.

"I do," she said. "Though a dagger is of little enough help when a great oak is holding a sword to your throat."

"A great oak?"

"Your arm," she said as the sun began to fade away. "I've never seen an arm so thick and . . ."

Unfortunately, she stopped. Court would very much like to know what she would have said next.

"I am sorry for that," he said finally. "I'm sorry for all of it. Marion, if I could give you the stone right now, I would. I do not want to cause you any further pain or distress."

She didn't answer, but her back, so stiff and straight yesterday, leaned casually against his chest. At least part of her trusted him, a boon he hardly deserved. He gently pulled her head toward his shoulder, and she accepted his invitation. Shifting a bit, she found a comfortable position and settled against him. Court resisted the impulse to lean down and kiss her head. Instead, he lifted his chin and stared ahead. Waiting and watching until it finally came into view ahead in the darkness.

Camburg Castle.

6

At first Marion didn't know where she was. Waking abruptly, she sat up in a large, canopied bed and looked at the light streaming through the one lonely arrow slit above her. She jumped from the bed and made her way toward the door. Nearly stumbling on something, Marion looked down and almost squealed with delight. How had her belongings come to be here?

A knock at the door had her running back to the bed. Lucky thing since the maid who entered the room was followed by four young male servants carrying . . . a tub! Pulling the coverlet over her, Marion watched as they carried it to the center of the room.

"My lord thought you'd be wanting a bath and a gown, my lady."

The maid, a girl of no more than ten and nine, held a gown high in the air.

"'Tis lovely," she said, curious who it belonged to. A former guest perhaps? She had been given the impression Camburg was a modest estate, but the sprawling square fortress was anything but. Everything was hazy after Court shook her awake on his mount, but the memories of last eve slowly came back to her. Her men had not yet been spotted.

"What is your name?" she asked the maid as she watched the servants carry buckets of deliciously hot water into the chamber.

"Elaine," the girl replied, nimbly preparing her gown. By the time the tub was filled and Elaine handed her a large piece of lavender soap, Marion forgot everything. Her quest for the stone, her longing for the man who should be her enemy. All of it fell away as she closed her eyes and reveled in the thought of clean skin. She had not had a true bath in more than a fortnight, and the pleasure of the prospect was akin to . . .

Nay! She'd not think of that kiss.

But of course she would. It had occupied her thoughts ever since. At first the passion and intensity had startled her, but her surprise had melted away. She'd not once thought to stop him, for her body ached for the very thing he offered. Though it was wrong for too many reasons to count, his lips had felt—

"My lady?"

She focused on the maid, who handed her a drying cloth.

Turning her attention to getting dressed, Marion rushed to dry her hair and get into the gown. The sooner she could get dressed, the sooner she could eat.

The only time Marion had been this hungry before was the night of the banquet her father had commissioned in her honor. Excited, she'd entered the hall at Ormonde only to realize he'd intended for the banquet to pressure her into choosing a suitor. When Marion saw all the young men seated in their hall, she'd decided not to eat that night, or the following day, out of protest. She'd been quite young, and foolish.

As she dressed, Marion learned that Elaine had joined her aunt and uncle at Camburg the year before, after both of her parents were killed in a raid. A familiar tale along the border, and one Marion was accustomed to hearing from her own people. But in their stories, it was the English who destroyed families and were to blame for their current troubles.

Belatedly, she realized Elaine did not seem bothered that she was Scottish. She would certainly not remind her of the fact now.

As soon as Marion was dressed, Elaine escorted her down a long corridor and down a winding stairwell. The great hall was bright and well decorated, filled with red and yellow striped banners and fine tapestries. Ten trestle tables were lined up, set for the morning meal. And as she entered the room, every single one of the men and women sitting at them turned to stare.

That was the reception she'd expected.

She paused and stared back, but she found her eyes drawn to the far end of the hall. How could she have missed him earlier?

Court stood and walked around the high table toward her. He looked nothing like he had the day before. The growth on his cheeks gone, his hair freshly washed. Clad in a fine surcoat of black and gold, Court looked every bit the lord.

By the time he reached her, all eyes were on them. Bowing, Court extended his hand. When she took it, the same feeling came over her as when she'd awoken in his arms the day before.

The mad notion that she never wanted him to let go.

"Well met, my lady." He guided her toward the high table.

"Good morn to you, my lord," she responded formally.

When they sat, it was just the two of them.

"Do you have no visiting nobles?" she asked. The high table at home was nearly always full. Her father had always been fond of entertaining despite the danger that lurked just outside their castle walls.

"Just one," he said, pushing his trencher toward her with a wink.

Eventually, the others went back to their meal, though Marion caught a couple of men and women glancing at her covertly, eyes narrowed, as if she were the enemy.

Which, of course, she was.

"Camburg's hall is . . ." She looked up at its wooden beams and around to the whitewashed walls. ". . . splendid." And she meant it.

"Richard adored this castle," he said. His tone was warm, as it always was when he spoke of his former mentor. "When he put me in charge of it, I was truly shocked. At the time, it was one of many properties he owned, but with the exception of Kenshire, I believe it was his favorite."

"At the time?" She picked up a piece of bread and ate without reserve.

167

"Sara has since given many of the Caisers' holdings back to the crown."

She was about to ask why when he continued.

"To appease Lord Lyonsford"—he looked sideways at her—"the man to whom she was betrothed."

"Betrothed?"

Court frowned. "When she fell in love with her husband, Geoffrey, she was betrothed to the Earl of Archbald."

Marion's hand froze halfway to her mouth. Something about how he said her name . . . her husband's name . . . "You are in love with her."

He did not appear pleased about her observation.

She was right!

"*Was* in love with her," he finally corrected. "I care for her, of course, but she is married now."

Marion thought back to what he'd said before. And while she filled her stomach, she pieced together that which he had not told her.

She had an idea of what may have happened. "Richard gave you Camburg to get you away from Kenshire. Away from his daughter."

Court's face twisted in a way that told her she was right.

"But why? You said he loved you like a son. That he—"

"He did." Court scowled at the cheese on their trencher as if it had gone bad.

"So why did he—"

"Richard had plans for her. Bigger plans than a young knight with nothing but an ancient title and no land to go with it."

The pain in her chest came without warning. And the strangest thing about it was that Marion could not tell if it was sympathy for a man who had been deemed an inferior match for the woman he loved, or the knowledge that he had loved that woman so deeply that it continued to affect him.

Either way, it did not concern her.

The stone. She had to remember her purpose here.

"I'm sorry," she murmured, finishing her meal.

They continued to sit in silence until the hall began to empty.

"I've been away," he said finally, "and need to meet with my men. As soon as yours arrive, I will send for you."

Her plan. She needed to get that stone before he attacked Scotland.

"And I may walk the grounds, speak to people here?"

He looked at her oddly. "You are not a prisoner here, Marion. You may leave at any time. When your men arrive—"

"Nay," she said, much too quickly. "We have an agreement."

"One I mean to honor."

He stood, and she did the same. "Elaine can show you—"

"I will find my way," she assured him.

"Very well," he said with a slight bow. "Until we meet again."

He walked so quickly from the hall, Marion wondered if perhaps she'd offended him. The thought pained her, but in the end, it hardly mattered. She needed to learn all she could about her Englishman. And either convince him to forgo the attack or get him to let his guard down enough for her to take what was hers.

She meant to have the stone. She meant to do her duty as its guardian.

\#

While he should have been preparing for one of the most important battles of his life, Court found himself pacing the ramparts of the castle Richard had entrusted to him so many years ago. Even a brutal training session could not get visions of him and Marion together out of his mind.

So many strange things had happened to him over the last few weeks, from the appearance of the mark to the pull of the stone. But none had taken him more by surprise than his feelings for Marion.

It was more than desire. He'd known that from the moment she walked into the great hall that morning. The sight of her had nearly poleaxed him in the gut.

Forget Marion. Victory is within reach.

Almain had promised him Halbury Castle just to the east of Camburg. Moreover, he'd hinted that he would arrange an advantageous match for Court once he completed this mission.

Forcing his mind back to the upcoming battle, Court envisioned Moordon Castle, an ancient keep once held by the English. The castle had fallen into disrepair after a raid more than ten years ago, which had forced the English owners back south. He knew not who currently held it—it could be any number of Scottish nobles and clan chiefs, from MacAdder to Douglas as the new owners. It hardly mattered. His scouts had confirmed the king's regent's assessment of the situation. Moordon existed on a skeleton staff, and its strategic location was ideal for the raids that may be necessary if—or when—war broke out once again along the borders.

And yet . . . he found himself thinking of what Marion had said. Sara and Geoffrey certainly wouldn't approve of his actions. And such a measure was as likely to cause a war as to stave one off. And while once appealing, the thought of a titled bride no longer appealed.

Do not be foolish.

Defying the king's regent, losing a potential stronghold . . . he simply could not do it.

The sun had set long ago, but Court could not bring himself to attend the evening meal. He should not force Marion to eat among strangers, but seeing her again in that shape-hugging gown, the epitome of nobility and grace . . .

Skipping the meal was the right thing, for both their sakes.

Court descended the stone stairwell and strode through the square courtyard lit only by torches along each outside wall. He navigated the large well in the center of it all and made his way into the main keep.

Damn. The hall was still filled with retainers and servants alike. Avoiding the entranceway, he made his way along a long corridor and nodded to the guard at the top of a winding stairwell that led to the lord's chambers. Was he a coward for avoiding her? Aye, but a coward who knew his own weaknesses, and Marion was one of them.

He pushed open the door of the chamber and was about to pull it closed behind him when a voice stopped him.

"Court?"

Oh God, no. Not here.

He turned, reluctantly, and instantly regretted it. The desire to reach for her—to touch her—was almost impossible to ignore. He wanted to smooth out the line of worry between her brows, make her smile. Or better yet, flush with pleasure.

Marion looked confused. He didn't blame her.

"My lady," he said, trying not to look at the expanse of creamy skin her gown revealed.

"I thought to speak with you at dinner. I'm worried for my men."

He was as well. They should have arrived before them, which was why Court had sent three of his own men north to see what they could discover. Oddly, he did not want her to know that. The thought of her knowing that he cared should not bother him. But it did.

"I'm sure they are well," he said. "And will be along anytime."

Her frown indicated she did not agree, but Marion inclined her head in parting and began to walk away.

Lord watch over him, he was about to make a bad decision. A very, very bad decision.

He reached out and pulled her back to him and inside the chamber. With one hand, he closed the heavy oak door, and with the other, he reached up to pull her face toward his own. Capturing her lips, Court branded her with a searing kiss.

She kissed him back with such wild abandon Court was left breathless when he pulled away to look at her.

"This cannot end well," he said, warning himself as much as her.

"I agree," she said, her arms wrapped around her shoulders.

"I will not stop the attack," he said softly, knowing the words might push her away. Half of him wanted them to; the other half wanted this moment to last forever.

"I am a virgin," she said, "and must remain such for my husband."

It was as if she'd doused him with water from the River Esk, frigid even now during the summer. "Husband?"

Was she betrothed, then? To whom?

"The man I will marry," she said, looking at him as if he'd gone daft.

Court backed away as if burned. "Who?"

She stared at him blankly.

"When?"

Understanding finally dawned, and Marion lifted her chin, a sure sign he was about to receive a tongue-lashing.

"I am betrothed to no one," she said. "I just meant . . . it is one of the many, many reasons I should not be alone with you in your bedchamber now."

She is not betrothed.

And what in God's bones was wrong with him? Would it have made a difference if she were?

Aye. It would have mattered. When he touched Marion . . . even when he simply looked at her . . . one thought ran through his head: *mine*.

He took a step back toward her and captured her neck from behind. "We have established that this is foolish and wrong. But by God, Marion, I've never wanted anything in my life more than I want to kiss you again. To tear off that gown of yours and cherish what lies beneath it."

To make you mine in truth.

When he brought her head toward him this time, the kiss was gentler. While their tongues tousled, Court finally allowed himself to explore the maddening desire that she'd awakened in him.

Dipping his hand beneath the fabric of her neckline, he reached lower until his hand was able to cup the round, beautiful breast below. Taking it firmly in his grasp, Court teased her nipple with his thumb as he continued to show Marion with his mouth how deeply he needed her. When she moaned beneath him, a kitten-like purr that instantly hardened his cock, he released her breast and prepared to replace his hand with his mouth.

Trailing kisses from her mouth downward, he shoved the fabric on her shoulder aside and continued his exploration. He didn't dare open his eyes. The sight of her breast beneath his mouth might crack his already-thin resolve to leave his Scottish noblewoman a virgin this night. But by the time his mouth finally reached her hardened nipple, Court was not sure how long that resolve would last anyway.

Marion grasped his hair at the back of his head and pulled him closer. He met her demands, nipping and squeezing, showing her exactly how much pleasure she could expect from him that night.

When Court finally backed up and gazed into her wide, clear green eyes, he felt an unmistakable tug on his heart.

"We cannot continue," he said.

Marion licked her lips. If she did that again, there would be no turning back.

"I've never felt like this," she said, her honesty so endearing that Court couldn't decide if he wanted to ravish her or protect her for all eternity.

"There's something between us, Marion. If it were not for the stone, for your position—"

"My position?"

He stepped back and ran his hands through his hair.

"You are an earl's daughter. And I—"

"You believe *that* is the biggest problem between us?" The moment was gone. Thankfully. Marion righted her gown and crossed her arms. His feisty Scottish lass had returned.

"That . . . and the stone."

"Nay." She shook her head. "Not the stone. Your stubborn refusal to see what is in front of you. The 'peace' you talk of so fondly is about to be ripped to pieces by the very person who claims to cherish it."

"I have no choice," he ground out, tired of this argument. Tired of fighting with her. With himself.

"You always have a choice."

With that, she pushed against him, ripped open the door, and left.

A good thing, because Court had nearly made the biggest mistake of his life.

7

He had nearly taken her virginity.

Four days later, Court climbed the stairs that led to Camburg's round hall. Named by the lord who'd once ruled here, a man with no heirs who'd allowed the castle to revert back to the crown, the round hall was nothing more than a circular chamber atop the east tower. The four windows gave him the best—and most well-lit—view in the castle. Staring out of one shuttered window, Court could see as far away as the small village they'd skirted on their way back from Scotland. Beyond that and slightly to the north, he could see the land that would become his once Moordon was captured.

He would continue to hold Camburg for Kenshire, but he could finally begin a life of his own rather than one loaned to him. One that did not include a blasted stone and a redheaded woman who tormented his thoughts every moment—waking and sleeping. Or her prickly guards who had arrived two days earlier, along with the men he'd sent to find them.

Court pushed his surcoat aside and reached down into the pouch he carried at all times. Pulling on the gold chain, he lifted the emerald stone and laid it out on his hand. This simple stone was responsible for all that had transpired since he awoke with the mark. Without it, he never would have met Marion.

Turning it over in his hand, Court felt nothing out of the ordinary. And after speaking to the elders of Camburg over the past few days, he was no closer to learning more about his own role in Marion's legend.

Sounds filtered to him. Court tightened his grip, hiding the stone from view as the door creaked open.

"Marion."

The sight of her took his breath away, affecting him as potently as if he'd not avoided her for days. The green overtunic above her cream-colored kirtle matched her eyes.

"'Tis a wonder you remember my name." She closed the door behind her, looking around the room. Using the candle she'd brought with her, she proceeded to light each of the three wall torches.

"I hadn't noticed the dark before. 'Tis usually quite light in here."

She placed the candle on the small table beside them.

The nearness of her was almost unbearable. *This* was why he'd been taking meals in his solar. Why he'd been meeting and training, leaving Marion to explore. Why he'd been unable to sleep. Unable to think straight. Unable to do much of anything except wonder what it would be like to give in to temptation. To toss Marion onto his bed and spend an entire night pleasuring her.

"You've been avoiding me."

There was no use denying it.

"We need to talk, Court."

For one wild moment, he envisioned himself laying waste to the contents of the table before them, clearing it to make way for Marion's luscious body.

"Court?"

He had to get out of here.

"I can't—" He tried to move past her, but this time it was she who stopped him.

"Please."

Her hand branded him, the linen shirt not enough of a barrier against the heat of her touch.

"I need to know how long we'll be here," she pressed. "How long until—"

"One more week." He could no longer deny her. Not when she stood so close, not when she was touching him. He turned as her hand fell. "One more week and I will be gone. Afterward, the stone is—"

"Gone where?"

"Marion, please." It was his turn to beg.

"I know about Halbury Castle."

Light flickered across her skin, illuminating her faint freckles as well as her eyes, which reflected every bit of the judgment he deserved.

"And?" he said, his voice harsh.

"That is why you are intent on this mission. Not because you are 'following orders.'"

If she had approached him with caution, it was gone now.

"Not because Almain is the king's regent."

Kissing her was not the only way to stop her from saying it aloud, but it was one way. And so he kissed her with every bit of the pent-up desire he'd felt over the past few days. His body was immediately engulfed in a raging battle, one he was not certain he'd win.

One he didn't want to win.

#

When his lips touched hers, Marion cursed herself for a fool. She'd intended to confront him about his planned attack, not to end up in his arms again. But the passion they shared for each other had changed her, and she found it difficult to go back to playing the earl's innocent daughter. She was not the woman who'd set out on a quest to become the next protector of Scotland. She was a woman who understood desire, who could recognize the fluttering deep within her body for what it was. One who, despite her best intentions, would not stop this dangerous course.

With every flick of their dueling tongues, Marion was pulled deeper and deeper into an irreversible decision. One that would infuriate her parents, change her future, and bind her to the man she'd sworn to overcome. Despite the implications of lying with a man that was not to be her husband, Marion could not seem to pull herself away.

When his mouth moved from her lips to her neck, Marion tossed her head back to give him greater access. Since her arms could not fully encircle his broad chest and shoulders, she did the best she could, gripping his tunic and clinging to him lest her legs give out under her.

"So sweet," he murmured against her neck.

She'd come here to confront him about the attack.

Not for this.

At least, that was the story she told herself. But the way her body responded, the things he made her feel . . . some of her, maybe all of her, had hoped their last kiss would lead to more.

When he abruptly pulled away, the loss was immediate. One moment, his hands and lips were on her . . . the next, he crossed the room toward the door.

He locked it.

Her heart skipped a beat.

Turning, Court stood by the door and simply watched her. She took in his tunic, opened wide at the collar allowing for a peek beneath. His expression was predatory and male, one that sent a shiver down her spine.

She thought he would say something then, but instead he moved to the table at the center of the room, swept its contents off with one swipe of his arm. A ledger went flying to the ground, and before Marion could see its final destination, Court was in front of her. He picked her up easily and carried her to the edge of the table. When he positioned her in front of him, she could feel the most intimate part of him pressed against her stomach.

He lowered his head once more, both hands gripping the back of her head, as if she needed encouragement. Every thrust of his tongue, movement of his hips, made her want more. She returned his kiss greedily.

"Something . . . ," she tried to say. But how could she describe this new pressure in her core? This tingling deep within her that longed to be set free?

He tore his lips from hers and looked into her eyes. Ever so slowly, his hand moved back down until it reached the hem of her kirtle. Lifting both it and the undertunic up at once, Court closed his eyes. A primitive sound escaped him as soon as his hand found her bare flesh.

Still looking into her eyes, he pushed aside each barrier until he reached the part of her no one else had ever touched.

Marion should have been embarrassed enough to break eye contact, to turn away. She held his gaze instead, mesmerized by the dance of his fingers on her skin.

"What are you doing?"

Court's only answer was a slow, sensual smile that made her insides pulse. His smile deepened as he slid his fingers inside her. With his free hand, he opened her leg as he pressed and withdrew, circling and flicking his fingers.

Marion was lost.

Gripping each side of the wooden table, she resisted the urge to close her eyes, wanting to see his face, wanting to watch his expression as it changed from pleasure to . . . something else. No longer smiling, Court looked at her with an intensity she recognized. This was what he'd looked like the day she'd warned him about the reivers. Determined, resolved. But this time, the only threat was that she'd lose her heart to the enemy.

"I've imagined doing this every night since waking with you pressed against me."

Marion tried to breathe.

Court lifted his chin, his hand pumping faster now. "And this is just a taste."

The intensity of his gaze, the intimacy of his fingers inside her, she wanted to hold on to this moment forever. But Marion simply couldn't. She did close her eyes then, pushing her hips toward the delicious sensations that were building and building . . .

"Come for me, sweet Marion."

A pulsing sensation at her very core gripped her like a violent wave, turning her around and around so that she couldn't tell up from down. Squeezing the table, trying to catch her breath, Marion finally found her way. Now the sensations were like an ebb and flow, still pleasurable but not threatening to drown her.

When she opened her eyes, Court seemed quite pleased with himself. He licked his lips, leaving a trail of wetness behind.

"Don't do that," she said, unable to look away from his wicked lips.

When he raised an eyebrow rakishly, Marion knew she'd said the wrong thing. This time, his movement was deliberate. His tongue not only darted out, but it captured the lip below. She simply could not look away.

"You shouldn't have told me you liked it."

She reached up to one of his biceps and squeezed, giving in to another one of her curiosities. He was as hard as the table she sat on.

"Who said I liked it?" she teased, not wanting their easy banter to end.

"You did ask me to stop."

"And I also asked you not to attack my people," she said, aware her words would ruin the moment, but unable to stop herself. "But you did not reconsider."

"A discussion for another day."

"Another day? When the attack is imminent?"

He looked as if he'd argue with her. Instead, he took a step back and held out his hand to assist her off the table. "Tomorrow?"

He stood so close that Marion could feel the heat of his body.

"You'll not disappear on me again?"

Court lifted his hand and laid it on her cheek. For a man so large, his touch was surprisingly gentle. "I don't make promises that I do not intend to keep."

You've made none to me.

But it was better than nothing. "Aye," she agreed. "I look forward to it."

Unfortunately for her, she looked forward to more than just their discussion.

8

"All is ready, my lord."

Court's captain and most trusted advisor, who had been with him since he left Kenshire, bowed as he began to leave. "Shall I send in the Scot?"

Court nodded. The leader of Marion's small band of men, Kenneth, had requested an early audience with him. He entered the solar and did not waste time on a greeting.

"How much longer must we stay here?"

"I don't believe, sir, that is any of your concern."

"I have been charged with—"

Court stood and took a step forward. "With following your lady's orders. And she told you, quite clearly, you are to remain at Camburg for a fortnight, at least. And await further orders."

Kenneth scowled. "I cannot stand by with my lady a prisoner—"

"Prisoner? Is that what she told you?" He knew she'd said nothing of the sort to her man. It was obvious he simply did not trust her judgment, which for some reason infuriated him.

"Not precisely, but—"

"But you think to take control of a woman you serve, one who clearly has the intelligence to carry out her duties."

The look Kenneth gave him was so full of contempt he had no doubt the man would have attacked him had it furthered his cause.

"I suggest," Court said when Kenneth turned to leave, "you speak to Lady Marion if you have further concerns."

He left and Court sank back into his seat. Before parting from Marion last eve, he'd promised to find her before his training session. It was time to do just that, but she wasn't going to like what he had to say.

Delaying, Court thought about the evening before. The raging need to be inside her, claim her, the uncontrollable urge to be the first to show Marion what could come of the passion that he'd awoken in her. It couldn't be, no matter how much he wanted it. The attack, the stone . . . if only their circumstances had been different.

It was for the best that the attack would be over soon. If all went well, he'd be gone less than one week. And then he could give her the stone and return to his normal world. One of his own choosing. Though not, unfortunately, one which included Marion.

He rose and after a brief search found her in the great hall . . . playing chess?

"Your move, my lady."

A young knight named Marcus sat across from her. And though the hour was still early, the men's training not yet begun for the day, Court nearly ordered the knight out of the hall. Marcus looked at Marion the way any man would regard such a beautiful woman. Unbidden, a vision of Marion in the round tower, her head back, hair streaming all around her, assaulted him.

"You wished to speak to me?"

Both she and Marcus startled at his tone. Sensing his displeasure, the knight scrambled to his feet and left them alone. Or as alone as they could be in a crowded great hall.

"Only if you can manage a civil conversation, my lord?"

He was tempted to say that he could not.

"Come."

Without waiting for her, angry at himself for his reaction to a simple game of chess, Court led her out of the hall and down a secret

CECELIA MECCA

passageway. Descending a few stone stairs, he opened a door, which led to—

"A garden!"

None used this path but he. Shielded from the rest of the herb and flower garden, this patch of greenery and the small courtyard surrounding it was a rare private space. One he wanted to share with Marion.

"'Tis lovely," she said, her hands gliding across the coralbells as she walked.

It is you who are lovely.

"Why are you so cross with me this morn?"

Not prepared for the question, Court scowled in answer. "I am not—"

"Aye," she cut in. "You are."

She wore the same riding gown, now laundered, as when they'd first met. Her hair, no longer flowing freely, was clasped back on both sides, a simple twist holding the remainder in place.

He couldn't very well tell her the truth about his ill-considered jealousy. Instead, he broached another equally delicate topic.

"I know you hope that I may reconsider the attack—"

"But you will not," she finished for him.

"My orders—"

"What would happen if you did not follow these orders?"

She asked too much of him.

"I would suffer. Kenshire would suffer. You yourself could not answer what you might do in the same circumstance. Not to mention Almain could . . ." He stopped. What would the regent do exactly?

"But you would suffer most of all. Without your precious Halbury, you would not have your land and title." Her chest rose and fell with indignation.

"You think that's all I care about?"

"Am I wrong?"

Court shook his head. "You'd never understand."

"Try me."

He knew she'd do anything, say anything to stop this attack, and yet he found himself opening himself to her nonetheless. "I loved her," he said. *Stop, Court. Don't make a fool of yourself.*

But if he didn't, she would push and push, and either he'd succumb or he would be forced to ignore her until she had the stone. But he'd tried that, and it didn't work.

Marion was not a woman to be ignored.

"Lady Sara," he said, the words like acid in his mouth. "But I was not enough. Richard loved me, cared for me, but he never intended me for his daughter."

"But you are a knight, a lord—"

"A title given to me by Richard."

"Surely he—"

"Knew what I did not yet understand. I was foolish, but after this raid—"

"You will be the very same man I stand before now."

"No," he said. "You're wrong. I will be the man who was generously rewarded for obeying the king's regent. Land, title, an advantageous marriage."

She pursed her lips. "So that is why you've waited, even though Lady Sara has long since married."

"Waited?"

"I wondered why someone like you was not already wed."

"Someone like me?" The edge was gone from his voice, and he sounded weak, plaintive. He should have never opened his mouth.

"Someone strong and protective. A champion for the weak, one who is disciplined, if not a bit arrogant, and who clearly knows how to please a woman."

She took a step closer to him.

"You please me well, Sir William, Lord of Camburg."

An instant jolt of lust was followed by an ache in his chest that felt as if it would tear him apart. He had not asked for those words.

"Don't, Marion."

She took yet another step toward him.

"Why?" she asked.

The answer was too painful. He longed to be with her, but he could not go through it all again. Even without having to answer to Almain . .

. even if she wanted them to be together, her father certainly would not. It was easier for him to turn the conversation back to her.

"What of you? As the daughter of an earl, you must have had enough marriage proposals to be wedded and bedded thrice over by now."

"Wedded, nay. Bedded . . ." She shrugged her shoulders.

She deliberately goaded him.

Court reached for her and pulled her toward him. "You have not—"

"And what if I had?"

The thought of Marion lying with another man . . . "No."

Her scowl was fierce and instantaneous. "You've no claim on me to say such a thing."

"And yet I'll say it just the same."

When he brought his lips down on hers, neither of them softened the impact. The kiss was rough and uncompromising. Court reached for her back, her hips, and brought her even closer, showing her the evidence of his words.

"I want that claim," he said, gasping as he pulled away.

She didn't even hesitate.

"Then it is yours."

#

After an eternity, Marion finally gathered enough strength to pull away. She could not think with Court's lips on her own. This was the second time she'd come to speak to him of the attack—and ended up in his arms instead.

Trust the stone.

Court was not the enemy. He could be if she didn't stop him, but the same stone that had given Marion her ability had been guiding her all along. They were not enemies. Court meant no ill toward her, or even to her country. Not truly. If he had, she would have sensed it. He only thought to follow orders—in part because he wanted that which he already had. He simply hadn't realized it yet. He may have been given Camburg, but even that had been earned. Court was already a man to be admired. There was nothing left to prove.

Court still held her shoulders. "You don't know what you're saying."

He looked terrified. Understandably so.

His expression softened. "Marion, I—"

A brief knock landed on the door, and it then swung open.

"My lord. A visitor has been spotted approaching the gates."

Marion looked at Court as the many possibilities ran through her mind.

"Who?" Court demanded, his eyes locked with hers.

"The king's regent," the guard said with more than a tinge of fear in his voice.

"Edmund of Almain."

The man nodded his acknowledgement and then turned to leave. "Aye, my lord."

The implications of her failure to convince Court to abandon the attack finally began to penetrate.

And now it was too late.

9

What was Almain doing here? This was not part of the plan. Court's mind raced as they walked toward the hall together.

Then it is yours. The only thing more surprising than Marion's declaration was his own. He *did* want that claim.

"We don't have much time," he said, pulling Marion into an alcove just before the hall's entrance. "There are only two ways a man can claim a woman. And neither of those are acceptable for us. I spoke rashly—"

Marion reached out and took his hands. The familiar gesture nearly tore Court in half.

"As did I," she said. "But how can we deny there is . . . something . . . between us?"

"Mayhap that something is the stone," he said. "A connection forged because of it." It was a thought that had entered his mind on the sleepless nights he'd spent away from her.

When he looked down to where it lay, her gaze followed.

"May I?" she asked.

He could not deny her. He disengaged one hand and took the stone

THE PROTECTOR'S PROMISE

from its pouch, pulling the gold chain upward so that the emerald green shone and spun. He handed it to her. While passing it, a strange jolt coursed through his body. Judging from her expression, she had felt it too.

"It belongs with me," she said.

You belong with me.

With the chain still wrapped around her delicate fingers, Marion reached for his hand once again. When they joined hands this time, the chain between them, Court saw a glimpse of the two of them in this same pose. They wore different clothes, however, and Marion's expression was one of contentment, not concern. The vision left him as quickly as it had come.

"You've had another vision," she guessed correctly.

"Aye," he said, unable to bring himself to describe it to her. He could not allow himself to hope. How could they have a future together when Edmund's decree stood between them?

If he attacked Moordon, he would lose her. If he didn't, he would lose everything he'd worked to achieve. And perhaps his head along with it.

Court leaned toward her, and when her eyes closed, he was nearly felled by the trust she put in him. He didn't deserve it. But he kissed her anyway. When her mouth opened for him and her tongue hesitantly explored his mouth, he pressed himself against her. Wanting to be closer, to feel all of her. The need to be inside this woman was so strong that Court vowed it would happen. She would be his, one way or another.

He broke the kiss and stood back, taking the stone with him. "Come," he said.

"What will you do?"

An agreement had passed between them, one he had initiated. But how that agreement reconciled with his mission, Court could not begin to contemplate.

"We must go," he said, turning. He had no answers yet.

"We?"

Marion followed him into the great hall, where his guest was due to arrive at any moment. Perhaps Edmund could be convinced of another

CECELIA MECCA

way, but he didn't dare voice such a hope to Marion. For if it didn't work . . .

"Stay with them." Court gestured to the men who stood on both sides of the entrance.

Marion, who was clearly no less confused than he was by his inclusion of her, stood to the side. He walked toward the high table and took a seat in his usual place, opposite the chair that had been positioned in front of it. Court nearly laughed at Marion's attempt to mesh with the others. She might as well be dancing in the middle of the hall. She was like a lone white cloud in a sea of blue, evident from every direction to all who chanced to look. Beautiful and untouchable but certainly noticeable.

They didn't have to wait long. Court heard Almain's retainers before he could see them. As they streamed into his hall, he counted no less than thirty men.

When Almain entered, Court stood and waited as the short, beady-eyed earl made his approach. Bowing as the man came closer, he silently rued that he should have to be subservient to a man who had never served in battle, never once bloodied his own hands.

"Well met, my lord," he said, straightening.

Rather than respond, Almain looked around the hall with an assessing gaze.

"You do well by Camburg," he said.

"To honor the memory of Richard, I would do anything," Court said. And meant it.

"The girl and her husband are lucky to have you."

Lady Sara was no girl, and he was the lucky one to have their support. But Court remained silent. Almain was both older and, if the rumors were true, crueler than the new king. He was not a man to be trifled with.

"You must be tired from your journey," he said, still unsure why that journey had been made. "Would you like—"

"What I would like," Almain said, "is to know when Moordon Castle will be ours."

#

Nay, it could not be!

Moordon Castle? It had no men to speak of—certainly not enough to pose a threat to Camburg, or England—and it would have long since fallen into disrepair if it weren't for her father.

Did Court know it was theirs? Is that why he'd refused to reveal the location to her?

When Court's guest had walked into the hall, a chill had coursed through her at once, so powerful it had nearly brought her to the ground. Certainly her ability had grown stronger since the mark had appeared and she'd first come into contact with the stone. But this was . . . indescribable. When the English earl had walked by her, she'd struggled even to stand. Marion had no doubt this man intended to do harm. To her? To her country?

And then the man had mentioned Moordon, and thankfully, she began to feel herself once more. Because she would have to act, and quickly. Her own cousin had been sent to Moordon when the king granted it to her father asking for him only to restore the ancient holding to its former glory. But why the regent would want—

Its position.

Moordon was not valuable, but its position at the threshold of strategic holdings was very much so. Did this mean Edward would break the thirty-year truce? Did he intend to wage open war with Scotland once again?

"Your Grace, I believe we should discuss—"

"Discuss?" Almain spat out, his contempt for Court's words apparent.

Marion's hands began to shake as she watched the proceedings. How could she have so completely misjudged him? She'd nearly given herself to a man who would attack her own people . . . What had she been thinking?

You were not.

She'd allowed the man who'd stolen the stone to edge his way into her heart. In doing so, she'd failed to fulfill her destiny. Marion had failed miserably at the one thing she was supposed to do well.

"Well," Almain pressed. "When do you attack? I've brought some of my own men to ensure victory. You still want Halbury, do you not? And an heiress to go with it?"

Court's eyes met hers.

"Of course, Your Grace."

The traitorous English bastard. The son of Satan. How could she have trusted him? Listened to him?

Fallen in love with him?

He could keep the damned stone. Marion had to warn her people.

She fled the room, running as quickly as her feet would carry her, out of the hall and into the courtyard. How could she have been so utterly foolish? She should have . . . what? Stolen the stone? Court was too intelligent to have allowed that to happen. Seduced him first and then stolen it? Injured him and taken it by force?

She chided herself even as the thought crossed her mind. But certainly the worst thing she could have done was wait around for him, trusting him and believing, even for a moment, that he'd begun to care more for her than his own ambitions.

Fool. You are a fool.

"Pardon," she said to one of the gatehouse guards. Trying to keep her voice calm, she inquired after her men.

"They are just above," a young knight, mayhap even a squire, said. He disappeared and emerged a short time later.

"What's wrong?" Kenneth said.

They didn't have much time. Moordon needed to be warned.

"We must leave," she said. "Now."

Without waiting for an answer, Marion rushed across the courtyard to the stables. She would find out soon if Court had been lying about her status here. Guest or captive?

"My men and I are leaving," she said to the stable master just inside the entrance.

Kenneth caught up to her as their horses were being readied.

"What is happening?" he demanded in his typical condescending tone.

She was having none of it. She would treat the man who protected her with his life with the respect he deserved if he could give her that same courtesy. If he could not, she didn't need him.

"Kenneth," she said, "that is quite enough. I will remind you that I am the daughter of Archibald Rosehaugh, 3rd Earl of Ormonde, and the Protector of the Stone of Scotland. You will either speak to me with the same respect you give my father, or any other man of status for that matter, or you may remain here, relieved of your duties to me and my family."

The other men arrived during her speech. The stable master and one of his hands gawked at them openly, and Marion couldn't blame them. By the time she finished, her voice likely carried back into the hall, where Court and the king's regent plotted her people's demise.

"Aye, my lady," he said. They stared at each other a moment longer, a new understanding dawning between them.

"Circumstances have changed, and we need to leave. Now."

Kenneth's eyes widened and he opened his mouth but promptly closed it. Instead, he gave her a quick nod and turned to the others.

"You heard the lady. Let's go."

Marion would have smiled had the situation not been so dire. In a flurry of activity, she and the men prepared to leave Camburg.

I may have failed to retrieve the stone, but I will not fail Moordon.

As she rode away from the stable and through the courtyard, Marion wondered why Court had allowed her to leave. Though she looked over her shoulder, once, twice, as they rode through the gatehouse and beyond, there was no sign of pursuit. Nothing.

And just like that, the stone, and the man to whom she'd inadvertently given her heart, were gone forever. She ignored the pull that tried to lure her back. The stone would not protect Moordon now.

She would.

10

Court watched as his unwanted guest was led from the hall.

He had to find Marion to explain. When she'd dashed out of the hall, Court had very nearly run after her. But he'd reminded himself of her words, her pledge, and trusted she would understand. Whatever happened next, they would be in it together.

He should have questioned Almain's motives earlier. But he'd been too stubborn, too blinded by his own ambition to see what was before his eyes. The stone had revealed the truth to him—everything had become clear as he spoke to the king's regent.

A vision had nearly knocked him off his feet. In front of his very eyes, Edmund of Almain had transformed from an elegant agent of the crown to a snarling, vindictive man. The man's eyes had narrowed as he looked at Court in greedy anticipation of the spoils at Moordon. As the vision peeled away, Court fully understood the ability the stone gave him for the first time.

He could see things as they truly were. Or in some cases, how they would be.

He wasn't sure how he knew, but Edmund's intentions were not honorable. Was it because Scotland would suffer or was it more than that? Either way, he had to find out. He also needed to speak with

THE PROTECTOR'S PROMISE

Marion, but first he would need to find her. It was only after he searched her rooms that Court's pulse began to race.

She wouldn't have left, not after everything they'd shared. Would she have?

Every step he took toward the stables brought him closer to the truth. Marion was nowhere to be found because she had left. Did she have so little faith in him? He'd agreed to Almain's plan for one reason —he needed to pacify him until he had an alternate plan. But had he ever told Marion he wouldn't make the attack? What precisely had he said to her?

A connection forged because of it.

Nay. That was not true. There was so much more than simply the stone between them. So why had he said it?

Because it was easier than facing the truth. Court had fallen in love with a woman who circumstance dictated was his enemy. One who likely despised him now.

Damn, Court. What have you done?

He needed to go after her, but he could not do that. Not yet. One of the most powerful men in all of England, powerful enough that he had been chosen as a regent to Edward, would be returning belowstairs for dinner, and Court needed a plan before then.

Preparations for the meal were already underway. What the hell was he supposed to do now? Almain expected him to lead an attack he was not prepared to conduct. He strode to a table where a handful of Almain's men sat. Court had to be careful, but he recognized one of them and could hopefully get information from him.

"Sir Roger, son of Lord Wellingstone?"

Lord Wellingstone was an honorable man, one who fought on the side of peace at the border. He assumed the son was no less.

The man looked up at him as conversation ceased around him.

"The same," the heavily bearded man replied.

"You serve Almain now?"

"Until my knight service ends, aye."

Almain's men would never betray him. To do so would risk the wrath of a man who could wreak havoc on their lives. That meant

Court could not be direct in his line of questioning, but he didn't need to be direct to discern if his suspicions were correct.

"And will you take Moordon with us?" he asked, keeping his eyes on the man's face.

The look that passed over Sir Roger's face—and the visages of his companions—told Court that none of them were particularly pleased about this particular mission.

"We will," he said only.

Court had his answer.

"Enjoy the meal and the hospitality of Camburg." He inclined his head to the others. "Good day, sirs."

With that, his course of action firm, Court waited for his guest to arrive. Ignoring the activity around him, he sat. And drank. Waiting for his future to be decided.

Unfortunately, a certain redheaded vixen distracted him from the task at hand. Instead, he saw her waking up beside him, felt her soft flesh beneath his hands.

"I want that claim."

"Then it is yours."

No matter what happened between them, or to him, Court did this for her.

And for the borderlands.

He had one hope. Robert Burnell, the king's chancellor and co-regent of England, was the only man who could challenge Almain and the only person to whom Court could appeal if he hoped to refuse Almain's request but keep his head.

When Almain finally reappeared and was escorted to the high table, Court did not wait for him to be seated. He'd finish this now.

"Before you sit, Your Grace," he said, not quieting his voice or caring who heard them. "I would know one thing."

The man's mask of confidence slipped. "Which is?"

"Does this attack have Burnell's full support?"

It was a guess. A wild guess at that. But with the cloud of his own ambitions lifted, Court could see so much more clearly.

And one glance at Almain told him his suspicions were once again right.

"What is this?" Almain's voice was tinged with anger, and perhaps a bit of fear as well.

"I asked if this attack on Moordon has the support of Robert Burnell."

"Listen to me well," Almain spat, "I am regent to Edward I, King of England, and you are nothing. Certainly no one to be questioning me. You will take Moordon Castle or see yourself locked in the Tower."

He'd expected the threat.

"For?"

"Treason. Disobeying direct orders from your king." Almain, furious, turned to look at his men. Though he'd brought several of them, Court had many more retainers who were already present. The man turned back to Court. "You will pay for this display. As will Kenshire."

He could endure threats to himself, but Court would not allow one against Geoffrey and Sara. They had naught to do with his foolishness, and they would not suffer for it, even if he did. "If it is peace you want, I will give it. My allies at the border will quell this unrest and uphold the Treaty of York. Is that not truly the goal?"

By speaking openly, he backed Almain into a corner. A very dangerous proposition, especially given the man's open show of temper, but the only one he had.

"That will not happen," Almain snapped. "When Moordon grows stronger, and it will, the Scots will push back into our own borders. They'll have the foothold they need to destroy us."

"Nay, they will not."

Everyone, including Almain, turned to look at the entrance of the hall where Marion stood tall and proud, engaging with a man who could summon England to war with her own country if he so desired. Even this far from her, Marion's voice was clear and strong.

God, she was magnificent. And judging from Almain's expression, very much in trouble.

\#

She'd arrived just in time.

Marion walked toward Court, trying to appear unaffected by the icy waves of air emanating from the man who stood at the back of his hall as if he owned both it and all of England. She'd learned from

Court's confidence, and if there was ever a time to appear confident, it was now.

"I don't believe we've had the pleasure of an introduction," Almain said, making clear with his tone how very displeased he was with her interruption.

Court obliged. "Meet Lady Marion Rosehaugh, daughter of the 3rd Earl of Ormonde—"

"And Moordon," she said, adding her father's most recent acquisition to his title. She arrived at Court's side and, turning to face Almain, continued, "I am also the betrothed of Lord Thornhurst, seneschal of Camburg Castle." She did not dare look at Court. "So I can assure you, my father will not declare war against his daughter's husband. Or any of his southern neighbors."

Almain's face turned a dreadful shade of purple and red at her declaration, but she forged ahead anyway. "He is very much committed to the thirty-year treaty, to the Days of Truce, and to peace along the border. Enough so to ensure its success with this marriage."

Marion did chance a look at her supposed future husband. His expression impressed her—he looked nothing like a man who had just learned about his own betrothal.

"Why . . . ," Almain sputtered. "You said you were prepared to attack," he finally managed, enraged.

"I could not understand why you insisted on this raid," Court pressed him. "It took some time for me to realize that your concern is for your own interests, not for England," he told him boldly. "But as you can see, there's no reason to pose this attack. Marion's father is—"

"I know who Ormonde is," Almain spat out.

The regent wanted to punish Court. A new chill ran up her back. This man intended to hurt the people she loved and, if allowed, would strike at the very heart of the treaty that had allowed some modicum of peace in the borderlands these last few decades.

When she felt Court's hand, Marion thought he was attempting to interlace his fingers with hers until she felt the chain.

The stone.

She took his hand then, and together they held the stone. In that moment, any vestiges of cold were gone, replaced with the exact opposite. A warmth so consuming it felt as if she and Court had ventured outside to stand under the bright summer sun. She wasn't sure if Court felt it too.

Almain stared at them, wide-eyed, and then turned to look at the men gathered in the hall. Marion had not noticed earlier, but Court's men looked as if they were prepared to fight at any moment. None had unsheathed their swords, but they were clearly ready to commit treason for their lord. For if they did strike down Almain or any of his men, it would be akin to an attack on the king himself.

Even so, Almain would be taking a great risk if he punished her love. He would be declaring, once and for all, that he was an enemy of peace.

The tension hung in the air for a long moment, and then without warning, Almain's chin rose and he addressed Court very differently than he had before. "Very good, Thornhurst. You've done well to avoid bloodshed and secure the western border." He nodded to them both. "Congratulations on your impending nuptials."

Marion thought carefully about her next words and decided to forge ahead.

"I do believe Halbury would suffice as a wedding gift."

For a moment, she thought perhaps she'd pushed too far. But when Almain threw his hands up in the air as if granting a wish, she smiled for the first time since entering the hall.

"Of course, of course. Thornhurst," he said to Court, "Halbury is yours."

Almain's men looked at him as if he'd gone mad, but she sensed no rush of cold from them. They had not brought any malintent to Court's hall. They'd only gone along with their leader.

"We shall stay to celebrate."

With that, he walked around the dais to the side where she and Court stood and sat next to Court as if he'd not threatened him moments earlier.

Would they really sit and eat with this man as if nothing had happened? It appeared so. But Marion was afraid to let go of the stone. What if it was controlling Almain's behavior? What if he reversed his position as soon as they released it?

Court finally decided for them, letting the stone fall into her hand as he pulled away. She looked at him as he walked around to the other side of the table. Following, Marion sat alongside him and caught Kenneth's glance. He had not known she would declare herself betrothed to Court. She had not known herself. But oddly, he did not look surprised. She smiled, hoping to reassure him and the others that all would be well. After the day she'd put them through, they were owed an explanation. And she would give it to them.

After she and Court had the opportunity to talk about what had transpired. And whether or not they were indeed going to become man and wife.

11

They must have appeared to Almain like any other couple, but he and Marion were anything but. She played the part well, smiling and laughing as if she'd not just set down one of the most powerful men in England. Court wasn't sure what to think of her performance, aside from being grateful for her timely entrance. But he needed to know her mind.

Now.

"If you will excuse us," he said, at the risk of further insulting Almain by being the first to leave. "I must escort my lady to her room. You will, of course, be shown to yours when you are ready to retire."

Almain lifted his goblet, a signal that his wine was not yet empty. "A splendid night to you both," he said, looking at his men. "I shall speak with you about Halbury in the morning before we depart."

Court escorted Marion from the hall then, pausing only briefly so she could have a word with her men. She took his arm as she followed him down a darkened passageway and up a spiral staircase.

"My bedchamber is not this way, my lord," she said beside him, her voice like a gentle breeze on a cool summer night.

"I know well where it is."

She followed in silence until they reached his destination. Opening the studded door that led to his own chamber and adjoining solar, Court gestured for her to enter. She did, and he was pleased to see his room had already been prepared for the night. Candlelight glowed from every corner of the room. Though large, it was sparsely furnished with only a bed, two chairs and a hearth, which was not needed on a warm day such as this one. Court needed little, though he aspired to much. And yet . . . now that he'd achieved that which he'd always wanted, his own castle and lands, he found the victory a hollow one. The only thing he cared about was the woman standing so close he could reach out and touch her.

But he did not.

If he laid a hand on Marion, they'd not have the conversation they so desperately needed to have.

"You came back," he said, unsure of where to begin.

"I did."

He couldn't do this. Court gestured for her to sit in one of the chairs, far enough that he could not reach her.

Once seated, Marion opened her hand and revealed the stone, entangled in the gold chain to which it was attached.

"Did you feel it?"

"Aye," he said. "It felt like I was seeing everything as it should be even without a vision. What happened?"

Marion looked down at the stone in her hand. "I do not know. From what I've learned, the stone has only ever been in the hands of the protector or the protector's nemesis, not both at the same time."

When she looked up, Court nearly lost his resolve not to touch her. She was so very lovely.

"I thought you'd betrayed me," she said.

He had assumed as much—and decided he couldn't really blame her. If she'd mistrusted him, he was to blame. "So why did you return?"

She looked at him with such intensity the hairs on his arm rose.

"I felt his malintent," she said, "when he walked into the hall. I should have known then that he was purposefully deceiving you, but you agreed to the attack so readily, and I was too angry to consider it logically. It was only after I calmed down that I reconsidered."

"Moordon is truly your father's?" He still could not believe it. He'd never heard of a greater coincidence, and yet mayhap it was not surprising at all given everything else that had transpired between them.

"It was recently bequeathed to him, aye. I thought for certain you knew that, at first, but then . . ." She shrugged. "I took a chance."

She had put everything on the line for him, and he knew it. He had done the same for her in the end.

"Marion," he began. "I'd not betray you. Now or ever. I don't pretend to understand the power of the stone, but I'm grateful to it for bringing us together."

Her smile touched his very soul. "I've never announced my betrothal to a roomful of witnesses before."

Court stood.

"If you meant what you said in the hall"—he reached out his hand—"I would be honored to have you as my lady wife."

She laid the stone down on the seat below her and took his hand, allowing him to help her to her feet. "I wasn't sure if—"

He couldn't wait any longer. Court leaned forward and captured her mouth with his own. She responded immediately, and before long, the kiss turned from one of a shared declaration to something much, much more.

This beautiful, incredibly astute woman who'd walked into his life only a week before was going to be his wife. And he couldn't wait any longer to make her his in truth. When he slipped his hand under the hem of her kirtle on both sides and pulled upward, she did not protest. Neither did she say a word when he did the same to her undertunic.

Standing before him in nothing more than a shift, Marion peered at him, waiting.

He discarded his surcoat and tunic more quickly than he'd ever disrobed in his life. When her eyes lowered to his bare chest, Court's cock responded immediately. When she reached out a tentative hand, Court captured it and placed it on his chest. Willing himself to take it slow, he watched her explore. She traced the lines of muscle in his stomach, and then the little minx actually trailed her fingers even lower.

"It is not always this way," she said, referring to his straining cock. Only a layer of hose separated her delicate touch from the evidence of his need.

He sucked in a breath. "Nay, it is not."

His eyes rose to hers, and what he saw there nearly brought Court to his knees. He'd wanted to go slowly, but it was just not possible. Lifting her up in his arms, Court carried her to the bed.

"You are sure about this, my lady?"

Laying her down, he then stripped the only remaining barrier between them save her shift. As he awaited her answer, Court stood beside the bed completely naked. Her gaze was not shy. His body responded to the mere suggestion in her eyes that she was indeed sure about what they were about to do.

"Very sure," she said, as if reading his thoughts.

He knelt beside her, lifting her shift up as she wiggled to allow the soft fabric to glide off her body. She slid it over her head, and he sucked in a breath at the sight of her round, firm breasts.

Then his gaze moved down to her hip, and he spied the small, dagger-like mark shaped exactly like his own. When she noticed where he looked, Marion stared at his own mark. After a moment, he was roused from his momentary fascination by one much more grounded in this world. He cupped her beautiful breasts as he studied her face, then lowered his head and took a small taste. Allowing one hand to wander between her legs, he used his tongue to taunt and tease her nipple until his hand finally found its mark. Already wet and ready for him, Marion gasped when he entered her with his fingers. Her reaction changed his plans. He'd bring her pleasure more than once this eve.

He lifted his head to watch her, and when she arched her back toward him and closed her eyes, Court whispered words of encouragement.

"I will please you well this night," he said as she began to find her first release. "And every night after it."

When the throbbing subsided, he reluctantly withdrew, moving atop her and replacing his fingers with the tip of his manhood. He throbbed, wanting nothing more than to be inside this woman, to claim her as his own. A rush of heat coursed through him as she gripped his arms, her passion answering his.

When her breathing returned to normal, he said, "If I do this, you will be my wife."

In response, she thrust her hips toward him, forcing him to guide himself deeper, to break through her maidenhood. Marion let out a gasp of pain and began to pull back.

"Nay," he said, moving his hands to both sides to support himself as he lowered atop her. Capturing her lips, slowly, passionately, he used his tongue to make her forget the temporary pain. When she began to move again under him, Court knew she was ready.

He started slowly and then circled his hips until she was moving with him.

"Oh God, Court I cannot . . ."

"You can," he said, willing her to feel as much pleasure as he did. He couldn't hold on much longer. The luscious body he'd imagined under him writhed and moved with him as if she'd done it many times before.

But she had not. Marion had never been with a man before, and he would be her first and last. The thought filled him with contentment, her moans the most beautiful sound he'd ever heard.

"Thank you," he said, watching her.

Marion's eyes flew open. "For what?"

"For choosing me." He pressed himself into her and moved in a way that he knew would help her find fulfillment. Sure enough, Marion cried out, the telltale throbbing his signal to let go. His release was so powerful that he met her cries with one of his own. Utterly spent, he collapsed on top of her, making sure his elbows were propped enough not to cause her discomfort.

They lay there like that until Marion twisted beneath him. Moving to her side, Court closed his eyes while he returned from whatever other world he'd journeyed to just then.

"Court?"

When his breathing slowed, he opened his eyes once again and turned his head. The sight of her, thoroughly ravished and looking more than a mite content, stirred his cock awake once more.

"Aye?"

"I enjoyed that very much."

He trailed his finger from her shoulder down to her breast and continued exploring the soft curves of her stomach, her waist, her hips. By God, if it truly was the stone that had brought him this perfect woman, then he would worship it all the days of his life.

"I'm glad to hear it," he said, "as we will be doing it often."

She turned then, propped her head on her elbow, and smiled. "I wonder if it's ever happened this way? If the stone has ever brought both protectors together in this way."

"Ah, so now I am a protector too?" When she reached out her hand and laid it on his cheek, Court's chest ached with a very new emotion.

"I did not believe so at first—"

"When I held a sword to your throat?" he asked ruefully.

She mimicked his earlier motion and let her finger fall from his face downward, toward his manhood. A shiver that had nothing to do with cold ran through him.

"I never felt cold near you. I should have known—"

"How were you to know I would love you . . . protect you and hold you dear for all the days of my life?"

When her eyes widened, he knew the words had penetrated. Just to be sure, he repeated them, only this time he added, "I love you, Marion."

In response, she looked down at his growing cock and then back up to meet his eyes. He laughed at her brazenness and pulled her atop him.

"And I love you. All of you," she teased.

Before he made love to her again, he would ensure she understood their position.

Lifting her hair to one side and placing it behind her ear, he reached up and held her beautiful face in his hands.

"If for some reason your father does not condone the match, we will run away. You are mine, Marion, from this day forward. And I am yours just the same."

When she licked her lips, he knew their discussion was at an end.

"If that is true"—she shifted her position to better prepare for what was to come next—"then I do believe I'd like to make love to you again."

Court was more than happy to oblige.

EPILOGUE

Halbury Castle, England

"My lord, my lady." The steward approached them just as Marion and Court were preparing to sit for the midday meal. "A visitor has arrived and asks to speak with you both."

Marion looked at her husband, wondering if he'd seen anything unusual. His visions came fairly regularly now that they were in possession of the stone, but she had not felt a premonition of malintent since encountering Lord Almain. Since they'd married and moved to Halbury Castle, none had threatened them, and her power had thankfully lain dormant.

A visitor was nothing unusual, so why did their steward behave so oddly?

"Show them in," Court said.

"She asks for a private reception."

Marion and Court exchanged glances. Though others may not have seen it, Marion glimpsed a slight crease in his forehead. If he was worried, then she was as well.

"Who is she?"

"She gave no name. But she—"

"Show her to the east tower chamber," Marion said, anxious to see who could inspire such wariness in the steward. If her parents had not just returned to Scotland after a brief visit to Halbury Castle, she would have expected they were the visitors. Marion smiled, remembering her parents' reaction—their joy that she and Court had found each other.

Suddenly, Marion knew the identity of their visitor. At least, she suspected she did.

By the time she and Court made their way to the visitor, she was convinced the Priestess of the Stone would be inside the private chamber to which she'd been shown. Marion squeezed her husband's hand and received a reassuring squeeze in return.

She was about to share her thoughts when they turned the corner and were greeted by a guard. Marion was still learning the layout of her new home and had not realized they were so close.

Court nodded to the knight standing at the door, and when they entered the room, Marion held her breath, waiting for the cold to come. But it did not, *would* not, for she had been correct. Would the priestess be angry at their decision? A familiar face smiled at them as they entered. It was strange to see her here, in this very ordinary room. The pools suited the priestess much more than this chamber.

"I apologize for the request," she started as soon as they walked into the room. "I cannot stay long."

Her lilting voice filled the chamber, and she smiled as she glanced down at their still-joined hands. Relief washed through Marion. She did not appear to be upset.

"I came to see if that rumor was indeed true."

Marion and Court exchanged a glance.

"This"—she waved a hand toward them—"has happened only once before."

Surprised, Marion asked one of many questions she had about their joining and the stone.

"I wondered about that, but how is it possible? We thought the stone might be responsible for bringing us together."

The priestess gave Court a stern glance. "Nay," she said. "Your seizure of the stone ensured only that Lady Marion would find you."

"Does that mean—" Court began.

"Your joining has nothing to do with the stone." The priestess looked at Marion then. "May I see it?"

"How did you—"

"I can sense it, as you can."

Marion let go of Court's hand and reached into the small leather purse hanging at her side. Pulling the stone out, she began to hand it to the priestess, but the ethereal woman shook her head.

"Nay, it is yours now." She looked at Court. "Both of yours. I keep it safe only when it awaits a new protector. At least"—she frowned at Court once again—"my ancestors and I usually are able to keep it safe. To see things as they truly are . . . that is a power I've never encountered before."

Marion squeezed Court's hand. No doubt he was confused, as she was, but it seemed unlikely the priestess would ever reveal how she'd known about their powers.

"But now that it is in your possession, you will protect it, together."

"What is my role?" Court asked. He'd asked Marion's mother what she knew about the stone and his role in protecting it, but she'd had no answers for him beyond what she had already shared with Marion.

"That stone," the priestess said as Marion put it back where it belonged, "is the lifeblood of Scotland. Most often, its nemesis intends harm upon our land. But now our interests are aligned with those of our southern neighbors. It is possible that the borderlands will suffer without your joint protection. And with it, the fate of both Scotland and England."

They were to protect the border. And peace along the border meant peace for their two lands. Of course.

"You came all the way here just to ensure the stone was safe?" Marion asked.

When the priestess smiled, a warmth filled the room.

"Your love, your union, and the power the stone has given you will guide you. May you both find joy in each other and in your protection of the stone."

With that, the priestess made her way around them, and as quickly as she had come, the woman was gone.

"I did not even say farewell," Marion said finally.

Court pulled her toward him, wrapping her up in his arms. "That was an ... interesting ... visit."

"Aye, very much so. At least we have some answers."

"And, more importantly ... privacy." Court's hand ventured from her waist to her backside, and when he squeezed gently and pulled her even closer, Marion knew they would not be eating for some time.

When he kissed her, her heart raced as if it were the very first time. So it was not the stone after all. They'd been brought together by something much more powerful.

"I love you," she murmured.

"And I love you," he said. "Do you believe me?"

She startled. "What kind of question is that? Of course I do."

Court frowned in mock sadness. "Ah, well that is a shame."

She pulled back and looked up at him.

"If you had not, I was prepared to prove it."

He was insatiable.

"In that case," she said, sliding her hand between them. "I'm not sure I do believe

you."

His slow, sensual smile confirmed that the meal would indeed have to wait.

"Then by all means, let me show you."

She looked forward to the lesson and hoped it would be repeated today and every day for the rest of their lives.

Go back to the beginning of the Border Series when Court visits Lady Sara at Kenshire Castle in THE THIEF'S COUNTESS: BORDER SERIES BOOK ONE.

ABOUT THE AUTHOR

Cecelia Mecca is the author of medieval romance, including the Border Series, and sometimes wishes she could be transported back in time to the days of knights and castles. Although the former English teacher's actual home is in Northeast Pennsylvania where she lives with her husband and two children, her online home can be found at CeceliaMecca.com. She would love to hear from you.

Become a CM Insider to receive a bonus chapter of 'The Thief's Countess,' plus other exclusive content including family trees, chapter upgrades and sneak peeks of upcoming Border Series books.

Become a CM Insider

ALSO BY CECELIA

BORDER SERIES

The Thief's Countess
The Lord's Captive
The Thief's Maiden

The Scot's Secret
The Earl's Entanglement
The Warrior's Queen

facebook.com/ceceliamecca

twitter.com/ceceliamecca

instagram.com/ceceliamecca

bookbub.com/authors/cecelia-mecca

goodreads.com/ceceliamecca

THE HIGHLANDER'S QUEST

A Sutherland Legacy Novella

ELIZA KNIGHT

Lady Julia's mission is to protect the young boy king. Sir Alistair has uncovered a plot to destroy Scotland. Together, they must fight a powerful enemy who hides behind a traitorous veil of secrecy...

ACKNOWLEDGMENTS

Many thanks to my wonderful editor, Kelli Collins! And to my amazing assistant, Kris, and my bestie Andrea, who proofread everything I write. Thank you to my beta readers and review team for reading my books and spreading the word. It was a pleasure working with Madeline, Cecelia and Lori on this amazing project! So many hours spent collaborating! You guys were amazing. Always, so much gratitude for my family, who are 100% there for me through every book. Thank you to my amazing friends Andrea and Corrina who travel with me to Scotland every so often to do research, allowing the details in my stories to come alive. And last, but never least, to you, dear readers, without whom the dream of being an author wouldn't exist.

Much love,
Eliza

PROLOGUE

Scottish Highlands
Eilean Donan Castle
1298

'Twas well past nightfall when they arrived on the bridge to Eilean Donan. Ronan Sutherland sent up a call to the guards to let them know it was no enemy who approached, and the gates were swiftly opened.

Half the men had returned with them, while Wallace led the other half in a chase for the vile Earl of Ross, who had been terrorizing the Highlands for years with his alliance to the English.

They were greeted in the courtyard by nearly everyone, including Robert the Bruce, who looked worried over the lack of those returning and stuttered William Wallace's name, until Ronan explained what had happened. He then gave his future king a serious look and asked to speak with him in private.

"I will also attend your private meeting," Julianna de Brus stated. Her shoulders were squared, head held high. The lass, if a hellion could be called by such a docile term, was the bastard half-sister of the Bruce, as well as his personal guard.

ELIZA KNIGHT

"Julianna..." Robert warned, but Ronan shook his head.

"She may, if 'tis all right with ye, my lord." Ronan couldn't take his eyes off her. Despite the bits of dirt smudging her creamy skin, she was still a vision. And nothing had scared the piss out of him more than seeing her quiver at the end of Ross' sword, and then finding her missing. Thank God she was no longer in danger.

"All right," Robert drawled, looking between the two of them.

The man must have started to put two and two together, because his face grew pinched, and if Julianna's earlier projections about her brother not wanting her to marry were true, they might be in for a bit of disappointment.

They were in love, and that was the simple truth of it. Ronan could not picture his life without her in it.

Robert beckoned them into the castle and they followed him up the spiral stair to his chambers. A fire blazed in the hearth and several candles lit the room. Ronan's stomach twisted with hunger, but he ignored it.

"Wine?" Robert asked, holding up a jug.

"Aye, please." Julianna gripped a cup from his table and held it out while her brother poured.

Ronan nodded and lifted his own cup, watching as Robert poured the red liquid with steady hands.

"Sit. Drink. Tell me what this is about."

Ronan and Julianna both took seats while Robert stood, arms crossed, and gave them a stare that might have cowed a lesser man. But Ronan was not a lesser man, and he knew what he wanted. Needed. Julianna. He loved her.

"I wish to offer for Julianna's hand in marriage." There, he'd said it.

Robert looked ready to throttle him, but at least no weapons had been drawn. However, Ronan wasn't entirely sure that he wouldn't be cast into the bowels of hell—the Bruce's glower was that staggering.

"I see. Julianna?" Her brother glanced her way, his expression unreadable.

I see? What the hell kind of response was that? Ronan tried not to frown but couldn't help his jaw muscles flexing with irritation.

"I wish to marry him, brother. With all my heart. I've served ye many years. Since we were bairns even. Now I am seven and twenty. 'Tis well past the time I marry." She turned to Ronan and smiled, her eyes twinkling. "And I love him."

Robert let out a disgusted grunt and whined almost like a spoiled child. "Truly?"

"Aye, brother." Julianna turned her attention back to the Bruce, and her voice grew stern. "I've not asked ye for anything afore. I've only lived to serve ye. Give me this one thing."

Robert walked away from them, toward the window. He opened the shutter and gazed out at the cloudless night sky. Ronan could have counted to a thousand in the time it took for Robert to finally turn his attention back to them.

"Ye have my blessing," he said softly. "Though a third-born son is well below your station."

Ouch. Ronan felt as though an arrow had slammed into his ego.

"Robert!" Julianna scolded. She gave Ronan's hand a squeeze and then stood, marching over to her brother as though she'd grip him by his ear and drag him outside to the stocks. "His station means naught to me."

The Bruce held up his hand, his face serious. "That is not the way I meant for it to come out. I only mean that Ronan must be elevated. He has proven his worth to me. To this country. And if he means that much to ye, then I would see him given his rightful due."

Ronan also stood. "My lord—"

"Dinna try to change my mind. I've thought about it. Had been thinking about it afore now. In a few months' time, we will move closer to the Lowlands to prepare for the invasion promised us from the English come spring. When we leave, the castle will be without a laird. Ye, Ronan Sutherland, will be the new Laird of Eilean Donan; in fact, all of Kintail. Ross has lost his privileges here, and I hope to see ye keep this castle fortified against him."

Ronan's heart felt ready to burst. "Aye, my lord. 'Twould be an honor. And thank ye. I love Julianna with all my heart."

"Good. Because if ye ever hurt her, I will make ye pay. Painfully."

Ronan blinked a few times, trying to assess how to react, but the

Bruce stepped forward and clapped him hard on the back three times, a grin on his royal face.

"When should ye like to marry?" the future king asked.

"Now," Julianna and Ronan answered at the same time.

Robert's head fell back and he roared a laugh. "Well, I see ye are both not too eager," he teased, his voice dripping sarcasm.

Julianna's face turned a ravishing shade of red, and Ronan felt a little heat creep into his own cheeks.

"Oh, come now," Robert chuckled. "Finish your wine. I will call for the priest."

Less than an hour later, Julianna and Ronan were sequestered in their wedding chamber, a table full of food, a jug full of wine and two hot, steamy bathtubs.

Man and wife.

I

June 10, 1329
Eilean Donan Castle

Her uncle was the king, and the king was dead.

"Ye'll need to leave right away." Lady Julianna Sutherland's pallor was ashen and sweat beaded along her brow and upper lip. Her once reddish-gold locks hung limp as though even the strands of her hair were too weak to do anything more than hang.

Julia, named for her mother, stared wide-eyed, disbelieving the order she'd just been given. "Leave? Now? But Mama—"

The Lady of Eilean Donan waved her hand dismissively, as though she'd simply asked her daughter to go and fetch the eggs from the hen house, and an attempt had not just been made on her mother's life. "Dinna sass me, lass. I'll be fine."

Julia shook her head hard enough that her hair, which matched her mothers, came loose from the knot she'd secured at her nape. "Da will kill me if I leave ye like this."

Her mother reached out a trembling hand and gripped onto Julia's shaky fingers, stroking her thumb soothingly over the knuckles. "My own sweet bairn, your da will be proud of ye, and he will understand. I assure ye, the poison has quite left my body now."

Julia tried to quell the slight shaking in her hands but nothing seemed to work. How was she supposed to do as she asked? Someone had just tried *to kill* her mother. Though Lady Sutherland had trained Julia in the arts of fighting and protecting others, there had been little she could do about a poisoning. Her mother told her it wasn't Julia's fault, and she mostly believed her, but still... It didn't matter. She couldn't leave. Her duty was here. Mama needed her. What if there was another attempt on Lady Sutherland's life? Julia was supposed to just up and leave? Preposterous! "Da will be back any day now, at least let me wait until he returns."

Her mother shook her head, then closed her eyes as though the movement made her dizzy. "There is no time to waste. The boy king needs ye."

The boy king. Wee King David II. Already a king at five years old, and no one would have thought it to be so.

Her mother's half-brother, King Robert the Bruce, God rest his soul, had passed away just two weeks ago near Dumbarton while on campaign with his men, after a prolonged illness. The country mourned him—as did all of Eilean Donan.

All his life, her mother had hidden behind a veil of secrecy, pretending to be a servant at the same time she'd taken care that anyone who got close enough to harm Robert was eradicated. All her life had been dedicated to keeping her brother safe, and in between her missions, she had managed to carve out a life with her husband, and birth just a single daughter—Julia—to whom she'd passed on her trade and skills.

But Julia was not an only child.

Before she was born, her father, Ronan Sutherland, the Laird of Eilean Donan, had adopted a son, Tad, whom he and Lady Julianna had raised as their own, and Julia considered to be her brother in full.

"Tad is due back on the morrow from his scouting mission. Please, let me just wait until then, Mama."

"If he is not back by the nooning, ye must go, my darling. King David is not safe. Already enough days have passed without him having a guard who isn't tainted with a personal agenda. The Earl of Moray wrote to me, personally requesting my assistance. I canna let him down. They need ye. This country needs ye."

Julia swallowed, trying to find the courage within to agree. It wasn't that she didn't want to serve her king, but it meant she had to leave her mother, who had been near death's door just the day before. But she could see that her mother was not going to budge and that there was no use in arguing.

What would be worse? Disobeying her mother and incurring her disappointment, possibly jeopardizing the king's safety? Or her mother taking a turn for the worse, or another attempt being made on her life, when none of her loved ones were there to care for her? How was Julia to make that choice?

"I know ye're struggling with this, my darling, but I promise ye. I will be well soon. I can feel it in my bones. And the king needs ye. If Robert were alive..." Her mother's voice broke on a sob.

The trembling in Julia's hand ceased and she squeezed her mother back, as she did want to be a pillar of strength for her mother. Perhaps if she just played along... "Where is the king now?"

"Dunfermline Palace, Fife."

"It'll take me at least a sennight to get there."

"That is why I must insist that ye leave as soon as possible." Her mother started to cough, her face turning red, lips blue, and Julia rushed to grapple with a pitcher of water by the bedside, pouring into a cup. She held it to her mother's lips as soon as her coughing fit gave her enough mercy to sip. "Thank ye, sweet child."

The courage seemed to have evaporated with her mother's coughing fit. Julia bit the inside of her cheek. She wanted to argue with her mother. To tell her this mission had come at the wrong time and someone else was going to have to take care of the bairn king, that she needed to remain behind and be with her mother.

But the way her mother looked at her then, with such pride, the way her mother held such confidence in Julia's ability to see the task through, had her holding her tongue.

"All right, Mama. I will leave as soon as Tad has returned, unless he has not returned by noon."

Her mother grasped her hand once more. "Thank ye. I know ye can do it. Go over there to my wardrobe. I want ye to have something."

It took an effort for her to let go of her mother's hand and walk across the chamber, but she managed it without tripping and called that a victory. The wardrobe creaked on its hinges as Julia opened it, recalling how as a lass she'd played inside the wooden structure, touching all of her mother's clothes, boots, slippers and, every once in a while, opening her jewelry box to admire the few trinkets she found there.

"In the back, there is a notch. Can ye feel it?" She coughed, and when Julia was ready to give up finding the notch to turn around and help her mother, she said, "I'm fine, keep looking."

Lady Sutherland was not one to be disobeyed, and so Julia continued to feel along the back wall of the wardrobe until she found a tiny nick in the wood. "I found it."

"Good, stick your finger into it and slide the panel open."

How had she not found this secret panel as a child? The melancholy of her mother's illness dissipated for a moment, replaced with excitement. She slid the wood out of the way, though slowly, as it was very tight.

"Come get a candle so ye can see," her mother called.

Julia grabbed a candle, shuffled the hanging garments out of the way and saw a treasure trove of objects that one did not typically see in their mother's wardrobe—unless one's mother was a secret guard.

Weapons and armor had been hidden behind the wood paneling. Swords, daggers, a bow and arrow, long pins, satchels with the contents hidden, and a beautiful leather-and-iron-studded corset vest with pauldrons to cover the shoulders, and matching forearm and thigh braces. There was even a small leather mask that would cover the bottom half of her face, only revealing the eyes.

"Mama," Julia breathed out in surprised, stroking the items with wonder. For all twenty-nine years of her life, these things had been kept a secret from her. "Why have I never seen any of this?"

Her mother let out a small, scratchy laugh. "When ye were young, I went out on missions while ye slept, or had ye whisked up to the nursery."

"But why? Ye taught me to fight, why not let me see ye in this magnificent armor?"

Julia turned to face her mother, watching as the older woman bit her lip, gnawing over what she wanted to say. "I suppose there was a part of me that dreamed ye'd never take up the sword. I wanted to protect ye, love. There was also fear. Children often say things they shouldna without realizing it. Your da and I couldna risk ye saying ye'd seen me in armor, when there was rarely anyone at the castle to know just who I was."

That made sense, and Julia couldn't fault her mother for trying to protect her and their kin.

"Why are ye showing me now?"

"Because, it is your time, my darling, and I want ye to have it."

"But what if ye need it?" Julia regarded her mother. Tears brimmed in the older woman's eyes.

"I am passing my legacy on to ye, Julia. Now it is ye who will guard the king."

Julia reached forward, her fingers brushing over one of the bracers. At the contact, a shock much like what she felt sometimes when she touched metal after a storm passed through her veins, and she cried out at the jolt.

"Try it on. I want to see ye in it."

With deference, Julia took down the leather corset vest with pauldrons first, slipped it over her head, and fitted the pauldrons to her shoulders.

"It tightens on the side, so ye never need anyone else to help ye put it on."

Julia lifted her arm and tugged at the laces on the side, tightening the armor until it fit and tucking in the extra length of laces.

"My God, child, it looks incredible on ye." Her mother's face beamed with pride.

Julia glanced down, wishing there was some way to see her reflection, but satisfied with the proud look on her mother's face.

"I can only hope to fill your shoes halfway, Mama."

"Ye will fill them more than twice, I'm certain."

Again, a jolt went through her limbs as she pulled the bracers and face mask from the back of the wardrobe and put them on. Fully dressed, daggers tucked into the bracers, a sword in the scabbard at her hip and another strapped to her back, Julia turned in a circle for her mother's approval.

"Ye're almost ready. There is one more thing. My hair pins."

Julia untied the face mask, letting it hang by her neck, and reached back into the wardrobe. The mask was going to take some getting used to as she found it hard to breathe with it on. She plucked the long pins that were held in place against the back paneling by leather loops.

"They are sharp," she said, pricking the tip of her finger.

"Aye, they are weapons themselves, but there is something that ye can put on their tips that will help put your enemies to sleep." Her mother struggled to sit up, and Julia rushed forward, putting the pins down on the side table as she adjusted the pillows.

"Are ye all right, Mama?"

"Aye, I'll manage. Now, go back to the wardrobe. In the back, ye'll find a tiny satchel. The scent is unpleasant."

Julia found the one she spoke of right away.

"'Tis filled with poisonous mushrooms. They have aged much and will be more potent. If ye boil the mushrooms, the juice can be used to slip into an enemy's drink or meal, but mind the amount, as it can be deadly. Also, the pins," she picked one up from the side table, "can be dipped in the liquid. Let them dry, and then put them in your hair. When ye stab a man with the pins, the poison will get into his blood. It willna kill him, but if ye ever find poison mushrooms in the forest, the fresh juice could."

Julia listened carefully to her mother's instructions, seeing the older version of herself in a whole new light.

"How many have ye..." She found her voice fading, her question on the tip of her tongue.

"I never kept count," her mother answered, avoiding her eyes, which could only mean that her mother knew just how many she'd killed, and didn't want to tell her.

Were there so many? Was she ashamed?

Julia leaned in and gently hugged her mother, not wanting to cause another coughing fit.

"I am proud to be your daughter," she said.

"And I am proud to be your mother." Her mother stroked her hair, and then very calmly said, "Ye can do this. I know ye can."

Julia was grateful for her mother's confidence, because she certainly wasn't feeling it so much herself.

LATER, IN HER ROOM, JULIA UNDRESSED, WASHED, AND WHEN SHE lay on her side on the bed, felt a sting against the front of her left hip.

What in blazes was happening today? Shock after shock and now this?

The candle beside her bed was still lit, so she flung back her covers, yanked up her chemise and looked at the red, enflamed mark. She must have been bitten by something. Zounds, but it hurt like the devil. She touched the mark, surprised that it felt warm. That was not a good sign. When bites were warm, they often got infected.

Rising from bed, she went to her wardrobe and pulled it open. She studied the vials in a wooden box she kept for healing purposes and found one to rub on her skin.

The sting subsided enough that she fell asleep, only to be awakened shortly thereafter by what sounded like the whispers of a dozen people in her chamber. She bolted upright, the light from her banked fire enough to see that she was quite alone. The whispers ceased abruptly.

But as soon as she lay back down, the murmurs sounded once more, causing her to bolt upright again.

Then, silence. Then more whispers. A vicious, taunting cycle.

Julia covered her ears with a groan, but the croons grew louder, and it was then she determined—they were coming from inside her mind.

Had her mother's poison somehow gotten into her skin?

Dunfermline Palace, Fife

ALISTAIR CAMPBELL LISTENED INTENTLY AT THE CHAMBER DOOR.

Ordinarily he would not consider himself to be a great spy, but in the past sennight, he'd become quite adept at eavesdropping, and doing so unnoticed.

Inside the chamber was the Earl of Moray's steward, Hugh, and a lady who Alistair had not recognized. She'd lured the steward up to her chamber some hours before, and when the man had not returned, Alistair took it upon himself to see what mischief the steward was getting up to.

The Earl of Moray was now, without a doubt, the most important man in the country besides wee King David, as he had been appointed as regent upon the king's death.

Both the earl and Alistair had been at the king's bedside when he passed away, and both of them had rushed to the royal bairn's side before anyone else could get to him. The queen had been beside herself at the death of her husband, but while she mourned her dearly departed king, she now had more to worry about—as did they all.

Whenever a child inherited the throne, the danger to his life was multiplied exponentially, and for King David, the danger was no less.

For his part, Alistair was in charge of the Earl of Moray's safety. He was his personal guard, and he took his job very seriously. For several months now, he'd had his suspicions where the steward was concerned. Hugh was a bastard not only to anyone with breath, but especially behind the back of his employer. The steward was often cruel to the servants, and even more so to the orphaned children who served the castle for a bit of food and a roof over their heads. Anyone who could be cruel to children had a black heart. But beyond his propensities for vile behavior, there was something more about Hugh that had disturbed Alistair of late.

Alistair was fairly certain that the steward had been skimming the coffers, but that was the least of his offenses. Before the king's death, Alistair had been hearing rumors of Hugh dealing with the English. With the ongoing war against the Sassenachs, to have dealings with them was treason, and the highest offense any Scot could make against his fellow man.

If word were to get out that Moray's own steward was dealing with the English, given the earl's past, Moray would be ripped from his new position as regent and sentenced to death for treason himself, even if he'd had nothing to do with it. That was the way of the world. One's past could always sneak up behind a man and condemn him for deeds he was innocent of committing.

Aye, there had been a time, over two decades before, when Moray had sided with the English, but it was only because he'd been captured by the bastards and sought a way to survive. As the nephew of King Robert, Moray's very life was at risk, had he not agreed to an allegiance to the English king. That had only been for a period of two years, until Moray had been rescued and brought back to the Scottish fold. Moray had been the very picture of a loyal vassal ever since, dedicating his life to his king and Scotland.

Now, the little piss-pot Hugh was trying to undo everything.

For the better part of the time Alistair had been standing at the door, there had been a lot of moaning and groaning going on. Lord help him, but Hugh certainly appeared to have quite a bit of stamina. Seemed unfair that a vile man like that shouldn't have a limp cock.

Finally, the moaning stopped and it sounded as though they were talking. Hugh was rather overly confident in the thickness of the doors, it would seem. He grew louder, boastful, until Alistair could hear nearly every word.

"He knows nothing," Hugh slurred, followed by the soft murmur of his companion. "I could easily get ye the jewels, my love, a pearl for each ear and diamonds that would nestle beautifully between your perfect breasts. The earl will never know, as he gave the task of taking inventory of the crown jewels to me."

Dear God, the man was going to rob the crown jewels for a harlot?

"Before the year is out, I expect a title," Hugh continued. "And then ye can suck the cock of a lord. Would ye like that, my beauty?"

"Ye're already a lord in my eyes," she said firmly enough for Alistair to hear.

Who the hell was she?

"Ye know what ye need to do then?" Hugh asked.

"Aye." And she murmured something unintelligible, followed swiftly by more moans from Hugh.

Again? Alistair rolled his eyes and grimaced in disgust.

Besides stealing the crown jewels, what the bloody hell was Hugh up to? For ballocks' sake, Alistair couldn't be in more places than one. He'd have to follow the harlot around in addition to Hugh, not to mention the earl and the king. Well, sleep was overrated, he supposed.

At the sounds of voices approaching in the corridor, Alistair melted into the shadows, keeping himself still and unnoticed as a lord and lady passed by on the way to their chamber.

Since the king's death, Dunfermline, once a quiet and peaceful palace, had become a beacon for anyone seeking favor—and every one of them could be considered an enemy of not only Moray but the king as well.

Mo chreach, but the next few months were going to be complete and utter hell. Right now, he had enough information about the crown jewels to go to Moray and accuse Hugh of going against his master, but that was only scratching the surface. There was definitely something bigger happening here, and he had to get to the bottom of it, before letting it be known that he was onto the bastard.

Alistair was not going to let anything happen to Moray or the king.

2

"Name?"

"Lady Julia Sutherland."

The guard atop the gate paused a moment, looking at her, and then studying the large hound by her side. She never traveled anywhere without Merida.

Overlarge, and with a sleek black coat, the dog often frightened anyone who saw her, which was partly the purpose of having her as a companion. Merida was a war dog, with the stamina of a retriever, the hunting ability of a terrier, and the power of a great large breed. She was a special mixed breed that Julia's father had stumbled upon and begun breeding at Eilean Donan. He'd given Merida to Julia about four years ago, after she'd been a bride for less than a day. Her husband, one of their clan, had died in a raid. Rather than marry again, she'd chosen to devote herself to her clan instead.

Julia never went anywhere without the hound now.

The guard shouted to someone behind him, then said to Julia, "Proceed. We've been expecting ye."

Julia had been prepared for that. When she'd left Eilean Donan the week before—after her brother Tad returned early in the morn—her mother told her that she'd already sent a messenger ahead to inform the regent of her arrival. The man would be expecting her to pay her respects to the king in the name of Lady Sutherland, the young king's aunt, who was too ill to attend him.

The earl had known her mother well throughout the years and, from what Julia knew of him, was kind. Towards the later years of the Bruce's life, he'd allowed those close to him to know his sister for who she truly was, the earl included.

The gates yawned open, allowing Julia to see that the inner courtyard of Dunfermline was a thousand times busier than she ever would have imagined. Julia dismounted and handed the reins off to a stable lad, then clicking her tongue to Merida, made her way through the throngs of people toward the front doors of the castle. Beneath her gown, she wore her mother's armor, which was fitted enough to appear inconspicuous beneath the flowing layers of her green and blue plaid *arisaid*.

It had been quite some time since she'd been to court, and the times that she had been were few and far between. Already the crowds were pressing in, the noise, making her uneasy. Intensified by that were the whispers that occasionally still sounded in her mind since that night at her castle. Beside her, Merida growled low in her chest whenever anyone got too near, only to be hushed by the snap of Julia's fingers.

Once inside the palace, a servant eyed the hound and looked ready to tell her to leave Merida outside, but then thought better of it at the low rumble of a growl.

"Hush now, pup," Julia murmured. "I am looking for the Earl of Moray."

The servant, eyes still on Merida, pointed toward the stairs. "Third floor. Second door."

Julia made her way up the winding stairs, encountering a number of lords, ladies, servants and other people on the way. Dear heavens, with the castle this crowded, how was she ever to keep a watchful eye on the king?

She found the second door on the third floor and was about to knock when the entry swung wide. She came face to chest with a mountain of a man who glowered down at her with such scorn that Julia might have backed up, were it not for how irritated his obvious contempt made her. His dark shoulder-length hair was slightly curled. And every angle of his chiseled features seemed to be arrowing down into his frown. A shadow of a beard lined his tanned jaw, and his aquiline nose appeared fashioned for looking down on others. The only part of his face that wasn't dark and broody, were his eyes, glittering green and full of suspicion.

"The earl is not accepting visitors." The man's gaze bore into her own, and his wide, firm mouth turned back into what looked to be a permanent grimace. Despite that, she couldn't help but admire how handsome he was, if not a bit frightening. "Best get back to the village."

Julia opened her mouth to tell him to get out of her way when he held up his hand, silencing her with that single gesture—more so from shock than actually obeying his command.

"I'm in no mood to be trifled with, wench. Best be on your way."

Merida growled at Julia's side, seeming to grab his attention for a moment, his eyes squinting down toward the hound.

"And take that beast with ye."

Julia stood her ground. "I'm expected. Step aside."

At that, the unfortunately handsome brute raised an ironic brow. "Ye're expected? By whom? The cook?"

Julia gritted her teeth, her fingers touching the tip of a dagger that was just enough past her wrist to brush her palm. She considered flicking it out and giving him a good taste of just how frightening she could be. "The Earl of Moray, ye great oaf. Now get out of my way before ye embarrass yourself further."

"Embarrass myself?" the warrior sputtered. Momentarily, his brooding expression changed to one of confusion.

Julia let out a long, annoyed sigh. "I am Lady Julia Sutherland. If my name doesna crack open whatever is left of your brain, perhaps the fact that I am the niece of our departed king will."

The man looked ready to argue with her. Perhaps to force her to prove who she said she was, but instead, with a narrowed gaze, he did step aside. But he didn't leave. He followed close behind her as she made her way into the room. If she stopped suddenly, she was certain he'd run into her.

"Ye make a good shadow," she said with a roll of her eyes, and ignored his low growl. The solar was empty. Flanking the hearth were two great chairs. A table in the center of the room was covered in maps and scrolls. Shelves along the walls were similarly filled with scrolls, books and various other pieces of parchment. A large desk was cluttered with more of the same. Other than the two of them, the room was empty. "Where is the earl?"

"Through that door." Her shadow nodded his chin toward a door on the far left beside the hearth.

"I can handle seeing him on my own, sir, or are ye afraid I might have come here for some wicked purpose?"

He didn't answer, which was answer enough.

"Fine." Julia shrugged. "Follow me. Climb on my back and I'll carry ye with me through the door. I dinna care."

He simply stared at her and, judging from the simmering look of fury on his face, he wanted to toss her through the window. Ignoring the hulking man behind her, she made her way deeper into the solar to the door at the opposite end and knocked gently.

"Who is it?" the earl called from within.

"Lady Julia—"

"Come, I've been expecting ye."

Julia resisted the urge to turn around and smirk at the oaf behind her. Would serve him right to know she'd been telling the truth this whole time. Instead, she opened the door and, while she did try to kick it closed behind her, the man managed to duck in, the wood glancing off an elbow and nothing more. Astonishing, given his bulk. He had to be six and a half feet tall, and his shoulders as wide as the door's frame. Mighty lucky of him not to have been hit in the head just then.

"Ah, Lady Julia," the earl said, ambling forward, his black hair tinged with gray pulled into a queue. His middle had grown rounder since the last time she'd seen him, and the injury he'd taken to his leg in battle years before appeared to be bothering him immensely. "'Tis good to see ye, my dear. How is your da?"

"He is well, my lord, thank ye for asking."

"I'm sorry your mother could not join ye here. I hope she gets well soon."

"We are all praying."

"Was it poison?"

Julia bit the inside of her cheek, glancing at the man behind her, wishing he would get the hell out of the room so she might have a private conversation.

"We are nae certain." That was a lie. They were completely certain that it was an assassination attempt, but they weren't certain who had done the deed.

Her mother fell ill around the same time as the king's passing, which had them all worried that perhaps the king had come to the same fate, but nothing could be proved, and so for now, the official word on the death of her uncle was the continued illness he'd suffered for months.

"Well, I wish her well all the same." The earl patted her awkwardly on the shoulder. "She assures me that whatever we need, ye'll be able to provide."

Julia felt the heat of discomfiture clear to her toes.

"And who is this?" She hooked her thumb over her shoulder, trying to change the subject in hopes of reminding the earl they were in mixed company.

"Ah, forgive me my manners," the earl said. "This is Sir Alistair Campbell, my guard. He knew your uncle well, and is perhaps even acquainted with your father."

"Is that so?" Julia gave Sir Alistair a withering look. It would appear Sir Alistair Campbell would not be getting off her back anytime soon. "He did not mention that when he allowed me entry."

The earl chuckled. "Sir Alistair is not a man of many words."

"I see." Julia turned around to face him. "Well, I shall ask ye directly then, Sir Alistair, do ye know my father, Laird Ronan Sutherland?"

Alistair's expression did not change at all. There was not even a hint of recognition in his eyes that he'd been addressed, so when he said, "Nay," Julia had not been expecting it.

"Well, there ye have it." She started to turn back to the earl to ask if the brooding warrior could be dismissed when he spoke once more.

"But I am acquainted with your cousins, Sirs Liam and Strath. And I met your other cousin, Lady Bella, at court some years past with her husband, Chief Oliphant."

"I am glad to hear it, else I might have offered my advice to Lord Moray that ye be dismissed on account of lack of familiarity." She winked at Lord Moray, who chuckled indulgently.

Julia was exceedingly glad that she'd been blessed with her mother's skill as a warrior, and her father's charm. Her father, too, was a great warrior, but differed so much in personality to her mother. Having both their skillsets helped her tremendously in the world, for she could often distract people with her wit and charm, before using her skills as a warrior to see whatever task needed doing, done.

Insolent, arrogant chit.

"What was that?" Julia said, whipping around to face Sir Alistair.

He raised another of those sharply arched brows. "My lady?"

"I heard ye say something."

Green eyes judged her. "I assure ye, I didna speak."

Julia frowned and turned back to the earl, who was looking at her with some concern. Zounds, was she hearing things again?

The murmurs that had started to buzz the night she'd taken her mother's armor had mostly ceased, and she prayed it wasn't picking up in earnest again to torment her.

"Apologies, I think exhaustion and hunger are sinking in."

"Aye, I'm certain, if ye made it here in a sennight. I'll call a servant to take ye to your chamber and see that a bath and a meal are sent up. In the morn, I'll take ye to see King David. He was excited ye'd be joining us, as he is so fond of your mother."

"I'll take her, my lord, if ye wish," Alistair broke in.

Earl Moray glanced over Julia's shoulder to Alistair and nodded with a faint smile. "Aye, that would be good. I've some urgent correspondence to get to, and my knee is paining me greatly today. Thank ye for coming, Lady Julia. Ye must know I am grateful to have ye here with us."

Julia curtseyed. "It is my honor, my lord."

Outside the earl's chamber, Sir Alistair stopped and crossed his massive, muscular arms over his chest. She couldn't help but admire his braw figure, and that was irritating. With arms like that, the man could have the strength of at least two or three men.

Merida did not like his stance and let him know by growling.

Sir Alistair made a sound with his tongue against his teeth and Merida sat right down without hesitation.

Julia kept her mouth from falling open but couldn't keep her hands from fisting at her sides. "How dare ye silence my war dog? She is here to protect me, and clearly saw *ye* as a threat."

"Perhaps I *am* a threat, my lady. Or perhaps it is *ye* who is the threat."

"That is absurd," she scoffed.

"Is it?" He raised a challenging brow.

She was getting mightily tired of his over-expressive eyebrows. What would he do it she shaved them off in his sleep? Perhaps a little lesson would be good for the arrogant arse. "What is wrong with ye? What have I done to warrant such suspicion? Ye saw that the earl was pleased to see me, that I was invited. Ye even know that I am the niece of King Robert, God rest his soul, so why is it that ye have decided to pick a fight with me?"

"I'm nae picking a fight." The glower and crossed arms said otherwise.

"Then what are ye doing?"

He pursed his lips. "'Tis my duty to protect the earl and the king, and I must examine every potential threat and every person who enters this castle."

"Well," Julia said, crossing her arms over her chest, mocking his stance, "I will have ye know that it is also my duty to do the same."

Sir Alistair grunted. "Follow me."

Was it her, or did he give the order regretfully? What was it he hoped she was? Why did he seem to want her to be the enemy? Was he expecting someone? Was he up to no good?

Entirely too many questions and not enough answers.

THE WENCH WAS UNQUESTIONABLY UP TO NO GOOD.

Despite the honest look about her gray eyes, there was something about the red fire of her golden locks that set Alistair on edge. What was she up to? Why was she here?

The earl had never made mention of Lady Julia before, nor that he was expecting her. Was she truly who she said she was? The earl seemed to recognize her, but Alistair had to acknowledge that his lord was aging, and with age came a slight decline in eyesight. There was at least some measure of possibility that the chit was not who she claimed.

Dammit, he didn't have time to spy on her as well. Already Hugh and his lover were taking up much of his time. As it turned out, Lady Melia was one of the king's new nursemaids, which was why Alistair had recognized her. That meant there was a woman entirely too close to the young king for his comfort. He'd been able to convince the earl to double the guards on duty around the king, as well as to give Alistair the task of handpicking who would be among them, but that didn't mean that Lady Melia wouldn't be able to see her task through—whatever it may be. It only took one weak man to relent, and then the king's safety was in jeopardy.

They reached the chamber beside his—the best way for him to keep an eye on this newcomer. "I will see that a meal and bath are sent up."

She rounded on him, all of the fire in her lithe body directed at him. The lass was a beauty, with angles in her face that reminded him of those on a goddess. Beneath the layers of fabric, he would bet a year's wages she was just as perfect. "And ye willna be surprised when I have ye test both first."

What the devil? "Test both?"

"The food and bath water." The tone of her voice made it clear she thought him an idiot.

"Ye wish to watch me bathe?" He said it in hopes of distracting her, but she did not even so much as crack a smile.

"I would be satisfied with ye resting your hand in the water for several minutes."

"I will not poison ye."

"Since ye were in the room with the earl and I, but ye seem denser than the stone walls, I'll remind ye what ye should have heard before. 'Tis possible my mother was recently poisoned. It is not beyond the realm of imagining that I might too be victim to such a tactic."

"And ye think I would be the one to do so."

"Perhaps not." She shrugged. "If ye will not test the food or bath, I will partake of neither."

"Then ye will starve."

Merida growled, and again, he made the sound he gave his own hounds, calming the beast.

"Perhaps your dog can partake first," he suggested.

"Why not your own hound?"

She would not stop fighting him on this, he could see. "Fine. I will do it."

"Thank ye." Lady Julia turned away from him and put her hand to the door, then whipped back to face him. "Will ye have my satchel sent up as well?"

"Ye've no more baggage than a mere satchel?" He narrowed his eyes again, once more suspicious. Who came to an indefinite stay with no luggage?

"I'm quite simple, ye will find, Sir Alistair. But if it is beyond your duties to fetch it, I will happily see about it myself."

"I will do it."

"And search through it, I'm certain."

He grinned. "Ye catch on quickly."

"As long as ye dinna try on my nightrails, I'm certain I dinna care." With that, she pushed into her chamber and shut the door in his face.

It was only then, facing the worn wood, that he realized his heart pounded a bit faster, that a feeling leaked within his veins he'd not allowed himself to experience in some time.

Interest. Desire.

And she'd not even flattered or attempted to flirt with him in the least. If anything, she'd only been too apparent in her dislike of him.

That only made him like her all the more.

The door yanked open when he'd reached the stairs, and he heard her call out to him. "Sir, cider if ye have it please, instead of ale or wine, when ye send up my meal."

Alistair nodded and continued on his way, not considering to ask why until he'd reached the bottom. He often denied himself any alcohol as well, as it kept him more alert. Was that what she was up to? Keeping alert?

Hell and damnation, who had just entered the castle?

3

Julia woke with a start from a dream of running through the mountains and plunging into the Fairy Pools on the Isle of Skye. She'd been there once before but could hardly remember it, since she'd been a child at the time. So how was it that her dream had been so vivid? The colors of the water the richest blue, and steam curling from the surface. In her dream, a bewitching voice had continued to chant, *Come to the Fairy Pools... Fulfill your destiny.*

Had that blasted ogre spiked her cider?

Sir Alistair had played along and sipped, taken bites and rested his hand in the tub. Nothing had affected him. Though his intense gaze had affected her greatly. A shiver passed through her at the memory, and she tried not to think of what it could mean. On her wedding night years ago, she'd felt shivers... But even those virginal reactions to a man she barely knew were nothing compared to the memory of Sir Alistair's glittering emerald eyes.

Julia rubbed at her temples, trying to swipe away the memories.

Back to the more serious allegation running through her mind... If he'd spiked her cider, he might have been immune to whatever was in it. Didn't most of the warriors drink enough whisky to knock her under the table?

Swinging her feet over the side of the bed, Julia attempted to wipe the cobwebs from her eyes. No light filtered through her window, save for the moon. It was still quite the dead of night. A little twinge on her hip reminded her of the mark she had there. She lifted the chemise, staring at the welt on her hip. A lot of the redness and swelling had gone down. Thank goodness for the oil she rubbed on it. But how odd, the welt was starting to almost take on the shape of a... dagger. So very strange.

Despite the late hour, she felt a call to check on the wee king. They'd yet to be introduced, but that didn't matter. She'd come to the castle for one purpose alone—to protect the royal child. And she wasn't going to shirk her duty, even if it was the middle of the night.

Julia shrugged into her armor, then her gown, and for safe measure, strapped her arm braces and daggers beneath her voluminous sleeves, just in case.

Merida sat, watching her dress, her head cocked to the side as if she had her own thoughts about what Julia was doing.

"Dinna judge me," Julia said with a chuckle.

Merida's tongue fell out of her mouth, panting, and her tail thumped the floor.

She didn't expect to need them, but there were some nerves that niggled at the back of her brain, and had the hair on the back of her neck standing on end. Was it Sir Alistair? The way he'd been acting definitely had her suspicious, and she didn't trust him at all.

The door to her chamber creaked loudly as she opened it, a beacon to anyone that she was departing from the sanctuary. She expected at any moment for a guard to leap from the shadows to demand to know where she was going, but the corridor was utterly silent. Torches were lit, every other one, along the wall. Free of cobwebs but not shadows.

She closed the door behind her as quietly as she could and tried to get her bearings. Merida stood right by her side, prepared to follow wherever her lady led her. There were only a few places a king would sleep. Either in the nursery, as he was still a wee thing, or perhaps beside the earl's chamber, so as to be close to his regent—or a third option was in the king's old chamber itself, as he was now the king.

Given the worry for the lad's safety, Julia determined he must be near the earl. She descended the stairs and crept her way past the second door that had been the earl's solar, to the door after, which she assumed was the regent's bedchamber. Pressing an ear to the door, she listened for any sounds—hoping none of them were the whispers in her head. There were the snores that sounded very much like that of an older man—and aye, she'd heard plenty of that at Eilean Donan. Determining that this must be the earl's bedchamber, she continued on to the door beyond it.

Surprisingly, there were no guards outside any of the doors. It was possible they were within the chamber, but she found it odd all the same. Wouldn't they want as many guards on the lad, and the regent, as possible?

Julia pressed her ear to the door, hearing none of the snores from the previous chamber, but there were the sounds of shuffling, as though someone moved about the room. The guards perhaps, or the king's nursemaids.

Merida let out a low warning—then promptly sat. What did that mean?

"What are ye doing?"

Julia jumped, her head knocking into something hard—or had something been brought down upon her head? Was she being attacked?

She saw black for a moment, the jolt of the blow reverberating in her jaw, before whirling around, vision still blurred, ready to fight.

A large man stood behind her, and before she lashed out at him, she realized it was Sir Alistair, and he was rubbing his chin. "Why'd ye do that?" he accused.

"Me? That was entirely your fault. Why did ye sneak up on me?"

"I'm not the one doing the sneaking. Clearly 'tis ye sneaking about the corridor."

"With ye right behind me." She touched the dagger at her wrist. "Explain yourself."

"I will not explain myself to ye. In fact, *ye* need to explain yourself to *me*."

"I will *not*." Oh, she was so ready to pull the dagger out and jab it right into his insolent mouth.

"Then I shall take ye to the earl, and ye can tell him yourself why ye've come sneaking about King David's chamber."

Aha! So, she was right! "For the last time, I'm *not* sneaking."

"Then what would ye call it? Skulking? Slithering?" He leaned closer on this last word, hissing it out.

"I'm nae a snake. I'm a lady, and I'm a... protector."

He frowned. "A protector? Of what? Gowns and bobbles?"

"Ye offend me, sir."

"And ye offend me by trying to lie. I'm nae a fool."

"Ye could have *fooled* me."

Julia crossed her arms over her chest and braced her legs, prepared to remain rooted in this spot.

"I'll ask ye once more," he growled.

"And once more, I'll avoid answering."

Sir Alistair made a move like he was going to lift her up, but she jabbed him in the ribs with her fist and kneed him in the thigh.

Merida jumped up to all fours.

The man grunted but did not double over; if anything, he seemed to gain strength from her hit.

Insolent wench.

"I'm not insolent," she countered, "I am loyal and determined."

He stopped what he was doing and stared down at her in confusion. "What did ye say?"

Julia repeated herself, finding it hard to concentrate with the way he was so intently staring at her.

"I believe ye," he said in a low tone.

She was prepared to argue with him some more. To fight him until he surrendered, but she'd not expected at all for him to cave so quickly.

"What?"

"I believe ye." He shook his head and ran his fingers through his hair.

Julia didn't know how to react. She regarded him silently, waiting for him to make the first move or to say more. *Know thy enemy.* Something her mother always said.

"Are ye protecting... the earl?" he asked her.

"Nay."

"Nay?"

"Nay."

He looked over her head, his chin jutting toward the king's door. "Ye're here for him."

Julia bit the inside of her cheek, mulling over in her mind whether or not she could tell him that much. When she'd first met him, she'd not been certain she could trust him, and she still wasn't fully prepared to give him her trust, but he had said he believed her. Had stopped fighting her, and there was an earnestness in his eyes that made her believe him.

"Aye."

Sir Alistair nodded. "All right. So, why are ye here now, in the middle of the night? Did ye sense danger?" He scanned the corridor, as if he too expected villains to leap from shadows.

Before she could answer, there was a small cry from within the chamber. They both jumped, and in their haste to get to the door, bumped into each other, losing balance and falling to the floor. For the briefest of moments, his entire hard body lined hers, crushing her into the wood planks.

But it was very brief, and soon he was off of her, twisting the handle and finding it locked.

He banged on the door but Julia stilled his hand, pulling one of the pins from her hair and picking the lock.

They burst into the room but it was too late. Lying on the floor were all the guards and two nursemaids. Their mouths foamed white—poison.

"The king!" Julia shouted, rushing around the room and not finding him there at all. Everything was in disarray.

She'd only just arrived, and already she'd failed in her mission.

※

ALISTAIR BURST THROUGH THE DOOR TO THE EARL'S CHAMBER TO find his overlord crawling in his nightclothes toward the door. His head was bleeding and he held onto his leg where blood seeped through his fingers. Clearly, whoever had taken the king had tried to kill the regent, or at the very least incapacitate him. Alistair wanted to stop to help the regent, but the king was a priority. For less than a breath, he stood still, trying to figure out what to do.

"I'll be back," he finally said, and the earl nodded his head emphatically and murmured something that sounded like, *Go.*

Alistair burst through the door, Lady Julia and her hound on his heels as they went back out into the corridor they'd just come through. There was no sight of anyone, and when he determined to go down the stairs, he turned to see the lady standing in the hallway with wide eyes, shaking her head.

"Not that way. This way." She turned and ran in the opposite direction.

"Where are ye going?" There was no way out down that way that he knew of.

She frantically twisted handle after handle, tears in her eyes, until she finally came to a door that opened.

Inside the unused chamber, a secret door had been left gaping.

"There." Julia ran to it, but Alistair reached forward to grip her arm, stopping her at the last second.

"Let me go first," he said, not wanting her to bear the brunt of whoever their enemy was...and confused as to why he felt this sudden need to protect her.

"I can protect myself," she countered, breathless.

"I know. Ye've proven that already. Still, allow me." He spoke fast. Clipped. Wanted to hurry; there was no time to waste.

She didn't argue but shoved both of her hands against his chest in indication that he should go.

He spun around and ducked into the darkened space, feeling along the wall and desiring that he'd have brought a torch. The steps were slippery and small, and with his overlarge feet, he found himself having to hurry down the steps in an awkward sideways pattern in order not to tip forward and over.

At last, they reached the bottom of the stairs—and a stone wall.

Alistair pushed with every ounce of power he had, but the barrier would not budge.

"Search for a latch," Julia said behind him, her fingers brushing his as she searched too. "They had to have gotten out somehow."

But there were no latches to be had. No stones that pushed inward. No levers. No notches. Nothing.

"Ballocks," he cursed under his breath.

"We missed something." Her voice sounded as panicked as his own.

"What?"

"I dinna know." The sound of her retreating steps was the only clue given that she'd gone back upstairs.

Alistair gave one more shove to the barrier, and then he, too, retreated, catching her just as she looked ready to come find him.

"Come quick." With rapid hand gestures, she hurried him forward and pointed, showing him what they'd missed before—the hearth no longer had a back wall.

"Wait, should we not first see if there is another?" He regarded the room, scrutinizing every tapestry and every exposed inch of stone wall.

"I already looked. This is it."

"Let's go then." Alistair ducked into the hearth, and this time, they encountered stairs going up. The narrow stairwell turned abruptly, and a door opened onto the battlements, the cool night air hitting them with force.

The ramparts were empty on this side of the castle. "Where are the guards?" Alistair said angrily.

Julia was peering over the side of the castle, toward the moat, and then looked at him with sorrow. "They are down there."

Alistair winced at the bodies below that he could see in the moonlight. "Whoever we are dealing with is strong."

"And knows well how to use poison."

He stared at her, and she nodded. "I think the same one who might have tried to kill my mother. They would not have known that I would come in her stead. Little good that did."

Alistair didn't understand what she meant exactly about her mother, but there was definitely a connection, and why was it that she seemed to read his thoughts? The lass was hiding something, but there was no time for him to find out what. Not yet.

They followed the line of dead guards that hadn't fallen over the wall. Each of them had a small dart in their neck, likely filled with poison. This was how whoever it was who'd taken the king was able to do so silently and without sending up an alarm.

Was Hugh clever enough to do this?

"The nursemaid," he grumbled. *I should have told the earl.*

"What about her? What do ye know?"

They ran to the other side of the ramparts, where another door had been opened. He couldn't answer her now, and she didn't ask, as they didn't want those they pursued to hear them.

Once they made it to the bottom, ending in the bailey, there was nothing but quiet.

"She must have had something to do with it."

A loud clank from the gates jarred them toward the gatehouse, where they found out Sir Hugh and a servant had left hastily with a messenger, as he'd gotten news of a close family member being near death.

"That was no messenger!" But he didn't tell them anything else. Instead he ran back toward the castle. He had to tell the earl what had happened.

When he arrived in the earl's chamber, Julia was not with him.

Ballocks!

Had she gone after the king alone? Or was she a part of this elaborate plan? A sinking feeling churned in his gut. It was awfully convenient for her to have just now arrived, and the king to disappear on that very night.

"My lord." The earl had managed to get to a chair and was sitting on it with a rag held to his head to stop the bleeding.

"Sir Alistair. What happened? All I remember is waking to a pain in my head. Someone attacked me while I slept."

Alistair grimaced. He should have been there to protect him. "The king has been abducted, and I believe Lady Julia may be involved. She's disappeared along with your attackers. I'm certain Sir Hugh and possibly his new nurse were also involved."

The earl paled, and took a lengthy sip from his mug. A dark bruise marred the side of his face.

"I canna believe 'twas Lady Julia. She would not have done something like this. Her family has been nothing but loyal. Protectors of the royal family. Hell, they are part of the royal family." The earl's voice was scratchy. "But Sir Hugh... something has been off about him for awhile now. I wish I could have seen it before now."

"He is guilty, I'm certain. I should have told ye. I've been watching him, knew he was up to something, but I was nae entirely certain what."

"'Tis not your fault. Go after the king. Bring him back. And find Lady Julia, too. Likely, she went after the king, as it is her duty. Dinna say anything to anyone. I dinna want the entire country in a panic."

"Ye have my word. I will leave at once, my lord. What about the dead guards? What will ye tell everyone has happened?"

"I will take care of it. I'll tell them there's been a breach of safety, and that ye've taken the king to a secure location. No one is to know that he is missing."

"Aye, my lord." Alistair crossed the room. "I will not let ye down. I will save the king."

And he was going to make Sir Hugh and whoever else was involved pay for their treachery.

4

Sneaking out of any place was easy—doing so with a horse and a hound was a different story altogether. Even still, Julia managed it with such skill, she was certain her parents would have thrown a feast in her honor.

And thank goodness she'd been able to do it, because if she'd had to get to the king by force, she wouldn't have hesitated to take a few lives along the way.

She raced along the moors, listening to the cries of the young King David that echoed in her mind. Were they real or manifested? She prayed they were real, that the whispers, the mind reading she'd believed to be a curse, were actually turning into something of a blessing. The young king had a running commentary going on in his mind that somehow connected with hers. Fear dominated him, but as a young lad, he also took notice of things that an adult mind would not have—clues that told her where he might be.

I want my mama. Why did they steal me? There's the cliff that looks like cat ears Papa took me riding by. I miss my papa. My king. Why is it so dark in the woods?

Julia refused to be terrified by the voices in her head. Most things didn't terrify her at all, which her father often said was a flaw. Having a little bit of fear made one more cautious and gave one the ability to protect themselves and others. However, fear was not something she often felt. And this new ability—hearing voices or mind reading, whichever it was; were they the same?—didn't faze her as it probably should. Upon realizing with Sir Alistair that she could hear his thoughts, she determined that somehow, miraculously, she hadn't been imagining the whispers.

But she couldn't hear everyone's constant thoughts, even Sir Alistair's, just glimpses and phrases.

Merida kept her nose to the ground, sniffing out the lad's scent. Julia'd had the forethought in the lad's chamber to grab hold of one of his shirts. Merida was an excellent hunter and could find anyone hiding, as long as she had their scent.

They journeyed through the night, having to stop to rest when the sun came up, but not for long, perhaps an hour or two, and then she was on her way again. Julia did this many times through the next day, traveling for five or six hours and resting for two or three. And by the third day, she was exhausted, her horse and the hound were exhausted, but she could still hear the lad. Hear him crying for his mother, for his nurses. Hear him commenting on a deer carcass that crows were eating, on a fallen tree. All things she passed by within an hour or two's time.

Ironically, she could not hear the voice of the king's captor. As much as Julia squeezed her eyes shut and focused on evil, focused on hands gripping a child, she came up with nothing.

When they stopped to rest, usually near water, whether that be a loch, burn or puddle, the animals sipped. While her horse fed on grass, Merida hunted for squirrels, and Julia foraged for berries, nuts and roots, since she couldn't risk a fire to cook any game—despite her loyal hound offering her several squirrels and a rabbit. Every few stops, she closed her eyes, but would quickly bolt awake.

Every step of the way, Julia fought off the rising panic, the great sense of failure. How was she ever going to face her mother? Anyone, for that matter, after this?

Failure wasn't an option.

She must save him.

As the days passed, she had a sense of someone following her. Thought a few times she might have recognized the sound of Sir Alistair's voice in her mind, but every time she circled back around, she found no one there. No traces of anyone.

If only she'd grabbed hold of something of his and could send Merida out. But, then again, she couldn't risk the loss of her hound's nose for a meddlesome warrior when the king was a priority.

The landscape they traversed was familiar, and soon she realized they were in her own clan's territory. When she stopped to rest, she could see the outline of Eilean Donan's keep tower. The lure to go home and check on her mother was intense and more than a handful of times, she got up, prepared to do so. But the moment she walked over that bridge, she was certain her father would force her to stay, and perhaps even send Tad out to find the king, along with an army of warriors.

She couldn't risk the enemy knowing they were being followed. And given she had Merida and the sounds of the wee king's voice in her head, she was his only chance.

That, or she was going mad.

Julia was just about to close her eyes for a few minutes respite before they continued on the hard journey, when the snap of a twig sounded behind her. Merida growled—but the ensuing click of a tongue had Julia leaping to her feet, prepared to cut Sir Alistair down where he stood.

A sword in one hand and a dagger in the other, she scanned the trees. Every rustle was a marauder; every light breeze was the breath of her enemy.

"Come out from your hiding place," she demanded. "I know ye're there."

Sir Alistair melted from behind a tree. His jawline shaded with a few days' growth of beard, his hair pulled back tight with a leather strap. Beneath his eyes were shaded purple from lack of sleep, but he was still a welcome sight. Relief flooded her, which of course then only irritated her. Why should she want him here?

Julia looked behind him. Had he walked all this way? Run? "Where is your mount?"

"Back a ways."

Julia frowned and raised her sword, pointing it toward his neck. "Ye wanted to sneak up on me. Ye failed. What took ye so long to make yourself known?"

Merida leaned into his thigh as he patted her head absently. He shrugged.

Julia rolled her eyes and put her sword back in the scabbard at her hip. As much as she would have enjoyed sparring with him, there wasn't the time.

"Ye're not going to kill me now?" he teased.

"Nay."

"Why did ye run off without me?" He leaned against a tree, picking a blade of grass and placing it between his fine lips.

Fine lips? There was something so alluring about the shape of his mouth…

Since when did she care a fig for a man's mouth? Never. Not even her husband for a day. None had given her pause until she'd met Sir Alistair. Wicked rogue.

Julia shook herself from whatever path her thoughts were taking and concentrated on the crease between his brows instead.

"I have a duty to protect the king, Sir Alistair. That duty does not extend to asking ye for permission."

"But I could have joined ye." There was an accusation in his gaze she didn't like.

"So ye have." As much as she tried to concentrate and possibly hear exactly what was going through his mind, his thoughts were shut off to her. Perhaps that was a blessing.

"Good point." He fingered the blade of grass, rolling it with the tip of his fingers before plucking it out of his mouth. "So tell me, Lady Julia, how do ye know where ye're going?"

She wasn't about to tell him about the strange ability that seemed to have taken over her ever since her mother gave her the mission of attending the king, so she nodded toward her dog.

"She's got a strong snout."

Sir Alistair grunted, his eyes perusing her in a way that made her shiver. His gaze lingered on her mouth, before flicking away toward the castle in the distance.

"Is that nae your home?"

"Aye."

"Then why are ye here?" Assessing eyes glided back toward her.

Julia crossed her arms, tapped her foot and jutted out her chin. Whatever it was he hoped to find out, she was not going to divulge anything to him. "I am not traveling for pleasure, in case ye've forgotten."

"But ye could get reinforcements."

"Why are *ye* alone?" she retorted. "Ye, too, could have traveled with reinforcements."

He grinned and took a step closer to her. "Ye're hiding something."

"I barely know ye, I'm certain there are a lot of things I'm hiding."

Another step, and he was crowding her space. She assumed that might be a tactic he often used, taking advantage of his size and hoping to intimidate others. But he didn't realize she'd a horde of cousins and uncles who equaled him in height and breadth, along with a brother, and not one of them ever succeeded in intimidating her with such measures.

Julia laughed then, having figured him out, and finding it to be quite funny. She leaned casually against a tree and shook her head.

"Do ye think I jest?" he asked, pressing his hand to a branch above her head and bending closer.

She could smell him then, and found it odd that in all the days he'd been riding after her, he still managed to maintain a scent that was alluring, and perhaps even a bit intoxicating. Woodsy and masculine, leather and just a hint of spice. She resisted the urge to close her eyes as she breathed him in deep. Och, but his scent alone was a distraction. How unfair. She was certain that she herself was not in the finest of odors. Maybe that would be enough to push him away.

"I think ye dinna realize I am not like every other woman." She sniffed and looked away, pretending indifference.

No luck, he leaned closer still, enough that she could feel his breath on her cheek. "What do ye mean by that?"

"Your tactics." She waved her hands toward his arm planted on the branch, his stance towering above hers. "They will not work. I will not be intimidated by your size and closeness."

"Nay?"

"Nay." She regarded him full on then with her fiercest expression, the one she used on the children at the castle when they ran amuck. The one she used on any Sutherland or Mackenzie warrior who got a little too close.

"Hmmm." His gaze went toward her mouth. "What does intimidate ye?"

"Nothing." Zounds, but the way he was looking at her *did* intimidate her, because right now, if he tried to kiss her, she was certain she'd surrender—and show just how weak she truly was.

"I actually believe that."

"Good." *Thank heavens...*

"So perhaps I need to find a way to distract ye."

Julia's mouth fell open in shock. What the bloody hell was he up to? "From what? Why would ye want to distract me from my mission? Do ye not want the king back? Is that it? Ye're working with the enemy?"

All humor left his face when she said that.

"Now why would ye go and say that?" he growled.

"Because ye're acting suspicious. Because ye're alone. Why is there not an army with ye?"

"Perhaps for the same reason there is not an army with *ye*, when ye and I both know very well ye've one at your disposal a couple of miles away." He nodded toward the tower of the keep jutting from above the tree line.

"All right, so it would appear we both seem suspicious. I can respect that."

"Then ye will tell me what ye're hiding?"

"I hide nothing that ye need be aware of."

He frowned again, and she had the sudden urge to smooth out those lines and press her lips against his just to feel what that was like. *Nay, nay, nay!*

"Then we'll travel together." The tone of his voice left no room for argument.

But Julia was not one to let others tell her what to do. Yet another of her flaws, she supposed.

"That will not be necessary. I work better alone."

"I'm not asking."

"And I'm not agreeing."

"If ye insist on being stubborn about it, I'll just continue to follow ye."

It was on the tip of her tongue to suggest he might not be able to, but threatening the earl's guard was not part of her plan. Besides that, even if she did fight him with everything she had, he was strong, and there was too much risk he might overpower her. Or tie her up, leave her to rot and take Merida to continue the journey.

Before she'd met Sir Alistair, she would not have said it was possible for her beloved hound to betray her, but it would appear this rogue was the exception.

"I am not agreeing, but I will not fight ye on it," she finally said.

A teasing grin covered his lips. "Och, lass, 'tis a good thing ye agreed."

She resisted asking why, but her curiosity got the better of her. "Why is that?"

He tapped her nose and said, "I suppose ye'll never know."

Without thinking, Julia jerked forward and bit the tip of Sir Alistair's finger. Not too hard, but firm enough to sting, at least she hoped.

"If I want ye to touch me, ye'll know it," she hissed.

Alistair's grin widened. "Ye're a feisty one, are nae ye?"

"I've been called worse." She shoved him away from her, and he relented, backing up a few paces.

"No doubt, my lady."

"Go and fetch your horse, else leave me to my rest."

Julia sat down, leaned against a tree and closed her eyes. The moment she heard him move, she peered at him through slitted lids to see that he was doing as she demanded, or at the very least, it seemed that way.

As she drifted in and out of sleep, she heard him return, but still he did not bother her. When she woke, perhaps an hour or so later, he leaned against a tree opposite her, and appeared to be asleep.

Julia stood, stretched and prepared to find a private spot when his voice caught her.

"Ye snore."

"Liar."

He chuckled. "All right, well then, ye talk in your sleep."

"Have I told ye yet to bugger off?"

Alistair opened his eyes and grinned. Why did he have to be so handsome? Have such a teasing manner? Och, but it was both charming and irritating at the same time.

"Stop jesting with me, warrior. We're on a mission, and there is a wee lad scared for his life. Now is not the time for making fun."

At that, the smile fell from his face, and Julia walked straight into the woods with her spine rigid, feeling slightly guilty for having rebuked him. But they had a duty to return the king. They needed to remain on task, and the distractions had to stop.

※

IF ALISTAIR HAD WONDERED WHAT THE OFFSPRING OF A GODDESS and vinegar might be, Lady Julia was the perfect specimen with which to compare.

And what the bloody hell was wrong with him? His eyes lingered on her retreating rear-end, round and lush. The woman was built for pleasure, and yet, she'd obviously been trained as a force to be reckoned with. The way she'd bit his finger...

Hell, he'd been lucky not to spend in his breeches at the touch of her tongue on his skin. He'd also been lucky to still have a finger when she was done. Her reflexes were quick, swifter than he would have guessed.

She was right, he did need to be more serious, and yet all he could do was tease and flirt, like some drunken adolescent ready to bend her over the nearest downed tree and take her for the ride of her life. Then of course, that thought led to her shoving him to the ground and riding him—which was probably much more her style.

Alistair groaned, shifting his sporran to cover the evidence of his desire that now pushed up against his plaid.

Guilt flooded him. The earl had tasked him with finding the king. Alistair had alluded to Lady Julia being a part of the abduction, but after following her for days and discovering that she didn't have the lad, and that she appeared to be tracking them, he'd realized his error.

Along the journey, he'd stopped at a remote inn and paid one of the stable lads to deliver a message to the earl, that read simply and cryptically: *It was nae her—AC,* so that she wouldn't be blamed or hunted down for his mistake.

He was still certain it was Hugh and the nursemaid who had left with the king, but who was the third?

The questions and possibilities were still mulling through his head when Julia returned to camp. Her creamy skin was flushed red, and she avoided meeting his gaze. She shifted with what he could only discern was embarrassment.

"Well, I would leave now," she said abruptly. "Perhaps ye'd like to relieve yourself afore we go?"

At her words, she blushed all the redder, and Alistair could only guess at her train of thought at having mentioned him relieving himself. He knew she'd meant to take a piss, but well, it was almost like she could read his mind... and knew he would have much rather slaked his lust with her writhing beneath him.

5

They traveled in silence the remainder of the day until they came to the coast looking toward the Isle of Skye—far enough away from Eilean Donan to not be noticed.

"They went across," Julia said.

Alistair guessed as much, with the way the hound was looking out toward the sea.

"They had a *birlinn* waiting for them." She glanced down the coast.

"How do ye know?" Alistair bent and touched the deep grooves in the ground where the base of a *birlinn* had been pulled out to the water.

She shrugged, but it didn't matter. He guessed she'd seen exactly what he did, the evidence was there before him. Still, she was holding back.

What was the lass hiding from him? He wished he could crack her open to figure it out, but she was holding steady and not giving anything away.

"We'll have to leave our horses. Steal a *birlinn*." She stroked her mount's mane.

"Or we could swim." Alistair swatted the chilly water.

"Swim?" She gave him a skeptical look.

"Aye. Our horses and your hound can do it. Can ye swim?"

"Of course."

"Let's do it." He shrugged out of his scabbard, slipping it beneath his horse's saddle.

She narrowed her eyes at him but then nodded. "All right." Then she bent to untie her boots, placing them in her satchel, her bare toes curling into the earth. "I dinna want to ruin my boots."

Alistair grinned. "And what about your gown? Ye dinna want to ruin that either."

He expected her to whip out her sword and threaten to cut his ballocks, but she surprised him by nodding. "Aye, ye're right, and it will weigh me down."

Alistair blinked, disbelieving, as she began to take off her weapons and attached them to her saddle so they wouldn't get lost, and then she was undoing the ties of her gown down the side of her ribs. *Mo chreach...*

"Well, sir, are ye nae going to undress?"

"I'll leave my shirt on."

She shrugged, tugging off her gown, loosened something beneath her chemise and tugged out a leather armored bodice. Next came bracers from her arms and thighs. Holy hell... He'd never seen a woman with armor, let alone that much. He found it... incredibly... stimulating.

Armor removed, she stood before him in only a thin chemise, the breeze causing the fabric to cling to the outline of her ravishing figure.

All the blood drained from his body to center in his middle. Bloody hell... It had been a long time since he'd been with a woman. Too afraid of the fairer sex's desire to simply get in his bed to get closer to the earl. For that had happened to him a few times. He didn't want to be at their mercy. So perhaps his desire for this wench was just that he'd been living like a monk for too long.

Or maybe it was that she was everything he could have wanted in a woman, and everything he'd never found.

The more he stared, the narrower her eyes went.

"Avert your eyes, else I think ye didna mean to swim at all, and only convinced me it was so in order to see me undress."

Alistair's throat was too tight to respond, so instead, he turned around and undid the pin of plaid and his belt, tucking them both in his leather satchel, then rolling up his plaid and tying it to the back of his saddle.

By the time he turned around, she'd already waded into the water, and was making sighing noises as she paddled forward.

"What are ye waiting for?" she taunted and started to swim, her hound and horse following. "'Tis not too cold."

Alistair grunted as he stepped into the chilly water. "Quite refreshing," he remarked. As a youth, he'd done a lot more swimming than time allowed for now. Despite their circumstances, he was looking forward to the swim for the exercise, the ability to wash away the grime from his skin, and to hopefully cool his overly heated blood.

They swam across Loch Alsh at a swift pace, and he found himself to be quite impressed with Julia's stamina. But he supposed as a lass growing up at Eilean Donan, surrounded by water on all sides, she might have even made this trek before. Her hound and horse did not seem in the least bit disturbed by the notion of swimming, and even seemed to know their own way, while his horse had at first resisted.

They made it to the other side in just over a half hour, and while he told himself he should avoid looking at her as she exited the water, Alistair could not pull his gaze away. Rivulets of water dripped down her arms and legs, clung to her lashes and made her fiery golden hair darker.

But it was the fabric of her chemise clinging to her curves, the water making the garment nearly transparent, that had him stunned. She could have been standing there naked before him. Her breasts were full, and tipped with tiny, hard pink nipples. Her waist was trim, and her hips rounded into long, firm legs. Alistair swallowed at the sight of flaming red curls nestled between those long legs.

"Have ye had enough?" she asked with a raised brow. "I could continue to stand here for your perusal, turn maybe so ye might paint my buttocks into your brain, or ye could tuck that sword back into your plaid and we could be on our way."

Alistair's face heated. Ballocks, was he blushing? The hellion had just made a comment about his erection. Which could very well have been just as transparent to her as her parts were to him, given he was also wearing a soaked shirt.

Clearing his throat, he tugged his plaid from where he'd tied it to the saddle and laid it out on the ground, making the pleats. He rolled himself into the fabric, belted it in place and tossed the extra flap over his shoulder, pinning it at his shoulder. By the time he was finished, she'd already tied her boots and was plaiting her hair.

God, she was gorgeous. And not because he'd just basically seen her naked. She wasn't the first woman he'd seen. But she was the most stunning. All of her. Body, mind, soul, spirit. Her fiery nature, her fearlessness, the way she sprang headlong into adventure, and dear God, *those breasts...*

"Oh, for the love of all things breathing, Campbell." She sounded irritated, and he couldn't be sure what exactly had her that way. The lass stomped around and shook her head, as though she had heard everything going through his mind. But that was impossible!

"Let us be on our way then, wench," he grumbled.

She marched up to him then, grabbed the front of his wet shirt, and tugged him forward, her lips crushing his with bruising force.

At first, Alistair was too shocked to react, but as her tongue slid into his mouth, his senses came flooding back with a wildness he was going to have a hard time containing.

Lady Julia kissed him like he'd never been kissed before. With passion, with vehemence, yet somehow, it all seemed so innocent. Alistair stroked her back, tucking her closer to him and diving his tongue in deep, wanting to consume all of her. Her breasts crushed to his chest, and he could feel the tempting points of her turgid nipples pressed against him. God, he wanted to nibble them. Torment her as she did him.

Her back arched, and she moaned, as though she too wanted to get closer. If he wasn't careful, they'd end up on the ground, making love right there in the open.

All too quickly, she was pulling away from him, the both of them panting.

"I was hoping that might get some of your lust out of your system, but it seems to only have made ye more... lusty." She eyed him wearily —and with a hunger that simmered in her gaze.

"What?" Alistair said, bemused. "Do ye think that's how it works, lass? Ye kiss a man and he doesna want ye anymore?"

"I had hoped."

"Ye've not done much kissing then."

Her eyelids shuttered down. "And clearly, neither have ye." Her gaze traveled to his middle, where his arousal pressed steel-hard against his plaid.

Och, but that was a shot at his lack of bedding women, wasn't it? Alistair grunted, refusing to let the hellion get to him—even if at that very moment, every part of him very much did not want to forget her.

"There's one thing ye ought to learn about men, lass, and 'tis that ye canna just go around kissing them, thrusting your tongue into their mouths and rubbing your wee lush body all over them, and expect them to walk away. 'Tis not how it works. Ye're liable to wake a sleeping bear, love."

"I'll have ye know, ye're not the first man I've kissed. Nor the first I've bedded. I'm not as naïve about the world as ye might think." Despite the last part of her sentence, the way she shuffled and the uncertainty in her tone had him wondering if she didn't doubt herself.

Her face flamed red, and he had to try very hard not to grab her up and kiss her again. At the same time, he wanted to know just who she'd been bedding. Lassies of her station didn't simply go around bedding men. Was that a boast without the evidence to support it?

Och, she might try to be a woman of the world, experienced in all things, but it was beyond evident that innocence was still a great part of her. Even if she was telling the truth.

As much as he wanted to walk away, maybe even toss her back into Loch Alsh to swim back to her family, at the same time, he wanted to pull her closer. To feel that lush body against his once more.

"Oh, for heaven's sake!" She covered her ears and shook her head. "Will ye just stop?"

"What?"

The lass let out a loud groan, whirled on her heels and stomped away.

Alistair stood there, dumbstruck, now more certain than ever that she could hear his thoughts.

And if that was the case, then she'd heard every lusty, wicked thing he'd contemplated when he looked at her, when he touched her, when her tongue slid seductively over his.

But how was that possible?

Was she just good at reading faces? He'd heard of her mother before. A great warrior. And Lady Julianna de Brus had aligned herself with Ronan Sutherland, another great warrior, and the younger brother of one of the most powerful men in the kingdom. The Sutherlands had fought in all the major battles, right alongside William Wallace and Robert the Bruce, and this lass was descended of these two powerful families. He wouldn't be surprised if she had superior people-reading skills.

Reading minds was far-fetched. Aye, there were plenty of legends and lore about folks who could do so, but those were just stories.

Alistair was a lot more logical than that. At least, he liked to believe so.

***

WALKING AWAY FROM SIR ALISTAIR WAS DIFFICULT, BECAUSE EVERY part of Julia's body wanted to wrap itself around him. To feel those hard, sensual muscles pressed to her frame, to have his lips sliding over hers, his hands stroking her back. Zounds, but her entire body was on fire with a yearning she didn't know what to do with.

She ached for more, feeling like there was an irresistible itch than needed to be scratched and she just couldn't reach it.

What would her mother think? Her clan? To know that she was allowing desires of the flesh to keep her unfocused? That she'd lost the king before she'd ever met him. That in less than a fortnight, she'd completely undone whatever her mother, father and relations had done for Scotland.

Did it matter now that her father and uncles had fought alongside the Bruce and William Wallace for the country's freedom? Did it matter that her mother had been the personal guard of the Bruce for nearly all her life? Nay, none of it mattered when she'd been able to singlehandedly destroy all they'd worked to protect.

Whoever had the king had not just taken him for fun. This was not some whimsical jaunt across the country. They had bad things planned. And it was only the frantic whispers of a little boy in her mind that let her know they'd not yet done the thing she feared worst of all.

These were sobering thoughts. After walking for over an hour in silence, they stopped to rest once more, the grass and heather-covered mountains of Skye rising up all around them.

"Where do ye think they are taking King David?" Alistair asked.

"I canna be certain, but I think they might be going to the Fairy Pools."

"Why?"

"Just a feeling." Her stomach clenched as she stretched out the kinks in her body. A restless energy filled her. A need to run and never stop, until she found the lad safe and sound and returned him to his castle and the regent.

"Do ye often trust your feelings?" Alistair asked.

Julia jutted her chin forward, and reluctantly looked at him. "What do ye mean by that?"

He shrugged. "A warrior's instinct is often right."

She swallowed, trying not to show that what he'd said affected her. "Do ye think me a warrior?"

"Is that not what ye claim to be?"

She nodded. "I just didna think ye took me seriously."

He frowned. "I admit I didna at first, but ye've more than proven yourself."

"Ye've yet to do the same." Julia watched with humor as the man did a double-take, jerking his gaze toward hers.

"Well, I will endeavor to prove myself worthy, my lady."

Julia burst out laughing. "So serious. I jest."

Alistair passed her a wry smile. "Did ye nae say this was no time for jesting?"

Julia turned somber for a moment, nodding. "I did. But I'm learning something along the way, and that is if I remain serious, I doubt myself." She shielded her gaze from his, looking toward her boots and the grass that covered the tips. "Already I've... failed."

Alistair cleared his throat. "Nay. Failing would have been to remain at Dunfermline, or perhaps to have returned to Eilean Donan and refused to leave the walls. Failures refrain from action. Ye but misjudged, and so did I. Which is why together, we'll make sure the king is returned to his throne."

Julia swallowed around the lump that had suddenly formed in her throat. "I appreciate that."

"We make a decent team." He winked, arresting her with that one conspiratorial expression. "For certes no other lass would have swam Loch Alsh with me."

Julia's face heated all the more. Her hair was still slightly damp from that swim, but her chemise had dried and the chill had left her skin. "I'm not like other lasses, Sir Alistair."

"That I know." He winked again. "Ye're better."

6

Julia's instincts about the king being taken to the Fairy Pools were realized a day later. Wee burns trickled in winding paths cut through the earth, the long fingers stemming from the pools themselves. The sound of waterfalls echoed on the wind.

Merida's sniffing grew frantic, and her pace increased as she ran forward and back.

"We're close," Julia said.

Around a bend, they were met in the road by a woman garbed in a flowing, hooded green robe. She stood in the center of the road, unmoving. Eyes on them. Her expression was unreadable. They halted their mounts, both of them stiffening. Merida sniffed around the woman's hem but didn't seem at all disturbed by her presence.

She looked like a priestess, the kind Julia had heard about in stories when she was a child. The kind she knew lived in an abbey nearby. Her mother had taken her there once to pray.

"Come." Her sharp gray eyes met Julia's. "We've been expecting ye."

Alistair sidled his horse closer in a sign of protection. "Who are ye?" he asked.

"I am the Priestess Daria, Sir Alistair Campbell, and I swear no harm will come to ye or Lady Julia."

He stiffened beside her, his leg touching hers sending a jolt through her body. "How did ye know our names?"

The priestess did not answer his question but turned her gaze back to Julia. "Come. We've been expecting ye," she repeated.

"I dinna like this," Alistair said in a low tone.

"Do ye trust me?" Julia met his gaze, touched his hand where it rested on his horse's mane.

"Aye."

"Then let us see what the priestess wants."

Alistair pressed his lips together tightly but nodded all the same.

Without waiting for confirmation, the priestess turned around and walked back up the winding road. The way her robes flowed in rippling green around her ankles made it look like she floated rather than walked.

The impression was mesmerizing, and a lightness centered in Julia's chest. She didn't know why she trusted this woman, but there was something about the voice that she recognized. Perhaps because it was so much like her dream where she was called to the Fairy Pools, the night of the king's abduction. Or maybe it was simply from memory. Perhaps Priestess Daria had been at the abbey when she'd come as a child.

There was a power in the earth, a magical pull that seemed to fill all of Julia's senses. She breathed in deep of the summer air, letting the slight breeze wash over her skin. She felt free here. At peace, as though what she'd come for was soon to be within her grasp.

Oddly enough, the closer they'd gotten to this ancient and magical place on the Isle of Skye, the less Julia had been able to hear Alistair's internal thoughts, but, too, the wee king's frantic thoughts were lessened. Was he asleep? Lethargic? Or was the power she'd been gifted with only temporary?

They kept on their horses, and at another bend in the road, a second priestess joined the first. More of them came after every twist, until six priestesses walked in a line leading toward the pools, the sounds of the falls growing louder, beckoning her.

They passed many smaller pools and trickling burns, crossed over them, and at last came within sight of a larger pool with falls tumbling down a rock face at least a story high from another pool above. The water was a rich blue, turquoise almost at its center.

The priestesses held out their arms, pointing toward the center of the water. "Within the pools is what ye seek."

"Dear God in heaven! The king!" Alistair shouted, leaping from his horse, but suddenly one of the priestess' was by his side, stopping him from jumping into the blue.

"Wait," the priestess ordered, her voice calm and reassuring.

Alistair looked ready to lift the woman off her toes and toss her into the crystalline depths, but then an air of peace came over his face, and he seemed almost to be sleeping with his eyes wide open.

Julia tried not to be disturbed by the sight of him like that, and instead dismounted herself.

"Ye have been marked," the woman said, meeting Julia's gaze. Her eyes were the lightest of blue, almost white, and her hair glowed white like the clouds above.

The mark... on her hip. Julia nodded. What did the priestess know of it? She'd been worried when they swam across the loch that Alistair might have seen it through her wet chemise, but if he did, he did not remark on it.

"Show us," several of the priestesses said, their whispers on the air silky and enchanting.

"What?"

"Show us," Priestess Daria said. "Sir Alistair canna see. He is in a trance. Trust us."

Julia glanced at Alistair, still trying to comprehend the look of serenity in his eyes. Slowly, she lifted the hem of her gown and chemise to show them the mark on her hip. What had once looked like a welt had completely formed into the lines of a dagger, faint but distinct.

"The dagger. She's the one," the priestess said to the others. "Go into the pools, child. There ye will find what has been seeking ye. The heart of Scotland. The one who holds the stone holds the soul of this land, the protector. Beware the contender, for they will try to destroy us all. The safety of the country, the soul of this earth, is in your hands now."

Julia's thoughts raced just as Alistair's had. Was it possible they'd truly come all this way, only to find wee King David's body at the bottom of the pools? What did they mean the heart of Scotland? Was that not the royal bairn?

Not wanting to waste another moment thinking rather than acting, Julia stripped off her weapons, gown, boots, armor and hose and dove into the pools' depths. The water looked warm and inviting, but was crisp and chilly as it washed over her skin, soaking through her chemise. She dove down to the bottom, able to see clearly as she went. She slid her hands over smooth rocks and earth.

What was she searching for? She didn't know. But there was no body—and then suddenly she felt drawn to her left. Swimming that way, something blinked bright in the depths of the pools. What was it?

Kicking her legs, she propelled herself forward, brushed away some of the sand, and saw with a surprise a green gem, the most vibrant emerald she'd ever seen.

An emerald. The moment her fingers brushed the gem, a great jolt burst through her. Shocking enough that she sucked in a lungful of water. With the gem clutched in her hand, she sputtered and kicked her way to the top, trying to force herself not to suck in more water as her body fought her mind in order to cough and expel the water already there. At last, her face burst through the surface and she coughed and coughed, floating on her back until the water was gone and she could suck in great lungfuls of blessed air.

Julia floated toward the edge, completely exhausted, skin tingling and body aching from having nearly drowned.

Alistair pulled her from the water, the priestesses nowhere in sight.

"What the bloody hell were ye doing in there?" he asked.

"What?" Julia looked around, trying to find the hooded women, but they'd disappeared. "Where did they go?"

"Where did who go?" Alistair glared down at her like she was mad.

Julia searched his gaze, trying to decipher if he was jesting with her. He wasn't. 'Twas as if he had no memory whatsoever of the women who'd led them to the pools.

"What's that?" He nodded toward her hand.

Julia lifted the gem, seeing that it was attached to a gold chain. "I... dropped it in the water." She didn't know what compelled her to lie, but it came easily. Without looking at him, she pulled the chain down over her head, tucking the emerald inside her chemise where it rested between her breasts.

Only then did she realize how very naked she must look in only her soaked chemise. Alistair was staring at her the way he had before when they swam across the loch—with intense longing. But there was no time to do as her body wished and return his longing with another bone-jarring kiss, like they'd shared before. So, she pushed to her feet and rushed toward where she'd discarded her clothing and tugged her gown down over her head. This time, she put her armor on over top of it. No sense in hiding it now.

"How did we get here?" Alistair was glancing around the pools as if he'd never seen them before.

"Merida, remember? We chased her here. False alarm I suppose." She rolled her hose up over her calves and slipped into her boots, tying one and then the other before she noticed Alistair was completely silent.

She turned around and saw him staring at the opposite bank of the pools, up a little on the rise where the falls cascaded.

"Not a false alarm," he murmured.

Merida was on all fours, growling, her hackles raised.

Across the pools was a small child, perhaps five summers old, staring at them with fear in his eyes.

"He says give it to him," the boy called out over the tumbling of the water.

"King David," Alistair started to hurry up the rocky rise.

"He says stay back." The wee lad held his hands out and shook his head. "Else he'll gut me." Tears tracked down the child's sweet face. "I dinna want my guts spilled."

"Never," Julia said clearly. "We'll not let him hurt ye." Then she glanced up at the rises that surrounded them, turning in a circle. "Come out and face us, ye cowards!"

Laughter sounded from behind the lad, and then a man appeared, along with a woman, and someone in a hooded black cloak. The man pushed the lad down the rise until they stood on the opposite bank of the pools.

"Hugh," Alistair growled, but Julia couldn't believe her eyes when she saw the woman.

"Lady Melia?" Julia's voice held all the surprise she felt, as well as the betrayal.

The woman across the pond, tall and graceful, smiled in a way that sent a chill down Julia's spine.

"It was ye." Julia's voice broke. This woman who had been a close confidant to her mother for so many years. A dear friend of their family. Slept in their home. Mourned with them. Comforted Julia when her first husband had died. "Ye poisoned my mother… and now ye've taken the king."

How was it possible that none of them had seen this coming before?

Melia shrugged daintily as though they were discussing nothing more important than the weather. "Everyone has to find a way to survive."

"Ye will not survive this," Julia warned, and she meant it. Whatever happened, she would see that Melia was put in her grave.

"Give us the stone." Melia put her hand on the king's shoulder. Both of them held the child still, and Julia could see from a distance that the lad was trembling.

"What stone?" Julia pretended not to know.

"The one ye're hiding between your breasts," Hugh said with a sneer. "Give it to the lady."

"Only in exchange for the king." Julia had to get him back no matter what. No stone was worth the price of his head, even if the priestesses seemed to think the emerald held the soul of Scotland.

"Aye. An exchange," Melia said.

Beside Melia, the man Alistair had called Hugh jerked to face her. "What? That was not part of the plan."

Ah, they had not discussed this before. A rift between the two of them would be to Julia and Alistair's advantage.

Melia lifted her arm daintily, snapped her fingers, and the man in the hooded cloak stepped behind Hugh, who flung around and tried to shove him away. The mammoth of a man reached forward, not fazed in the least by the blows Hugh tossed him, and lifted Hugh a foot off the ground by his head.

With a simple twist, he snapped Hugh's neck and tossed him to the ground as though he were simply discarding garbage.

"Such a waste," Melia said to the man's body. "I really did enjoy our friendship."

Beside her, King David burst into tears and Julia's heart lurched. The child had been through more than anyone should endure in a lifetime in just a few short weeks.

Julia pulled the necklace from her bodice, but not from around her neck. "Is this what ye're looking for?"

That got the vile woman's attention back. "Aye, indeed it is." Melia's eyes glittered with greed. "Let me guess, ye've got a mark on your right hip?"

Julia narrowed her eyes. "Nay."

Melia's smile faltered. "Interesting," she mused.

"Do *ye*?" If she could keep Melia talking as she inched slowly around the pools, maybe she could distract her enough that Alistair could sneak around the opposite side. Wishful thinking, probably, but it couldn't hurt.

"I do. And if ye dinna, then it means I am the rightful owner of that gem. The priestesses visited ye, did they not?"

"What concern is it of yours?"

"The fate of Scotland, of course." Melia grabbed hold of the bairn king's shoulder and yanked him closer to her. "His life."

"I will give it to ye, for the him," Julia rushed, keeping her gaze steadily on Melia and praying hard the woman didn't snap her fingers for the ogre to do to the lad what he'd done to Hugh.

"Good choice." Melia snapped her fingers at her behemoth, who started to trudge around the pools. "Get her little sheepdog."

Well, better that he was headed toward Alistair than anywhere near the boy.

"I said I would exchange the gem for the king, not that your ogre could come get the gem," Julia warned. "Bring King David to us. Or let me come get him."

Melia shrugged. "Well, if ye want to fight about it, send your own ogre against mine."

Julia flicked her gaze toward Alistair, who nodded once and then marched solidly toward the behemoth. With the two of them occupied, she could cross to the lad and get him to safety. Melia was not protected by her henchman anymore, but that didn't matter, clearly. Somehow, she'd been able to poison the guards and her mother. In all the days she'd been at Eilean Donan, she'd only ever watched Lady Sutherland and Julia train, never participated. But clearly, she'd been a force to be reckoned with. Julia had to be ready.

The emerald started to glow and grew warm. A sudden jolt of power grabbed hold of her from inside, seeming to have been beckoned by the gem. The man who barreled down on Alistair let out a frightening battle cry. But he did not speak—it was his thoughts. And everything he wanted to do, every move he was going to make was revealed to her.

"Duck left," Julia shouted.

Alistair didn't understand her at first, and just barely missed the blow to his head from the wastrel.

"Right!"

Alistair picked up on what she meant now, moving to the right, ducking beneath the henchman's arm, spinning, and landing his own blow on the ogre's back. A very impressive maneuver given his own brawny size.

"Pivot!" Julia continued to call out orders, and Alistair was definitely in the lead.

Then she noted that on the opposite bank, Melia was starting to retreat with the lad.

"Oh, nay, ye will not," Julia grumbled. She charged across the opposite side of the pools, confident Alistair could hold his own, and so could she.

Melia took notice of her coming—and pulled a small crossbow from inside her sleeve. So small, Julia had never seen the like.

"Good night," Melia said, pulling back the string.

"Nay!" Julia dodged, but not quick enough. A pinch sank into her thigh, and she grappled for it. A small dart jutted from her leg, like the ones that had been in the warriors on the wall. Searing pain came from the connection point, and then her leg buckled as the muscles went numb. She caught herself, kneeling, and trying to push up, but it seemed like her movements were slow and uncoordinated. No matter how much she thought of pushing herself up, her limbs refused to cooperate.

Glancing up, she met the wee lad's gaze and screamed, "Run!" At least her words still worked, even if it was an effort to push them out.

He was quick to do her bidding, but he ran toward the ogre and Alistair. Julia opened her mouth to tell him to run the other way, to warn Alistair, but her throat was tight and no words came out. Whatever poison had been in the dart was already working its way through her veins.

She prayed that Alistair took out the ogre before the lad reached him. Prayed that the priestesses could emerge from wherever they'd disappeared to and come protect the king.

Apologized—for once more, she had failed them all.

Melia reached her side as Julia fell fully to the ground. She didn't speak, but that didn't matter, because Julia could hear her thoughts. And as the vile witch ripped the gold chain from around Julia's neck, she let slip where she planned to go next.

7

"Wake, damn ye!" Alistair shook Julia's shoulders once more.

Her body was limp, and her head hung back on her neck as though no bones or muscles had ever had the power to hold it upright.

His heart was pounding, threatening to crack his ribs. It had been at least an hour since he'd seen her fall. With one blow, he'd knocked the bitch's henchman into the Fairy Pools. The man had sputtered, kicked, flailed, and then fallen under. He couldn't swim it was clear. The behemoth had yet to come out of it—meaning he likely wouldn't.

King David had leapt into Alistair's arms and he hadn't let go since. Alistair didn't blame the whelp. He'd been through a hell of a time of it. Though he didn't look to have been beaten or starved since he was taken, he was shaken, and had dark circles under his eyes from lack of sleep.

Alistair had seen Melia race away, and he would have gone after her, but leaving Julia in the state she was in, and the king to his own defenses, was not a plan he could be proud of. So off that wretched, vile villainess had run.

"Her leg," the king had said. "A dart."

Alistair had plucked the poison dart from Julia's leg, sniffing the metal shaft and wrenching away in disgust. Whatever Melia used to poison Julia had been enough to make her sleep, but not to kill her. Thank God, a small favor he was grateful for.

"Nurse did that to the men, too," the king explained. His young, concerned gaze rested on Julia. "Will she wake?"

Alistair nodded, not wanting to tell the lad how he feared the opposite could be true.

She was so lifeless, pale, her dark lashes a stark contrast to the milk of her cheeks. Her hand was limp and when he squeezed it, he strained to feel her squeeze back, but there was nothing.

The king scooted enough away from Alistair to lean over Julia, touching her cheek. "She is bonny. I saw her in a dream."

"Ye have met her before?" Alistair figured they must have met at some point, with Julia's mother being sister to the king.

"Nay, just in my dream."

Alistair frowned. A dream? Was Julia inside everyone's heads? Impossible. And how serious could he take the words of a lad?

The king sat back on his heels and plucked at the blades of grass beside him. Alistair was grateful the lad seemed for the moment to be more distracted and less disturbed.

Just then, Julia's eyelashes twitched, and her lids fluttered open. She stared up at Alistair in confusion, then bolted upright so fast she hit him square in the forehead, falling back down.

"Och, why did ye hit me?" she asked.

Alistair raised a brow and wiped at his painful forehead. The lass had a habit of slamming into him and then wondering why he'd attacked her... He might have laughed if he'd not just been worried about her dying. "Do ye remember what happened?" he asked.

"She shot me." Julia jerked upright again, but this time he was able to get out her way in time. "Where is the king—"

"I am here, my lady," the wee lad said, taking Julia's hand in his. He brought it to his lips and kissed her knuckles. "A pleasure to make your acquaintance."

The move was charming and adorable.

Forgetting the pretense of him being a royal, Julia grabbed him up in her arms and squeezed him to her. "Thank God she didna take ye away."

"Thank ye, my lady, and Sir Alistair for rescuing me. Can I go home now?"

Julia nodded with a laugh, her eyes meeting Alistair's. The relief he saw in their depths made his own heartbeat slow.

"We did it," she murmured.

"Aye." He stood and held out his hand, pulling her to her feet. She wobbled slightly, and he slipped his arm around her waist to hold her steady.

"I need water." Julia licked at her dry lips.

"I've some on my horse."

"The pools will do." She moved to kneel and sip, but Alistair stopped her.

"I wouldna," Alistair warned. "Our friend is in there."

"Friend?" She passed him a quizzical look.

"The monk."

"Oh." She eyed the king. "Would ye like to go for a horse ride?"

"Can I ride on my own?" The lad's face split into a wide grin and he puffed his chest.

"We've only two horses," Julia said.

"Ye ride with him, and I'll ride on my own. I'm quite skilled." King David knelt and stroked his tiny hands over Merida's head. "Can I keep her?"

"How about we let ye ride on your own horse, and I get to keep my dog?" Julia said with a laugh.

The king smiled brightly. "All right. I suppose I can agree to that."

Alistair lifted the lad onto Julia's horse, and then took her by the hand. She was trembling slightly, the effects of the poison no doubt.

"'Tis probably best if I ride with ye." She gave a nervous smile. "I'm afraid I'd be no good with the reins."

"It'd be my pleasure to care for ye, lass." Alistair resisted the urge to pull her to him, to thrust his hands through her still damp hair and breathe in her alluring scent.

"I am grateful."

Alistair lifted her onto the horse, forcing himself to ignore the way her curves felt beneath his hands. He swung up behind her, whistled to her hound and then directed the king to guide the mount beside him.

"We must go to Eilean Donan," Julia said, a tremor racking her body. "Melia is headed there. And my mother…"

"How do ye know?" He reached for the water skin. "Drink."

"I heard her." Julia tipped the skin back and drank deeply, gulping.

Alistair nodded. "Ye can hear people's thoughts." He tensed when she nodded back. Aye, he'd been able to surmise as much, even if he'd been fighting it for days. But having her confess that it was indeed true affected him more than he realized it would. He wasn't sure why, but he felt… betrayed. "Why did ye not tell me?"

"It is new," she said softly. "I had hoped it would go away."

"New? How new?"

She shuddered again, and he tucked her closer against him.

"I started to hear some things before I came to Dunfermline. Just whispers, and then they grew stronger."

"Can ye hear me?"

She shook her head.

"Ye lie."

"Nay."

Alistair gritted his teeth.

"When we arrive at Eilean Donan, I will have my father send his army with ye to Dunfermline with the king," she said, her voice resigned.

"And ye will accompany me."

She shook her head. "Nay. I have proven I am not cut out for the life my mother so nobly led."

"What are ye talking about?"

"I lost the king at Dunfermline within hours of arriving, and I could have lost him again by the pools when Melia shot me." She touched her neck. "I lost the gem the priestesses gave to me for safekeeping. I have destroyed Scotland."

Alistair decided that whatever poison had been on the dart still flowed in her veins, for she wasn't making much sense. "Sleep now, I'll wake ye when we stop to rest."

"If I sleep… I canna protect the king."

"Let me help." But he needn't have argued, for she was already softly snoring in his arms.

Alistair listened to the wee king chatter as they rode for several hours. Even when they stopped, and he laid Julia, still asleep, on the soft grass, the lad continued to talk about everything. The water, the clouds, the dog, his father, the castle, an insect. The lad was a never-ending stream of words.

Merida curled up beside her mistress, resting her head on the lass' chest and moaning woefully. Even in her sleep, Julia wanted to care for the animal. She lifted a limp hand and pressed it to the back of the dog's soft neck.

Alistair wanted to be angry that she'd lied to him about hearing his thoughts—even if she admitted to hearing others. But he was finding it hard to hold that grudge. He was finding it hard to think anything but good things about her. She might see herself as a failure, but he saw her as a great heroine. Without her, he wasn't sure they would have found the king. He just had to convince her of that somehow.

WHEN JULIA AWOKE, THEY WERE NEAR THE SHORE OF LOCH ALSH. The sky was gray and hazy with the setting sun.

"How long did I sleep?" She pushed up on an elbow and glanced around at the makeshift camp Alistair had prepared for them.

Alistair grinned. "Welcome back. Ye've slept for a few hours. How do ye feel?"

Thank goodness it wasn't longer. Even still, a few hours was more time they didn't have. "Much better now." She glanced at King David. He looked a lot less weary, and the dark circles beneath his eyes were gone. Alistair had been taking good care of the boy.

"Good, ye look better as well. The coloring has returned to your face." Alistair smiled at her kindly.

King David grinned from ear to ear and launched himself into her lap. "Ye're awake! My protector!"

She wanted to correct him, but the smile on his face was too precious, so instead she ruffled his hair. "I'm glad to see ye're well, Your Highness."

The lad giggled.

"We'll rest here for the night," Alistair said, "then figure out a way to cross in the morning."

Julia nodded and sat up a little straighter, setting the king down beside her.

"Are ye hungry?" the wee lad asked.

"Famished." Her belly rumbled in reply, and the king laughed.

"Did ye hear that?" he asked her, as though she might not have.

Julia tickled him. "Better feed me, else I grow a taste for royal bones!"

"Hurry, Sir Alistair! Feed her!"

Alistair passed her a chunk of jerky and a bannock cake. "I regret we've nothing tastier."

"This will do just fine." She bit into the jerky, sighing at finally having something to eat. The mirth left her and she gave Alistair a sober look. "Has there been any sign of Melia?"

"None that we have seen, nor your hound."

Julia hoped she'd heard the woman's thoughts correctly, hoped that she was still headed to Eilean Donan, where she'd been headed before. Julia had lied when she'd told Alistair that she couldn't hear *his* thoughts. And she felt extremely guilty for deceiving him. She should tell him the truth. Should try to figure out a way to block his thoughts from her own.

"I have a confession," she said, after they tucked the king into a warm plaid for the night with Merida curled by his side.

"Aye?"

"I lied." She settled on the plaid beside Alistair, legs crossed and leaning back on her elbows.

Alistair, who had been sitting in a similar position, rolled to his side, also propped on his elbow, and gazed intently into her eyes. "I know."

She let out a sigh. "How?"

"Ye might be able to read thoughts, but I can read your body language."

"I might have guessed."

Alistair shrugged. "'Tis no matter."

"Well, in any case, I owe ye my thanks. As soon as we arrive and the king has had a chance to rest, ye're welcome to go about your way."

"I canna. We are a team, ye and I. I canna imagine being without ye. Ye've grown on me." His green eyes slid toward hers and she felt herself blushing.

It was an effort to block his thoughts, but one she was learning to master quicker than she supposed.

"Not because I can tell ye which way to duck or swing?" she teased.

He grinned, emotion in the depths of his gaze that touched her deep in her heart. "Nay, love. Though I now understand why ye blushed every time I thought of your lovely breasts."

Julia playfully slapped him on the arm. "Ye're incorrigible."

"'Haps, but I canna tell a lie. They really are lovely."

With that, he placed a hand on her waist, and tugged her close. When he kissed her this time, there was nothing of the biting urgency of before, but it was still filled with an intense passion. A hunger that quivered and trembled beneath the surface, trying to break free, but held back by chains.

Warmth filled her, wrapped around her at the touch of his lips and the enfolding of his embrace. Julia entwined her arms around his neck and scooted closer, her hip touching his. Then he was pushing her down to the plaid, his body half covering hers as his tongue took possession of her mouth.

She sighed against him, her fingers tugging at the wild, dark locks that had come free from the confines of the leather strap he tied them with each morning. So soft against her skin. She massaged his scalp, lifting her knee to rest it against his, slowly opening herself up to him more than she knew she should.

Everything about kissing him felt good. Nay, not just good, incredible. Fascinating. Enchanting. She wanted more of everything. Julia matched the stroking of his tongue with her own, crushed her breasts to his chest, and marveled at the tingly tightness of her nipples and the sparks of pleasure that were firing between her legs.

Alistair groaned against her mouth, the vibration sending a jolt of lust racing in her veins. To make it all the more potent, she could hear everything he was thinking.

Delicious.

So hot, warm, supple.

God, I want to part her legs and put my cock—

Julia gasped, arching her back, wanting him to put it wherever he was about to think of before the desire for him to do so knocked his thoughts from her brain. Nay, she couldn't invade his thoughts, had to control it, even as she felt herself swiftly unraveling.

"Wait," she murmured. "We canna." Och, but they were the ugliest words she'd ever uttered, because she very much wanted him, all of him.

"I know," he groaned, stilling above her.

Their chests pressed together, hearts pounding in unison. She flattened her hand on his chest, wanting to dig her fingers into the sinew, to stroke up to his shoulders and pull him down against her again. To say the hell with it, and let him have her.

Alistair tugged her lip between his teeth, his eyes looking into hers, with the dusky light darkening them from green to black. Then he sighed as he rested his forehead against hers, his breaths coming heavy and in tune with her own. She wanted so badly to be closer, to be one with him, but given their young charge slept just a few feet away, and that Alistair's kisses had already distracted her enough, Julia knew that would be a bad idea.

"This is not the end," he murmured.

"I hope not." She bit her lip, feeling slightly self-conscious at having just confessed as much. Her gaze slid to the safety of his shoulder rather than revealing all the emotion she felt through her eyes.

"I meant more than just kisses, love."

Slowly, she shifted her eyes back to his, allowing him in. "Aye. I want ye."

"More than that."

Her mind raced with the jumbled thoughts of her own and his crashing, and the emotions she felt that pummeled her and made it hard to quiet the sounds. "Tell me. Tell me out loud."

"I want ye for my own. Together, we'll fight off everyone who would try to destroy wee King David's life. Anyone. And every night, we'll finish the day together. As man and wife."

"Married..." she mused. The idea... Fear and excitement all at once. When she'd married before it had been about an alliance between the Mackenzies and Sutherlands. There had been no love in it. Julia had been determined to serve her family. But when he'd died... she'd decided to never marry again—unless she could have what her parents had. Love. Was that something she could have with Alistair?

"Aye." Emotion made them both tense, as words that were on the tips of their tongues were held back for fear of rejection. "Do ye wish to marry me?"

Julia paused, marveling at the sensation of love that swirled in her gut. When had that happened? Was it when he'd first sparred with her in Moray's chamber? When he'd followed her? Teased her? Kissed her? Or when she'd feared for his life at the pools? Or when he'd lovingly cared for her after the dart left her mindless for days? Probably all of it.

"Verra much. I want to marry ye."

She curled up beside him, her gaze toward the loch and the lights she could see shining in the distance from the tower of Eilean Donan. Zounds, but she hoped they arrived in time. They'd already lost enough light that Melia could have arrived and done the damage she'd set out to do in the beginning.

Hoped they could save her mother and toss Melia into a deep dark hole.

Hoped that a life with Alistair truly was within her reach.

8

They walked along the shore, leading the horses to keep them rested for their swim, rather than riding them. With a young charge in tow, Julia and Alistair had determined that finding the shallowest place to cross would be the least dangerous. Once they found a shallow crossing, the plan was to put the king up on the horse while she and Alistair swam across.

Dew soaked the tips of their boots and the hem of Julia's gown. The wee king walked stoically beside them, as all royals were taught from birth, but whenever he saw a bird or a pretty flower, he stopped to admire them, the way any child would. Watching him made Julia smile, and it made her sad at the same time. He was an innocent still, so young and impressionable. Thank goodness Moray was regent, and there were plenty of good people, including the Queen Mother, to support King David, but if he were to fall prey to the wrong hands, or a more sinister regent, what then? All his beliefs since the day of his father's passing were going to be skewed depending on the views of those who cared for him.

"Is that a *birlinn*?" Julia asked, shielding the sun from her eyes so she could get a better look.

Ahead, she spied what could have been a large fallen tree, or a small boat, maybe a canoe, hard to tell with the rising sun glinting off the water and making the world seem so bright, and all around the shapes of things became black blobs of haziness.

Alistair, too, shielded his eyes. "Aye, I think so. A canoe mayhap."

Julia glanced at him, urgency flooding her veins. "We need to take it."

"Aye." Lifting the king up onto a horse, they hurried forward to find that a small, roughly made fishing canoe had indeed been left by its owner, not too long ago. Though it had been flipped upside down to keep it from floating away if the tide came in, the bottom surface was still slick with loch water, as though they'd only just gone.

Julia scanned the shore, rises and any place a man might hide, and found nothing but the gently waving grasses and trees. She tried to close her mind off to every sound, straining to hear any whisper of a thought from someone hiding out there, but came back with nothing.

"We need to hurry, else they come back," Alistair warned. "Unless ye can hear…"

Julia shot him a look. "I canna. And ye need to keep that to yourself, sir," she flicked her gaze toward the king, "else the whole world will think ye and I have both gone mad."

"Understood, my lady." He winked at her, and they shared a brief smile before he was telling the king their plan.

"I love boat rides," the king said.

"And we hope this one doesna disappoint, Your Highness," Julia said.

Together, she and Alistair flipped the boat right side up and pushed it toward the water.

Before it was too deep, they lifted the king inside, and Julia joined him, followed by Merida, who had grown quite fond of the lad. Having him ride in the boat was safer than on top of a swimming horse, and would keep them all mostly dry.

Julia kept hold of the horses' reins, leading them into the water as Alistair pushed the boat. As soon as it was drifting, he climbed in and picked up the oars, dipping them into the loch and propelling them across the shore. Little sprinkles of water danced on Julia's hand where she held it against the rim of the boat. Mist burned off the loch's surface with the heat of the sun.

"Do ye think I could get a hound like Merida?" the king asked, his arm wrapped around the dog who so very much enjoyed the attention.

"I do." Julia grinned and nodded toward the towers of Eilean Donan in the distance. "Our clan breeds her kind, and that is where we're headed. We'll see if there is a litter, or one coming soon."

"I would like that." The king beamed and buried his face in Merida's neck.

"'Twould be an honor for ye to have one, Your Highness." Julia tossed Merida a hunk of jerky she'd been saving for her. The hound was being so incredibly patient with the wee lad, almost as if she knew just how important he was.

The king grinned from ear to ear, and nodded, his hand resting on Merida's head, who looked equally proud to have served her king as Julia was in regaining him from the hands of a madwoman.

Julia just prayed they got to the castle in time. No one at Eilean Donan knew of Melia's treachery. She would be admitted without question and given access to Lady Sutherland, possibly—and most likely—alone. Julia hoped it wasn't too much to believe that her mother had fully recovered in the time that Julia had been gone from their holding.

Alistair met her eyes from where he sat on the opposite end of the small boat. He might not have the ability to read minds as she did, but he definitely was adept at reading *her*. She could tell by the expression of concern on his face he must have known what she was thinking.

"When we arrive," she said, "will ye take the king to the hound hold? I'll send my brother Tad down to help."

Alistair nodded, understanding that she wanted the king to be protected and in a place where Melia would never look. He'd be surrounded by guards, both human and hound alike, and once her brother was with Alistair, the king's guard could explain what had happened, and they could quietly alert the rest of the castle to the threat while Julia went in search of her mother.

"Aye." He winked at the king. "What will ye name your new hound?"

"Well, it depends." The lad tapped his chin. "If 'tis a male, I will name him for my father, Robert, and if 'tis a female, I shall name him after my mother, Elizabeth."

Julia couldn't help but grin at the honor the lad was bestowing on a beast, and suppress a chuckle at what his mother might think of a hound being named after her.

Suddenly, the king looked at her, his eyes filled with both curiosity and sorrow. "Do ye miss your father?" he asked.

Julia startled. The lad had lost his father so young, he must have thought all fathers died when children were little.

"Ye will meet him shortly. I missed him while I was away."

"He yet lives?" The king's eyes widened. "He must be verra old."

Julia bit her lip to keep from laughing and Alistair snorted trying to hold his in.

By the time they reached the shore, Sutherland and Mackenzie warriors, the clans to which the castle was held, lined the shore.

"Sister?" Tad stood in the center of the line, and as soon as he'd uttered the word, the men stood down. Her brother was tall, though not as tall as her father, and wide, full of muscle. His ginger-colored hair was long, and he had a beard that she often grabbed hold of and tugged to tease him at the length. He had eyes the color of tree bark, that were serious one minute and dancing with merriment the next. He reached for her, pulling her into his embrace, and she couldn't help but sink into him for just a second.

Her brother eyed Alistair cautiously, and, a little more curiously, his gaze fell to the boy.

"What's going on?" Tad had a look on his face that said he didn't like what he saw, found it extremely suspicious.

And that expression matched his thoughts. *She's had a bairn, in secret, and with this great oaf.*

Julia said nothing until they'd disembarked the boat. Alistair climbed out first, handing her down, and then lifting the king, who slipped his hand into hers. As they approached the shore, Alistair was immediately surrounded by Sutherland warriors. She kept her hands on the king's shoulders, showing the men that the lad had her protection. Merida nipped at the ankles of a few men who crowded a little too close to Alistair. There was time to tell them all later that Alistair would be joining their clan as her husband, but now there were more pressing matters.

"Brother, we've a special guest." She looked down at the boy, who stared her brother full in the face.

"I'm the King of Scotland, King David II, and ye are my subject."

Tad raised a brow, looked taken aback, but quickly regained his composure. The men all started to bow, but Julia stopped them.

"Dinna." Her tone was sharp, and they quickly stood straight. She glanced up at the castle, unable to see who might be watching. "We must keep his identity secret for the time. All of ye," she said staring around at the warriors, "hold your tongues. Has Lady Melia returned?"

"Aye, she's with mother. Lovely of her to pay a call after hearing of mother's illness."

Julia shook her head frantically, dread filling her belly. She had to get to her mother—now. "Nay, she is the one who poisoned mother!"

Tad started to whirl around. But Julia grabbed his arm.

"Take the king with Sir Alistair, his guard, to the hound hold. Take the men with ye. Send a messenger to Da if ye must. I will deal with Melia."

Tad looked ready to argue, but Julia left him no choice when she thrust the boy his way. "Go."

Julia took off at a run, and she was slightly surprised to see that Merida was right beside her. She ran across the bridge, feeling sluggish as she went, as though the length of the bridge only grew longer the faster she tried to run. Her mind was playing tricks on her, she knew, but still it was frustrating.

At last she reached the small bailey, ducked through the wide great oak doors, too panicked to acknowledge the men on the ramparts who called down a greeting, and ran up the stairs, past several startled warriors. Into the barracks she flew, and then up another flight of stairs to the great hall.

Her father stood with several men before the hearth, startled to see her. He took in her stricken look, and before she could even ask where her mother was, he was pointing toward the winding staircase.

"Upstairs," he called, and hurried toward her as Julia slipped into the alcove that led up to the laird's chamber.

The door was barred; the handle jiggled worthlessly in her hand. Beyond the door there were the sounds of scuffling and grunting, as though two people struggled.

Oh, dear God, her mother... They were fighting! She could hear her mother asking *why*, begging Melia to just sit and talk, and wasn't certain if it was aloud or in her head.

Julia imagined her mother, weakened from Melia's previous attempt on her life, struggling to sit up. Searching for something, anything, that she could use as a weapon. Finding only a cup full of tisane and a candlestick. Julia prayed this was only in her mind, and that her mother could somehow reach a deadlier weapon.

"Melia! Mama! Open the door." Julia pounded against the wood with the flat of her hand while she kicked at the bottom, then moved back to kick at the handle, hoping to somehow gain enough force to break the bar that blocked her out.

There was a thud, and soft murmurs, but still neither woman acknowledged her. She pounded some more, felt the touch of her father's hand on her shoulder as he resumed her punishment on the wood—and then they both paused when the sickeningly sweet voice of the murderess called through the door.

"Wouldna ye like that, wee princess? Say goodbye to Mama."

Melia's laughter oozed through the timber panels. The sound was neither jovial, nor evil, but rather eerily singsong, as though Melia were finding great joy in whatever she was doing beyond the barrier.

"Dinna touch her! Open this door!"

9

Within two slams of his body against the door, Ronan Sutherland splintered the door and heaved himself through the shattered frame with Julia, a few warriors on their heels.

They both stilled immediately, when instinct bade them fight. Julia's heart pounded so loudly, the whooshing in her ears drowned out all other noise.

Her mother lay on the floor before the hearth in nothing but a nightrail. Blood dripped from a gash on her forehead, and she looked to be asleep. Pale and frail.

Worse still, Melia stood over her mother, a sword drawn and held at the back of Lady Sutherland's neck, and a grin of satisfaction on the vile bitch's face. The emerald necklace she'd stolen from Julia glowed bright green against the fabric of her gown, settling between her breasts. Julia could feel the gem's power pulling her in closer, as though the stone desired her above Melia, who was clearly the anti-protector.

But the only way to get it off that woman's body was if she were dead. And Julia couldn't kill her until she got her away from her mother.

If the gem had gifted Julia with a special heightened sense—like hearing others' thoughts—and she was supposed to be the protector of Scotland, what power had been gifted to Melia as a contender? Was Melia able to read thoughts too?

As if in answer to her question, Melia lifted the hand that did not hold the sword, and showed she was holding the tiny crossbow that she'd used on Julia before. Though Julia wore her armor, there were plenty of places where she was not covered, and if the miniature crossbow was powerful enough, the poisoned darts could pierce through the leather she wore.

"When I got the call from the stone, I suddenly could make poison from anything. And I figured out how to make this quaint delivery weapon." Melia gazed upon her tiny bow with pride, adding a fresh dart. "It really has helped me tremendously. And your dear mama was so kind as to help me test it out at first. I must say, I am underwhelmed with *your* power, Lady Julia."

"Ye dinna know what power I possess." Julia could barely speak through her clenched teeth. Beside her, her father was edging closer to her mother. The men at their backs stood rigid, ready to take on Melia when called.

"Does it matter? I've defeated ye more than once now."

Julia was not interested in bantering, and clearly neither was her father. He started to charge Melia but with one pluck of her finger, a dart was flying his way.

One of the guards jumped in front of the dart, and Julia screamed. The dart landed in the warrior's chest. He crumpled to the ground, eyes closed, and Julia prayed it only left him sleeping for a short time like it had done to her.

"Anyone else care to give my little friend a try?" Melia asked, waving it around?

Now was the time to distract Melia from her desire to kill Lady Sutherland.

"Give me the necklace." Julia held out her hand and stalked forward. The power of the gem, and the bond she herself had to it, sent a wave of fire up her arm. "I will not let ye destroy this country or take another life."

At Julia's advancement, and perhaps also feeling the stone heat,

Melia was distracted enough to remove the sword from Lady Sutherland's neck. "Too late. I hold its heart in my hand. And the king, wherever ye've stashed him, will go up in flames."

"Ye'd kill a young lad?"

"Is he truly a lad? Or a vessel? A symbol of all that is wrong in this country." Melia shook her head. "The king should have married *me* when he had the chance. That little whelp could have been *my* child. *I* could have been regent."

Julia narrowed her eyes, not understanding at all what Melia was talking about. Had she been a lover of Robert the Bruce, or had she only wished she was?

Julia was more inclined to believe Melia had high aspirations that never would have come to fruition. There was a madness about her eyes Julia was surprised to have never seen before.

"Give me the necklace." Julia took another step forward. Behind her, her father's racing thoughts suddenly stilled, and she hoped it was because he'd seen that the sword was no longer pressed to her mother's neck, but the tip had been put onto the wooden floor beside her. "Allow my father to go to my mother."

"Are ye jesting? Ye simply dinna understand the situation," Melia said, rolling her eyes and lifting the sword once more. "My, ye might be brave, but ye're dumber than the wood beneath our feet."

As the fiery pull of the stone grew in heat in Julia's body, a searing pain shot across her forehead. She gripped her temples and cried out. With a vengeance, she could hear all of Melia's thoughts, loud and clear.

I will kill that bitch. And her mother. I will kill them all.

Nay! Julia shouted in her head.

Melia grimaced, then groaned across from her, dropping the sword as she grabbed for her own head. She fell to her knees.

Through the pain in her skull, Julia charged forward, coming to a sudden halt when Melia lifted the crossbow and pointed a fresh dart at Julia's mother, who still lay unconscious by the hearth. Ronan Sutherland slid across the floor, blocking her mother from Melia's vision, planting his own body in the path of her poisoned dart.

"Nay!" Julia ground out, hands fisted at her side. "Put it down." She enunciated each word slowly.

Melia suddenly dropped the bow. And stared at the discarded weapon in horror, then back at Julia.

"Ye...Ye..." the woman stammered.

But Julia still didn't understand exactly what was happening. Had *she* done that? Had she been able to control Melia somehow? Force her to put the weapon down?

There was only one way to find out. Julia concentrated all of her energy on Melia. "Give me the necklace."

Melia reached up and yanked the gold chain from around her own neck and held it out to Julia. The look of outrage on her face grew more grotesque and she sputtered, spewing out vile curses.

Dear God in heaven... Julia *was* controlling Melia with her mind.

Ignoring the horrible things Melia was saying to her, Julia continued her demands. "Drop it and sit on the bed."

Melia did exactly as Julia said, and behind her, the gasps from the warriors and her father echoed in the room. They had no idea of the powers Julia had been gifted, and probably wondered what in bloody hell was going on.

Julia picked up the emerald and tucked the gem and broken chain into the bracer at her wrist, feeling comforted by the warmth of the stone.

The pain in her head had not receded, and a warm trickle of blood fell from her ear at the same time she saw it mirrored on Melia's own skin. Whatever power she had over Melia's thoughts and impulses was causing them both to bleed.

The urge to pummel the woman was great, but that would not satisfy Julia. If anything, it would only cheapen what should be a victorious moment. Julia picked up the tiny crossbow and tossed it into the fire. The moment the poison hit the flames, it sparked a vibrant purple and then was gone. Melia's shouts of outrage could have toppled the stone walls.

"Untie the bed curtain," Julia ordered.

Despite her mouth continuing to spew venom, Melia did as she was told.

"Hold still." Julia wrenched Melia from her seated position, using the ties from her mother's curtain on her bed to bind her wrists.

Cradling his wife in his arms, Ronan was calling for a healer. Julia was relieved to know that her mother was not dead.

"Ye will be hanged for this," Ronan shouted.

Julia met Melia's eyes, and the woman smiled, her gaze never leaving her. "Ye can kill me, but as long as there is a protector, there will be someone *like* me. That gem will not belong to ye forever. The king will fall. The country will be ruined, and all will know ye had the power to stop them—and failed!"

Melia's words caused Julia to falter. Failure was her biggest fear. But she'd proven herself over the past few days, shown that she had what it took to uphold the auspicious position she'd been given. With Alistair's help, she'd been able to save the king. And for now, Scotland would be safe.

"I dinna think we will kill ye," Julia said softly. "For I'd rather ye spent the rest of your days, knowing that I was victorious. That the country thrived, and the king lived long into his years, while ye rotted away in a cell as nothing and nobody."

Angry tears filled Melia's reddened eyes. If she'd not been so filled with hate, she might have been beautiful. Where had all the hatred come from?

"Take her to the dungeon." Julia turned away from the woman, handing her off to one of the guards.

She went to her mother's side, where her father bent over her limp body, whispering against her ear.

As soon as Melia and the guards had gone, her father asked, "How did ye know?"

Julia fiddled with the chain falling loose of her arm bracer. "She told me. The woman had abducted the king, and when we found her at the Fairy Pools, she told me she planned to come here and finish what she'd started with Mama. I came as soon as I could. I wish I'd been here sooner."

"The king?" Her father straightened, her mother still in his arms.

Julia nodded. "He is here. With the hounds. He wants one."

"We've just had a litter, but—" Her father shook his head, still trying to comprehend everything Julia had said. "Lady Melia... abducted the king?"

"Aye, she was posing as a nursemaid. It was fortuitous of Mama to have sent me when she did." Julia told her father everything that happened as he carried her mother toward her bed and laid her down, stroking her brow.

"And what happened just now, with her suddenly doing everything ye commanded?"

Julia shrugged. There were some things that even an intelligent warrior like her father, who had likely seen and heard it all, might still not understand. "I think she knew she was caught and there was nowhere for her to run."

The Laird of Eilean Donan still looked perplexed, but he accepted what she said with a simple nod, then he looked back at his wife.

"I hope your mama will forgive me. I let that monster up here." His voice was tight, making it sound like he was choking on emotion, and Julia didn't blame him one bit.

"Ye wouldna have known any different. I'm sorry for failing at the pools, giving her the opportunity to come here in the first place."

Ronan Sutherland shook his head, taking his wife's pale hand in his, the backs of her knuckles scraped and bruised from fighting off Melia. "I thought they were friends."

Julia squeezed her father's shoulder, sitting down beside him on the bed. "So did I. She fooled us all."

"Do ye believe what she said about the king? That others will come? Was she a part of a faction?"

Julia shook her head. "Not at all. I will make certain that he is protected, along with Sir Alistair. No one will take him away again."

"Tell me about the necklace." Her father tucked her mother's blankets around her, then stood, tugging Julia up with him. He hugged her tight, then held her at arm's length as though searching for injuries.

"It belongs to Scotland."

"She stole that, too?"

"Aye." Julia leaned into her father, letting him believe that the jewel was part of the king's own coffers. "I will return to Dunfermline with the king."

"As ye should."

"I thought I failed him, and Mama." Julia glanced back toward the bed, willing her mother to open her eyes, but she slept on peacefully.

"They are both safe because of ye. The country is too, and they dinna even know it." Ronan Sutherland held her at arm's length, and caught her stare, searching out her face for answers. "Who is Sir Alistair?"

Julia blinked, forgetting that her father did not know him, and that she'd mentioned him at all. "He is the Earl of Moray's personal guard, and protector of the king as well. We made this journey together. He helped me save the king. He saved me, too. I owe him my loyalty and life."

Her father chuckled. "Ah, I had hoped for something else."

Julia bit her tongue. After what had just happened, she knew now that she could never marry Alistair. Not if there was ever going to be the possibility that she might be able to take over his mind the way she just had with Melia. She'd never be able to forgive herself, and she wouldn't allow him to forgive her if she did.

"Nothing more," she said, unable to hide the hint of sadness in her voice, or the cracking sound of her heart breaking.

10

Alistair's palms were sweating. His palms never sweated. Well, not until he'd met Julia. What was it about this lass that made him nervous? Had him questioning his self-confidence and the affect he had on women?

For certes, he knew she wanted him. She'd told him. She'd even said she'd marry him.

But there was something else he wanted from her—and it wasn't just the physical things he desired. He needed to tell her what was weighing heavily on his mind.

Alistair reached up to knock on the door, but it opened swiftly before he got a chance. The sight of her stilled his heart. Julia stood in her thin nightrail, long fiery golden locks falling down her back in waves. The lights from her candle and the hearth shined around her, giving her an angelic look at the same time it allowed a little too much to be revealed through her barely there gown. An angel and a vixen all at once.

"Did ye hear me… thinking?" he asked, eyebrow raised, feeling a hint of heat in his cheeks.

"Not in the way ye think." She slid her dagger from behind the door, where she'd been hiding it, and gave him a sheepish grin. "I just heard someone lurking. I didna realize it was ye."

"Do ye always answer your door with a weapon?"

Julia shrugged, then reached forward with her dagger-less hand and tugged him inside.

"Where is the king?" she asked.

"Asleep with the men in the barracks. Merida is guarding him, along with his new pup, Robbie."

Julia grinned. "He's a sweet lad."

"Aye. But, that is not the reason I've come."

Julia licked her lips, eyes darting around his face in a panic. "Before ye say anything, I must tell ye that I canna marry ye, Alistair."

Sorrow filled her voice, and he could see her struggling, the muscles in her body tensing as she backed away from him. He tried to ignore the sharp pang to his chest that her words gave him.

"I wasna lying when I told ye that I wanted to," she continued, leaning the dagger against the wall by her door. "But, after what happened earlier today, I canna attach myself to anyone. The power that I have... 'tis too great. I couldna live with myself if I were able to bend your will to mine."

She explained to him what had happened in her mother's chamber, confirming what he'd heard from the men who'd not been able to stop talking about it all evening.

Alistair reached for her, and when she tried to back away, he thought about letting her, remembering when she'd told him when they first met that if she wanted him to touch her, she'd ask. But he couldn't let her just back away from what they had. Couldn't let her deny the feelings he'd seen in her eyes, the feelings he felt keenly in his heart.

"I came here to tell ye that I love ye. That I dinna want to wait to make ye mine. I dinna care that ye can read minds. Or that ye're afraid one day ye might control mine. Already ye've got me under your spell. And it's an enchantment I want, love. Do ye nae see? I'd lay down my life for ye, and I'd give up the ability to think on my own completely if it meant that ye would be my wife, for I know that with ye by my side, the rest of my days would be complete with happiness."

Anguish wrecked her features. "But I dinna *want* to control ye. I *like* who ye are, I *love* ye, too, and that is why I canna do that to ye."

Alistair shook his head, and this time he did grasp her hands, and she didn't pull away but stepped closer, hope shining in her eyes.

"We'll work together to harness the gift ye've been given. To bring it out when needed and put it away when not. Together, remember? Ye and me."

Julia swallowed, the tender knot of her throat bobbing, and he wanted more than anything to pull her into his arms and bury his face in her hair.

She gazed up at him, vulnerability plain in the curves of her face and the glittering of her tear-filling eyes. "Are ye certain?"

"More than I've ever been certain of anything in my life."

"And if I turn into... *her*?"

He knew exactly whom she meant by *her*. That vile wench who'd tormented them the past sennight and more. "Ye could never be her."

"But if I am, will ye lock me away and throw away the key?" Shining gray eyes searched his.

"Nay." Alistair was firmly in denial that he could ever do anything to harm her, even if she was threatening to take over his entire intellect.

"Then I canna marry ye." Julia backed away, shaking her head.

But Alistair tugged her back. "Fine, if I agree that, should ye become an evil murderess, I'll lock ye away, will ye marry me?"

A wide, satisfied grin spread over her face. "Aye!" She wrapped her arms around his neck, hugging him tight, and he was then able to bury his face in her sweet-smelling hair as he'd wanted to.

Alistair lifted her up and twirled her about the room. "On the morrow, I'll ask your father, and we'll be wed."

"On the morrow." Her eyes grew heavy-lidded and a wicked grin covered her lips. "But tonight... tonight ye shall be mine."

Alistair stared at her in shock, fairly certain of what she was inviting him to do. "I canna. 'Twouldna be right."

"We plan to marry, aye?"

"Aye?"

"Then why is it not right?" She nuzzled his nose with hers. "I am your wife. Ye are my husband. There, I've said it, and now 'tis true. Take me to bed, so we might finish what we started by the loch."

How could he argue with that?

Alistair carried his almost-wife to the bed and laid her out on it, staring down at the dusky pink of her nipples beneath the creamy white of her nightrail, followed by the dip where her navel was, and the fiery curls that shadowed the fabric between her legs.

"Ye're so beautiful. Like a breath of fresh air in a smoking building, or the first rays of sun on a frozen earth."

She smiled up at him, let out a soft laugh. "Ye've become a poet."

Alistair unpinned his plaid and unbuckled his belt, letting the fabric of his plaid fall, leaving him only in a shirt. "I only say what I see."

"And your body says the rest." Her eyes were on the part of him that swelled with hunger for her.

He lay down on the bed beside her, leaning up on his elbow, much like he had beside the loch. She lifted her knee toward his hip and tucked herself closer. "Dinna make me wait."

"Have ye...?"

"Aye. Once, a long time ago." Julia told him of her marriage. How it had not lasted more than a night before her husband was killed in a raid. She told him how she'd cared for the man, but that their marriage had been one of convenience. That Alistair was the first man she'd truly been in love with.

Alistair breathed out a sigh of relief, not just that she'd only been married before out of convenience, but that she was not a virgin. If this had been her first time, he was afraid she would not have enjoyed it. But knowing that the barrier had been broken by another before him, did not leave him with a sense of jealousy at all for the man who'd claimed it, but instead with a sense of gratitude, because that meant tonight, she would feel only pleasure.

Julia leaned up, capturing the back of his head with her hand and tugging him to meet her lips halfway. She kissed him deeply, hungrily, thoroughly. His almost-wife was full of a passion that matched his own.

He stroked the length of her legs, skimming the nightrail up until his fingers touched the bare skin of her leg, and then her hip. She gasped into his mouth and made a crooning sound that drove him wild.

"What's this?" He traced his finger over a birthmark on her hip that looked a hell of a lot like a dagger.

"A birthmark," she said.

"A dagger."

Julia grinned and pressed her finger to his chin, tipping him back up for another kiss. "Aye, a dagger, marking me as a protector."

"Ye never cease to amaze me, love." Was she confessing to him that the mark had something to do with her power? What had happened at the loch? He could have contemplated it more, but at the moment, he did not want to. Instead, he wanted to love her. To sink inside her.

Alistair slid his mouth from her lips to tease the points of her breasts through her nightrail that jutted with clear need for attention. He swirled his tongue around the tips, and reveled in the arch of her back and her guttural moan of pleasure.

Julia's hands thrust into his hair, tugging hard in a silent demand for more. Alistair answered with a growl under his breath. He wrenched the gown from her body and stared down at the creamy perfection of her skin. The sight of her was too much not to taste, and he lowered his head to gently nibble some more at her delicious nipples.

As he licked at the taut peaks, his fingers danced their way over her hip, her belly, to slide tentatively over the warm heat of her center. *Mo chreach*, but she was incredibly hot, like fire, and so unbelievably slick. He stroked over the nub of her pleasure, and she moaned, bucking her hips forward.

"I want to feel ye on my skin," she said, pulling his shirt up his back and over his head. She splayed her hands across the expanse of his back. Och, how he loved that she touched him, explored him.

Alistair continued to stroke between her thighs, and her moans and gasps increased, along with the frantic rocking of her hips. She was going to find her release on his fingers, and that knowledge made him all the hotter. It took only a few more swirling strokes of his fingers before she was crying out, her thighs clamping against his hand, and her entire body shook.

"That's it," he grinned against her breast, sucking her nipple a little harder to drag out the pleasure.

"Oh, Alistair, my love," she crooned.

God, he loved her. So damn much. The emotion of it consumed him, made him shake a little as he leaned up to take her mouth once more. "I love ye, sweet lass," he said against her mouth.

"I love ye, too," she answered back, pressing her hands to his cheeks and gazing deep into his eyes. "I never thought I could feel this way."

"I am honored to be the one ye bestow it upon."

He kissed his way back toward her lush breasts, and then lower, over the plane of her belly, the curve of her hip. Her feminine scent teased his senses, made his mouth water.

"I'm going to pleasure ye with my mouth." When he kissed the very top of her mound where her soft curls began, Julia gasped and clenched her thighs tight on his head.

"Nay, dinna," she murmured.

"Aye, I'm going to, and ye'll like it, I promise." He met her gaze, still hazy with pleasure. Her cheeks were flushed, lips parted.

He pried her thighs open and breathed hotly over her folds, watching the way she bit her lip to try to stifle a whimper. "If ye dinna like it, I will stop, sweetheart."

"All right... but I think ye're right... I liked that already.

Alistair chuckled and then dipped his tongue in again, teasing her folds with the tip. He nuzzled, probed, licked. Julia's muffled whimpers grew to full-out cries of pleasure, her hands fisted in the coverlet, knuckles white. With his thumbs, he pealed her folds open, giving him fuller access to her nub of pleasure. God, she tasted like heaven. He suckled her, flicked his tongue over and over, nuzzled her folds, made love to her with his mouth like he'd never made love before.

Julia's thighs shook and she clenched. One fist unlatched from the coverlet to bury in his hair, holding his mouth to her center. She writhed beneath him, and when he slipped a finger inside her wet heat, her muscles squeezed him tight. She was so close...

Alistair didn't stop, but continued his intense ministrations until Julianna broke apart in the ultimate surrender.

"Alistair!" she cried out as her body shook violently, eyes wide, mouth open in surprise, cheeks flushed pink.

He smiled in pure male satisfaction. "I told ye, ye'd like it." He gave her one more full lick for good measure, chuckling when she let out a surprised cry of pleasure.

She nodded slowly, licking her lips. "Aye... Verra much. Can I... do the same to ye?"

At the thought of her luscious lips wrapped around his length, Alistair's cock surged. Already he throbbed against the mattress, and he knew he would not last if she took him in her mouth. "Next time," he croaked.

"On our wedding night," she said with a wicked grin. "Ye'll not be able to escape me then."

"Ye're a vixen. I want ye so verra much," he whispered.

"Take me." Julia lifted her hips in invitation.

Alistair groaned, and moved to kneel between her warm thighs. Hands pressed to the insides of her knees, he stared down at her, all flushed and ready for him. With a tilt of his hips, his cock pressed against her slick entrance. He surged forward, burying himself to the hilt in one full thrust.

She was exquisitely tight, surrounding him at once in a cocoon of pleasure. He fell forward onto his elbows and pressed his forehead against hers. For a moment, he was paralyzed, unable to move. He just breathed, trying to focus, to shove off the release that hovered on the verge of exploding.

"That feels so good." She nibbled his neck and wriggled beneath him.

If she kept doing that... Alistair claimed her mouth, trying to distract her and himself for just a moment, but she flexed the muscles of her sex and tilted her hips up even farther. He groaned.

"Dinna move," he begged.

"Am I hurting ye?"

Alistair groaned. "Nay. Just the opposite."

"Oh, so ye're saying this," she lifted her hips again, "feels good?"

"Och, aye. Too good."

She moved again, lifting her legs higher around his hips.

Alistair tried to hold out, tried to keep his control, but the way she was moving beneath him was more than he could handle. He withdrew, then plunged back inside with increasing speed. He wanted to go slow. Wanted to drag out their pleasure, but she felt so damn good... And she was moaning, her fingers clasping his back, hips rising and falling to meet his. Julia was a natural at lovemaking. A natural at tormenting him with pleasure. He'd never been with a woman who fit him so perfectly.

He tried to keep his pace measured, calculated to draw out her pleasure, but the vixen grew only more demanding. As soon as he felt her sex clench tight and begin fluttering, Alistair knew his intent to make love to her for hours was lost. He gritted his teeth and plunged ahead, riding out her climax.

"Oh, so good, Alistair," she gasped.

Tremors shook her body, and his own shivers took hold, pleasure radiating from the base of his spine and surging forward. He quickened his pace, thrusting deep and hard until his release hit him like a gale force, crashing into him with a power he'd never felt before. A primal moan of ecstasy thrust from his throat, as his entire body shuddered against hers.

Conscious not to crush her, he held himself upright on his elbows, but let his forehead rest against her shoulder, breathing in her feminine floral scent as he waited for his breaths to steady. Making love to Julia had been like nothing he'd ever experienced before. And he was going to get to do it again, every day for the rest of his life.

"Julia," he murmured, then kissed her lightly on the lips, stroked back the strands of hair that stuck to the sides of her face. "I love ye..."

"I love ye, too, husband of mine."

His entire chest swelled as he gazed into her beautiful face. "Mine forever."

"And ever."

Want more books in the Sutherland Legacy? Check out THE HIGHLANDER'S GIFT! Want to read Julia's parents' story? They fell in love in THE HIGHLANDER'S LADY...

ABOUT THE AUTHOR

Eliza Knight is an award-winning and *USA Today* bestselling author of over fifty sizzling historical romance and erotic romance. Under the name E. Knight, she pens rip-your-heart-out historical fiction. While not reading, writing or researching for her latest book, she chases after her three children. In her spare time (if there is such a thing…) she likes daydreaming, wine-tasting, traveling, hiking, staring at the stars, watching movies, shopping and visiting with family and friends. She lives atop a small mountain with her own knight in shining armor, three princesses and two very naughty puppies. Visit Eliza at http://www.elizaknight.com or her historical blog History Undressed: www.historyundressed.com. Sign up for her newsletter to get news about books, events, contests and sneak peaks! http://eepurl.com/CSFFD

ALSO BY ELIZA

THE SUTHERLAND LEGACY

The Highlander's Gift
The Highlander's Quest

PIRATES OF BRITANNIA: DEVILS OF THE DEEP

Savage of the Sea
The Sea Devil
A Pirate's Bounty

THE STOLEN BRIDE SERIES

The Highlander's Temptation
The Highlander's Reward
The Highlander's Conquest
The Highlander's Lady
The Highlander's Warrior Bride
The Highlander's Triumph
The Highlander's Sin
Wild Highland Mistletoe (a Stolen Bride winter novella)
The Highlander's Charm (a Stolen Bride novella)
A Kilted Christmas Wish – a contemporary Holiday spin-off
The Highlander's Gift — coming soon!

THE CONQUERED BRIDE SERIES

Conquered by the Highlander
Seduced by the Laird
Taken by the Highlander (a Conquered bride novella)
Claimed by the Warrior
Stolen by the Laird
Protected by the Laird (a Conquered bride novella)
Guarded by the Warrior

THE MACDOUGALL LEGACY SERIES

Laird of Shadows
Laird of Twilight
Laird of Darkness

THE THISTLES AND ROSES SERIES

Promise of a Knight
Eternally Bound
Breath from the Sea

THE HIGHLAND BOUND SERIES (EROTIC TIME-TRAVEL)

Behind the Plaid
Bared to the Laird
Dark Side of the Laird
Highlander's Touch
Highlander Undone
Highlander Unraveled

WICKED WOMEN

Her Desperate Gamble
Seducing the Sheriff
Kiss Me, Cowboy

UNDER THE NAME E. KNIGHT

TALES FROM THE TUDOR COURT

My Lady Viper
Prisoner of the Queen

ANCIENT HISTORICAL FICTION

A Day of Fire: a novel of Pompeii
A Year of Ravens: a novel of Boudica's Rebellion

facebook.com/elizaknightfiction

twitter.com/elizaknight

instagram.com/elizaknightfiction

bookbub.com/authors/eliza-knight

goodreads.com/elizaknight

THE HIGHLAND GUARD AND HIS LADY

LORI ANN BAILEY

To protect Scotland, she must eliminate her greatest enemy. But when the challenge begins, will he forgive her for destroying his family?

ACKNOWLEDGMENTS

For Barb Massabrook, a warrior with a true Heart of Scotland. Special thanks to my editor, Jessica Snyder for her diligent attention to detail and amazing work. And as always, for my best friend, my husband, for his love, support, and for understanding when the story calls and I get that far off look in my eyes and forget what we're talking about that I still love him and he's my real-life hero. My kids, for encouraging me and being proud of what I do. And for you, the reader who picked up this book and gave me a chance to share a piece of my heart.

1

Edinburgh, Scotland
Holyrood Palace – Royal Residence
January 25, 1567

Captain Duncan Douglas, distant cousin to the king consort, Lord Henry Darnley, and thus infant Prince James, paced outside the door to the babe's room as Mary, Queen of Scots, spent time with her son. Movement down the hall caught his attention. A lass. One he'd never seen.

He'd been in his position long enough to know all the nursemaids and servants who were allowed in this portion of the castle and this red-headed stranger was not one of them. She wore a cream embroidered jacket over a green fitted corset that cinched in at the waist, accentuating her curves, not standard servants' attire.

He took a breath to command her to halt, but the lass stopped, glancing down at a large tome she carried. Using her teeth, she removed a glove from one hand, then laid it across the book. Her slender, bare fingers traced the cover as she worked to balance the book on one arm, and her lips moved in a steady whisper that eluded him. She was lost in her own world and never looked at him.

Was she talking to it? And what the hell was she doing here? In the seven months he'd held this position, he'd never seen the lass. She did not belong.

Straightening his shoulders, he was about to call out to ask what business she had here, but before he could, her mouth fell wide in apparent shock and she spoke out loud as she shook her head. "Nae. Ye shouldnae write things ye ken arenae true."

The lass didn't look up as she started down the hall again, directly toward him and the prince's chamber. Maybe she was addled. Such a shame considering the animation on her face and the slight blush on her cheeks, as if she'd just come in from the cold. She was bonny.

The stranger reached the prince's door and pivoted, turning to open it with the hand that had been touching the top of the book. She meant to walk in without permission, completely ignoring him though he stood within an arm's length.

He grabbed her ungloved hand and she shrieked, dropping the tome as he twisted her around and backed her into the solid wood door. The book fell to the floor, landing flat with a loud bang that rivaled the sound of a cannon blast as it reverberated through the stone hallway.

"What is yer business here?"

The lass's jaw tightened. Her eyes, he could see now, were a shade of green that matched her corset and they focused on his lips a moment before lifting to his gaze, anger flaring in their dark depths. She attempted to pull free.

Catching her other hand, he pinned her to the solid frame. He held her firmly but gently, not wanting to hurt her delicate wrists while needing to keep her restrained. The position felt intimate, but he'd acted on instinct and years of training. Until he knew her purpose, she was a threat.

"Unhand me, brute." She brought her knee up, skimming his manhood as he swiveled to block the blow. Despite the maneuver, he still felt the force of her impact and was just able to maintain a grip on her. Hell, the wee lass had courage to attack a man with a sword—or, then again, she could have something loose in her head.

"Ye have no business here," he asserted between gritted teeth.

"Aye, I do." She squared her shoulders, tilting her chin up.

The door swung in and the lass stumbled backward, but before she fell, he snaked his other arm around her and pulled her close. Och, it was a mistake. Her curves were welcoming and his defiant man parts stirred to life despite what she'd almost done to him. Fresh lavender filled his nostrils as his hand rested on the slope of her hip.

"What was that noise?" the queen asked as her regard narrowed on him then roved up and down the lass's back. Her brow rose. "Duncan?"

"We seem to have an intruder, Yer Majesty." The lass twisted to pull free, but he swung her around in the other direction to keep her away from the queen.

"She's no intruder. Lady MacKinnon is my translator." Mary smiled and pointed at the book on the floor as if its presence should make the lass's appearance something normal. She pivoted to the woman still caged close to his body, her gaze lighting. "I see you are already hard at work."

Stunned the queen knew her, he let the woman slip from his grasp as she dropped into a deep curtsy. "Aye, Yer Majesty." A delightful flush stole onto her pale face, this one deeper than the one caused by the outside cold.

Footfalls sounded from the end of the hall and Duncan turned. His replacement had arrived for his shift, smirking as he studied the lass's curves.

She rose and addressed the queen. "I'm so sorry. I must have made a wrong turn. This place is so big and I havenae had time to learn my way around."

"Holyrood Palace is quite large. Duncan, can ye show Lady MacKinnon to her room and make sure she has everything she needs?" The queen's lyrical tone held amusement at his mistake.

"Aye, Yer Majesty." He stiffened and bowed.

"And, Lady MacKinnon, please join us again for dinner. I'd love to hear about your work."

"Aye, Yer Majesty." Lady MacKinnon curtsied once more, and his gaze caught on the curve of her long, elegant neck and the thick gold chain she wore. He'd obviously just accosted a woman of some influence. Thankfully, she and the queen seemed to have forgotten his display, although he could still feel her cool, smooth skin in the tingles on his fingertips.

It had been his duty to stop the lass. How was he to know the woman was a guest at the royal residence?

He'd been out with his cousin Henry last night, and they'd dined at an earl's home nearby. Too bad the queen and her husband weren't on the best of terms or he may have had the chance to meet Lady MacKinnon the previous evening...or at least know she was coming. Although he couldn't blame Mary. He didn't enjoy Henry's company when the man was plied with whisky either.

If Henry and James weren't the closest thing to family he had left in the world, he'd find other acquaintances, but he quite enjoyed keeping an eye on the queen and her bairn. He'd not been present the night his cousin had persuaded men to help kill the queen's counselor, but he'd heard of the brutal incident and the threats Henry had made to Mary, so he felt it his duty to protect the young queen from his kin.

Kneeling, he picked up the large book, which was covered with unusual symbols on the front and writing in a language he had never seen. The volume probably weighed half a stone or more. He also scooped up the lass's glove and held it out. She took the soft material and slipped it back on.

"Duncan, will you be with my husband tonight?"

"Nae, Yer Majesty."

"Then you may join us as well," she lilted with her slight French accent as soft cries erupted from the infant within the room. "Now, please help Lady MacKinnon find her room." The queen turned, shutting the door, and the babe's sounds softened before dying away altogether.

The lass glanced up at him, the light in her eyes darkening as she straightened her spine. Ignoring her disdain—though who could blame her, he'd practically assaulted her—he swung toward his replacement. "Ye were late again."

"Sorry, Duncan."

But he was already turning away. He would have to see the guard moved to another position, but he was not prepared to scold the man in front of the queen's guest.

"This way, Lady MacKinnon." He held out a hand to indicate the way toward the back stairs and waited for the lass to move before falling into step beside her.

※

Duncan, the very large Highland guard who had nearly attacked her, stirred her curiosity. His fierce, assessing gaze sent chills to the back of her neck while at the same time it intrigued her. Leslee MacKinnon, niece to the MacKinnon laird, wasn't accustomed to men looking at her as if she were something to be desired. She wasn't familiar with their consideration at all.

The MacKinnon men back home on the Isle of Skye believed her mad and steered clear of her. Sure, this one had thought her trying to break into the royal rooms, but she'd seen the guilt there when he discovered she was only lost and not someone with a nefarious purpose. Then she'd noticed the spark of interest.

"May I have the book, please," she asked.

"'Tis a heavy one. I have it. Where is yer room?"

Irritation took root. "If I kenned that, I wouldnae be standing here with ye."

He stopped, and his warm hazel gaze met hers. "Please accept my apologies. I was not aware there was a guest in residence and I was doing my job."

She flattened her palm against her chest, sheltering the stone that lay hidden beneath her shift as a warmth soaked into her skin. She understood duty and protecting something precious.

His words were sincere. She wasn't as adept at reading people as objects, but the regret in his stare was genuine.

"Ye are forgiven."

"Where are ye visiting from, Lady MacKinnon?" He pivoted and continued down the hall, clearly confident that she would follow his broad shoulders and the deep chestnut hair that gently brushed their tops. She shook her head. She wasn't here to look at a man. She had business to attend so she could get back to Skye and away from the busy streets of Edinburgh.

She struggled to keep up with his long, lean, muscled legs. He had to be a good head taller than she. Intimidating. But she'd held her own against him. If the queen hadn't opened the door, she would have found a way free. But Her Majesty had opened the door, and this man had wrapped his arms around her, held her in a way no other ever had. It brought gooseflesh to her skin to remember the smell of wild woods and something all male on him.

"I'm only here to help decipher this old text, then I'll be on my way back to Skye." That was true enough.

Stopping at the bottom of the stairs, he held up a hand, palm facing her, and she obeyed again as he peeked into a room and spoke to whomever was inside. "The queen has a guest here to decipher texts. Where is her room?"

While he waited for the reply, she inspected her surroundings, hoping to find her bearings. It was quite frustrating, but since she spent so much time avoiding objects, she paid less attention to her environment.

"This way." He was standing in front of her again, a strange smile on his face as he studied her.

She suddenly needed to defend herself, but why should she care? Everyone back home thought her mad already. Why did the opinion of this man matter? "'Twas dark when I arrived last night."

"Yer on the other side. Actually, just a level below my quarters, and I was confused my first week here as well. Ye'll get used to it."

Och, hopefully not, but his kind words eased the tension. She didn't wish to be here more than two weeks, although as long as she could spend the majority of her time cloistered away in the abbey or her room she would do just fine.

Spending the evening dining with the queen had not been something she wished for.

Paying close attention to the route they traveled, she was mesmerized by the thick, warm tapestries and the opulence of the palace. Her uncle's castle was impressive, but this place made his home look dull and small.

They reached a staircase in the back corner, and she paused for a second, memorizing the details of the painting hanging at the bottom so that she would know her way back. Fascinated, she moved closer and absently removed her glove. When her naked fingertips touched the painting, the world around her faded.

Suddenly, she was the artist as he created the portrait—thinking his thoughts, steadying his canvas while her hand brushed strokes of color onto it. She knew his pride in this work.

"You look lovely," James the V, King of Scotland, said as his wife, Mary of Guise, walked into the room, round with their only child.

The queen waddled over to the artist, sidling up beside him. "It looks just like you." Excitement bubbled in her voice. The queen started to say something else, but Leslee was being led away as a hand on her shoulder gently pulled and her fingertips fell from the painting.

"Lady MacKinnon." The thick Highland burr sounded concerned as she blinked to bring her surroundings back into focus. It was the prince's handsome guard.

"Och, I'm so sorry. I was just lost in the artist's work." She glanced back at the painting, hoping he wouldn't question her further. She didn't want the people here to think her addled.

"Nae, 'tis fine, lady. I just didn't want ye to get lost again." Was he teasing her? Her cheeks heated. If he'd just let her hold the book, she wouldn't have been drawn to the portrait. He smiled and winked at her then continued on.

Following him up the stairs, she replaced her glove, determined not to touch another item. And yet she focused on all the marvelous paintings and tapestries on the walls rather than their course. It wasn't until they were walking down a hall that she realized she'd not paid attention as closely as she should have, so she concentrated on remembering the rest of the route. At three doors along on the right, he stopped and turned the knob, pushing the door in then standing aside for her.

"My room?"

"Aye, my lady. Did ye think we were going to my room?"

This time she was certain the flush on her face must be visible. Men didn't typically tease her, but there was something about his mischievous jest that warmed her skin.

He followed her inside and she turned to tell him he had the wrong idea, but he moved across the small space and carefully set the religious text down on the small table that would work as her makeshift desk.

She shivered as his attention returned to her. "'Tis cold in here."

Pivoting away, he glanced at the small fireplace then back to her. "Will ye be spending the day alone in yer room?" Was he asking for an invitation or just curious?

"Aye." The reply sounded raspy as if she'd not had a drink yet this morning, but she had thankfully been able to find the great hall in time to break her fast before retrieving the old manuscript from the abbey.

"I'll see to getting ye some peat and a fire started. This area in the palace sometimes gets drafty and I dinnae wish to disappoint the queen by letting ye take ill." Of course he had not been interested in her.

What about this man threw her off balance?

She only nodded and looked away, ashamed at where her thoughts had taken her.

Moving toward the door, he twisted back around just before easing it shut. "Welcome to Edinburgh, my lady." The words rolled over her like the vibrating purr of a kitten.

"Thank ye," she said just before the door shut behind him, leaving her alone with her work.

2

It had taken the rest of the afternoon to tear his thoughts from the mysterious lass who'd nearly felled him with one blow of her knee. Venturing into the lists to train with his men this afternoon, he'd attempted to put her from his mind, but his thoughts kept returning to the beauty who was at her desk directly below his room as he tried to puzzle out what about her intrigued him. She'd seemed proud but aloof, educated yet at the same time innocent. Her cheeks colored readily, and he'd baited her just to see the flush on her pale skin.

He never teased anyone.

But now, sitting so near her in the queen's private dining chamber, Duncan had the time to study her as she conversed with Mary. She wore the same gown she had earlier in the day, and he wondered how she'd found such a deep shade of green to match her eyes. The only thing different about her appearance this evening was that her earlier confidence seemed slightly shaken without her book as a shield, and her two gloved hands fidgeted like she couldn't wait to run from the room.

The lass's hair, still pinned up as it had been this morning, looked lovely, but a few red spirals had escaped, and she had a small dark smudge under her ear. He was tempted to wet a napkin to trace the spot—no, he wanted to do it with his finger. It appeared to be ink, and the fact that she could read and write other languages made him want to hear if she could speak them as well.

She wore no cap to indicate she was married, and he wondered why such a bonny, intelligent woman wouldn't be taken. Surely the men of Skye weren't daft or immune to those full pink lips and the way she blushed easily when provoked.

Despite her innocence, there was something strong about her. Defiance radiated from her and she didn't easily follow his commands. After losing his family, he'd been sent to King's College in Aberdeen and spent years proving himself, knowing the other nobles would stomp on him due to his lack of a title if he let them. His ability to lead had garnered him a position of trust as captain of the Royal Guard, and he was accustomed to others obeying without question.

Still, there was something refreshing about the small lass challenging him. No one had questioned his authority in years, but it had taken her only seconds to prove she wanted the upper hand.

Finding a break in the conversation and wanting her focus on him, he asked, "How did ye come to ken so much about ancient texts?"

It worked.

She turned her focus on him alone, and a small thrill rushed through his body as the others at the table turned their attention to the queen and kept up a dialogue with her, essentially handing him Lady MacKinnon's sole consideration.

He scraped his chair closer to hers, and her cheeks once again flushed. Perhaps from the honeyed wine that had been served tonight, but he preferred being the reason. Despite himself, he reached for the pitcher of wine, pouring her a glass, just to see if he could turn the light pink into a deep rose.

"I picked up other languages at an early age, and my uncle had me frequent the convent near our lands often because the nuns there offered to tutor me. I've been helping them for as long as I can remember."

"Was it lonely?"

"Och, nae. They all fawned over having a willing student." Her smile lifted up to animate sparkling eyes as she reached for the wine and took a sip.

"Did ye nae miss being at home?" A pang of loss intruded, and he pushed it away to focus on the lass in front of him.

"Nae. No' at all. I have five siblings and so many cousins I cannae count them. 'Twas nice to have a place to go and call my own."

At the mention of her family, an irrational jealousy swept into his chest, but he squashed it down.

"And how is it ye became a guard for the prince?"

"Hard work and discipline." He'd like to add a family tie, but despite their distant relation, his cousin, Henry Darnley, the king consort, barely paid him any heed.

"Do ye always carry the sword around with ye?" Her gaze traveled to the broadsword he had strapped to his side.

As a guard, he was allowed to walk the palace with a weapon. He suspected Mary wanted him here because Darnley and his companions had murdered her friend and most trusted advisor, David Rizzio, in front of her in this very chamber just a few short months ago. The queen and Henry had been estranged since.

"Aye. 'Twas my father's." A familiar lump formed in his throat and he swallowed to relieve it.

"I'm sorry. Is yer father no longer with ye?"

"Nae. He and my mother have been gone a long time." Along with the rest of his family, but he wanted to keep the conversation light. Tonight, her company, her pretty eyes, lessened the weight of their absence that he'd carried for years.

Tonight, he wasn't quite so alone.

"I'm sorry to hear that. I'm sure they'd be proud of who ye've become."

He'd never thought of that, but she might be correct. He nodded, and a few moments of silence passed as they both gave their meals a bit of attention while he let her words play in his head.

"Thank ye," she said when her emerald gaze returned to his.

"For what?"

"Seeing to a fire in my chambers and making me feel welcome."

He nodded. "How is it ye dinnae have a husband?"

She froze then, her gaze darting to his, then dropping to her gloves as she wrung her fingers in her lap. Surely, there must have been a scandal, because she was too intelligent, too bonny to be unclaimed by a man.

She took a large gulp of her wine, as if looking for the courage to speak, deliberated a moment, then straightened her spine. "I am no' a prize to be won. My sisters will find their husbands first."

He opened his mouth to disagree when one of his guards burst into the room, bowing to the queen. "Pardon, Yer Majesty, Captain Douglas is needed."

"Yer Majesty?" he queried as he bowed his head.

"Go, Duncan." Mary nodded.

"Pardon me, Lady MacKinnon." He rose, and she nodded. Pivoting and moving toward the door, he presented a deceptively calm façade. His men never came for him during the evening.

Once in the hall, he learned one of his men had taken ill and the rest were out drinking and couldn't be trusted with the prince's safety. He'd be guarding the babe until the next man's watch.

At his post an hour later, he watched as Lady MacKinnon exited the queen's apartments and sashayed in her full skirts toward the stairs. At least she was headed in the right direction.

After the next guard appeared, he navigated the chilled halls to his own room. His fire burned as if someone had been in not too long ago to refresh the peat for him. It was unusual, but not unheard of, so he closed and bolted the door. Unlacing his boots, he slid them off and moved them to the side, once more looking at the flames.

Removing his sword, he laid it across the table and froze. Draped across the back of one of his chairs was a lady's skirt. His heart raced. It looked like the one Lady MacKinnon had been wearing. Nae, she didnae.

His breath caught.

Turning to the bed, he found curly red tresses splayed across his pillow. The woman who wouldn't leave his thoughts was now beneath his covers.

How much had the lass drunk? She must have accidentally taken the extra flight of steps to his room.

Easing forward, he took in her soft features. Around her neck she wore two chains—one made of gold he'd noticed earlier, which now dipped into her chemise so that he couldn't see where it ended, and one of what looked like iron with a coin on it.

Not recognizing the currency, he turned to his night table, lit the candle and pivoted back toward the sleeping lass. The mythical unicorn stood proud and tall on a coin he'd never seen before, so he reached forward, gently, careful not to wake her, and flipped it over. A dagger was embossed on the opposite side, and the coin was cool against her warm skin.

Hell, he had to get her out of here. His body was already thrumming to life with the desire to climb in behind her and wrap his arms around her small waist, pull her to his fevered body. But she was a guest of the queen and he was a guard.

The lass should have known better than to come to his bed, and that was probably why she was unwed. Had she wandered into another man's bed, and he'd taken advantage of her? The thought angered him, but he didn't take the time to analyze it. She had to go.

Standing before he could change his mind, he spun to place the candle on his night table. He strode toward the door to open it, then returned to his bed. He slid the covers from her and was hit by the sweet smell of lavender.

Scooping Lady MacKinnon in his arms, he drew her close and inhaled sharply. She was light, but her warm weight was intimate, and it stirred in him some primitive need to keep her safe. She nuzzled into him, sighed, but she didn't wake. His cock hardened instantly, so he darted for the door and then down the flight of stairs to her room.

Pushing in the door, cold air assailed him. Her fire had gone out. Continuing on, he moved to her bed and, balancing her slight weight in one arm, he drew back her covers then gently lowered her onto the mattress. She sighed and sultry, sleepy eyes opened and focused on him.

She smiled, and his body tightened with desire.

"Go back to sleep now, Lady MacKinnon. Ye just went to the wrong room."

"Leslee."

"What?"

"Call me Leslee." Then her eyes shut again.

Tucking the covers around her, he shivered, then turned to the hearth to get some warmth back in her room. He couldn't leave her in here when it felt as if she were out in the night air. He'd see to it tomorrow that someone kept a constant watch on her fire so she didn't freeze.

Duncan stopped. How was it that he felt so responsible for the lass? If anything, he had to distance himself because she would be returning to Skye and he wouldn't be going anywhere.

As he left her room, pulling the door shut, he stepped out to find two of the queen's maids wandering the hall. They took in his bare feet giggling and obviously whispering to each other about his departure from the queen's guest's room.

Hell, what would Mary have to say about this? Would she believe him innocent of any wrongdoing?

LESLEE'S HEAD ACHED AS SHE SAT UP. THE ROOM TILTED, AND A pounding assailed her senses. Someone was knocking on a door down the hall, but they may as well have been shouting in her ear. Och, she knew better than to have too much wine.

After Duncan had left the dinner table, she had lost interest in continuing her conversation with the queen and her acquaintances. Instead, she was preoccupied with both thoughts of the guard and her task ahead, so she had another glass of the deep red liquid. When she'd left, she barely remembered how to get back to her room.

Rising, she stretched, determined to fight her way through the fuzziness because she had work to do. Once this book was translated and she retrieved the other, she could return home. A proper meal to break her fast would be helpful in allaying the pain in her head and allowing her to focus on her work.

She picked out a gown with a rose corset and a skirt with rose-and-green embroidered flowers on the material, then glanced around the room for her gloves. Panic assailed her, and for the next few moments she searched, unable to find them.

She must have been addled enough to take them off in the queen's dining room last night, but there was an extra pair in her trunk. It wouldn't do for everyone here to think her crazy. When she was safe at home, she didn't mind the unbidden images from the past that bombarded her when she touched an object, but here she had to use caution. They'd been so frequent since coming into her full power that she could barely control the urge when an object called out to her.

The priestess at the Fairy Pools had told her she would become stronger and be able to control them. But since accepting the stone she now wore around her neck for safekeeping, she hadn't been able to fight the impulses without a buffer in place.

Her slippers were missing as well. Och, her head pounded now. What had she done with everything from last night?

Donning her less comfortable pair, she rushed from the room, determined to have a bite and get done with this business so she could get home where everything made sense and was safe.

She took the stairs to the main level, surprised when it was only one flight. Strange, she'd thought her room another floor higher last night.

She easily found her way to the great hall where people were already scattered about, talking and eating. Taking a plate from a table set to the side of the room, she filled it with eggs, cheese, and bread, then walked to one of the empty long tables and eased into a chair.

A mental list of what she'd need for the day occupied her thoughts as she ate. Paper, ink, and some more peat to keep her fire going. The men in the abbey had already agreed to let her work sequestered alone in her room and she was thankful for it, but it meant she would need to seek them out when she required more supplies.

She'd also need to stop by the kitchens to see if she could take her afternoon meal in her room, then the evening one down here with the others. She would avoid the queen's invitation from now on because dining with her took too much time and she would have to see Duncan.

Something about the way he looked at her made her think she

LORI ANN BAILEY

could be normal again, that a man might want her. But he would think her crazy too if he knew her secret. And he was the prince's personal guard. He'd never come to Skye to live with her and she couldn't stay here.

No, it was best if she kept her distance. She wanted to see the braw man more than was proper. As though conjured from her very thoughts, she caught a glimpse of him at the corner of the room. His focus landed on her and her pulse quickened.

As his regard lingered on her, she felt her cheeks warm. His mouth turned up and he leaned into the wall to watch her. The casual gesture heated her further as her thoughts turned to what it would feel like to kiss him. She'd watched him during dinner and the few times she'd come upon him, and she had the impression he did not share his smiles freely. The thought that he might be interested in her caused her breath to shallow, and she was about to tear her gaze away when he pivoted and left the room.

His abrupt departure left her feeling chilled. Had she imagined his interest? She focused on her meal and tried to block him from her thoughts, but that was unsuccessful when he reappeared a few minutes later.

Moving toward her, he stopped by her side as a slight fluttering started in her chest. "Good morn to ye, Lady MacKinnon."

"Thank ye, and the same to ye, Captain Douglas."

Leaning closer and kneeling beside her, his hand rested on her gloved one, and she shivered. He was so close she felt light-headed despite her seated position. He moved in, so that only she could hear as his warm breath washed over her ear. "If ye need a tour of the palace, I'll be happy to show ye around."

Her chest rose and fell as her body tightened. "I think I have it now, thank ye."

"Are ye certain?" His brows rose like he didn't believe her.

"Aye." She swallowed.

"Ye look bonny when ye blush."

She opened her mouth to say thank ye, but the words were lodged in her throat. He laughed, a comforting, pleasant sound, then he rose.

"Have a nice day, Lady MacKinnon." He swiveled and was gone

before she could reply, leaving her wondering what his intentions had been.

After eating, she pushed thoughts of the handsome Highlander from her mind and made her way to the abbey for her requests. On her way back to her chamber, she almost took the second set of stairs before remembering that she was only one flight up. Thank heavens she'd paid attention this morning, because it would be embarrassing to walk into someone else's room.

Closing the door behind her, warmth in the air told her someone had already been in to replenish her store of peat. Her slippers and the missing garments from last night were laid out on one of the chairs, and her gloves were placed across the tome she was getting ready to work on as if they had been there all along. She peeled long, white silk from her hands and glared at her favorite pair.

Picking one up, she was tossed into someone else's world. Captain Douglas.

Duncan closed a door to a room that looked identical to hers and peeked down the corridor. She counted as he passed two more doors. In his hands, he held familiar items as he darted through the hall and to the stairs, then down one flight, where he peered around the corner again before bolting to another room. This time it was her chamber, and he laid the items out just as she'd seen them. The vision disappeared when he placed the gloves on the text and turned to leave.

She dropped her glove, the food in her belly turning as she remembered being cradled in his arms, then telling him to call her by her given name. And he didn't take advantage of the mistake she'd made. How had she thought he might desire her?

She'd gone to his room the night before and he'd carried her back. Och, she had to finish her work and get home because he wouldn't think her a witch, he would think her a harlot. Resolving to keep her distance from him before she could make more of a fool of herself, she dedicated herself to her task.

3

Duncan hadn't been able to stop himself, but when he'd seen Leslee breaking her fast, red curls escaping her attempt to tame them and tumbling around her face, he'd remembered the vision of the silky strands spread across his pillow. And then he'd remembered the feel of her in his arms and he'd wanted to touch her one more time.

He momentarily lost his mind and found himself dangerously close to her in public. Taking her hand in his, he couldn't resist whispering teasing words in her ear, all in an attempt to darken her cheeks. Then, he discovered the caress hadn't been enough, and he'd wanted to peel the gloves from her fingers and feel her bare flesh. But she was a lady and he was a man of honor, he couldn't be so bold again.

After his display, he didn't see Lady MacKinnon for almost a week —it helped that he avoided the steps he knew she would take and kept his distance from the abbey. He hadn't been invited back to the queen's dining chamber so he couldn't say if the lass had been there. Regardless, it was best that he stay away since he didn't want any damage to the lass's reputation. He had tracked down the queen's maids and asked them not to spread rumors. Luckily, they seemed to be kindhearted lasses who would keep their tongues still.

But, every night as he fell asleep, he thought of the lass just below him and how her light weight had felt good in his arms. Leslee, she had said. He fought the urge to seek her out and make that pretty shade of rose creep onto her cheeks.

Now, as he paced outside the prince's room, the door swung in and the queen tiptoed out. She stopped just short of him. "Duncan."

He stood straighter. "Aye, Yer Majesty."

"My husband will be present for dinner tonight. I would like for you to dine with us." Her implied meaning was clear as she looked at his sword. She wanted someone she trusted in that room tonight. Her husband drank too much, was arrogant, and seemed to destroy everything he touched. The man may be his family, but he'd not been raised with the same values that had been treasured by Duncan's parents.

"Aye, Yer Majesty."

Then a hint of a smile crossed her lips. "I haven't seen Lady MacKinnon. She's been so busy. Would you please see to it that she joins us as well?" Mary's eyes twinkled, and he knew then that the maids hadn't been as discreet as he'd wished. He didn't know why he thought they would have kept it from the queen, a woman known to favor tales of love.

"Yes, Yer Majesty." She turned to go then peeked back over her shoulder. "She would be a treasure to have nearby. Maybe you could see to that." This time she almost laughed. At least he could be thankful the queen wished to push them together instead of being angry about him ruining the poor lass.

Only a short while later, he was outside Leslee's room, ready to escort her to the queen's private dining chamber. Knocking lightly, an odd thrumming reverberated in his chest as he waited for her reply. When she faced him, the breath was sucked from his lungs. She inhaled, and her cheeks flamed to life. Somehow, that relaxed him.

"Lady MacKinnon." He bowed.

"I believe I told ye to call me Leslee."

"Och, so ye do remember then?" The blush deepened and he wanted to move into her space, touch his lips to hers just to see if they would taste as sweet as they looked.

She swallowed and slid out of the room, careful to keep space between them. "Aye, but just barely. Why did ye no' tell me what had happened?" She started down the hall and he followed.

"I wanted to spare ye the embarrassment, and there was nae real harm. Except that two of the queen's maids saw me leaving yer room in the middle of the night." She stopped, causing him to bump into her, and he coiled his arm around her waist to keep her from pitching forward.

He couldn't make his arm release her. The smell of lavender, mixed with ink and paper, drifted through his nostrils. He'd never imagined those scents together, but it was like she was a precious flower that had been hidden away between pages and he'd just discovered her in a mysterious library.

His head was so close to hers, he tipped his lips to her ear and whispered, "Are ye well?"

She nodded, and somehow he was able to convince his body to let her go. They continued down the hall.

"It doesnae matter. I'll be gone soon anyway."

"What?"

"The maids. 'Twill nae matter. I'll be gone soon, and they can gossip about someone else."

"Nae. I talked to them. Yer reputation is safe."

Glancing at him, she gave a thin smile. "Thank ye for trying." It was evident she thought everyone would already know.

"How is yer work coming along?"

"Nicely. I've made quite a bit of progress."

"Tell me of yer necklace." She froze again, but his time he was beside her and didn't run into her. When he turned to look at her, she'd paled and taken on a defiant stance, as if she were ready to fight her way back to her room.

"The coin." He pointed. "I've never seen a unicorn on one." The tension left her body. Then her hand rose as her long, gloved fingers stroked the coin.

"'Twas a gift from a friend. She said it would protect me from evil."

"From what?"

"Those who would wish me harm."

"Does it work?"

"I dinnae ken, but it makes me feel safer just having it. I pray I never need to find out."

At the entrance to the queen's dining chamber, the door was already open, so he stood back and let Leslee enter. She chose a chair on the far end of the table and he slid in next to her. The queen smiled at them then turned back to talk to another guest.

Duncan took a breath to speak to Lady MacKinnon, who tensed and scanned the room before leaning back and pressing her hand to her side. He was about to ask what was wrong when his cousin sauntered into the room, Henry's good looks and easy smile not hiding the fact that he'd already been drinking. Mary scowled but seemed to calm mildly when Henry bent and whispered something in her ear. The man had an uncanny knack for appeasing her with only a few words. He fell into the seat next to his wife, rubbed at his hip as if he had an itch, then reached for the nearest cup.

Duncan had the oddest urge to hide Leslee, to protect her from Henry's vulgarity even as his cousin's contemplation roamed over those seated at the table and stopped at the bonny lass. Fixated on her, Henry's head tilted to the side. Duncan slid his hand onto her leg, a shield to whatever his cousin was planning, and she surprised him by taking it in her own.

"And who is this, Duncan?" Henry pinned him, a little bit of an edge to his voice. He didn't want to answer, but his cousin's requests always pulled at him. Many times he'd wanted to tell the man no, but something had stopped him, maybe family loyalty or his status. Just as his mouth fell open to reply, Leslee answered.

"I am Leslee MacKinnon of the Isle of Skye." She'd straightened her spine and drew her hand free of his, a gesture showing she believed herself to be in control. She looked as if she would draw a sword, ready to battle the king consort. The only other person he'd seen stand up to Henry had been the queen's advisor, the very one that Henry had killed. Chills spread down his back. "And who are ye, sir?"

"I am Henry Stuart, husband to the queen, but most people call me Lord Darnley."

"'Tis a pleasure to make yer acquaintance, Yer Royal Highness." How did she manage to sound civil and defiant at the same time?

"Ah, and what brings you to Edinburgh?" Henry leaned back in his chair, cool confidence radiating from him.

"I am translating an old text from the abbey."

His cousin only nodded. "Are you familiar with the tales surrounding the Fairy Pools?"

"Aye, I am." The edge was back in her tone.

"And do you believe them to be true?"

"I believe enough to ken that there are evil men in this world."

"Let's have a toast to evil men." Henry laughed, and everyone lifted their cups and drank. Everyone except Leslee, who kept eyes as sharp as a dirk pinned on his cousin.

"Interesting." Henry set his cup down leaned back once more, allowing Mary to draw him into a conversation. But he kept a close watch on Leslee while they spoke.

Dinner was a strained affair, between Henry's forced joviality and Mary's barely contained annoyance. Leslee fairly vibrated with tension, and Duncan resented that he could do nothing to soothe her in such a public setting. He slid his foot across to rest alongside hers, the only silent support he could provide. And she nudged hers against it in response. Even so, before dessert could be served, she excused herself from the meal, citing an early start on her work in the morning. She was out the door before he could object or offer to escort her to her room.

Then Henry stood as well, and Duncan prepared to disobey all protocol in his haste to protect Leslee.

THE MARK, WHICH HAD APPEARED ON HER HIP WHEN SHE'D BEEN called to be the Protector, still prickled upon exiting the room. She held her hand over the Heart of Scotland, which lay safe against her chest, attached to the gold chain on which she'd found it. Leslee crossed the landing and was at the top of the stairs when long fingers clamped onto her wrist, stopping her attempt to flee the oddly charged dinner. Turning, she met the cold, cruel eyes of Lord Darnley. He had sent chills down her spine the moment he walked into the queen's chamber.

"Unhand me."

He did not loosen his grip. "What is your true purpose here?"

"To help decipher a text."

"We have others that can do that." His head quirked to the side.

"Let me go." He did this time, and she darted for the stairs, but he dodged, cutting in front of her, blocking her progress.

"Come, have a drink with me." Strange vibrations emanated from the words.

She almost accepted even though she had no desire to.

"Nae, I need to retire so I can do my work tomorrow."

"You are an intriguing lass." He was silent a moment, glaring into her eyes, then he tried again, the vibrations stronger. "Come have a drink with me." But her resolve had strengthened as well.

"Nae."

Duncan rounded the corner. A scowl on his face, his stare bored into the queen's husband.

"Lady MacKinnon, I was told to escort ye back to yer room so ye dinnae get lost again."

Jumping on the opportunity, she backed toward him, weaving her arm through his, and instantly she could breathe easier. "Thank ye. I think I have it now, but let me lead to show ye I have mastered the treacherous turns of the palace. Good night, Lord Darnley."

She practically hauled Duncan down the stairs in her haste to retreat. Chills exploded on her back, and she looked over her shoulder to see Darnley's focus fixed on her. She swiveled back around and fought the urge to shudder.

When they were out of earshot of the queen's husband, she glanced at the man who had made her feel safe with very few words. "Thank ye. I dinnae ken why he followed me."

"'Twill serve ye well to stay away from him. He's my cousin, but I wouldnae want to leave an unwilling lass alone in his presence."

"He's yer cousin?"

"Aye. Distant, but family nonetheless."

"I ken he's the king consort, but 'tis as if he expects everyone to give in to his wishes without thought." She absently scratched at the mark on her hip as the tingle faded, no longer sending a warm warning through her.

"Aye. He's always been like that. I apologize for his behavior. 'Tis one of the reasons the queen and he arenae on good terms."

"Is it true that Lord Darnley killed the queen's advisor in front of her?"

"Aye. But dinnae overly worry. He's no' staying at the palace and I'll keep an eye out for ye when he is here."

"I think 'tis best I get my work done and be on my way back to Skye."

"How is yer work going? Ye have been quite busy. I havenae seen ye."

Was he watching for her?

The thought of him wanting to know where she was sent a thrill rushing to unfamiliar places. This man had also gone out of his way to see to it that others wouldn't gossip about her. Her heart fluttered.

Her hold on his arm had pulled him up close to her and his proximity was doing strange things to her nerves. She steadied her resolve to finish this text and get home right away. She couldn't let this attraction turn to anything more, regardless of her draw to Duncan. It was the loneliness she sensed in him that intrigued her. She wanted to fill that void for him and put back the pieces of whatever he'd lost.

This man belonged here in Edinburgh, and she could never live around all these strangers. Still, silly childhood fantasies of a husband surfaced, and she cursed her traitorous mind for thinking it possible. She had more important things to guard than her heart. Her fingers brushed across the necklace hidden in her shift. The strong chain held the Heart of Scotland, an emerald that protected the very well-being of the nation.

They had made it to her room. She reluctantly drew her arm from his and turned. "Thank ye."

His eyes were dilated and intense, focused on hers only to dip and linger on her lips before his regard slowly returned to hers. Her heart beat faster as his hand rose, fingers grazing her hairline while his thumb traced her cheek.

He leaned in, closer, his head tilting toward her. She let her lips fall open as her breathing stopped, and she fell into something that felt like a trance, a mesmerizing need to see what would happen next, to learn if his lips were as soft as they appeared. She closed her eyes as she turned up to his mouth, only scant inches away now.

Unwelcome voices carried from somewhere far away, and he backed away abruptly as she opened her eyes. *No, come back.* She was numb and breathless and didn't know why. She wanted to know.

Glancing around, Duncan focused on their surroundings to make certain no one had seen the display. The voices continued but became more distant. No one was in sight. And she wanted the moment back. No one had ever looked at her like that, with need and desire blazing behind his dark eyes. For a moment, that lonely, battered soul of his looked at peace, but it was now gone.

"I'm sorry," he said and then pivoted, dashing away before she could think of a response.

Opening her door to a fire-warmed room, she ducked in, closed the door and bolted it before her senses returned. She'd almost given in to the unfamiliar urge to draw him in. Och, she had wanted to kiss him. She'd never find a MacKinnon that didn't think she was crazy, why not give in?

She knew the answer. Her life wasn't her own and her country depended on her to not be so careless.

4

Duncan hadn't seen the lass who had haunted his dreams, no, his every waking moment too, for days now. Well, that wasn't quite true, he'd kept watch on her from afar when she broke her fast each morning, but he didn't dare get close to her again.

He apparently lost his senses along with his control when she was near.

He'd almost kissed her. In the hall, no less, where anyone could see. She deserved better than that. And what would the queen say? Although he had a suspicion Mary had a plan to encourage something between them, Leslee was still a guest and a lady.

His honor wouldn't allow him to give in to these feelings without intending to make her his bride, but that was something he currently could not do. He had responsibilities to the prince, and she seemed eager to go home.

Sitting in his usual spot in the great hall, one that afforded him a view of the whole room, he'd collected an ale and was waiting for some friends when he saw her appear. She held a long rod as she made her way out of the palace and into the cool, late day air. Curious, he rose and followed her weaving path through the city streets.

A moment of guilt spattered against his thoughts, but he brushed it away. He had already served his shift for the day, and with the lass's sense of direction she may not find her way back. And it would be dark soon. He was doing Leslee a favor.

After passing several streets, she stopped and asked a lass with a small child a question. The woman pointed, giving her directions. Leslee followed them, then repeated the process several times, until she eventually ended up at Greyfriars Kirk.

He followed her inside and took a seat in the back, watching as she approached one of the religious men near the altar. After a brief conversation, Leslee slid onto the first bench while the man sauntered toward the back. She waited for close to half an hour for someone to reappear.

He was losing his patience and wondering if he should make himself known when a Highlander he recognized returned to speak with her. Not a man of the church, rather it was Clement Litill, a lawyer known to the queen. He and Duncan shared an interest in books on the occasions he'd visited the castle. He was a Protestant convert held in high regard with both the Church of Scotland and the aristocracy.

What would Lady MacKinnon be doing meeting with this man?

As Leslee stood to greet the esteemed lawyer, a stab of anger poked at him because she returned the smile the man bestowed on her. Could she have been meeting with Litill all this time? On the days he'd avoided her, had she found a man who would win her heart?

But then Clement held out a book. Hell, this wasn't some secret rendezvous, this was about her work. He didn't want to acknowledge what had come over him, but he knew it was raw jealousy. What was wrong with him? The lass didn't belong to him, didn't belong here.

This tome was much smaller than the one he'd carried to her room that first day.

They spoke a couple moments more before Clement retreated the way he'd come. Leslee stood still, her gloved fingers trailing the book's binding reverently. She drew the volume in and held it close as if it were a long-lost friend. Curious.

She placed it in a bag he'd not seen her bring and draped it over her shoulder, then retrieved the stick she'd brought and swiveled to head turned to him, concern in his eyes as if he felt responsible for the younger man. "Run. 'Tis a palace guard."

Duncan stepped up as the leader staggered back as fast as he could, pain etched on his face with each step. "If I ever see any of yer faces again, ye will wish for a quick death."

"Aye, sir, ye'll never see us again." The arse had come to the corner and he took off around the nearest building, the other two presumably already gone to safety. She had to admit that with Duncan's broad shoulders and imposing voice he made a fine guard.

Stomping over to her, he lashed out. "What the hell did ye think ye were doing coming out here at night?"

Now that the threat was gone, she couldn't speak. Her gaze bounced around the buildings, the lights, and the wretched smell of the city streets stung her nose. Her stomach churned as the memories came flooding back, drowning her in fear.

"I, I—" Och, hell, she had to get over this.

Her hand went to the emerald around her neck. She had a duty and it required her to be stronger than this. She couldn't let silly childhood fears consume her. Taking a deep breath, she let go and reached out to take the hand Duncan offered to help her up, keeping hold of her staff with the other.

"I had business to see to. I didnae intend on being out in the dark."

"If ye feel the need to come back out here and get lost again, come find me first." The clipped words hurt. He had been nothing but a gentleman until this moment.

Then it hit her.

"Were ye following me?"

"Aye."

"Why?"

"I saw ye leaving, and I was concerned ye would become lost."

Her head spun, and she wasn't sure if it was from the fall she'd taken or the new suspicion that took root. Had that really been his reason or had he been doing his cousin's bidding? Now that she'd had a couple days to think about Darnley's behavior, she had a suspicion that he may be the one the priestess had warned her about, the villain she would have to face to protect the Heart of Scotland.

His hand rose, tilting her chin up to meet his gaze, he studied her. "Are ye hurt?"

"I don't think so. I'm just a little shaken." That wasn't exactly true. Her whole body trembled.

"Let's get back."

She nodded as his hand slid down and took her gloved one. She'd never held a man's hand like this before. It was comforting, and as they walked, she was shocked to discover there was something magical about all the lights of the city and being here.

No, it was being here with him.

"How did ye learn to fight?" He sounded shocked that a lady might know how to use a weapon.

"I have brothers. They taught me."

"And ye chose a rod."

"'Tis easier to carry than a sword."

Not knowing what triggered her admission, her mouth fell open and the words came tumbling out. "I don't like cities."

"Why is that?" There was no judgment in his reply, only curiosity.

"When I was a child, my family went to Inverness. There was a festival going on and the streets were crowded. I was separated from my family." Her chest tightened.

"Och, I could see how that would be frightening as a child."

"Aye, but 'twas no' the worst of it. It took two days for them to find me. In that time, I wandered the streets looking for them, for food, and having to fend off men who wished me harm."

"That is terrible."

She didn't tell him the worst. She'd been able to defend herself against danger, but her abilities had started to develop then too. Touching items had become hazardous because someone else's memories and experiences flooded her senses. She'd not known what was happening until she'd made it back home and confessed her secret to the nuns, who had told her it was a gift from God. When she later told the priestess at the Fairy Pools, the woman had explained her destiny to her.

"I can see why ye might dislike the city then. Why did ye go to see the lawyer?"

"What lawyer?"

"Clement Litill." He sounded angry again.

"'Twas the other part of my reason for coming to Edinburgh. I was sent to retrieve a book from Greyfriars. I'm almost finished translating the other one and can go home."

"How long?"

"Just a few more days, I think."

They walked most of the way back in silence, holding tight to each other, and by the time Holyrood Palace came into view she was no longer trembling. As they neared the palace, Duncan's hand dropped from hers, and she realized for the first time since the confrontation that it was bitterly cold out.

He escorted her to her room. As she turned to say thank you and good night, he surprised her by opening her door and ushering her in, following and closing the door quickly. Ah, he was worried about being seen with her again.

Glancing at the fireplace, he smiled. "Good, they've been keeping it stoked for ye."

"Aye. I have been well cared for here."

Placing her rod against the wall near the door, she moved farther into the room and took the bag from around her neck, setting it on the table, then peeled the gloves from her fingers, laying them on top.

Why was he still here?

Duncan strolled over to the fire, poking at it then adding a piece of peat. She needed him to go. He couldn't be in here looking at her like that because it made her want to ask him to stay. She enjoyed his company and found herself wanting to know more about him. Something about this man called to a part of her no other had, but she still wasn't certain he could be trusted.

She couldn't let herself get closer to him without knowing how loyal he was to Darnley, and she wouldn't know that unless she used her gift. If she did, he may be like the others. He might think her mad, but in order to protect the stone, she had to know that his best interests lay with Scotland—not his distant cousin and a family lineage that included England.

When he returned his attention to her, she avoided his gaze

because she couldn't decipher what was in his eyes. Instead, she scanned him for anything that might give her a read. His tartan was crisp, newer, and probably spoke of his days here in the palace. She needed earlier than that. There was no way of knowing his pin's age, so she settled on his sword. It seemed like the thing he would have had the longest.

Now, how to get her hands on it? Oh, she had it.

"Can I ask for yer help with something?"

"Aye. Of course ye can."

"Will ye help me move the table toward the window? The light from the window will be better on my eyes while I'm trying to work."

"Aye." He crossed the space, easily picking up the small table and moving it to the spot she'd indicated. As he set it down, she came up behind him, just wanting a quick touch. If she was in and out of the vision fast enough, he'd never know.

Her hand brushed the hilt of his sword, and her fingers started to vibrate. She was beckoned into a vision, and her heart plummeted, submerged in grief as she sat holding the weapon in her lap on the side of a road. Carnage surrounded her. Dead. They were all dead. His whole family.

It had been his father's sword, and Duncan had plucked it from the ground near his father's body once he'd awoken. He'd waited for help and needed protection if the bandits came back to finish him off. His head pounded, and the blood from the blow he'd sustained had dried and stuck in his hair.

"Lady MacKinnon." Her name flitted in the distance.

He sat there overnight, hoping someone would come to help, memories of his childhood swirling in his head—all the wonderful things that were now lost, the games he'd played with his siblings, his mother reading to him, his father teaching him how to use this very sword.

"Leslee."

Her eyes stung as her hand fell from the hilt.

"Leslee." She blinked, and when her vision focused, it was to find his eyes filled with panic. Och, she'd been in the vision too long. He'd think her mad.

"Are ye well?"

She nodded, and she wasn't sure if the tears she held back were because of his loss or because now he would look upon her with disgust. But he didn't. He took her arm and guided her to the bed, urging her sit.

"Did ye hit yer head? Ye looked as if ye were about to fall over."

She nodded, and it was partially true. When the man had tackled her on the streets it had jolted her head. "Should I call for a healer?"

"Nae. I'll be fine. I just need a little rest." But his hands were already reaching forward, removing the pins from her hair. The curls bounced free, around her shoulders, down to her waist. As his fingers delved into her hair, she nearly sighed at the tingles erupting in their wake.

"What are ye doing?"

"Checking to make sure ye arenae hurt."

Och, she wasn't hurting, quite the opposite. She swallowed and allowed herself a quick glance at his mouth. When she looked back up, he studied her interest in him. She licked her lips.

A deep, husky sound escaped his throat and then his mouth was on hers and her body tilted, melting into his warmth. A surge of desire ran through her as the intimacy of the embrace intensified. His hand dropped from her head to circle her waist, and he drew her into his lap.

Here she was at the perfect height for him to deepen the embrace, and he did as her mouth opened to him. His tongue dived in to tangle with hers. New waves of need pulsated through her as she gave in willingly to the caress. Her arms enveloped him, trying to get closer, trying to find out what it was that her body craved, what the more was, because she wanted it.

Suddenly, he was retreating, setting her aside and standing. Her head felt fuzzy again and it wasn't from the vision or the jolt she'd taken, it was the lingering effect of his touch. Why had he backed away? Had he realized she wasn't normal?

He was breathing heavily, while she couldn't breathe at all. Tearing his eyes from her, looking toward escape, he asked, "Are ye certain ye are no' hurt?"

"Aye."

"Then do me a favor. Dinnae leave the palace or abbey again without coming to get me first. I'll make sure ye are safe."

All she could do was nod as he stomped toward the door. He put his hand on the handle then turned back over his shoulder. "Keep yer door locked. My cousin will be in the palace some this week with this wedding coming up. I dinnae like his interest in ye."

As the door shut behind him, she was left cold and wondering if Duncan didn't like that Henry might be interested in her because he was jealous or because he had figured out what she was and deemed her unworthy of Lord Darnley's attention.

5

Thankfully, no one was about when Duncan left Leslee's room. It had been so hard to pull away. He hadn't wanted to. He had wanted her, still wanted her, didn't think he would stop wanting her, but it wasn't meant to be. He'd seen the fear in her eyes earlier, even though she'd tried to hide it. She would never be happy in the city, not after what she'd been through and not now that she'd been attacked in Edinburgh.

Her kiss had been heaven. It had been innocent and trusting, and he'd almost gone too far. He had gone too far. Retreating down the hall, he decided it was best to put distance between them before he did something he couldn't take back. If he took it any further, he knew he wouldn't be able to let her go and it would destroy who she was to be forced to stay.

Over the next few days, he continued to purposely keep his distance. She appeared to do the same, spending more and more time sequestered in her room with those books. Hell, he'd kept away, but that didn't mean he couldn't ask the servants about her.

When his cousin was about, he kept a close watch, making sure the man kept his roaming hands far away from her seductive curves. Yes, he'd felt them when he'd pulled her onto his lap. Even now, as he thought about it the longing to claim her for himself grew stronger.

He was just finishing his shift with the prince when the queen appeared. "Please let Lady MacKinnon know I would like her to join me for dinner tonight. She is leaving soon. I've talked her into staying through the wedding so that I can have a sufficient number of guards to see her home."

"Aye, Yer Majesty."

"Please escort her and be vigilant with her tonight. We have many guests here, and I fear for her virtue without a chaperone. Her family was to return from a visit to Stirling to take her back, but she has sent word to them, and I agreed to have her escorted back since she is near completing her task and eager to return home."

At the thought of facing her again, it should have been dread coursing through him, but it wasn't. Avoiding her recently had been torture, and now he had no choice. His blood pumped faster, and the thrum running through his veins was excitement.

"Also, my husband will be present this evening and I'm afraid I've already had word that he's been drinking. I don't know how Henry talked me into letting him back in, so I want you at dinner as well."

"Aye, Yer Majesty." He bowed and pivoted to make his way to see the woman who hadn't left his thoughts since the first time he'd laid eyes upon her.

Moments later, he was knocking on the solid wood of her door. She didn't answer. Maybe she was asleep. Turning the knob, he was surprised to find the door unlatched as it swung in slowly.

She was sitting at the table he'd pushed to the window, her long red curls hanging loose down her back, apparently absorbed in her work. The door clicked when he shut it, but she didn't turn, so he walked around toward her front to avoid startling her.

As he moved closer, he caught a glimpse of her small feet under the table. They were bare, the sight reminding him of the home he'd lost and how he and his brothers and sister would run around their home without shoes. There was something intimate about it. He swallowed and looked closer to see she wore nothing more than a shift. His heart thudded loudly. She hadn't noticed him yet. Should he leave?

while attempting to close the lid on the memories that he'd tried desperately to keep hidden away.

※

HE HATED HER. IT WAS THE ONLY EXPLANATION FOR THE FEAR SHE saw in his eyes. No, perhaps he thought her insane like others who had seen her read an object. Would everyone else in the palace think her crazy now? She thought he might be discreet, but she'd also thought he could handle the truth.

She'd never tried to explain her gift to someone before, but maybe she'd gone about it the wrong way. It had never mattered what others thought of her, but she had been compelled to tell Duncan. If she'd only locked the door, she could have spared them both this. Now she would have to leave knowing the connection she'd felt between them had been severed.

Och, he was coming back, and she had to spend the evening with the queen again. Squaring her shoulders, she sat at the dressing table to start on her hair. This was not about her. She had more important things to worry about, things that required she leave Edinburgh as quickly as possible.

She hoped Lord Darnley wouldn't be at dinner. The man made her stomach churn.

She chose her gown with the deep green corset, the one that made her feel confident. Two more days. That was what she had promised the queen and she could do it. But no more.

A while later, nerves calmer, a knock sounded at the door. Closing her eyes, she took a deep breath before opening it. Duncan stood tall and proud, stiff, and the light that normally shone in his eyes when he spoke was missing. "Ye should latch yer door when ye are in the room."

She nodded and moved out into the hall, aware of a gulf separating them. She longed for the night they had walked hand-in-hand back to the palace. He'd probably never touch her again now that he knew her secret...well, one of her secrets. She still couldn't tell him about the stone at her neck that would protect Scotland from its foes or that she was responsible for its safety.

They'd almost made it to the queen's chamber when he spoke. "Ye should stay near me. My cousin will be here, and I dinnae like the way he looks at ye."

"Aye." She didn't want to be next to Duncan, but she knew deep down that Lord Darnley was trouble and she must avoid him at all costs. On cue, as they stepped into the room, the mark on her hip started to heat and tickle as the man's cold eyes landed on her. It was as if he sensed her as well. Was he the one she'd been warned about?

The chamber was filled with people she'd not seen before, probably here for the wedding, and thankfully most of the seats near the queen and her husband were occupied.

Duncan's hand reached for hers, and she flinched. Lord Darnley's lips quirked up on one side, a maniacal, twisted grin. His unabashed contemplation followed her as Duncan led her to the opposite side of the table, as far away from their hosts as possible.

The first course was served, and she reached for a cup of wine, careful to only take a small sip—she would not lose her senses tonight.

Duncan leaned in and whispered, "Do ye wear the gloves to prevent seeing things?"

"Aye. I do. They are like a shield."

"Can ye no' control it then?"

"Most of the time, well, I've gotten better about it, but I thought 'twould be safer here where I dinnae ken people to make sure I kept to myself and didnae show people."

"I agree. 'Tis best not to let anyone else ken." And she wasn't sure what she heard in his voice. Fear, disgust, a hint of protectiveness?

"The queen tells me ye will be leaving soon."

"Aye."

Would she have contemplated staying had he accepted her gift? She couldn't. Not as long as Darnley was here, especially if he was who she suspected. It fit, the queen's husband being from England, he had only come to Scotland to wed Mary. If he got his hands on the stone, he'd take it away and Scotland would suffer. She wouldn't let that happen.

The way Lord Darnley was watching her, he had a suspicion of who she was as well.

"I've never been to the Isle of Skye. What do ye miss most about it?"

"My family," she said without thinking. How insensitive after what she'd seen, after what she'd made him relive tonight.

"I'm sorry. I didnae..."

"'Tis alright. It's been a long time. I still miss them."

She placed her hand on his and he didn't retreat.

"We were close."

"I saw that too." She pulled away, hoping he wouldn't shut her out, but also not wanting to give him the opportunity to draw back first.

He surprised her. "What else did ye see?" She glanced around. It was loud, and she'd already had to raise her voice.

"I'll tell ye in private. I dinnae wish to talk about it here."

He nodded.

The lass next to her started a conversation with her and she was drawn in for the rest of the meal. Her mark stung, raw and inflamed the whole while, but she kept her gaze from Darnley's. Only once did she venture to look his way, and she saw the obsession and anger there. All directed at her.

Suddenly, Duncan's hand was on her leg, warm and reassuring. "I think 'tis time we get ye back to yer room." Food and wine were still being brought out, but she didn't object. "The queen willnae mind, there are too many guests for her to have time with ye."

"I would like that. Thank ye."

"Let me go tell her." He rose and made his way to the queen, leaning down to whisper something in her ear. Mary smiled, then glanced at her and nodded.

Duncan was once again by her side, pulling her chair out and then escorting her to the door.

"Is the queen trying to reconcile with yer cousin?"

"She is angry that he killed her favorite advisor. I dinnae think she will forgive him, but he has a way with words, and she keeps letting him back in."

"Why would he do such a thing?"

"The man was the only one in a room that would stand his ground against Henry. Everyone else adores him and follows his commands without thought."

"Even ye?"

"Aye, sometimes. I find myself wondering why I'm doing some of the things he asks, but then I remember he is my only family."

They were close to her room now and she had to know, so the question spilled from her lips even as her body tensed, waiting for his reply. "Do ye think me mad?"

"What?"

She stood tall, remembering what the nuns had told her. God had given her this special gift. It was nothing to be ashamed of, she should be proud.

"That I can see the past."

"Nae. I think 'tis a miracle." His hand rose, caressing her cheek as his sapphire gaze studied her. And for a moment she thought he would lean in and kiss her right there in the doorway outside her room. Her breath caught, and her mouth fell open, but instead he took a deep breath and shook his head, putting more distance between them.

But he didn't leave. They stood there a moment before he asked, "Will ye tell me more of what ye saw?"

"Aye, if ye wish it."

"I do, but I need to go get something first." She nodded, and he closed the distance again, but he reached around her to open the door.

Pushing it in, he instructed, "Lock it until ye ken 'tis I outside. There are too many strangers lurking about."

"Aye." And with that, he was gone.

6

Returning from his errands, Duncan paused outside Leslee's door to remind himself that as much as he wanted to have her, she didn't belong here. He had to keep his hands and his mouth to himself, because if he touched her again he might not be able to stop himself.

Knocking lightly, his breath caught when she opened the door. She'd let her red curls down and they bounced around her shoulders as her pink lips opened in a welcoming smile. Some man would be lucky to come home to her each evening, but it wouldn't be him. The thought caused a longing in his chest, so he only nodded at her when he strolled in.

She'd removed her gloves, and he took special notice of her long, slender fingers, the ones that God had granted favor to. He knew many people would call her a witch, but there was something genuine and pure about her. He'd known she was special the first time he'd seen her.

A pitcher of wine in one hand and two cups stacked in the other, he set the items on the floor near the fireplace and turned back to watch her shut the door. "Latch it. Ye really should keep it latched all the time, especially with so many people about."

"Aye. I've learned my lesson."

He nodded then yanked a blanket from the bed and folded it in front of the dancing flames as well. Next, he removed his boots and placed them next to her slippers.

"Sit." He motioned to the pallet he'd made.

Thankfully, she smiled and didn't object. He wanted to watch her in the firelight, enjoy her company for the last little bit of time they had together. Sitting by the fire was comfortable and safer than near the bed.

Taking a seat on the floor next to her, a sense of peace washed over him. "I was hoping ye would do something for me." He held up a box he'd picked up when he went back to his quarters.

Curious green eyes sparkled in the light. "What is it?"

"Some things that belonged to my family."

"Ye are certain ye dinnae think I'm mad?"

"Nae, I think ye are a miracle."

"But ye couldnae leave fast enough when…"

"It wasnae ye. Och, I didnae want ye to think that. It's just that I've tried to push the memories of my family away for years. When I was sent to school, I had nothing to cling to but being the best at everything. I couldnae let their memories haunt me."

His heart hurt at the admission. He'd not even realized he'd tried to forget them, and now he knew it was why he had sought out Henry. He wanted that connection to family. He missed it.

"I had to be by myself to deal with the memories. I had pushed it all away and it came crashing back when ye reminded me."

Leslee closed her eyes and when she opened them he could swear there was a sheen of moisture in them. But it wasn't sadness—he couldn't place it.

"I've never told anyone before because anyone that has seen it happen has accused me of being a witch." Her gaze drifted down to her hands.

"Nae."

"Ye asked why I was no' wed. No one wants me because they are scared of me." She still wouldn't meet his stare.

"Och, they are fools. Ye are special. I kenned that the first time I saw ye."

She glanced at him then. "Thank ye."

He didn't know who had made her feel less than a miracle, but he wanted her to know she was special, wanted her to always have the look she wore right now. She had a confidence that was buried just beneath the surface and it only came out when she felt threatened. He wanted her to wear it all the time.

"Now, what did ye bring? I've never done this for anyone, but I'll see if I can get something."

He couldn't imagine people shunning her for this amazing gift. No wonder she kept to herself, despite her curious and questioning nature. It must have been hard for her.

"But dinnae fear for me. While the vision is happening, I won't really be here."

"I will try no' to worry."

"Can I have a cup of the wine first?"

"Aye. I think I'll let ye have some. After all, ye are already in yer room, and I ken I willnae find ye in my bed later." Not that he would mind, but he wouldn't have the willpower to carry her back anymore.

Color flushed her cheeks, and he was happy he had put it there. Hell, he wanted her back in his bed, wanted her by his side, so they could sit like this every evening. But he knew that they lived two different lives and it wasn't meant to be.

She sipped on her wine then set the cup down and glanced back up at him. "Now what's in the box?"

His fingers started to tremble as he flipped the lid up. He'd not opened it in years. Setting it in front of her, he breathed deeply. "These belonged to my mother, father, brothers, and sister."

"I don't ken how many I'll be able to read before I tire, so which do ye want me to start with?"

Peeking inside, he retrieved his mother's pin. Leslee cupped her hands in a welcoming embrace. He hesitated for a moment, but she smiled and nodded.

Placing the tarnished, silver family crest in her palms, he couldn't resist the urge to touch her fingers as he closed them around the precious object. Something he wouldn't trust with anyone else.

She held it to her heart and closed her eyes, waiting...well, he wasn't sure what she was doing. Then her eyes reopened with a glazed, distant look. Not knowing how long it would last, he felt helpless and couldn't quell the worry that came over him.

Moving to his knees, he skirted over to rest behind her, wrapping his arms around Leslee's waist and drawing her close to his chest. She leaned into him, her eyes still unfocused, and his heart opened. There was something so intimate about what she was doing for him, and she'd placed all her trust in him when she was at her most vulnerable.

It wasn't long before he heard a sigh and then her hands lowered. She glanced over her shoulder, her lips turning up as she continued to let her body rest against his.

"Are ye well?"

"Aye." She shifted, his arms loosening with the movement, but she didn't go far as she let her light weight fall back onto his chest. He took the moment to breathe her in. "'Twas yer mother's."

He nodded, afraid if he said something she'd hear the vulnerability pulsing through his veins. Leslee continued to hold the brooch in her palm as her other hand rested on his knee. The caress so light, it felt like a gentle breeze, tickling and soothing at the same time.

"I saw her telling ye and yer little brother tales of Robin Hood. She was an amazing storyteller and she loved it. She especially loved how yer eyes would widen and follow her movements."

Images ran through his head, memories he'd not dared to relive since that day, and he held on to Leslee to keep him grounded, to save him if he fell.

"I saw her pretending to have a bow and then ye asking for one. Then I saw her telling yer father about it when he returned to the room which had a tapestry of the tree of knowledge hanging on the wall. Ye look so much like him, but ye have yer mother's eyes."

Cradling her near, he nuzzled his head into her neck, treasuring her and what she'd just given him as he fought the sting in his eyes. He'd forgotten it all, but now it came flooding back.

"Was that all?" His voice shook.

"Aye, but if I try again another time, I could see something different. It changes every time."

He nodded, and even though she couldn't see, he knew she'd felt it. Her finger circled his knee, sending waves of soothing vibrations through his leg, and he wanted to melt into the touch.

"Would ye like for me to do another?" He just wanted to hold her, cherish her and what she'd just given him, but their time was limited.

"Are ye sure ye are no' tired?" His mouth was so near her ear, and she tilted slightly as if his voice called to her. Temptation to kiss her there tore at him, but he couldn't do that to her. He backed off a little, unable to find the strength to remove himself entirely.

"Aye."

"Then, yes."

They went on for a couple hours, and he savored each tale she told, each memory and revelation that reminded him of who he was and where he had come from. He continued to hold her, and when she eventually went limp against his chest, her eyes closed, he knew they were done. He held her a few more minutes before scooping her up and carrying her to her bed.

She was still fully clothed, and he was tempted to remove her gown so that she could sleep comfortably, but it would be an abuse of her trust, so instead he loosened the laces of her corset. After laying her down, he retrieved the blanket from the floor, shook it out and covered her.

Placing a soft kiss on her forehead, he inhaled the sweet scent of lavender clinging to her and knew it would always remind him of her.

He collected his box and put another piece of peat in the fire before picking up the wine and glasses. On his way out, he took the extra key hanging on a hook by the door. No one was in the cold, dark hall when he left, so he secured the latch and slid the key back under the door to ensure he wouldn't be tempted to come back and claim her for his own.

WAKING TO THE SUN SHINING THROUGH THE WINDOW, LESLEE WAS

surprised to see how high it was. She'd slept most of the morning. Using her gift usually made her tired, so it would only make sense that after she'd pushed herself these last two weeks and then spent the late evening hours reading for Duncan, her body had needed some rest.

As much as she wanted to stay here with him, she couldn't remain close to Lord Darnley, who was most likely the enemy the priestess had warned her about. Although she would always remember what she'd shared with Duncan last night. They fit—there was no other way to explain it. No one had ever made her feel so at ease when reading. She usually locked herself away so no one could see, but with Duncan, she felt comfortable, even respected.

She'd fallen asleep at some point, which had been a huge mistake, but it had proven she could trust him because the precious stone around her neck was still there. He had not attempted to take it, but she still couldn't put herself between him and his cousin, not knowing what family meant to him. If he were forced to choose, he would have to side with Darnley, and that would destroy her.

She changed clothes, found her key by the door, and made her way down to see if she'd missed the morning meal. Thankfully, with the palace packed and preparations underway for the wedding today, there was an abundance of food laid out. Filling a plate, she ate quickly, then made her way back to her room to finish the text. She'd be done by noon and would be able to leave first thing tomorrow.

After finishing, she let her mind drift to last night. Would she see Duncan again before leaving? It might be best to avoid him because her emotions were twisted when it came to him.

Closing the book for the last time and collecting her papers, hands full, she managed to open her door and slip out. She needed to make her way to the abbey and let the men who had sent for her know that she was done and hand over the last of her translations. Strolling down the hall, she breathed a sigh of relief that she could return home. Entering the staircase to head down, her mark suddenly burned.

She froze. Her hands were full and there was no way to retrieve her staff before he appeared.

"Lady MacKinnon. So this is where my wife has been keeping you."

Of course Darnley knew, she could think of no other reason for him to be in the guest quarters.

"Greetings, Lord Darnley, I need to get these to the abbey." She cut to the side, acting as if he were any ordinary man, but her blood raced. If he was after the Heart of Scotland, she stood a better chance at defeating him out in the open.

He slid in front of her, blocking her retreat. "Lady MacKinnon, surely you can take the time to converse with one of your hosts. I've heard you have excellent manners."

"Why do ye no' escort me then?" She tried to sound casual, but she was already looking around for anything that would double as a weapon.

He didn't move. The smell of spirits enveloped him as if he'd washed in them this morning.

"I hear you are going back to Skye."

"Aye, 'tis time to go home."

"Do you have the stone?" Strange sensations floated around her as if she too had been imbibing in whisky.

"I'm sorry I cannae help ye with that." She clipped in the most defiant tone she could manage, ready to smash him in the face with the heavy book if need be. She could find a horse and flee, but would she be able to outrun the guards when they came looking for the lass who assaulted the king consort?

"Give it to me." He crowded into her space.

Standing her ground, she said, "Ye are mistaken."

"Interesting. How is it you can ignore my command? Give me the stone." Vibrations pulsated in waves toward her with the words, but she could almost feel them fall to the ground as they bounced from her.

"Ye must have me confused with someone else."

"No. I do not. I can feel it. It's calling to me and my mark burns when you are near. You are the guardian."

She didn't deny it. She stood taller, knowing that he was the one she'd been warned about. If she could get to a weapon and get him away from the palace, he wouldn't be a threat. The key was to get to him on her own ground, or even neutral territory.

She felt naked before him without her staff. She'd trained for this, but if she killed the queen's husband in their own palace, she would be arrested and authorities would take the stone. They had to be somewhere private if she was going to confront him.

Suddenly, his hands were on her shoulders, pushing her back into the wall. Book and papers tumbled to the ground with a boom that echoed through the stairwell.

"Give it to me."

"Nae." She kicked out at him, but he had the advantage of height and strength. He pinned her leg with his own.

"Then I'll take it."

One of his hands released her and he twisted to grab at her neck, but before he could get a grasp on the chain that held the emerald, she slammed her knee into his groin. He cried out in pain and doubled over.

She turned to run for her weapon, but his hand closed around her arm while the other pulled back to strike her. She watched as, midway through his attack, a hand caught his, yanking Darnley off her and pushing him back.

"What are ye doing, cousin?" Duncan's broad shoulders were drawn back, and he positioned himself between her and Darnley.

The king consort's face darkened, and he glared back and forth between the two of them before Duncan continued to scold him. "I think ye have had too much to drink. Ye may want to go get cleaned up before the wedding. Yer wife is expecting ye there."

"You will give it to me." Darnley's eyes pinned her with hatred and insanity. If he got his hands on the stone, he would destroy Scotland. She couldn't let that happen. The crazed man's glare drifted to Duncan, who looked torn, but fierce. Darnley's mouth moved to issue a command, but Duncan beat him to it.

"Go get sobered up, Henry," her savior spat at the madman.

The king consort clenched his fists but must have decided he couldn't take them both on at one time. "I will have it." A sick smirk appeared, and he looked to Duncan then back to her as if he'd already hatched some evil plan in his head. Finally, he turned and made his way down the stairs.

"Are ye hurt?"

"Nae. I'm fine." She bent to collect the precious pages of her work strewn all over the floor. Duncan reached down for the book then helped her retrieve the rest. "I'm sorry about Henry. He usually does not pursue lasses that have told him no."

"Ye cannae help yer cousin's behavior." The fiery mark on her hip finally faded, and she felt comfortable that the threat was a reasonable distance away.

"Can I help ye with anything?"

"I need to put it all back in order then take it to the abbey. Will ye escort me?"

"Aye. The prince is in good hands today. I am free."

"Thank ye." She started back toward her room and Duncan followed.

He sat at the table watching as she went through the papers to make sure they were in order then he escorted her to deliver everything and accompanied her back to the room.

They were alone again, and as he checked her fire, she remembered the security and peace she'd experienced in his arms last night. She'd never felt that connection with anyone. Likely never would again. She would treasure every moment she had spent with him.

But she wanted more, one more night to take with her, to hold on to and cherish, before she went back to her solitary life where she watched her family marry and have children. They didn't have the same responsibility as she, but it didn't stop her from wishing she could have that too. This was her one chance to experience love.

Decision made, she ambled toward the door, ensuring it was locked. When she turned back, his gaze was fixed on her. Strolling up to him, she put her hands on his heated cheeks then rose up on her toes to place her lips on his.

He groaned as his arms circled around her, drawing her in, consuming her, and taking her out of time, out of place. Knowing she could trust this man, she let everything go as Duncan's mouth claimed hers, the possession calling to that innocent part of her that believed everything was possible. She pushed away any doubts.

He pulled back, breathless, his eyes dilated as they devoured her.

"Leslee, if we..." But she didn't want to hear that there would be regrets—she only knew she would regret not giving in to the emotions he elicited in her.

"Shhh. I want this. I want to be with ye, Duncan."

"If we—"

She cut him off again, pressing her mouth to his. It didn't matter that he couldn't go back to Skye with her. Right now was all she needed.

7

Och, he'd never before been so affected by a lass, but he knew somewhere deep inside it was right. They would be happy together. He would make sure she was well cared for, even if they had to find a small place outside of Edinburgh and he had to hire someone to escort her to the city when he wasn't available.

And he would protect and care for her, even keep his cousin away from her. She was his. From this moment on, they belonged together.

As his tongue danced with hers, peace and desire washed over him. For the first time since he'd lost his family, he knew where he belonged. With Leslee.

Still, he would not force her into life here with him, so he asked one more time. "Ye are certain this is what ye want."

"Aye. I've never wanted anything more." And those words drove him over the edge.

His mouth drifted across her jaw, placing kisses along the route as he made his way to her long, gently sloping neck. Her hands were on his ribs, and as he nipped at her skin, she clenched his sides, holding on, arching into his touch.

His fingers worked frantically to remove her jacket and corset as he continued to lavish his attention on her throat, then he tilted his head to whisper in her ear. "I've dreamt about doing this from the night I found ye in my bed." He nibbled on her lobe, and she turned into him, giving him better access.

Peeling off her skirts, they fell to the floor, and he took her by the waist, swinging her up and away from the discarded material. He set her on the mattress, where she removed her slippers and stockings as he unbelted his sword, laying it just under the bed for easy access if needed, then he tore his own clothes off, dropping them to the floor.

When his gaze returned to hers, she stood and removed the pins from her hair. As the fiery curls fell to her waist, his cock throbbed. He took her mouth in another kiss as his hands drifted down, sliding over her curves and to the hem of her shift. Grabbing the soft material, he broke the embrace and pulled the garment up and over her head.

His mouth watered as he let the shift drop to the floor, his regard roaming from her swollen lips down to her pert breasts and the green stone nestled between them. The emerald reminded him of her eyes. He wanted to take in all of her, and his stare drifted farther to find an unusual birthmark on her hip. It almost looked like a dagger.

Curious, he moved closer, placed his hands on her hips, but as the warm flesh of her bare body heated his, the urge to draw her nearer intensified, and he encircled her waist with one arm. Leslee's hands clasped onto his hips, then slid behind his back, urging him near as her bare breasts brushed against his chest. He dipped his head to claim her mouth again. She tasted of honey, and as the heady lavender scent that clung to her reached his senses, he was enthralled.

Lifting her and drawing her closer, his mouth still on hers, he backed her to the bed, then gently ended the embrace before easing her down onto the plush mattress. Her eyes studied him, curiosity, warmth, and need, but if she were nervous, her emerald gaze didn't show it.

This attraction had moved so quickly between them, but it felt right, and he knew he wanted her as his wife. He recognized what Leslee would be giving up and had to know, just once more, that it was what she wanted. "Are ye certain?"

"Aye."

Her eyes were dilated and needy, drawing him in and making him forget everything but her and this moment. But he didn't want to rush this, he wanted their first time to last, so instead of climbing on top of her, he said, "Back up a little."

She did, and he climbed onto the mattress next to her, resting on his elbow and looking down at her as he let his other hand rest on one breast. She moved into the touch, and his manhood protested the slow pace he was striving for, wanting him to sate the throbbing urgency. Instead, he leaned down as he cupped the firm mound, his mouth placing gentle kisses then licking at the peak of her engorged nipple. She arched into him, and he couldn't help but smile at her eagerness.

Edging upward, he let his mouth trail kisses to her neck, the gentle slope beckoning him farther under her spell as she tilted to give him better access. As he lavished her with affection, he let his hand drift down, across her belly, to land in a mass of curls at the apex of her legs, only stopping for a moment to let his fingers play in the soft hair.

He reached down to feel her core, and his lips once again met hers, delving and tasting the potency of her desire while he trailed one finger up and down her slick and ready center. She arched into him, and something like a plea escaped through their embrace.

That sound was his undoing. He pulled back, fascinated by the bliss on her face as he continued to massage her center. Leslee's green gaze met his as a pant escaped her lips and he knew she was about to reach her climax. He wanted to be inside her when that happened. Feel her clench around him and draw him under with her. He slid his fingers down, spreading her thighs apart as he rose to position himself between her legs.

Taking his cock in his hand, he slid it up and down her passage, soaking up the proof of her arousal, the contact sending urgent waves of pressure and need crashing over him. Some semblance of awareness kept him from thrusting into her with abandon, rather, he let the head of his penis penetrate her warm sheath and slowly drove in. Buried to the hilt, pleasure he'd never felt assailed him at the same time she gasped and clenched his sides.

"'Tis normal. I've been told it willnae hurt ye again."

He remained still until she gave him a tentative smile, but instead of pulling out and thrusting back in, he gently rocked back and forth, terrified of hurting her, yet unable to stop moving completely. Their hips ground together, and before long Leslee's gaze filled with desire once more.

As he continued to move, small pants escaped from her lips and, suddenly, she was falling to pieces beneath him. Her eyes focused on him, hands gripping his hips as she held on, letting the pleasure pull her under. It was the most beautiful sight he'd ever seen.

Her tight passage clenched around him. He withdrew slightly, returned to the warmth and then did it again. Faster as she continued to hold on and the pleasure spiked, pulsating through him as he spilled his seed inside her.

He stayed there, soaking her in, this miracle he'd been lucky enough to find. Eventually, his arms started to tire, and he moved back to her side, but he didn't release the connection completely, letting his hand trail up and down her curves. Tracing her breasts and her belly.

"Ye are beautiful."

"Thank ye." She closed her eyes and arched into his touch. "That was wonderful."

"Aye. And we can do it anytime ye like. Mayhap tomorrow we can look for a cottage outside of the city."

Her lids flew open.

"What?" She came up on her elbows and his arm fell from her side. The sleepy, sated look he had been enjoying on her face turned to panic.

"For when we wed. We can't stay here," he tried to reassure her.

"Nae. We cannae wed." Something in his chest stabbed at him as a strange numbness started to invade.

"Ye said ye understood if we did this we would marry."

"Nae, 'tis no' what I meant."

"I asked several times." Anger and confusion mixed together, threatening his control.

"I am going back to Skye tomorrow."

※

LESLEE COULDN'T STAY HERE. SHE THOUGHT HE KNEW THAT. NOT

once had she agreed to wed him and make a life here. He hadn't even asked. Aye, what they'd just done was beautiful and amazing and had made every concern disappear for a few moments, but that wasn't who she was. Strengthening her resolve, she repeated to herself that she was the guardian and she didn't belong here, even as a hole was torn in her heart at the realization that a life with him would be incredible.

"I cannae stay." Sitting up completely, she attempted to climb over him to retrieve her clothes.

His hand caught her arm, gentle but firm, "Why?"

She turned away at the disappointment she saw in his gaze. Taking her chin with his other hand, he softly tilted her face to his. "Please, tell me why. Trust me. I'm prepared to make ye my wife."

"Ye willnae believe me."

"Try me."

Her mind drifted back to the day she'd discovered she was the new guardian of the stone. She'd felt intense vibrations coming from the earth and had an overwhelming desire to go to the Fairy Pools. It had been a long ride on her palfrey to get to the place she'd once visited as a child. Heather and thistle dotted the landscape, and she was mesmerized by the purples and lavenders as she drew near.

Finally dismounting near the water, she removed her slippers and stockings. There wasn't a soul around, so she drew off her gown and laid it on a nearby rock. Dressed only in her shift, she waded out into the magical place and felt a peace and purpose wash over her, as if the cool water had somehow soothed her very being.

But it wasn't enough. An unknown force beckoned her toward the falling water as her hip started to burn. Lifting her shift to be certain a bug had not bitten her, she discovered something that looked like a raised birthmark on her hip. It appeared to be in the shape of a dagger, yes, it definitely looked like a dirk, pointed down, and it wasn't raised, it was flush against her skin. Following the direction, her eyes caught on something glistening in the water.

Reaching down to grasp at the object, surprised when her hand caught on it, she withdrew a chain of gold, a beautiful green stone dangling from it. Pulling it close to inspect it, energy radiated from it, thrumming like a heartbeat.

She stepped out of the pool to sit on a large, flat stone jutting into the water. Who would have tossed away something so wondrous? The thought crossed her mind that it might belong to the Fae and perhaps they would punish her for removing it.

She dipped the stone back into the water as she debated what to do. Just then, a woman appeared on the rock opposite her. She wore a long cape of dark green that matched the velveteen gown she had on beneath.

The priestess began to speak about her destiny, but Duncan pulled her from the memory.

"If 'tis the city, it willnae be a problem. We can live farther out. I promise to keep ye safe." The pleading in his voice broke her heart, but she couldn't. The priestess had made it clear that day, her life was not her own.

She shook her head.

"Can ye no' trust me?"

"If 'twere just Edinburgh, 'twould no' be a problem. 'Tis yer cousin."

"Henry?"

She cringed at his name. "Aye."

"I ken he can be hard to accept. Ye will never have to see him."

"Nae. He will come for me." This man was willing to give her his life, his future. He accepted her gift and had proven he could be trusted. But how to explain it all?

She slid off the foot of the bed so she wouldn't have to climb over him. Donning her shift, she took a deep breath and a leap of faith. "I didnae come to Edinburgh only to translate the text. I have another reason."

Stepping over to the table, she picked up the bag she had slung over the chair, reached in and pulled out the small book she'd retrieved from Clement Litill. The man had discovered it among his large collection of volumes and had somehow notified the priestess it required safekeeping so that the information it contained wasn't exploited.

The woman had appeared to her not long after, presented her with the coin necklace and instructed her to come to Edinburgh to translate the text. But most importantly, she was to retrieve the book and bring it home so it could be secured.

"I came for this." Holding it up, she eased back over to the bed, sitting beside Duncan as she held the precious volume to her chest.

"If I give ye this information, ye cannae tell a soul. 'Tis for the safety of Scotland." He nodded. "Can ye promise me?" Doubt crept in, but this man had proven he could be trusted.

"Aye, I promise."

Flipping open the pages, she turned to the relevant passage and started to read.

While beautiful and ethereal in her wildness, Scotland held within her so much power, she could very well tear herself apart. To ensure Scotland's safety, an ancient order of druids decided to safeguard her very heart.

They made a stone of the purest emerald green, protected by a necklace wrought of gold, and locked her soul within, imbuing it with magical properties no mortal could ever destroy. For every generation to come, the soul of the stone would select a protector, a woman with a pure heart and the ferocity of a warrior. Upon her death, the immortal stone would then seek the security of its next protector.

But the battle of light and dark is as old as time, and nature has a way of balancing itself—whether for good or evil.

When the reach of the stone stretches toward its next guardian, so too does the call echo out to the opposing force, a man whose heart is set on reclaiming Scotland for his own purposes. Both guardian and nemesis receive their mark and are drawn toward the stone that lies in wait within the glittering shallows of the fairy pools, guarded by the Priestesses of the Stone.

Scotland's darkest days will emerge if the stone should fall into the wrong hands.

The fate of the chosen is a never-ending battle for the stone, Scotland's life-blood, between the protector and her adversary. For when one dies, a new struggle will begin again until the end of time.

"This is why I cannae stay. I am the guardian."

Silence met her admission. After a moment, he reached over, clasping her hand in his.

"I can help protect ye and Scotland." The words were sincere, and she wanted to think it could be, but she had to destroy his closest family member in order to fulfill her duty.

"Nae. Ye cannae." She shook her head.

"Do ye no' have faith in me?"

"'Tis no' ye. 'Tis yer cousin who is also called to the stone. He willnae stop until he possesses it. I must leave, and when he comes to claim it, I will fight him on my own lands."

"Nae, I cannae believe it. I'll keep Henry away from ye." His words were soft, as if he were trying to grapple with her story and determine if she truly was mad.

"Here, if I harm him, I will be sent to prison, and I dinnae ken what will become of the stone. 'Tis a risk I cannae take." She stared straight into Duncan's eyes, making sure he understood the gravity of her conviction.

"He will follow me, and when he comes for the stone, we will fight 'til one of us is dead. I willnae let him have it."

8

Duncan didn't know what to say. Before Henry's slide into spirits, debauchery, and murder, his cousin had been charming and well-liked. Leslee wanted to kill him, which shouldn't surprise him, because as of late, most people didn't tolerate the king consort's presence, but hell, she really meant it. This was no jest.

Mind whirling around what she'd just said, he let his thoughts relive the last two weeks. He'd not once found Leslee to be dishonest. In fact, she had trusted him with two of her most closely guarded secrets. And Henry had shown a strange interest in her, but he'd been drunk and Leslee was a bonny lass. Although Henry had an abrasive personality, he'd never seen his cousin go after a woman the way he had attacked her.

The passage she read came from a book given to her by a person considered to be one of the most reputable men in all of Edinburgh. It had said something about a mark. Was that what he'd seen? Taking the volume from her hands, he set it on the small table beside the bed, and reaching back over, coiled his arm around her waist, pulling her over his body to lay her back down on the bed. She squealed with the unexpected movement.

"What are ye doing?" She pushed at him, on edge and tensed to defend herself if needed.

"Can I see?"

He reached for the end of her shift and drew it up to inspect what he'd seen earlier but had been too excited to examine. She tried to sit up. "Ye had a mark." Up on her elbows, her gaze riveted on his, a steely determination in her green eyes, she nodded, and he glanced back down and continued to lift the material.

On her hip, a reddish-brown spot just slightly larger than a coin caught his eye. He let his fingers drift to inspect it. Tracing the outline, he realized it was flush with her skin as if it had always been part of her, and it was in the shape of a dagger, tilted slightly with the point aimed down toward her toes. "Were ye born with this?"

"Nae. It appeared when the stone called out to me." Sitting all the way up, she met his gaze, and it was clear that she believed what she said.

"The emerald ye wear. That's it?" Her hand drifted to the stone buried beneath her shift, hidden from view of the public. Most people that possessed a rock of such beauty would proudly wear it out in the open.

"Aye. 'Tis crucial to Scotland that I protect it."

She'd not lied about her gift. Would she deceive him about this? He couldn't see a reason for her to do so.

"And Henry?"

"He is the one who would take it for his own gain. If he takes it to England, we are all at risk of famine and plague."

"How do ye ken 'tis him?"

"When I am near him, the mark starts to burn. It's like a warning signal." She glanced away and took a deep breath—bolstering her courage to give him some other shock? "There is something else ye need to ken. I think he controls people with his words. I dinnae ken how he does it, but he tried it on me and was angry when it didnae work."

There had been times he found himself questioning some of the orders his cousin had given, but he followed Henry's requests out of duty to his family and in deference to his cousin's position as king consort. He'd seen the queen do things he'd thought she'd never agree to because Henry had a charm about him that had people wanting to please him. He certainly didn't have some magical ability to bend people to his will.

Before he could finish his thoughts, Leslee spoke again. "If he gets the stone, he'll be unstoppable. It will enhance his abilities."

"That's insane."

She yanked her shift down and jerked away from him, scurrying off the bed. Hell, he'd offended her. Knowing her history, he should have chosen another word. Guilt stabbed in his belly, but he couldn't wrap his mind around what she was saying.

"Please leave. I will be gone tomorrow, and ye will nae longer have to deal with a mad woman in yer midst." She reached to collect her gown.

"'Tis no' what I meant." He stood, wanting to draw her in for an embrace, but she retreated.

"Aye, 'twas. Now go." She pointed to the door and continued to draw her skirts up around her waist.

Everything had been perfect only moments earlier. A pain erupted in his chest. Would he have to choose between his family—what he'd lost during childhood, desired for years, and finally found again in Mary, James, and, regrettably, Henry—and the woman who made him feel whole?

Quickly dressing, he stepped up to her and drew her in. She protested, but only for a moment as he wrapped his arms around her and held her close, breathing in her scent, memorizing it. Was he going to lose her?

But she was correct to push him away because he needed space and time to think. How could this all be true, and what was he to do? Releasing her, he strode toward the door. "Stay here and keep yer door locked. I'll be back in a few minutes."

"Nae. Dinnae bother," she spat as she pulled her corset over her shift.

LESLEE HAD TO SEE THE QUEEN ONE LAST TIME SO SHE GRABBED HER staff, slid open the door and made her way to the queen's chamber only to learn once she'd arrived that the wedding celebration had started and she had missed Mary.

Placing her hand flat on the wall outside the royal chamber, she breathed deep, frustrated that her perfect afternoon had turned into a mess. An unexpected vision assailed her, almost knocking the breath from her body as the mark on her side erupted in flames.

Lord Darnley's thoughts raced into her skull, invading and sending a spike of pain through her head as he stood with one hand braced on the wall.

Mary's ability to resist my power is increasing. I need to get to the Isle of Skye to find the stone the druid told me of. If it works, I can walk right up to Queen Elizabeth and have her abdicate the throne. Then I'll have it all.

He punched the wall with his other hand, and she could feel the rage, ambition, and insanity surging through his veins, intensified by the whisky he'd been drinking.

First, I have to get rid of Rizzio. Why is it my words don't affect him? That's fine. He'll be easy to take care of, then he'll stop poisoning Mary's thoughts against me.

Then he pushed away from the wall, and the pressure in her chest eased.

Och, she'd forgotten to put her gloves on. Glancing around, she took in her surroundings, hoping no one saw her. This vision had been short, and the man down the hall guarding the prince's door was looking in the other direction.

Knocking on the door again, the maid she had just spoken to answered. "Is it possible to leave the queen a message? I'll be leaving in the morning."

"Aye. I'll show ye to her desk."

"Thank ye."

She sat down as the maid scurried off to perform some other task. This time, when her hand skimmed the desk, the queen's thoughts flitted into her head, but they seemed scattered and from different moments in time. They all had to do with her husband.

Something is wrong.

I have to get away from him.
Why do I keep taking him back?

The thoughts disappeared, and she finished her letter to the queen, thanking her for being a gracious hostess and wishing her well in the future. Then she hurried back to the safety of her room, determined not to leave until morning, when she would meet the men escorting her home.

9

Duncan ambled back toward the palace after finishing a dram of whisky at the nearest tavern. He'd only had one, just enough to calm his nerves and help him think clearly. It hadn't helped. He wanted Leslee but he needed his family, and he could see now that whether he believed her story or not, *she did* and that was enough to prove there was no way she would stay here with him.

At least he'd been able to come up with a plan, buying him time to sort out the jumbled emotions that held him in their grip. Entering the palace after the wedding ceremony, knowing Mary would be in the great hall entertaining, he made his way in that direction. He found the queen at a table on the raised dais, dining on roasted pig and root vegetables.

Henry, who only a year ago would have been a fixture at her side, had been relegated to stay at the home of a noble, not invited to attend the ceremony or celebration. His cousin had fallen from her favor, and she had gone to visit him at the Old Provost several times since he'd arrived in Edinburgh. He'd only been at the palace the two times she'd let him dine with her. Although they seemed to be working toward a reconciliation, Duncan wasn't sure it was possible, and he had a strong suspicion that she harbored feelings for another man.

When he knelt beside Mary, she turned and smiled at him.

"Yer Majesty, I have a boon to ask of ye."

"Yes, Duncan, what is it?" Her cheeks were rosy and filled with mirth, either from joy for the couple or an excess of wine.

"I'd like to be one of the guards to escort Lady MacKinnon home." He'd never asked the queen for a favor, but this was the only way he could think of to give him the time to decide what to do. Heat crept up his neck to his cheeks as she gave him a knowing grin.

He couldn't just let Leslee leave, but he also knew she wasn't going to stay. And what if Henry did come for her? He'd deal with that if—or when—it happened.

"She is a remarkable woman," Mary stated. "Do you think she might persuade you to stay on the Isle of Skye?"

"I havenae thought that far ahead, Yer Majesty, but I do ken I'm no' ready to see her go."

"You have my blessing, Duncan. I am sure your men will guard James well in your absence."

"Thank ye, Yer Majesty." He started to rise, but she caught his arm.

"If you love her, make sure you dinnae let that go. You may never find it again." A hopeful sadness shined in her gaze, and he knew she was remembering her first husband, the one she'd lost so soon after their marriage. He also understood she was giving him permission to court the lass, but did he love her? Could he after the short time they'd known each other?

"Aye, Yer Majesty." She removed her hand, putting it back in her lap and nodded at him. He rose and turned to leave.

Rushing to his room, he ticked off the items in his head he would need to pack. He guessed he'd be gone one or two months, depending on weather. This time of year had short days with weak, wintry sunlight for travel. All the better, because he would spend the nights with her and somehow convince her she should come back, that he would protect her from his cousin.

Entering his room, he found Henry sitting at the small table near the fireplace. "What are ye doing here?" He took the chair opposite the king consort.

"I need your help, cousin." The words vibrated through his ears, tickling them with the request.

"Aye, Henry. What can I do for ye?"

"You will bring Lady MacKinnon to me at the Old Provost's lodging at midnight." The request seemed wrong, but he couldn't refuse the order. "Tell her there is something magical there and she must see it before she leaves."

"I can do that, Henry."

"Do not let her know you are coming to see me. I want it to be a surprise." His cousin leaned in closer, glaring into his eyes and as the words rolled through him like a steady wind.

"Tell her ye have something special to show her before you leave. Do not mention my name at all." Henry stood, and he followed.

"Aye." He was compelled to agree, despite the nagging feeling in his head that something was wrong.

"And, Duncan, do not tell anyone else of your destination."

"Aye, Henry." His cousin turned away and strolled toward the door, a lazy confidence in his strides.

Henry pulled open the door, peeked down the hall, then disappeared, shutting the portal behind him. Duncan was left with a peculiar foreboding as he set to packing his belongings, confusion clouding his thoughts.

Just before he left the room to retrieve Leslee, he placed one last object in his bag, the box of mementos from his family. Then he set his packed items by the door for easy retrieval in the morning. He was ready to start this journey and see where it led, but in the meantime, he had a request from his cousin, so he headed for Lady MacKinnon's room.

Knocking, he waited for a reply. Nothing. Then he knocked harder and tested the door. It was bolted. Leslee's sleepy, questioning voice, filled with suspicion, came from the other side of the thick wood.

"Who is it?"

"'Tis Duncan. I need to see ye."

A few moments later, a click registered as the key turned, and she slowly opened the door. Pushing his way in, he was mesmerized by her, curls tumbling around her waist, staff in hand, ready to attack had he been a threat. She looked every bit the warrior chosen to guard some mythical stone, and he so wanted to believe it for a moment.

"What do ye want?" She closed the door and eyed him warily.

"I need to show ye something. I ken 'tis yer last night here, so 'tis the last chance." He didn't know where the words came from. All he really wanted was to lay her back down in that bed and hold her.

"Duncan, I need sleep. I leave quite early."

"'Twill no' take long, besides, I need to tell ye something."

"I dinnae wish to go tonight."

"But it's something magical. Ye have to see it." Other than her ability to see the past, he couldn't think of any magic he believed in. Wasn't that the problem? Och, his thoughts were so jumbled. Why did they have to go?

She must have taken pity on him because she set down her weapon and started pulling on the gown she had laid out for in the morning. "Very well. Give me a moment."

Grabbing her staff, she pushed open the door, then locked it behind her. He was happy to see her taking precautions. Why was he taking her out again? He couldn't remember, but his feet started, and he followed.

"What is it ye wished to tell me?" Leslee had thought she wouldn't see him again after asking him to leave earlier. She'd had the most amazing afternoon with him and had given him her complete trust, then he'd said she was mad.

"I'll be going with ye tomorrow." She froze, and he looped his arm through hers, tugging her along.

"Why? Don't ye have to be here for the prince?"

"The queen has given me leave to escort ye home." Hope blossomed in her chest at his admission. Did he truly wish to spend more time with her? She admired this man, his hard work and dedication to the royal family, his protective nature, but most of all the way he made her feel treasured and worthy of affection.

Reaching the bottom of the steps, she recalled how the afternoon had ended—he'd called her insane. She shook her head. He was like the others. As good as it felt to be in his arms, she couldn't accept him if he didn't believe her.

"But why would ye choose to do such a thing?"

"I think 'twill give us a little more time to understand one another and figure out where we need to go from here."

"My place is on Skye and yers is here. There is nothing more to discuss."

"What if ye are carrying my babe?"

They were out in the cold air now, and his words, emphasized by a blast of frigid wind, chilled her, leaving her raw and vulnerable. She hadn't thought of the consequences of taking Duncan to her bed. "Then ye will be able to come visit whenever ye like."

"Nae. I want more."

She did too. She wanted Duncan with all her heart, desired that he return to Skye with her, leave this place and always stay by her side. But she also wished he could trust her, and she accepted that no matter what she wanted, nothing was more important than guarding the stone.

If he were willing to escort her home, maybe she could talk him into staying. Maybe with time, he would accept that she was being truthful about Lord Darnley. They continued to walk through the darkened streets in silence, the only noises an occasional animal, rowdy tavern patron on his way home, and her staff tapping the ground as they traveled.

"Where are we going?"

"There." He pointed.

"'Tis a kirk?"

"Aye."

"But 'tis late to go to such a place. What did ye want to show me?"

"Something magical," he said vaguely. He squinted and shook his head as if he wasn't quite in agreement with what he was saying. Odd, because Duncan was always so deliberate and assertive about his plans.

Entering an old house at the edge of the small compound, he guided her up the stairs and knocked on the entrance to the second room on the left. Unease stabbed at her as the mark on her side started to burn. The door swung in, and Duncan entered, pulling her along though she tried to tug free. Before she could see who was behind her, the door slammed shut.

Pivoting, she came face-to-face with her nemesis. Lord Darnley was ready and willing to fight her to death for the stone. She readied her staff, wondering what weapon he would draw against her.

Duncan stood next to the man, looking dazed and confused. He'd brought her here as a sacrifice to his cousin. She had trusted him, given him her secrets, her body and her heart. He had betrayed her.

Henry turned on Duncan. "You are late. I had given up on you."

"Why are we here?" Duncan asked.

The king consort swiveled toward him. "Stay where you are and keep quiet, Duncan."

His focus returning to her, she shivered and held her staff in front of her like a shield.

"I apologize for my state of undress. I had assumed my dear cousin had forgotten his orders." Lord Darnley waved a hand in front of himself, indicating his lack of clothing. He wore only a nightshirt, but his tone wasn't repentant, and the smirk on his face indicated he didn't really mind.

She kept her focus pinned on him, knowing he must be mad with lust for the stone. She'd hoped to fight him on her own territory, not in the confines of a small, rented room in a city where she could be sent to prison for harming the king consort. She briefly scanned the room to see Duncan had followed Lord Darnley's order and hadn't moved, but his head was angled toward his cousin with an angry, dazed stare. He looked as if he was attempting to break the man's hold on him. Or at least that's what she hoped he was doing.

"Now, give me the stone." This time his voice filled the whole room, waves pulsating at her as he tried to bend her to his wishes.

Breathing deeply, she drew on the strength of the stone. "Ye may not have it."

"Oh, my dear, you are wrong. I will have it, and I'll take your will before we are done here tonight."

Straightening her shoulders, she prepared for the fight, twirling her staff around to catch and hold it with both hands. Not taking her stare from the threat in front of her, she caught movement from Duncan as he shook his head and flexed his fingers as he continued to fight the spell.

"Why is it my power doesn't work on you?" His lips twisted as he studied her but made no move to get closer.

"Because I am the rightful protector of the stone."

"No, it's the same thing with Rizzio. He was immune as well, but he was easy enough to take care of. Give me the stone." His last words reverberated through the air in waves of command, knocking against her, but she resisted their draw.

"And what would ye do with the stone?" Maybe she could buy time. From the corner of her eye, she could see Duncan shaking his head, trying to gain an understanding of their conversation. If he knew the truth, he would fight for Scotland. She knew he was noble, even if he hadn't believed her.

"Why, my dear. It will help me hold the English and Scottish thrones. Elizabeth will abdicate at my will and my wife will have no choice but to obey my every command."

"Can ye no' do that without the stone? Go to England, use yer powers to take the throne, but the stone stays here in Scotland. Ye would harm her people. I cannae let ye do that."

"No. I need the stone."

"Yer power is fading the more ye use it on someone." The man's eyes darkened on her and she knew she'd guessed correctly.

"Once I have the Heart of Scotland it won't matter."

"Duncan, help me," she pleaded as she let her gaze drift his way. "Ye have to stop this. 'Tis madness to turn the stone over to yer cousin. Many in Scotland will suffer if ye aid him in his mad quest."

"Do ye think he has a choice?" Lord Darnley laughed at her as Duncan moved to stand between them. She prayed he saw sense now.

"Subdue her, dear cousin." She heard the vibrations echo through the room as the arse gave the order to Duncan. Then Darnley leaned back against the door and smirked at her as the man she'd come to care for blinked, apparently trying to fight the order.

Duncan twisted and closed the distance between them.

10

No. This wasn't right. Duncan didn't want to hurt Leslee, but he couldn't shake the command, so he reached out to grab her. Her staff swung down on his arms, and a smack rent the air. Hell, that stung.

Shaking out the burn, a little clarity returned. How had he gotten here? Had his cousin truly found a way to control his mind?

"Stay back, Duncan. I dinnae want to wound ye." He didn't want to hurt her either. Splitting pain stabbed in his head as he tried to reject the urge to hold her down.

"He is controlling ye. Ye have to fight it." Her green gaze pleaded.

He blinked. Yes, something was wrong here.

"Take her." His cousin yelled at him behind his back, and he was compelled to dive for Leslee again. She came down hard with her rod across his leg, and he buckled to the floor. Hell, she was good with that thing.

"Please, Duncan." Her eyes were glossy. He wanted to comfort her.

A door slammed behind him, and he spun to see his cousin's valet rush into the room, still in a nightshirt, but he'd wrapped a cloak around his body. "What's going on, sir?" The confused man looked at Henry.

His cousin turned to the man, anger in his glare. "Go get some rope." The order was barked out then he turned back to Duncan.

"Subdue her!" The words grated across his skin and into his nerves, an order he had to obey.

Standing, he drew his father's sword, but his hands trembled.

"Attack." The order from Henry echoed through his ears, and he couldn't stop his arms as they rose then came down in a hard swipe aimed at the woman he loved. A tear escaped from his eye as she held her staff aloft and blocked the blow.

"Nae, Duncan, this isnae ye." Leslee's words reached his ears, reached his heart, but he couldn't control his movements.

"Again," came the screech from behind him. And he struck again as Leslee blocked the blow, but her weapon splintered and cracked with the force of his assault, almost breaking.

Instead of panicking, she stood taller, more determined as she twirled her stick, going on the offensive. *Bam.* The rod smacked his head, and he stumbled back. Then she spun it in the opposite direction. As it whizzed through the air, she took a step forward, and the solid wood collided with his wrist. Pain exploded at the spot. He dropped his sword.

His wee lass was fierce and, despite her ire being directed at him, he felt proud. No other had ever divested him of his sword. He'd trained with some of the best men in all of Scotland, but the skill with which Leslee wielded her staff made her a worthy opponent. She moved as if she danced with her weapon.

He caught sight of the valet returning, a long rope draped over his arm. "Get her, William," his cousin ordered from behind, then there was a flash as the man ran for Leslee.

Pivoting, she struck the man in the arm, and he yelped in pain as he collapsed to the ground.

"Retrieve your sword and stop her." Angry words vibrated through his head, demanding that he obey. His hands shook as he scooped up his weapon, bringing it in front of him, ready to attack.

Leslee swung, connecting just a tad bit higher on his arm than she had before. It stung like hell, but he kept his grip. Then he rose and tried to stop himself even as his weapon came down in a slashing arc in front of her. His eyes stung and watered, he resisted Henry's orders, but it was no use. If she was hurt because of him, he might kill his cousin himself.

As his sword collided with her staff, the wood broke in two, and he realized everything she'd said was true. The legend she'd read to him, the stone she was protecting. He had to find a way to save her and the stone. He saw now that his cousin was nothing like the family he'd known. The man was evil and wished to destroy Scotland and the woman he loved with his cruelty.

With the clarity of truth burning through the haze in his mind, Duncan managed to wrench free from the spell just as Leslee's foot connected with his gut. He stumbled back and made it appear as if his sword flew from his hand to land out the door the valet had left ajar. He hoped it would be a start toward ensuring Leslee's safety. If he didn't have the weapon, Henry couldn't force him to use it on her.

"Take her," Henry shouted again, and he obeyed, charging toward the woman he'd hope would be his wife. Knocking her into the wall, he pinned her arms to her side. Her lavender scent beckoned him and gave him strength to keep fighting the orders pounding through his head. He wanted to tell her he wasn't going to let Henry hurt her or get her stone, but he was afraid if his cousin figured out he was starting to break the hold, he might intensify his commands.

"William, the rope. Duncan, sit her in the chair."

He breathed deeply. Though the lure of Henry's spell still urged him on, given a little more time, he'd be able to break it.

But until he found the right time, he had to show compliance. Leslee fought him.

"Duncan, ye cannae do this. He'll bring great harm to our home. Ye cannae let him have it."

Her eyes shone with desperation, hurt and betrayal, and it tore him to shreds. She continued to struggle, but he looked away, knowing he had to be strong for her.

Spinning her around, he forced her to sit in the chair that had been on the side of the room. Meeting Leslee's gaze once again, he held her there as the valet tied her hands behind her back and to the wooden seat. He found a glimmer of tears and defeat in her eyes. His chest ached.

"Now, how is it you have been able to resist my commands?" Henry moved closer, but Duncan didn't back away. The man was not putting his filthy hands on Leslee.

His cousin squinted and screwed up his face, pointing to the unicorn charm she wore. "It's that coin. Is it made of iron? That's how Rizzio did it too. He wore a cross of iron. I'll have to remember to watch for that in the future. But with the stone, I should be powerful enough to counteract it."

"Nae, the stone belongs in Scotland." She kicked out at him, and Henry backed away as if he were scared of her. After the fight she'd just put up, he couldn't blame his cousin for having some sense.

"Looks like you have lost, my dear." Henry put his hands on his hips and puffed out his chest.

"The stone will drive ye mad. Ye are already almost there. It willnae bring ye peace," she pleaded.

"You are wrong. It will bring me everything I've always wanted. I'll have both Elizabeth and Mary at my knees. Both thrones will be mine."

"Ye will destroy the peace in Scotland." Reproach sounded in her words, but his cousin took no notice.

"Maybe I'll even keep you as a pet for a little while." Anger surged through his veins at Henry's words.

"Now, where is the stone. It's on that chain, is it not?"

Leslee's stare pinned Henry with fury. His cousin backed up another step as if frightened of touching her then glanced at him. "Take her necklace."

BEFORE SHE COULD STOP HIM, DUNCAN GLANCED AT HER AND winked. He didn't appear to be under Lord Darnley's spell, but still he clutched the chain and pulled it from her neck in one swift yank. The force wrenched her head forward, and then it ricocheted back. She stared in horror at the man she'd come to care for stealing the thing most precious to her.

Pain ripped through her heart at the betrayal. He knew what he was doing. Not only had she failed Scotland, but she'd chosen a man who would see it suffer at his family's hands. Her eyes stung as she tried with all her might to free her hands from the tight bindings.

She was barely aware of Lord Darnley issuing the order to Duncan. "Give it to me."

Duncan laughed. "Cousin, ye will never have that stone. It belongs to Leslee and Scotland."

Glancing down, she saw that Duncan had taken the token the priestess had given her, the iron coin. He'd wrapped it around his hand like a shield and held his fist up to the king consort to witness. She wanted to weep with relief. She had made the right decision when she'd given her heart to this man, a true hero and protector of Scotland, but they weren't out of this yet.

The valet attacked Duncan from behind, but he easily twisted and drove his fist into the man's gut. The valet doubled over in pain and fell to the ground.

"Stop this, Duncan," Lord Darnley ordered, but Duncan advanced on him.

"How dare ye take my will away from me when I have been faithful to ye since the day my family died."

"Stop this, Duncan. Get me that stone."

Frantic vibrations echoed through the room, but instead of obeying, her Highland guard swung and connected with Lord Darnley's head. The arse collapsed to the floor, losing consciousness on his way down.

Suddenly, an explosion tore through the air, shaking the whole building. Duncan threw his hands out to keep his balance as the room tilted. The sensations from the blast left her shaking and confused.

Another bang, and then the muffled crackling of wood on fire reached her ears. She was blinking when Duncan scooped her and the chair up in his arms and darted for the door. He bolted down the stairs, the hall and then out into the fresh air. Placing the chair back on the frozen earth, he dropped to his knees before her. "Are ye unhurt?"

"Aye. Are ye?"

"Aye." Reaching down, he drew out a dirk, then moved behind her to sever the ropes at her wrists.

Stepping before her again, he released the dagger and placed his warm hands on both her cheeks, peering deep into her eyes. "Ye ken I didnae have control of what I was doing?" His plea was sincere.

"I ken."

"I would never hurt ye." Duncan showered kisses all over her face, pulling her close and holding her tight. She wrapped her own arms around him and drew him near. He had come through for her, for Scotland.

"Aye. I ken it."

A loud noise came from the building as if a beam had fallen, drawing her attention back to the door they'd just come through as a cloud of smoke whooshed from a broken ground floor window.

"I have to go back for them. I cannae leave them in there to burn."

"Nae. Ye cannae go back in there. 'Tis no' safe." Clinging to him, she hoped to shelter him and stop him from putting himself at risk.

"I have to. He is my cousin and the king consort. 'Tis my duty to protect him."

She understood his reasons, but the flames burned out of control and there was so much smoke. She held him tighter. How would he even see to get to them?

Leaning back, he glanced down at her. "If we make it through this, I will go to Skye with ye. I want ye as my wife. I will stay wherever ye are." His lips crashed down on hers, intense desire and relief seeping from them into her. Overwhelmed with a need to cling to him and keep him safe, she realized she loved him just as he said the words, "I love ye."

Taking her hand, he turned it palm up and dropped her coin necklace in the middle, folding her fingers around it. "Stay safe." He pulled free to run into the inferno behind them.

Seconds felt like hours as she waited for him to return. She could hear the voices of others gathering in the streets, but no one entered the courtyard, perhaps, like her, fearing another explosion. With each passing moment, her stomach knotted tighter and her breathing shallowed. Finally, a figure emerged, but it was large and awkward. Until he was closer, she hadn't realized it was Duncan with a man slung over each of his shoulders.

Kneeling, he placed the valet's body down, and the cloak he wore fell to the ground near the chair. He then carefully laid Lord Darnley down beside the other man. Both were still only clothed in their nightshirts.

Duncan coughed and struggled to clear the smoke he'd inhaled from his lungs.

"I couldnae catch my breath. The air was so thick. I barely found them."

She moved closer and noticed no rise and fall of the men's chests, just as men began shouting for buckets and water. "I think they are dead." She glanced at Duncan, knowing the news would come as a blow. But before she could judge his reaction, he was grabbing her hand and drawing her away from the men and the commotion, into the shadows and out of sight.

Once they were down the street, he drew her in close. "If they are dead, ye cannae be found near them. We have to make certain ye are able to leave for Skye tomorrow."

They maneuvered the back streets of Edinburgh to make their way to the palace, where drunk guests still milled about as music echoed through the great hall. Avoiding the crowd, Duncan guided her to her room.

"Collect all yer belongings. Ye will be staying with me the rest of the night."

She didn't ask why. She saw by the way he watched her that he was afraid he'd almost lost her, heard in his voice the worry that he himself could have harmed her. She knew because she felt the same way. Escorting her to his room, he bolted the door and dragged a chair over to a place in front of it as well.

While he stoked the fire, she undressed to her shift and climbed into Duncan's bed. He followed, but she noticed he placed his weapon within reach. The last she'd seen of it, he was tossing the sharp blade out of Lord Darnley's room. "How did ye find yer sword?"

"I nearly tripped on it when I went back in for Henry. 'Twas easy to scoop up and sheath."

"Do ye think we are still in danger?"

"Nae, but it doesnae hurt to be safe."

"I dinnae think anyone saw us."

"On our journey to the Isle of Skye, I'll make sure to purchase ye another rod."

She smiled. "It does appear ye owe me one."

"I'm so sorry." Wrapping his arm around her, he drew her near. "I tried so hard to fight the command. It would have destroyed me if I'd hurt ye."

"Nae, I kenned ye had no choice. I'm sorry ye lost yer cousin." She rested her hand on his chest. Lord Darnley had been a horrible person, but he was Duncan's family and he had to be grieving at the loss.

Leaning up on an elbow, she met his eyes, before lowering her head to claim his lips in a kiss. When she pulled back, she fought the sting her eyes as she said, "Thank ye."

"For what?"

"For no' believing I was crazy and for saving me."

"I'm the one who put you in danger to begin with."

"True, but maybe ye can make that up to me." She dipped again to kiss him, this time running her hands through his hair. When she withdrew, they were both breathless. "Make love to me."

And he did, long and slow, until she fell apart beneath him. As they lay together sleepy and sated, Duncan turned to her.

"Will ye marry me?"

"I've never thought of marriage. Never thought of leaving Skye."

"Ye dinnae have to. I will go wherever ye are. I love ye, Leslee MacKinnon, and I never want to lose ye."

"I love ye too, Duncan."

"Is that a yes?"

"Aye, it is. I will marry ye."

They only slept for a couple of hours before they rose and made their way out of Edinburgh. She didn't mind the lack of sleep because she was going home with the man she loved, and the Heart of Scotland was safe for another generation. Not only had her nemesis been defeated, but she now had her own Highland guard to help her protect the precious stone and the people of Scotland.

EPILOGUE

MacKinnon Lands
Isle of Skye, Scotland
April 1567

They were back on the Isle of Skye before news reached them that the Earl of Bothwell, a man who wanted the queen for his own, may have been responsible for planting the gunpowder beneath Henry's room and initiating the blast that led to his and his valet's deaths. Duncan and Leslee were lucky to have made it out of the building alive.

He only had a brief regret that he would never really know his distant cousin, Prince James. But he had more than that now. He had Leslee, and as protector of the Heart of Scotland, she was even more precious to guard than the queen herself.

Leslee had gone through his box, regaling him with tales from his family's past and giving him details about his parents he'd never known. She'd also told him stories of his father's bravery as she read the sword he'd retrieved when he'd gone back into the burning building. Not only was she the best link to what he had lost, but he had gained so much. She had a large family who had all welcomed him as if he were one of their own.

For a wedding gift, she'd presented him with an iron necklace and a coin just like hers. Now, as he glanced across their bed at his wife in his new home, he thought of how fortunate he was.

"What are ye smiling at?" he asked.

She laughed as she sat up, inching closer, running her long fingers over his bare chest.

"I never imagined I would be lucky enough to find a man who wanted me despite my ability and the stone."

"They were all fools." He scooted closer, draping his arm over her bare waist.

"Ye ken what else I never imagined?"

"What's that, love?"

"That I'd be able to help ye find a family once again." She nestled into his side.

"Oh, aye. Yer family has been welcoming."

"'Tis no' what I'm saying." Her face radiated as a huge smile lit her lips, and her attention tilted up toward his.

"Then what?" He rose up and placed a quick kiss on her lips.

"Ye are going to be a father."

His breath caught. He'd spent his whole life longing for a place he belonged, and he knew deep in his heart that no matter where they lived his home was with Leslee.

"Och, I love ye, lass."

"And I love ye too, Duncan."

And in that moment, he had everything he'd ever needed—a home, a wife he adored, and his own family.

ABOUT THE AUTHOR

Lori Ann Bailey is a winner of the National Readers' Choice Award and Holt Medallion for Best First Book and Best Historical. She has a romantic soul and believes the best in everyone. Sappy commercials and proud mommy moments make her cry.

She sobs uncontrollably and feels emotionally drained when reading sad books, so she started reading romance for the Happily Ever Afters. She was hooked.

Then, the characters and scenes running around in her head as she attempted to sleep at night begged to be let out. Looking back now, her favorite class in high school was the one where a professor pulled a desk to the center of the room and told her to write two paragraphs about it and the college English class taught by a red-headed Birkenstock wearing girl, not much older than she, who introduced her to Jack Kerouac. After working in business and years spent as a stay-at-home mom she has found something in addition to her family to be passionate about, her books.

When not writing, Lori enjoys time with her real-life hero and four kids or spending time walking or drinking wine with her friends.

Visit Lori at http://loriannbailey.com/

ALSO BY LORI

HIGHLAND PRIDE SERIES

Highland Deception
Highland Redemption

facebook.com/Lori.Ann.Bailey.author

twitter.com/labaileyauthor

instagram.com/loriannbailey

bookbub.com/profile/lori-ann-bailey

goodreads.com/LoriAnnaBailey

Made in the USA
Middletown, DE
24 July 2018